THE DAY OF THE WOLF

D1089494

THE DAY OF THE WOLF

ERIK HARALDSSON

C. R. MAY

COPYRIGHT

This novel is a work of fiction. The names, characters and incidents portrayed in it, while at times based on real figures, are purely the work of the author's imagination.

It is sold subject to the condition that it shall not by way of trade or otherwise, be lent, resold, hired out, or otherwise circulated without the writer's prior consent, electronically or in any form of binding or cover other than the form in which it is published and without a similar condition including this condition being imposed on the subsequent purchaser. Replication or distribution of any part is strictly prohibited without the written permission of the copyright holder.

Copyright © 2020 C.R.May
ISBN 978-1-9996695-3-9
All rights reserved.

In Memory of Thomas William May

GLOSSARY

Brynja - A mail shirt.

Drekkar - A large warship similar to a skei but heavily orna-mented. A dragon ship.

Ealdorman - A high ranking royal official holding civil and military duties directly from the king. The English equivalent to the northern earl or Scandinavian jarl.

Gesith - An English rank similar to the Scandinavian huskarl.

Hird - The armed retinue of a Scandinavian warlord or king.

Huskarl - House-man. A bodyguard or retainer to a powerful chieftain, jarl or king.

Jarl/Earl - A regional lord responsible for administrating a province on behalf of the king for whom he collected taxes, duties and owed military service.

Knarr - An ocean-going cargo ship.

Skat - Tax, tribute.

Skjald-borg - Shield-fort.

Skei - 'that which cuts through water.' A large sleek warship mounting thirty oars and above.

Snekkja - 'thin and projecting.' A small warship mounting twenty to thirty oars.

Styrisman - The helmsman on a ship.

Svinfylking - Swine or Boar-snout: a wedge shaped attacking formation used in battle.

Thane - A minor nobleman in Anglo-Saxon England.

Úlfheðnar - A wolf-hide warrior, similar to the more widely known berserk or bear-shirt.

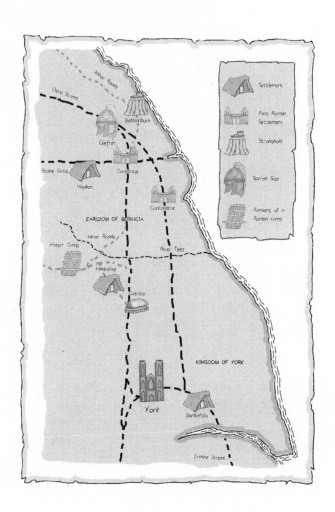

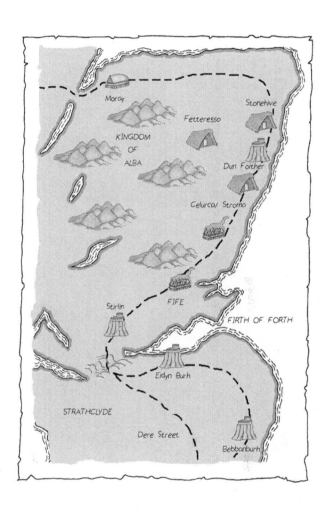

PART I

THUNDERBOLT

1

BARDOLFSBY

Wessex

Spring 952

'The sunshine is pleasant.'

'Yes, it is.'

'And the fields are nice.'

'Yes, they are very nice fields.'

The pair, archbishop and king, returned their gaze to the road ahead as the awkward silence returned. Of all the things Wulfstan had done to safeguard the independence of his homeland during his long and dutiful life, the long ride south with Olaf Cuaran must rank up there with the most disagreeable. Most folk in the kingdom of York were aware that the two leading men had little time for one another. It was an open secret that the prelate had come close to delivering up the nape of Olaf's neck to Erik Haraldsson's axe blade only four years before, when the Church of St Wilfrid had burned and king Eadred's armies had harried the land. Now they were on the final leg of their journey, summoned to appear before the southern king; only Wulfstan among the riders knew the instruction to be a ruse.

The archbishop's gaze took in the rolling hills as they rode. Lambs gambolled beneath a sky rend by swifts and swallows: in the middle distance shirtsleeved rustics broke off from their labours to gawp. The Northumbrian closed his eyes, savouring the scent of the hedgerow — bluebells and lady's smock — but as the sun warmed his old bones and he began to doze, the idyl was shattered as an exclamation from the man at his side cut the air. Wulfstan's lids flickered, his eyes following the dusty track until they picked out a knot of horsemen resting in the dappled shade of a hornbeam. Olaf exchanged a smile with his leading huskarls as the West Saxons urged their mounts into a trot. 'I was beginning to wonder,' he said, as the guards' hands went instinctively to the handles of their swords. 'Whether this kingdom contained any men who knew something of the world beyond the crest of the nearest hill.'

It was obvious even from distance that the Englishmen were men of importance, very likely the local thane and his hearth companions by the fineness of their appearance and the quality of their mounts, and the archbishop began to relax as Olaf's outriders moved to intercept what must be an escort sent to usher them before the king. Wulfstan watched them go, allowing himself a smile as he came to accept he had done all he could to delay the meeting between the two men.

The ride to Winchester had taken the best part of a week. Knowing what was to follow Wulfstan had told king Olaf that he was leaving his own armed retinue back at York. Made wary by a lifetime spent dodging enemies and assassins, the king had reacted to the news by increasing the number of his own guards for the long ride south. A hundred of Olaf Cuaran's finest troops, his heavily armed huskarls, had accompanied the two leaders down Ermine Street, denuding the garrison at York of the majority of its experienced fighters and leaders. Told by the Winchester ealdorman that king Eadred was at his estate in Wantage, Wulfstan had spent a very agreeable night as an honoured guest at the bishop's palace while Olaf and his men had attempted to drink the burh dry in time honoured fashion. Now, two days later, it would seem they were finally drawing near to their goal.

Despite the furore which would undoubtably follow when his scheming was laid bare, Wulfstan was confident he could weather the storm. He had done so many times before he reflected as the horsemen came together on the road up ahead, and the old archbishop allowed himself a gentle snort of amusement as he pictured the faces of the men riding in column to his rear when they came to realise the truth. Betrayed and angry or not, what could they do to a man of his eminence in a most Christian land? String him up? Lock him away?

With the identity of the powerful force come into the shire confirmed and reassured of their peaceful intent, the young West Saxon and his *gesith* were soon up with them. The Northumbrian cast them a flinty glare. These were men who would have been party to the harrowing only a few short years before; but the meeting was cordial, no doubt the arch-bishop reflected with a barely concealed scowl, due to the fact that Cuaran was king Eadred's lackey. Told that the royal estate stood at the head of the adjoining valley Olaf increased the pace, but as Norse thoughts turned to ale and feasting, Wulfstan's own were far closer to home.

Bardolfsby - twelve miles from York

Shouts and cries drifted downfield, but Erik paid them no heed. The day was going just as he had planned. 'They may look the part,' he cried as he paced the sward, 'but put yourself in their place. Last night they hit the straw as happy as a dog with two cocks.' He bared his teeth in a grin as the morning air filled with laughter. 'Olaf Cuaran, the lord who had their oath had gone south and taken his meanest, toughest warriors along for the ride. The men who always got the girl: the cosiest spot next to the hearth; the choicest cut; finest ale. For the next month or more they were to be the best source of silver in York.' He shrugged, and the rumble of laughter began again as he added with a smirk. 'Two cocks or not, a girl's got to eat.'

Erik threw a glance across his shoulder. The last spearmen were spilling from the place where the road to York exited the tree line, the leaders who had survived the horrors of the night pushing and shoving the laggards into line as they came face to face with the army of Erik Bloodaxe. Erik looked back as he continued. 'Then suddenly all was chaos. Shouts and screams in the night — the clash of steel on steel — a moment of befuddlement until their minds caught up with their senses and they knew. The bastards in York had turned on them again — it was to be every man for himself. Strange flags on the walls: the town has fallen. Grab what you can and look for your mates, get yourself into the largest group you can and force a passage down to the river.' Erik's voice rose in pitch as the men hung on his every word. They may be in the ascendant now, but the tidal flow of shifting loyalties and alliances in the lands of the Norse meant there were very few who had not experienced a gut-wrenching moment of betrayal.

'The ships were gone or tied up tantalisingly close on the far bank of the Ouse,' Erik continued, 'but the larger warships, Olaf's sleek *dracca* and *skei* were downriver at Riccall, and they clung to the hope as they jogged the eight miles and the first blush of dawn lit the eastern sky that the ship guard was still in place.' Erik smiled his war smile and gave a shrug as the faces behind the gaily coloured shields turned as one to a nearby copse. 'They were half right,' he said, 'the guards were there — mostly hanging from tree branches or bleeding out into the soil, the ships gone south with their captors: axe Norse; spear Danes; shipmen of the Sudreys and Orkneys.' Erik flicked a look at the enemy and back again. 'So now they are come to a field of death. All that remains is to fight their way through us, overtake the ships and sail away.' King Erik threw them all a final look as the earlier humour fled. 'We have been through the plan, and every man among us knows his part. Now, let us do what little needs to be done and break our fast in York.'

The army buzzed with anticipation as Erik made his way to the centre, setting up a steady rhythm as spear shafts beat against shields and the braying of war horns filled the air. The skjald-borg opened up to admit their king, and within a few paces the men of Erik's guard were closing around him as Sturla Godi hoist the bloodied axe banner of Erik Haraldsson and proudly took up position to his lord's rear. A hundred yards to the north, the enemy were beginning to cross the field where a meander in the River Ouse pinned the road against the woodland edge. The early morning sun reflected dully from helm and spear point as they came, and Erik ran his eyes along his own battle line for a final time as the distance between the armies shrank.

Thorstein was at the king's side, and the huskarl spoke as

the first javelins flew. 'Do you think they will do what we want?'

Erik nodded. 'Even if they miss the fact that the line is weaker next to the river, the buildings on the terrace and the lie of the land will channel them that way. There would be little point breaking our line only to get held up again fighting among the huts and alleyways to our rear — they want to take ship and be away. They have just escaped a massacre and run for miles wearing what arms and armour they could snatch up in the confusion, they are tired and dispirited, without their usual leaders and desperate to escape. You will see,' he said with a look, 'as soon as our line begins to curl back on itself and they think they are making progress their fears will get the better of them, any semblance of order will vanish like morning mist and they will become a rabble.'

On the field ahead Cuaran's fugitives were breaking into a run as Erik's fighters braced to receive the charge. Even disorganised and taken by surprise, these were men who had honed their fighting skills among the highlands and islands of northern Britain and Ireland, lands which rarely knew a time of peace. They were dangerous men made more-so by their desperation, and any chatter petered out as spears were couched, axes raised and the defenders prepared to fight. Moments later the lines crashed together with a sound like summer thunder, and Erik looked on in satisfaction as the men arrayed before him took a backwards step before throwing their shoulders into the boards and springing forward to regain their former position.

Erik ran his eyes over the faces of the attackers as spears began to saw back and forth, the closest little more than a dozen paces before him now. If the spittle-flecked snarls told the story of their wretchedness it was obvious to the experienced defenders that the runaways from York were lacking leadership, each man or small knot of friends throwing themselves forward onto the Haraldsson shield wall in an uncoordinated frenzy. Satisfied there appeared little chance of a breakthrough Erik let his gaze wander down to the riverside, and his spirits leapt as it became obvious that the carefully worked battle plan was developing as he had hoped. Helgrim Smiter had followed Erik's gaze, and he drew a smile from the old king's son as he repeated a saying of Harald Fairhair. 'First win the battle,' he said proudly. 'And then fight it.'

The pair were not the only ones to notice that the defending shield wall at the water's edge was beginning to curve back upon itself, as the full weight of the attack hit home. As he had hoped, men eager for a quick victory had taken the route which had offered the best chance of escape, the slope of the land adding impetus to the charge. Already the spearmen immediately to their front had seen what looked like the breakout they desperately needed if they were to survive the day, and Erik felt the pressure ease on the fighters before him as the enemy peeled off and rushed away downslope to exploit the breach. He nodded as the trickle became a flood and the break widened. 'You were right,' he said, 'my father knew a thing or two about fighting wars. A good battle plan is worth an extra ship's company or more in the clash of shields.' Erik glanced towards his bodyguard as men roared and steel clashed at the riverside. 'And enough about men to pluck a young lad from the hird, and make him the youngest huskarl in Avaldsnes.'

Helgrim flashed a proud smile as they watched the enemy stream away. 'That happened longer ago than I care to recall, lord. But I was as proud to give my oath to your father as I have been to serve you all these years.'

The riverfront had opened up now as the Haraldsson line curled back upon itself, and Cuaran's remaining men were stampeding southwards along the bank as the hope they may yet escape the carnage of the day drove every other thought from their minds. Erik glanced at Sturla Godi as they went. 'All set?' The banner man spat to clear his mouth as the battle horn came up, filling his lungs as he fixed his eyes upon the king. The moment Erik's head dipped the horn spoke, the *yip-yip-yip* rolling across the meadow as the furore made by the escaping men followed them south. Immediately the battle line turned, the spears and shields pivoting to follow the backs of the fleeing enemy as the trap slammed shut. Erik raised his chin to peer southwards; already the furthest fugitives were drawing to a halt, the realisation that they had been out-thought obvious even from a distance as the men desperately began to reorder themselves into some semblance of a battle line. Sturla's horn sounded again as the swimmers among the fugitives tossed weapons and armour aside, throwing themselves into the flood in their frenzied efforts to escape death or enslavement.

A nod from Erik and the war banner circled above them before dipping to the West. Seeing the signal Erik's crewmen whirled about the king's position, rushing across to anchor the eastern flank against the halls, outbuildings and paling that were the settlement of Bardolfsby. With the enemy herded together on the sloping ground before them, Erik took the opportunity to peer across their heads to what Cuaran's men now knew was the main defensive line on the far side of the village, out where the open space narrowed as a woodland spur forced the roadway almost down to the water's edge. Packed shoulder to shoulder ten men deep, Erik's sons and their crewmen were an impenetrable wall of razor sharp steel and gaudy shields, the flags of the brothers: Gamli; Harald; Guttorm and Sigurd — even young Ragnfrod taking his place in the battle line for the first time wooding the air above them. Erik held his position on a gentle rise surrounded by the men of his hird, while the jarl brothers Erland and Arnkel Torf-Einarsson led the men of Orkney down to help seal the trap.

At the river javelins and arrows were picking off the last of the swimmers, and as the current gathered up the bodies and began to carry them downstream, the resistance of those left on the eastern shore finally collapsed. Spears, swords and axes began to clatter to the ground as the survivors of Olaf Cuaran's garrison at York bowed to the inevitable after a night and morning spent fighting for their lives, battle-weary men opting to take their chances either in captivity or in attempting to buy their freedom from the victors rather than face a certain and bloody death.

Thorstein sniffed as Erik's army filled the riverside with their chants of victory. 'That's that then — I make it a hundred or so men in the prime of life. That should bring in a tidy sum for the lads when they are sold at the slave market in Hedeby.'

Erik nodded. 'Yes, let's be away, my sons can take care of things here. The city will be in uproar, we must support the earls and let the people see that there is more to today's happenings than a rising against the pretender, far more than a change of flag flying above the king's garth.' Erik ran his eyes across the field before him, totting up the number of horses available to them. 'It looks as if we have enough mounts for the three crews here to ride directly to the city. We will add the Orkney men to our own lads and head off as soon as the manacles begin to go on.' A look back to the south confirmed that the Erikssons and their crews were already moving in, stacking the discarded weapons out of reach of their former owners and beginning the task of parcelling up Cuaran's men into those with a future of sorts and others whose wounds, age or disfigurement would make them harder to sell on; men who were already beginning to sense that they had witnessed their last dawn. As Sturla Godi and Thorstein moved away to spread the king's orders, Erik and Helgrim made their way across to the horses. Erik stole a glance at his huskarl as they walked. 'You mentioned a saying of my father's before the attack,' he said. 'I sometimes wonder how Harald Fairhair would judge my efforts to live up to his name.'

'King Harald would be proud lord,' Helgrim shot back. 'I served you both and I know that to be true.'

Erik was still unconvinced. 'Even though I was driven from the kingdom he fought so long and hard to bring beneath his sway?'

'Lesser men valued the contents of their treasury over the weight of their oath,' the huskarl replied. 'Their allegiance was bought, not earned — there is no shame in betrayal.'

The pair paused, running their eyes across the riverside as they reached the place where the horses had been picketed before the battle. Sturla and Thorstein were making their way upslope as the men they had detailed to deliver the king's command scattered about the field. Helgrim spoke again as he raised his eyes to watch other men rushing to carry out the Erikssons' orders. 'Many think you the greater,' he said with a look. 'I have heard it said that not only was the loss of your Norwegian kingdom the will of the gods, but it was the making of you as a man.'

Erik scoffed at the praise. 'I doubt that!'

'Look at your sons,' Helgrim replied with a flick of his chin, 'working together for the good of their clan. They like and trust you Erik, not many kings can say that of their offspring. How was your relationship with your own brothers?'

Erik rolled his eyes. 'You helped me kill a few, and the ones we missed were at each other's throats.'

'The world is changing lord, and we are changing with it. Being driven from Norway meant that the boys were recalled from foster or never sent away at all, they grew to manhood with their father and mother in the bosom of their own family. They came to see you not as a distant figure, just a name to live up to or better if they wished to survive, but witnessed the love their parents had for each other and also for them; they took strength from that.' The big huskarl fixed his king with a look. 'You may think that I am going soft and I was proud to serve your father in his day, but those were wolf days Erik and Harald Fairhair was the biggest, meanest wolf in the pack. He ruled by fear and division, by setting men against one another be they jarl, hersir or even his own flesh and blood. You could never rule a Christian kingdom in such a way — the church would never allow it — and we need the goodwill of the clergy if we are survive and prosper in this land. You witnessed the grip the priest at Sheptun had on his flock, the day you prayed before the battle at Ceasterford. If you can win the hearts and minds of the parish priests, you can count on them to support your rule among the freemen, the men who will rush to fill your levy when the need arises.'

A gentle cough drew their attention away, and Helgrim flushed as he saw that Sturla and Thorstein had reached them some time before and were stood listening in. Erik's banner man threw his fellow huskarl a wry look before turning his gaze on the king. 'The men know what to do lord,' he trilled, 'and your sons are going to row the ships up to the city as soon as they have finished chaining the prisoners.' Sturla's eyes sparkled as they slid from king to huskarl and back again. 'That was a lovely sermon, lord. Perhaps we should get bishop Helgrim here back to York — before he decides to spend the rest of the morning baptising heathens in the river?'

Erik was at the paling where the horses had been racked-up before the final words were out. 'You are right,' he said as the knot was slipped, 'even if the words were spoken in jest. We need to get moving — whichever gods have your devotion, our fight today is but half done.'

2

RETURN TO YORK

The first sounds drifted down to the returning king as Erik came clear of the woodland edge, the harsh clamour of lawlessness as inhabitants settled old scores and snatched what they could from neighbours and the weak before the return of order. A mile ahead a pall of greasy smoke hung over the city of York, and Erik savoured the smell of victory as he threw Thorstein and Helgrim a look. 'Once we cross the Foss, split the men into groups of twenty and have them move through the town.' Erik did a quick tally up of the men immediately available to him as they approached the bridge. The first inhabitants of the sprawl outside the walls had seen the approaching column now and men, women and children alike were vanishing into huts and alleyways like startled mice. 'Our three ships' crews, added to those of Arnkel and Erland will provide three hundred or so spears.' A glimmer of mischief came into his eyes as he saw the huskarls struggle with the calculation. 'That will give us fifteen armed groups,' he finally added with a smirk as the guards gave up on the arithmetic and looked to him for the answer, 'more than enough to sweep the city clear of troublemakers.' Erik cast a look at the sky. The sun was approaching the second quarter, ideal for his needs. 'Have them clear the streets, and pass the word that until they hear differently anyone caught out of doors after midday today will be hung on the spot.'

The horses had carried them to the bridge as they spoke, and Erik dropped his gaze to the wharf edging the far bank as his guards clattered across to clear the way ahead. Four years had passed since he had last looked upon the weathered timbers, the day he had returned from annihilating the Kentish rearguard at the ford on the River Aire. He had made the mistake of thinking that his position of king was secure then, that the populace of the kingdom of York were as fervent as their archbishop in their desire to be free from rule by the southern English; but king Eadred's campaign that summer had cowed them, and with his support draining away faster than ale from a leaky barrel he had had the sense to take ship and live to fight another day. That day had now arrived, and he raised his eyes to drink in the view as the horse gained the western bank and his guards returned to ride at his side. Ahead, the stone gatehouse which was the King's Garth shone like a jewel in the morning sunlight, and rising beyond its crenellations the familiar twin towers of the cathedral reached skyward through cobwebs of smoke.

A group of armed men had gathered at the archway which pierced the garth, and Erik watched as Helgrim stabbed back his heels to lead a strong party forward. Even at a distance Erik could make out the identities of the leaders of the party astride the city gate, and a smile came instinctively as he saw a man raise an arm to hail the riders thundering towards them. Helgrim had exchanged greetings with the group before Erik drew near, and the restored king of York slowed his mount to a trot as his guards moved aside and flanked the ancient roadway. 'My favourite Englishmen!' Erik exclaimed happily as he came within hailing distance. 'You are a balm for my eyes.'

Oswald Thane was the first to respond, the archbishop's righthand man's features an image of joy at Erik's return after four years away. 'And you for ours lord king,' he replied. 'If only the archbishop were here to witness this moment.'

Erik alighted as the horse drew to a halt, his eyes flicking from Oswald to his companion and back again as he walked towards them. 'Has any news reached us from the South?'

Oswald shook his head. 'Not as yet, but there is little cause for concern. The southern king can only make recommendations in church matters, and has no say over the people of Northumbria despite his ambitions. If he harmed my lord in any way, the pontiff in Rome would declare him excommunicate and damn his soul to Hell.'

Erik chuckled. 'Perhaps we could persuade the pope to do just that. It should at least keep Eadred's armies in the South where they belong.' His eyes moved across to the man at Oswald's side, and he exchanged a grin with the bluff Englishman as they clasped forearms in the warrior greeting: 'Regenwold…'

'King Erik,' the big earl replied, the emotion of the moment obvious to those within earshot as he dropped his voice to an undertone. 'Welcome home.'

Erik lifted his eyes to the inscription on the archway above him. 'Six times acclaimed emperor…father of his country,' he read aloud, before dropping his gaze to encompass those around him. 'Well, I have ambitions to match this *Caesar Nerva Trajan Augustus*. He set his features into a look of determination. 'But much remains to be done, so let us make a start.'

Erik's hearth men led the way, the Northumbrian

spearmen pulling back inside the confines of the city as Erik and Regenwold followed on side by side. The earl's voice echoed back from the masonry as they walked. 'We followed your adventures keenly while you were away, lord,' he said. Erik threw him a guilty look, and the Englishman stifled a smile. 'The archbishop has eyes and ears working on his behalf throughout the city, particularly among the traders down in the new town.' Erik nodded that he understood. York was a trading hub, one of the most important markets for goods throughout the North and beyond. Men were always eager for news, if only to enable them to be among the first to take advantage of a profitable situation. 'So, Wulfstan knows all about my years away?'

Regenwold laughed. 'Yes, I am afraid so, but there is no need to worry. The archbishop once explained his feelings regarding the newly converted to me. He described the kingdom of York as a family of nations, and just like any clan you have to make allowances for the odd rascal they inevitably contain for the good of the whole.' He continued with a glint in his eye. 'Just because cousin Erik carries off God-fearing Irishmen and Franks to sell in the slave markets of Novgorod and Hedeby, does not make the fact of his kinship any less real. He believes that with time, patience and Christian forgiveness this wayward kinsman will one day come to see the error of his ways.'

Erik returned the look as they came clear of the passage-way. 'So this act of brotherliness is just Christian charity? It has nothing to do with the fact that trading in thralls is one of the surest ways to fill my hulls with gold and silver?' The humour in Regenwold's expression vanished as quickly as it had arrived, and Erik laid a hand on his trusted earl's arm as the warriors formed a cordon around the square. Profitable or not, the captives had still been fellow Christians. 'I made the mistake before of attempting to rule here without the means,' Erik explained patiently. 'A lack of silver weakens a king's authority as surely as a weak arm in battle, but I have learnt that lesson well. Every raid, every battle over the past four years, was fought to amass treasure. Now, with my ships and halls in Orkney and Jutland filled with good silver I have assembled an army — not just to reclaim the king helm of York, but to bring the lands beyond the River Tees back under Yorkish rule. You told me once you had a dream, to reestablish the ancient borders of the kingdom of Northumbria.' The king rested a hand on the earl's shoulder as they walked. 'Well, I share that dream, and now I have the means to make it a reality.'

Erik paused as the pair exited the gatehouse, running his eyes along the walls of the garth. All was as he remembered it; the old Anglian hall resplendent in its carvings of Christ and the saints abutting the Roman stonework, alongside the Óðinn tales picked out in fading reds and golds on the later extension added by the Danes in the last century. The sound of men and horses entering the gateway to their rear dragged Erik's mind back to the matter at hand, which was, he knew, securing the city. He turned to Regenwold again. 'Are all of Olaf Cuaran's men dead or in captivity?'

'As far as I can tell, King Erik. Practically all of the best troops accompanied him south to Wessex with the archbishop, and those remaining were only enough to guard the city walls and secure the garth here.' Regenwold indicated a moss covered lean-to further along the city wall with a flick of his head. 'Those we rounded up have been stripped of their weapons and armour, and are locked up in there.'

Erik looked. 'How many?'

'Three score and two, lord.'

'You seem very sure of the numbers.'

'I counted them myself.'

Erik laughed. 'Then it must be so. But try not to look so smug next time — it doesn't become you.'

Erik noticed that Oswald had crossed to the garth doors and was in conversation with the archbishop's house warriors, Morcar Thane, Oswy and Wystan — men the English called *gesith*. He exchanged a nod of recognition and a smile with them as he went on. 'So how many of your men are left within the walls?'

'Without counting those on the walkways and guarding places such as the garth, the prisoners and the cathedral, only about fifty or so.' Regenwold pulled a face. 'Earl Gunderic has men out sweeping the surrounding area for stragglers, but we couldn't make a move until we were sure that your ships were in the Humber.'

'You did well,' Erik replied with a reassuring pat on the arm. 'Helgrim is dividing our crews into groups of twenty. Most of them know the layout of the streets from their time here before, but four years is a long time and some of the men are new; if you can lend me a man to guide each group it would be a help. If we concentrate on the area within the city walls for now, we will bring order to the new town down by the Ouse when the Erikssons have brought the fleet upstream. I have given orders that anyone found out of doors within the perimeter of the city walls after midday will be hung without trial. Perhaps your men can help to spread the word?'

Regenwold smiled. 'It would be my pleasure, lord.'

'Oh, and at the same time,' Erik added as an afterthought, 'tell them to pass the word throughout the city that there is a reward of ten pennies for any of Olaf Cuaran's men who are still at large.'

Regenwold let out a low whistle. 'Ten silver coins per head? Rounding up a couple will be enough for a healthy

ewe, or a full month's wenching with the ale thrown in —
that is very generous lord.'

Erik smiled. 'Not so generous as it seems. I shall make it
back and more when I empty their purses, sell their weapons
and armour, and then pack them off to the slavers down by
the docks. It is a small price to pay to win back the populace,
plus it should dramatically reduce the chance of my getting a
knife between the ribs from one of Cuaran's stragglers
looking to make a name for himself before he pitches up in
Óðinn's hall.'

'I will see to it straightaway,' Regenwold replied with a
dip of his head. Erik was about to go when the Englishman
stopped and turned back, a smile lighting his face as he did
so. 'It is good to have you back, lord,' he said. 'Even rascals
can be sure of a welcome at the family hearthside.'

The earl moved away as the square resounded to the
sound of the king's laughter, and as faces were turned his way
Erik indicated that the remaining guards come to his side. At
the archway Helgrim Smiter had begun to divide up the first
crews, and as Thorstein and Kolbein came up the king hailed
the archbishop's men as the Norwegians approached the
king's garth after four long years away. 'Earl Regenwold tells
me that the majority of Olaf's men are safely locked up. Is the
garth completely empty?'

'There are a half-dozen trusted men, lord,' Morcar
replied. 'Making sure that no one is tempted to make off with
the contents of Cuaran's strongroom, plus a few thralls in the
kitchens.'

Erik's face lit up. 'Has anyone taken a look inside this
strongroom?'

'I took a peek,' the Englishman admitted, 'just to ensure
there were none of the usurper's men hiding inside. The room
contained several large chests, but they are locked and bound

by heavy chains so I could not look inside them. Whatever Cuaran had accumulated since he arrived must still be there I guess. The king's garth was the first place we took this morning — most of the men within it died before they were fully awake.'

Erik nodded. 'That was good work, I was hoping I would get to add Olaf's stockpile to my own. Once we are secure and the queen is here, I think a bit of a share out is in order.' Erik had long since learned that the promise of a purse of silver or an arm ring lifted the spirits of even the surliest of men, and the Englishmen guarding the doorway beamed at the news. 'I will send a half-crew to bolster your numbers until I return,' he added. 'It is important that I am seen throughout the city, so that no one is in any doubt who is king here.' Erik ran his gaze across the square as he walked back to the gateway. The crews who had accompanied him from the battlefield outside Bardolfsby were inside the walls now, their leading men busy parcelling up the spearmen and sending them through the roads and alleyways which ran away in all directions. The crew of the *Draki* were waiting patiently for his return, and Erik called out to his banner man as he came up: 'Sturla!'

'Yes, lord?'

Erik indicated the place where Morcar, Oswy and Wystan were still guarding the king's hall with a jerk of his head. 'Lead half of the crew over to the garth. It looks as if Olaf Cuaran has made a gift of his treasury — it would be a shame to mislay it so quickly.' Erik smiled. 'While you are waiting for our return you can sample the ale in the buttery, and check that the pantry contains plenty of provisions while you are at it. If you feel the need, send men out to buy in additional supplies — the crews have fought well, and I have a reputation for open-handedness to maintain.' Sturla nodded enthusiastically, and Erik turned his attention towards the centre of the city as his huskarl began to detail off those who would remain behind.

Helgrim had returned, and the king drew his leading guards about him as he prepared to lead those remaining into the heart of York. Fossgate stretched before him as he took up his place at the head of the column, the familiar dwellings and workshops which crowded the route throwing it into deep shade despite the approach of midday, and Erik exchanged a look and a nod with men at his side before stepping out. Within moments he had left the sun-drenched square behind, and as he plunged into the shadows his eyes stabbed the doors and alleyways to either side for any hint of treachery. Up ahead the first of the looters and cutthroats ferreted out by the crews were swinging lazily on makeshift gibbets, but Erik spared them scarcely a glance as the way opened up and he came to the crossroads at the centre of the city. A wheel to the right revealed the wide expanse of the main square, and beyond it the precipitous walls and towers of St Peter's Minster, the creamy coloured stone studded with blues and reds as the sunlight played upon the great widows there. It was here that Gunnhild had ridden at his side the day of his coronation, when she had helped to face down the barracking from Cuaran's place-men before joining the Erikssons to undergo baptism by the hand of Archbishop Wulfstan. The space was devoid of any kind of life this day, the populace of York well used to the dangers which stalked the streets when one king replaced another, and Erik walked boldly ahead despite his huskarls' obvious twitchiness at the danger posed by a bowman hidden in the storied buildings at the heart of the city. But no arrows came, the doors and shutters remaining resolutely closed as they marched, and soon Erik was climbing the steps to the cathedral and entering the stillness and serenity familiar to any who had cause to enter a house of the Christian God.

Oswald Thane reappeared at the door to the nave, the archbishop's representative now dressed in his finery following a predawn and morning spent in more warlike garb, and Erik reached behind his shoulder to draw Jomal as stewards came forward to collect his weapons. His face creased into a smile as did so. 'The city is quiet with no sign of opposition,' Erik said, flinching inwardly as his voice boomed throughout the cavernous interior. 'My loyal Englishmen did their work well.' The king's voice dropped to a more measured tone as he continued. 'I shall never forget it.' Erik moved forward to lay a hand upon the man's shoulder. 'You can help me one last time today, Oswald,' he said, 'if you would show me a further act of kindness.'

Oswald looked surprised. 'Of course King Erik, if it is in my power to do so I will aid you in any way I can.'

Erik snorted. 'Have no fear — 'tis no great thing.' His eyes took in the stout oak doors which flanked the vestibule to either side. 'I presume these doors lead up to the tops of the towers?' Oswald confirmed that they did. 'I wish to survey my kingdom,' Erik said. 'Is that possible from within?'

'There are stairways in both towers lord,' Oswald confirmed. 'Although only the northernmost tower has an uninterrupted view. The South Tower contains the great bell,' he explained, 'and the walkway which surrounds it is somewhat more precarious.'

Erik nodded. 'The North Tower will suit my needs well.'

As the pair crossed to the door and Oswald fumbled with his keys, Thorstein and Helgrim moved to fall in at the king's side: Erik held out a hand to stay them as he gave voice to a command. 'I would be alone with my thoughts lads,' he said as he patted the hilt of his short seax. 'If there are any enemies hiding up there I still have this to protect myself, and if I should fall within the confines of the cathedral walls it could only be the Will of God.'

Ahead Oswald was fumbling with a keyring the size of a blacksmith's fist, and as the correct key was teased clear of the bunch to grate in the lock, the door was pushed inward and Erik passed through into the room beyond. The big door closed with a boom which reverberated in the void sending pigeons and rodents scattering about the space, and as he craned his neck to peer upwards through a gentle rain of feathers and muck his eyes slowly grew accustomed to the gloom. A wooden staircase hugged the tower walls as it climbed upward through a latticework of supporting beams; high above specks of dust drifted slowly in the soft light streaming in from the wind holes high above. Erik climbed, marvelling that mere men could construct such a thing for the umpteenth time, and within a short while he broke out from the murk and into the full light of midday.

He crossed to the eastern casement first, the breath catching in his throat as he peered out across the rooftops of York far below. There, beyond the line of Fossgate he had recently travelled, out beyond the walls and the brooding stronghold of the king's garth, the ships of the fleet were tawny pinpricks on the waters of the Ouse as they walked on slender oars towards the city.

A few paces later he was gazing south, his eyes following the line of the old Roman road to the distant marshes which straddled the River Humber. Beyond it lay the old kingdoms of Wessex and Mercia, and of the Danish Five Boroughs too. Ancient enemies, they were now under the sway of the king in distant Winchester, and if his return had taken the giant by surprise Erik knew that could not last. Since King Athelstan's day the leader of the West Saxons had laid claim to the king-ship of all the English people in Britain, from the Southern Sea to the Firth of Forth. They would march north again, but Erik would be ready this time when they did.

Westwards the hills lay under a drugget of clouds as grey as any wolf, but it was the view northwards which had caused him to climb to his lofty perch, and Erik rested his palms against the gritty stonework as he raised his chin to look. Out beyond the woodlands of the Wolds, past the silver line which marked the meandering of the River Tees, stretched the vales and moors of the old kingdom of Bernicia. An earldom since the Danish invasions in the last century, the rump of Northumbria was still ruled by the old English rulers from their rocky fastness at distant Bebbanburh. But it was a throwback now, a distant echo of a time when warlords could carve themselves a small kingdom from the chaos which had followed the order of Rome, and their Englishness only attracted the avaricious gaze of the southerners. Divided thus York and Bernicia must fall, swallowed up by either the Scots to the north or the English beyond the Humber. Archbishop Wulfstan, that champion of northern independence knew it, and so too did Erik. But let them make their plans the Norseman mused, as he gazed out across the lush fields and tree covered hills of his kingdom; he had not wasted his years in exile — with his treasury replenished and his army rein-forced, he now had plans of his own.

3
___

BEASTS OF OÐINN

The king left the stony setts, his spirits soaring as he felt
the spring in the wooden boards and his thoughts
turned to ships and the sea. In the six weeks which had passed
since his return, Erik had tightened his grip on the city and
the surrounding countryside as his Norwegians and the loyal
English earls had driven the last of Olaf Cuaran's oath sworn
beyond the borders. News had reached York of archbishop
Wulfstan's arrest, and strong war bands under trusted men
had been sent across the Humber to look for signs of attack;
everywhere they rode they had found only a land at peace,
and Erik had recalled them gratefully as the long days of high
summer approached.

Content that the kingdom was under no immediate threat
he had sent word to Orkney, and his eyes came alive at the
sight of his queen as the ship came about and pointed its snub
bow into the Foss. Prone to seasickness as she was, Gunnhild
had come south in the more stable hull of a trader's knarr, her
youngest sons Sigurd and Ragnfrod escorting her in their
skei. With no sign of danger at home Gamli had gone too, the
long sleek hull of the *Vindálfr* sweeping the seas clear of

27

shipping as the little flotilla hugged the coast of Alba and Bernicia.

The trader was coming alongside now, the styrisman scattering coots and grebes like windblown leaves as he dragged the tiller to his chest and the ship swung in. Erik walked forward as the strakes nudged the landing stage, the mooring ropes flew, and the gang plank met the jetty with a clatter. Gunnhild was the first to cross, and Erik's face broke into a smile of welcome as he watched her approach. 'Hail Erik Haraldsson,' she said as she came closer, 'the rightful king in York restored.'

Erik's eyes drank in her form as she approached. If her childbearing days were behind her Gunnhild still had the body of a woman far younger in years, and Erik looked on appreciatively as the silks and gold which clad his queen stood out in stark contrast to the more earthy colours of those all around. He took her hand, and all thoughts of grand speeches flew from his mind at the closeness of her after a springtime away and he uttered the words they had waited so long to hear. 'Welcome home my queen…'

Gunnhild was a proud woman, the daughter and wife of kings, and he knew that she would be struggling to hide the feelings of elation she felt at her homecoming in front of her lessers. But her features softened at the words, and as her eyes began to moisten the king knew that the quicker they took the short ride to the garth the easier it would be for her. Exile, he knew, had been far harder on the queen than himself — four years spent on a gale blown rock off the western coast of Orkney while he had been off with their sons every summer, plundering any land which offered a coastline or estuary as they fought to restore the family to their rightful place in the world. They mounted quickly, and Erik paused only to exchange nods of greeting with his returning sons before he urged the horse into a walk.

Gunnhild was serene at his side, and Erik cast his thoughts back over the time in York since his return as the horses moved ahead and his sons mounted up to follow in their wake. The takeover had been remarkably smooth he reflected, as the populace crowded Fossgate and cheered his name. Familiar with the sound of sword fighting in the dawn and the meaning behind it, the inhabitants of the city outside-the-walls had already settled old scores and finished their robbing by the time the fleet had arrived following the battle at Bardolfsby. The Erikssons had led their crewmen through the maze of streets and alleyways in a show of strength, but the only sign of man had been the odd unclaimed corpse and they had joined Erik in the garth by mid afternoon. Erik snorted as he recalled the time. Even a morning in a place like York without a king would produce a month's worth of rulings when authority returned, but the backlog was behind him now and he could leave the rest to Gunnhild. Tonight they would celebrate her homecoming, and in the morning he would ride once more to the southern border, sniff out any hint of trouble brewing there and plan his next move.

ERIK DREW rein at their approach, waiting patiently for the scouting party as they pearled the waters of the ford to urge travel-weary horses the final half mile. The king ran his eyes over the riders as they came. The River Aire had washed the road dust from legs and flanks, but the unmistakable signs of a hard ride still coated men and beasts in a dusting of greyness, and Erik made a call that ale be passed forward as the horsemen recognised the king's banner and began to slow their headlong dash. He flicked a look skyward as he waited.

The vault was the mackerel blue of a perfect day, and Erik watched the gyrations of the swallows and martins with joy as they slashed the heavens before swooping down to reap the summer bounty a hand width above the meadow. Erik hailed the leading rider as they reined in before him. 'Hauk,' he said. 'Welcome home — what news?'

'All quiet lord,' the scout replied. 'There is no sign that the southerners are mustering for an attack.'

Erik nodded. 'How far did you ride?'

'We have been out just over a week,' Hauk said. 'The farthest we rode was to a place called Werchesope, a hamlet a couple of days' ride south of here, but we made sure to comb the countryside to east and west and question the inhabitants thereabouts.' He shook his head. 'Beyond that is a vast tract of woodland the locals call *Scir Wudu* — home to far more deer and wolf-heads than regular folk, we would discover nowt there. Nobody has heard a word — there has been no hint of a call-out or any orders to gather supplies to feed an army on the march. Nothing to suggest that campaigning is in the air.'

Thorstein was resting a skin of ale on the horn of his saddle, and Erik indicated that he toss it across to the thirsty scout. 'Here,' he said, 'rinse the dust from your throats. We were about to stop and eat — we have fresh white bread and cold meats on the wagons. Join us and I will find a firkin for your lads, it will be enough to start the day until you can reach York and celebrate your safe return properly.'

Hauk beamed at the invitation. Scouts rarely drank anything more potent than small beer while away from the main army, the success of the errand and very survival depending on keeping their wits sword-blade sharp at all times. But a nine gallon barrel of the finest Yorkish ale should be a good start to the homecoming celebrations, and Erik smiled at the looks on the faces of the men before him even as he envied them their youthful appetite.

Erik urged the horse forward with a jab of his heels, and as the scouts parted the riverside flanking the crossing place at Ceasterford opened up before him. The weather here had been just as flawless four years before, the day they had trapped the English rearguard with their backs to the ford and cut them down almost to a man. It had been Erik's greatest victory on English soil, but heavy fighting lay ahead if he was to realise his dream, and with his coffers full and the kingdom bristling with spears he ached for the war to begin again. Helgrim's voice cut into his thoughts as they reached the causeway, the ancient road known as the Roman Rigg shimmering in the heat as it ran down to the ford. 'That is a good place to stop, lord,' he said. 'Nice and flat, and far enough from the bone field.'

Erik looked. A grassy terrace cut across the roadway, the southern boundary falling away sharply where it joined the floodplain. 'Yes,' he agreed, 'have the wagons pull over.' He slipped from the saddle as the Orkney brothers rode forward. Erland and Arnkel were kin now through the marriage of Erik's daughter Ragnhild to their older brother Arnkel, and he had promised that he would show them the battle site that morning. The king and his leading warriors had gone shield to shield with the Kentishmen during the fight, far too closely engaged to gain an overview of the battle. But Erik's banner man was also his skald, and Sturla Godi came across to lead them down to the scene of the fighting as Erik slipped from the saddle. He turned to his huskarls as they dropped to the ground all around him. 'Go and grab something to eat boys,' he said with the flick of a hand. 'I am just going down for a look around.' Erik tossed the reins of his mount across to Kolbein as he turned to go. Ahead Sturla was already in full flow, the skald's arm arcing around as he described the moment of Gamli Eriksson's flanking attack which had finally broken Kentish resistance. A knot of Orcadians were hanging on every word as Sturla described the fight, and Erik passed by unnoticed as he walked down to the place where the front ranks had stood that day. From here the bone field radiated out to east and west like ripples in a pond, the more distant showing just how far the last of the fugitives had travelled before they were ridden down by the Norse reserve under Arinbjorn and his men. His foster-brother was back in Norway and settled into his inheritance now that Thorir had died, rarely venturing abroad having made his peace with Erik's half-brother King Hakon. Erik had toyed with the idea to visit him at his hall in Fjordane more than once during the past four years, or even the king in Avaldsnes to make his own accommodation with Hakon and revisit the scenes of his youth. But he had known it was folly; there was nothing for him now back in Norway — whatever the gods had in mind for Erik Haraldsson it lay here, on this side of the sea.

A familiar voice broke onto his thoughts, and Erik turned to throw his huskarl a smile as he took the proffered food. The pair stood shoulder to shoulder in silent companionship as they ate, with only the muffled words of Sturla Godi drifting across from the far roadside to compete with the high pitched *chir-rup* of the swallows above.

Helgrim was the first to break the silence, his voice not much more than a murmur as his eyes remained fixed upon the scene of fighting. 'You came as close to Valhöll here as anywhere, lord.'

Erik nodded as he recalled the fight. 'The backwoodsman — I misjudged him and almost paid the price.' He snorted. 'It is a lesson to us all. The old hags care nothing for pomp and reputation — when the time is ripe and the shears sharpened, they will snip your life thread whether you are faced by king or thrall.' Erik cast his eyes to the south. Beyond the drainage ditch which edged the causeway the bones of a defeated army lay in drifts. Four years in the open and the depredations of scavengers had been enough to strip the flesh from them, but the tattered remains of clothing and the odd patch of buff coloured hide still added a smidgeon of colour here and there. 'I thought that I might seek out his remains,' Erik said suddenly. 'To carry him away for a Christian burial.'

Erik's maudlin tone drew an immediate response. 'It is not like you to think too deeply about the fate of your enemies Erik, and it would not sit well with the men if they knew.' Helgrim teased out a grisly piece of meat from his meal and tossed it aside. Within moments a magpie had hopped across to carry it off. The huskarl placed a friendly hand on his lord's shoulder as he prepared to go. 'I am off back to the lads, lord,' he said. 'Do your thinking and leave it here, the men look to you for leadership in more ways than one *Erikr Blóðøx*. You are a battle winner, a lord of war — that is why they follow you.' He smiled as he turned to go. 'If they had wanted to follow a deep thinker they would have become novices or skalds.'

Erik rolled his eyes at Helgrim's advice, but a quick look at the crowd filling the terrace as he watched the big huskarl go confirmed the wisdom of his words. Most were happily at their cups, hunks of meat or bread in hand as they swapped tall-tales and quaffed ale with their friends. But more than a few heads were turned towards him, a solitary figure now that Helgrim had gone, and he knew that the number would grow with every moment away. A dozen paces to the West, Sturla was still describing the fight to enthusiastic Orkneymen and he thought to walk across — but a king sometimes needed to be alone with his thoughts if he was to govern well, and he knew that this was such a time. Away to the Southwest a dark cap of clouds was building over the higher ground of the Peaks; beyond it lay the heartlands of king Eadred's kingdom of the southern English. Erik's return and the manner of it had been a humiliation for that king — archbishop Wulfstan's disappearance was proof of that. That there would be a reckoning was obvious despite the king's ill health, and Erik ran through the steps he had taken to preserve his own kingdom as he watched the distant rainclouds gather.

Gamli was already back at sea, Erik and Gunnhild's eldest son leading a strong force south along the coast to guard against any reaction from that quarter. If no opposition was forthcoming they had agreed between them that his son would sail as far as the Thames, waylaying traders sailing to and from London in an effort to discover what preparations were being made there to challenge Erik's return to York. Despite the fact that he had been shorn of the best part of his army, Olaf Cuaran must still be considered a threat — especially as he had the backing of the southerners. In addition his old enemy also had kin in Dublin to turn to for succour, along with widespread holdings within Cumbraland in Britain's north-west. Harald Eriksson had left York that morning to scour the western hills, but it was the journey made by Oswald Thane on which Erik pinned most of his hopes, and he sent an invocation to Óðinn and Christ that the archbishop's experienced go-between be successful in his endeavour. Sent north the moment that Erik's position in York was secure, Oswald had been tasked with persuading the earl of Bernicia, the fellow Englishman Oswulf Ealdwulfing, to form an alliance with Erik's kingdom of York, a wide ranging cooperation which would not only help both leaders to counter the military threat presented by the powerful kingdoms of England and Alba which bordered them, but enable the pair to take the offensive. For far too long, ever since the fall of York to Danish Vikings in the previous century and the subsequent division of Northumbria into its ancient regions, the lands between the Humber and the Firth of Forth had been riven by division. Thus weakened they had provided easy pickings for the burgeoning powers of Alba and England, a weakness they had been quick to exploit. But Erik knew that if the earl could be persuaded to remake the old realm, to restore the Northumbrian kingdom of old, then it would be they who held sway over the island of Britain and the centre of power would return to the city of York where it belonged.

Erik cast a last lingering look to the south before turning aside. The time away from the men had helped to clear his mind, and reinvigorated by the steps he had taken to safe-guard the kingdom he began to make his way back along the Roman Rigg. At the roadway's edge Sturla Godi was still in full flow, and Erik marvelled at his craft as the skald's words hung in the sultry air:

> *The Rigg lay narrow under the feet of men;*
> *the mail clad troop burst forth into battle.*

> *When the iron-grey úlfheðnar rushed down,*
> *slavering beasts of Óðinn;*
> *great was the slaughter at Ceasterford.*

Within a few short paces he was nearing the riverside terrace and its cargo of Norse. Erik watched as conversations trailed away at his approach, and mindful of their gaze he painted on a grin as he passed the horses and left the roadway. The men brightened to see their king in high spirits, the earlier concerns now chased away as he moved through the crowd, hailing them by name and lauding their kin. The nagging concern that he had abandoned the archbishop to his fate still tugged at his conscience, but there was little he could do until he received news from the South, and satisfied now that he had done all within his power to safeguard his land he crossed to his friends and took up a cup of his own.

4

HREYRR CAMP

Erik crossed to the window, the morning sun warming his face as he rested his elbows upon the sill. Cupping a hand to his mouth he called out to the guards on the roadway below. 'Stand fifty paces from the wall, and remember; no-one is to come closer than that under any circumstances until I tell you otherwise.'

The sentinels nodded that they understood, and Erik watched as their leader began to pace out the distance. As the spearmen began to shoo the travellers and bystanders away, Erik stepped back into the shadows of the king's garth and turned his face to the men sat there. 'Let us have these closed too,' he said with the waft of a hand. 'The fate of us all could very well rest upon the decision we take today. The fewer men who know our plans the better, even guards have ears.' The king crossed to the high seat and took his place, watching as the sunbeams which lined the floor were snuffed out one by one. Erik gave Gamli a nod of thanks as the final screen closed with a clatter and the motes of dust dancing in the air before them disappeared from view, waiting until his son had regained the bench opposite before flashing the group a smile. 'Everyone got a drink?' The raised cups and horns told him they had, and with Arinbjorn back at his hall in Norway, Erik paused to run his eyes along the men who remained from his most trusted companions. The Erikssons: Gamli; Harald; Guttorm; Sigurd and Ragnfrod alongside his own huskarls: Thorstein Egilsson; Helgrim Smiter; Sturla Godi and the ever loyal styrisman Kolbein Herjolfsson. The Orkney men Arnkel and Erland were there, brothers of the jarl Torfinn Skull-Splitter. The English trio Regenwold, Morcar and Oswald Thane had proven their loyalty time and again over the years and he was glad to have them alongside his Norse. Erik fingered his beard as his mind sifted the names. A dozen men he could count on, almost half of them kinsmen, may not appear so many after a lifetime spent dispensing gold and silver from his gift-stool, but it was a reflection on the loosening of the ties of honour which bound fighting men he decided, rather than any fault of his own. The words spoken by Helgrim Smiter came back to him, the day they had crushed the fleeing garrison of York earlier that summer. He needed the help of the Christian church now to rule effectively, the teachings and lessons of the priests were chipping away at the old loyalties which bound fighting men together in a brotherhood of warriors, eager to tread the rainbow bridge as a company. He was growing more convinced by the year that the wolf days of Harald Fairhair and Erik Haraldsson were drawing to a close, as what churchmen called "civilisation" closed in on every side.

Erik's eyes came into focus as his mind returned from its wanderings to be met with a line of quizzical expressions. He gave a snort of embarrassment at the lack of attention at such a time, raising his own horn to drain the contents in a single draught in the time-honoured sign that the council of war had begun. The equally customary belch and slap of the lips out of the way, Erik refilled the horn from the pitcher at his side and addressed the men. 'So, it seems that the expected retaliation for the king of York regaining his rightful throne is to be an invasion, not from the South as expected, but from the people to the North. Oswald,' Erik said with a nod in the Northumbrian's direction. 'Would you share the news you received today, so that we may look to our response?'

The archbishop's thane answered with a nod, and rising from the communal bench he took the floor; a final swig from his ale cup and he addressed the room. 'As you are all well aware, my lord and patron has been detained by king Eadred in the South for what I am informed they are describing as: "certain accusations which have often been made to the king against him; that he connives at the shifts of allegiance of his compatriots."' Oswald threw them a smile which was reflected back by those present; 'that would be us. As you also know,' he continued, 'the archbishop still has many friends within the southern church, so although his confinement in the old Roman fortress at Iudanbyrig may be frustrating to a man of his intelligence and energy, it has its uses. His gaolers talk freely about matters of statecraft unaware that the archbishop has friends close by who can deliver messages to us here in York. It would seem that king Eadred's health is worsening, almost by the day, and as such we can rest assured that we are safe from attack from that quarter this year. However the archbishop has discovered that the southern king has required Mael Colm mac Domnaill, the king of Scots, to honour the agreement made several years ago by his brother king Edmund following the invasion of and subsequent seeding of both Strathclyde and Cumbraland to his kingdom of Alba.'

As the men remaining on the bench began to chatter at the revelation, Erik rapped the ale horn on the arm of the high seat to gain their attention. 'Listen up! Grizzled veteran or not, the king of Scots and his whelps will not be coming alone.'

Oswald acknowledged his king's intervention with a nod and continued. 'Archbishop Wulfstan has sent word that he has discovered that king Eadred has shipped large quantities of silver north to pay for the participation of earl Oswulf and his Bernicians in the coming invasion.'

A growl came from the men lining the bench, but Erik held up a hand to still them. 'It would seem that we may have the answer to the messages of friendship we have been sending to the earl in Bebbanburh over the course of the summer, but let us not jump to hasty conclusions. A powerful army is about to attack us here in the kingdom of York and the quickest, most direct path they can use to reach us is along the Roman roads which cross the northern earldom.'

'The last time the Scots came south under old king Constantine,' Oswald offered, 'the Bernician thanes who hold lands in Lothian, north of Bebbanburh, joined forces with the invaders. Earl Oswald remained holed up in his coastal fortress, but at least he refrained from adding his army to the host so there may be hope of an alliance yet.'

Erik nodded. 'If the earl does take southern silver and joins the invasion, we shall give him the benefit of any doubt for now.' Erik paused and swept those sat opposite with a look of determination before continuing. 'As soon as we beat back this attack, we shall redouble our efforts to bring the Bernicians over to our side. Experience tells them that they have every reason to fear the power of their northern neighbours and their puppet-masters in Winchester and London. That may well have held true in the days of Olaf Cuaran and his kin who sat in York in days gone over, but their complacency may well work to our advantage and it falls to us to prove them wrong.' Erik smiled a rapacious smile which was reflected back from the faces opposite. 'Thankfully we are about to be handed the perfect opportunity to do just that.' He turned his eyes to the earl. 'Regenwold — how do we usually respond to a northern invasion?'

The earl hauled his giant frame from the bench and moved across to take the floor as Oswald regained his seat. 'The war arrow is sent out as usual lord,' he replied, 'and the army musters in my earldom — along Dere Street just north of my hall in Catrice. It's a short hop from there to the border at the River Tees, as you will recall from the time we rode it together.'

Erik nodded that he did. The weather had been sullen the day they had ridden to mark the borders of his new kingdom five years previously — rainy and windswept under a cloak of leaden clouds. The fast flowing river and absence of any useable bridge made an ideal bulwark against an invader and he could see the sense of it, but it was a gutless approach to warfare and his mind was already working on a plan as he pushed the earl for more. 'Do we ever move across the river to confront them? Or are we always on the defensive?'

Regenwold's mouth became a line and he shifted awkwardly. 'The Great Army rode over the land of course, back in the last century, but the last time that a major battle was fought in Bernicia was over thirty years ago when I was a lad. Ragnall ua Ímair came from Ireland and defeated the Scots and Bernicians at a place called Corebricg on the River Tine, and then came south to rule here in York for a couple of years before he died. Naturally on his death,' he said with a look of exasperation, 'Northumbria split again.'

Erik set his features into a scowl as his mind continued to sketch out a plan for the upcoming war. 'That depends on the mettle of the king here in York. What can you tell me about this place Corebricg?' Erik asked the Englishman. 'Why did the fight take place there, is it another river crossing?'

Regenwold took a sip of ale before replying. 'Three important roads converge at that point lord; Dere Street itself passes through on its way to Lothian, a good Roman made road leads north-east to Bebbanburh and another called Stane Gate skirts the southern side of the wall of Hadrian to Cair Ligualid, the main town in Cumbraland.'

Erik's eyes flashed as the battle plan began to come together in his mind. He ran his gaze along those seated opposite as he attempted to control any outward signs of the excitement which was building within, but his face creased into a smile as he saw that Harald Eriksson too had realised the opportunity which was presenting itself. If Erik's second son was thinking along the same lines the plan was sound — the young man's mind was as sharp as a blade. He turned his face to Oswald Thane. 'The archbishop is certain that we will be facing the combined armies of Alba, Strathclyde and Cumbraland, and in all probability earl Oswulf too?'

The man nodded. 'That is the information I have lord. I received the correspondence this morning and hastened here to share the news.'

Erik switched his gaze. 'Regenwold, where is it most likely the men from Cumbraland and Strathclyde will join their Scottish overlords?'

'King Dyfnwal of Strathclyde should lead his host east-wards to link up with the Scots at the northern limit of Dere Street and head south together. Despite the fact that Cumbraland is ruled from Strathclyde, I doubt that the men levied there will also take the same route.'

Erik shared a look with Harald. 'No, it is unlikely,' he agreed. 'That would mean they would be marching in a great circle, north, east and back south, ending up practically where they began, tiring out the army and using up valuable provisions.' He turned back to Oswald. 'When did Wulfstan's letter say that the enemy intended to assemble?'

'On the Feast of the Exaltation of the Holy Cross, lord.'

Erik rolled his eyes, drawing a rumble of laughter from those present.

'This month King Erik, the fourteenth day of September; they clearly have it in mind to carry off or burn the harvest as part of their treaty obligation to the English king.'

'And when does this exalted feast occur?'

'Nine days from now lord.'

'But the archbishop did not mention where this meet up was to take place?'

Oswald shook his head. 'I am afraid not, no lord.'

Erik raised his eyes to take in those opposite, and was gratified to see that more of the men sat there were realising his intention to carry the fight to the foe. 'Nine days...' he breathed, drumming his fingertips on the arm of the high seat as the plan hardened in his mind. 'Regenwold,' he said finally as he reached his decision. 'What size force can we expect to face from Cumbraland alone?'

'Three, maybe four ships' companies.'

'So — two hundred men at most?'

The big man nodded. 'Cair Ligualid is the only settlement of note in the entire region. Most of the men are hill farmers in the valleys and dales, a few Norse and Angles but mostly Britons whose ancestors were tending sheep thereabouts before the Romans came.'

Erik switched his gaze. 'Oswald, change into your travelling clothes and be ready to leave York at midday — you are riding with me. Everyone else,' he said with a ravening look. 'Listen closely: this is what I intend to do.'

· · ·

Erik slipped from the saddle and arched his back, blowing out as the muscles protested and a joint somewhere made a loud crack. He was well past his half century on Midgard now, but he consoled himself with the thought that that still gave him thirty or forty more years if he were to outlive his father. Whether he would need that long to fulfil the Finnish sorcerer's prophesy and gain his fifth and final crown remained to be seen, but another realisation surprised him when it came as the image of a white haired Erik Haraldsson secure in his garth in York came into his mind — he cared far more for the wellbeing of the folk in this kingdom than he ever had for those in the fjords and uplands of his motherland. Oswald Thane was having a last word with the scouts, and Erik waited patiently until they looked his way. 'All set?'

A chorus of youthful voices assured him they were, and Erik smiled a fatherly smile as he prepared to set them loose. 'Remember, we are all counting on you. Stick to the uplands and keep as far away from folk as you are able. As soon as you locate the enemy hightail it back to us here with the news, but for the sake of us all don't get spotted. If we can catch them by surprise we shall have a great victory, but if they are ready and waiting it will be our bodies feeding the eagle and the wolf. It's forty miles from here to the road we expect the Cumbrians to travel to the muster, so you will have to move fast if we are to have any chance of intercepting them. But you were chosen because you are the best,' he added with a look, 'and I know you will repay our trust.' Erik jerked his head to the north as the scouts stretched their backs to sit a little taller in the saddle at their king's praise. 'Off you go then lads,' he said as the riders hauled the heads of their mounts around, 'and deliver them up to our blades.'

As the band of riders whooped with joy and spurred their horses northward, Erik exchanged a smile with Oswald as they watched them go. 'To be young and invincible again, eh?'

The Northumbrian stood kneading the blood back into a travel sore rump as he shot back a reply. 'And able to ride day and night without feeling like you have just wrestled a bear.'

Erik snorted and looked back to the South. Erland was leading his Orkney men in through the gap in the ancient ramparts to join his brother Arnkel and his war band; the men of the *Draki* were already picketing the horses, pitching tents and clearing a space for the campfires. Satisfied that all was in hand, Erik indicated that Oswald Thane follow him across to the high point near the south-west corner as the first fire steels sparked. A rectangular ditch and bank had been thrown up by men long since gone to the grave, and perched upon the high point a stone built watchtower stood sentinel over the road which passed its base. Despite its age the bank was steep, and Erik scrambled up to poke his head inside the doorway. A floor ankle deep in the detritus of centuries lay underfoot, and Erik craned his neck to peer upwards as Oswald made the summit. Milky white clouds drifted slowly across a rectangle of blue, the square holes in the walls the only remaining evidence for the beams which had supported the stair, upper floor and roof long ago. From a sheltered cranny a screech owl and her chicks glowered down at the unwelcome visitor to their world.

Oswald's voice sounded at his shoulder. 'It's a pity the stairs and upper level have rotted away, but there is still a commanding view to be had from here.'

Erik ran his eyes around the interior a final time before ducking out into the soft light of late afternoon. Below him the raiding army of Erik Haraldsson, what his Northumbrian subjects called a *here* in their English tongue, had all but settled in for the night, and the king felt the old thrill of a life

45

on campaign returning as he inhaled the heady odour of horses, fighting men and woodsmoke.

Oswald was still speaking at his side, an arm jabbing out as he described the landscape which surrounded them to the king. 'Over to the south-east you can make out the higher lands of the Dales in our own country, lord, with the River Tees snaking its way down to the sea beyond Miydilsburh.' Erik looked. The day was fine, and the waterway shone like a silver chain as it meandered through the verdant lowlands on its way to the coast. Oswald turned on a heel to point north-westwards. 'And behind us,' he said, 'you can see the mountains of Cumbraland in the distance.'

Erik nodded as he gazed at the far horizon. 'I have seen them often enough from seaward. Let us hope that they do not discover we are here, or all our plans will lay in ruins.'

The Northumbrian moved to allay his fears. 'I doubt that any travellers will venture this way, lord; everyman and his thrall will know that war is coming — they will stay put until the fighting is over if they have the sense they were born with. Besides, if they did tread this route they would get a life-ending surprise if they ran into us.'

Erik dropped his eyes to the encampment. The Roman road which had carried them here cut through the earthen walls just to the south before heading west into what Oswald had informed him was the Vale of Eden. Erik estimated that the old ramparts of Hreyrr Camp stood roughly a dozen feet high, and in addition to the places where the roadway cut the walls a further nine openings were spread around the perimeter. The pair crabbed down the slope as the sun sank, the air cooled, and the first cooking smells drifted across to entice them away. Erik pumped the knowledgeable old Northumbrian for more information as they walked. 'It seems like a big camp to protect a lookout station.'

'No, this is what they called a marching camp King Erik,' Oswald replied. 'It was constructed at the end of the day's march by the Roman army as a refuge in hostile territory. The following day they would build another, then another and so on. This one,' he said with an expansive sweep of an arm, 'was constructed in the first century when the empire was still expanding into the lands of the northern tribes. The signal station and road came later — that is why they cut through the earlier groundworks.'

Erik was impressed. 'So, it's nearly a thousand years old? As old as my garth in York? Remind me to congratulate the next Roman we meet, it is perfect for our needs — we can see for miles, remain hidden, and it is easily defended if the need arose.' Up ahead, Erik's huskarls had finally noticed their lord was missing and were making a search of the tents and horse lines. He gave Oswald a nudge as they walked back into camp. 'I have escaped my minders,' he said with a smirk. 'Watch them try to act as if they were unconcerned when they reach us.'

Kolbein was the first to catch a glimpse of Erik through the crowd, and Oswald chuckled at Erik's side as the styris-man's involuntary gasp became a face saving cough. 'These walls are almost a thousand years old,' Erik volunteered as Kolbein reached them.

'Is that right, lord?' came the pithy reply. 'Well, well, who would have thought?'

Erik chuckled. 'I take it you are unimpressed, old friend?'

Oswald attempted a different tack. 'They were built soon after our Saviour walked the earth,' he said with an obvious sense of wonder.

'Yet they sit upon this hilltop, so the hill must be older,' Kolbein replied with a shrug. The huskarl paused and lifted his chin as the flash of sunlight on metal caught his eye. Erik and Oswald followed suit. A few miles to the north the scouts were crossing the skyline, before first the horses and then the outlines of the riders began to sink from view as they descended the back slope. 'So the ramparts were thrown up when Christ walked among us you say? But the hills have been here since Óðinn and his brothers formed the earth from the body of a frost giant.' Erik fought to suppress a smile as the old heathen made it plain whose beliefs he considered the more wondrous. 'If it's being impressed you are looking for, I would suggest that you take your nose out of books for a moment, and recognise the beauty which surrounds you.'

5

VÍSUNDR

The horse whinnied, raking the ground with a hoof as the warrior slipped the crown over his ears and secured the buckle. Thorstein looked up from tightening the belly band on his mount and threw Erik a smile. 'Another one less than happy with the early start.'

Erik tutted. 'He will have to get used to it like the others,' he said. 'If a dawn start is good enough for the rider it is good enough for him. Besides,' he added with a casual glance to the east, 'he has had a full day's rest, and he *is* sharing the trials of a king. He should be grateful to be in such exalted company.'

The upper edge of the rampart had gained an ochre fringe as the new day dawned bright and clear, and satisfied that all was secure Erik hauled himself into the saddle. Even mounted the walls of the fort towered above him, and Erik's eyes squinted to pierce the gloom as he cast a backwards look to check that all was ready. Hundreds of horses and their riders were coming together in the centre of the fort, the shadowy shapes moving slowly beneath a vaporous brume as the breath of man and beast plumed in the chilly air. Satisfied that the column was forming in his wake Erik turned the head of his horse to the north, urging the beast into a trot as his eyes worked to pick out the chosen gateway. Within moments he had passed through, the sound of hoofbeats falling away as he left the enclosure and came out onto the ridge line which would carry them to war. He slowed the horse to a walk as he did so, trusting the animal to pick its way across the boggy ground which flanked the wall on this side. Hoping to remain undiscovered for as long as possible they were travelling without remounts; a thrown rider, a twisted fetlock or knee and they would have to leave a man behind, and Erik knew that he would need each and every one of them in the fighting to come.

Beyond the circuit of the ancient walls now, Erik cast a look across to the east. The sun was an arc of flame on the horizon as the sky horses Arvak and Alsvið hauled their charge into the firmament. Erik shielded his eyes from the glare with the ledge of a hand, dropping his gaze to soak up the beauty of the moment as the horse walked forward. Down below in the farms and settlements of Northumbria not a trace of light yet lit the earth as men slept through the darkness of the witching hours, and Erik watched in wonder as Sol rose little by little and the sunlight crept slowly down the flanks of the Pennine hills. Somewhere down there in the night the army of the kingdom of York were at their rest, and Erik scanned the dark in a vain attempt to pinpoint their campfires. The Erikssons were there as they led their hirdmen north on Dere Street, alongside the English and Danes from the kingdom itself under the command of the redoubtable Regen-wold. Erik sent an invocation to Óðinn that they were strong enough without his presence to keep the hired swords and Viking freebooters in check until the fighting began.

The mire was soon behind them, and Erik's mind recalled

the moment he knew that his plan stood a good chance of success as he waited for the army to make firmer ground. A brace of scouts had been spotted by the lookouts coming in at a canter late the previous evening, the dark forms of their cloaks streaming away to the East as they emerged onto the ridge top and caught the full force of the westerly blow. Before Erik could reach the gateway the riders were inside the fort, searching out the king to make their report. The army of Cumbraland had been spotted, just where they had hoped it would be, and Erik was calling a council of war before the young men had had time to quench their thirst. It was forty miles or thereabouts to the Roman road called Stane Gate, but the scouts assured him that the enemy column was encumbered with foot soldiers and wagons and moving forward at the pace of the slowest. Barely a dozen miles from their own muster point at Cair Ligualid when spotted, the Cumbrians still had thirty to travel until they met up with the their king at Corebricg. Oswald Thane had confirmed that three days still remained until the day of the Feast of the Exaltation, and it was the work of a moment to realise that the enemy leaders planned to cover the distance to the meet at the leisurely pace of ten miles a day. Brought along for his local knowledge Oswald was riding in the lead group with Erik, and the king turned to the thane as the last of his *here* came clear of the bogland. 'Oswald,' he said. 'Do you stand by your reckoning?'

The Northumbrian nodded enthusiastically. 'Haydon lies just a few miles to the south of Stane Gate and only ten miles or so from Corebricg. It is the perfect place to overnight and arrive at the assembly point on the appointed day King Erik,' he replied. 'There is a grassy shelf above the ford large enough to accommodate an army and the river itself to act as a defensive ditch. The men expect to be fighting soon and there is a fine church at the high point to cater for their spiritual needs.' He threw Erik and his huskarls a smile as he fished inside the purse which hung from his belt. The coin flashed in the rays of the morning sun as it spun end over end before it was snatched back from the air. 'I have a purse of the new silver pennies of Erik Rex, the king in York, bearing the sword of war and the cross of Christ,' he said as he held the disc up to the light. 'If any man cares to match it, I am happy to wager we shall overtake the enemy there.'

Bolstered by the Englishman's confidence, Erik turned back. The last of the riders were on firmer ground, and a quick check to the north confirmed that the scout who was to lead them back to the assembly point was waiting patiently. His partner from the previous day's ride had left as the first grey light of the pre dawn had lit the sky, sent east to find the main army of York to brief the earls and the Erikssons of the king's plans. If they could work together to surprise the enemy at the muster they should have the victory. If the ploy failed and they were discovered or the battle was lost Erik mused, it would need to be a fighting retreat to the banks of the River Tees and hold them there.

Erik raised an arm, and the signal was acknowledged by the young man up ahead as he hauled the head of his mount aside and put back his heels.

THE SCOUT TROTTED back to the king and drew rein. 'Here lord,' he said, 'this is the place.'

Erik looked across the river. A rough track climbed northeastward from the valley floor until it became lost among the trees. 'And that leads to the eastern side of Haydon ford?'

'Within half a mile of the causeway itself,' the youth replied, 'and there is plenty of tree cover where the men can watch and wait for the main attack to go in. I am sure of the distances lord,' the young man added as he sensed Erik's hesitation. 'I scouted the route myself when we were still searching for the Cumbrian army. I remembered it when it became clear that they were making for Haydon, and I thought that we might need to deny any escapees the chance of carrying word of the attack to the main army at Corebricg.'

Erik slipped a silver ring from his forearm and tossed it across. The young scout beamed. 'Good work,' he said, 'you did well. But there is something else I want you to do.' Erik looked across to Thorstein. 'Choose twenty men to go with our friend here. I want them to wait for the attack to go in, and then move out from cover to defend the ford.'

Erik raised his gaze, away to where a westering sun had now dipped from sight below the hills; it had been a hard day's ride and it was growing late. Ideally he would have found a quiet valley and holed up for the night, attacking in the dawn when most men were snug in their tents and weary guards were distracted by the smell of breakfast cooking after a lonely vigil; but the main enemy encampment was too close, the margins of success and failure too slight to risk delay. What if the Cumbrians broke camp early? Or horsemen from Corebricg rode west to establish contact with their friends? It was the eve of the Holy Day now — King Dyfnwal of Strathclyde must be awaiting the arrival of his spearmen on the morrow so would expect them to be close by, even if they had neglected to send word ahead. Erik let his gaze wander down to the riverside as he thought. The men were taking good care of their mounts before seeing to their own needs as any good horseman should, the animals slaking their thirst after a hard day as men flicked small stones and any other debris from their hooves with the point of a knife.

His concentration was broken as Thorstein arrived with

the chosen men, and Erik quickly ran his eyes across the group as they awaited his orders. A dozen young fighters eager to make a name for themselves with a stiffening of old hands to add experience and discipline: Thorstein had chosen well. The king pulled a stern expression to emphasise the importance of the task as he addressed them. 'You know what to do lads?'

'Yes, lord,' they chorused.

Erik nodded. 'Thord here will guide you. I would have sent more men but we are likely to be outnumbered as it is, and I have already used the rest of the scouts to seal off the route down from Stane Gate. If any escape our attack, it is up to you men to ensure that none get away across the ford.' He paused, pinning the fighters with his gaze to emphasise the importance of their task. 'If they slip past you they will warn the main army up ahead of our presence, and all our efforts here will go to waste — it is vital for our success they none get through alive.'

The chosen few gave stern nods in reply. 'You can count on us lord.'

Erik acknowledged them with a nod of his own and they were away, splashing through the small river that Oswald Thane had told him was known as the Allen. Erik thought back on the day as he watched them go. They had done as well as any men could and he understood just how well suited the old Roman marching fort had been for their needs, but as the sky continued to darken overhead he could not help but wish the distance had been a little less. Keeping to the high moors they had made good time that morning, the miles going beneath the hooves of the horses at a giddy rate, and by midday they were dropping down to cross the valley of the River Wear. An hour later they were in Allendale, picking up the scout who was now wearing a silver arm ring for his initiative for the long ride north. A little later more scouts had come in to confirm that the Cumbrians were pitching their tents at Haydon, and Erik's mind began to work on the details of the upcoming attack as the outriders rode alongside and described the enemy encampment.

As the detachment was swallowed by the greenwood, Erik returned his attention to his leading men. Arnkel and Erland had come forward to join them while the king had been busy with the small group, and a quick glance to the West confirmed what the lengthening shadows and the cool-ness of the evening air on Erik's skin was already telling him: they were running short of time. 'The scouts tell me that we are five miles from the enemy camp,' he said looking back. 'Three miles ahead the Allen empties into larger river called the Tine. As luck would have it we are close to a place where it is spanned by a stone bridge, and on the far bank there is a wide track which shadows the Tine and leads directly to Haydon and the enemy camp two miles downriver.' Erik's gaze moved from face to face, thrilling at the war-lust etched on each and every one as he began to describe the enemy encampment. 'The Cumbrians are concentrated on a grassy area on the eastern edge of the settlement, between the church and the river.'

Erik cast about the water's edge for an aid to help him illustrate the attack plan. Scooping up a stick he scored marks in the dust, rattling off the details as he did so: 'Tine — bridge — camp,' he said as the leading men gathered around. 'Here is the ford where the river curves to the north, just downstream from Haydon itself.' He lifted his head to look at the Torf-Einarsson brothers. 'I want a three pronged attack, so we will remain in our crews.' Erik sketched a rectangle flanked by twin horns. 'Think of a *vísundr*, the bison of our homelands. That is myself and the men of the *Draki*,' he said tapping the central block. 'We are the loins. I will drive directly through the centre of the camp and kill everyone we find.' He glanced up as the men surrounding him nodded in unison. 'Arnkel, you are the right horn: take your Iron Beards in a sweep along the riverbank. Erland you are the left: head up towards the church with your men of the *Valkyrie*.' Erik looked from Orkneyman to Orkneyman. 'Don't join in the attack until you are sure the net is closed. As soon as you have linked up, move into the camp and kill everyone you see. Detail a few riders to keep a lookout for any we miss, but remember I have sent a score to the far side of the ford ready to mop up any that do sneak through in that direction, so don't chase after them or any remaining scouts you see closing off the path which leads back to Stane Gate.' Erik tossed the twig aside and swept them with his gaze. 'If anyone can capture flags or war banners that will be a bonus, but try to keep them clean and in one piece — they will help with our deception during the main attack on Corebricg in the morning.' Erik's eyes moved from face to face as his voice became a snarl. 'Strike like a thunderbolt. Make sure that every Cumbrian is dead before we lose this light completely — if word gets through to the main army that we are in the area, it will be us who are surprised and slaughtered on the morrow. Any questions make them quick — we must hit them before it grows too dark.'

Sturla moved forward to point with the toe of a boot. 'The bridge up ahead, lord,' he said. 'I know that it is a couple of miles from the camp, but now they are settled in for the night do you think they might have thought to set a guard?'

Erik's eyes widened. 'That is a very good question. Obviously it was unguarded when the scouts came back that way, and it's still unlikely even if they are aware of its existence. As far as they know there is not an enemy spear within fifty miles — it's both the reason for our long ride today and why my rump feels like it's been kicked by a mule. But you are right,' he continued as his quip broke the tension among them, 'it is best to be sure. Go and tell one of the scouts to ride ahead and check as quick as he can. If we don't hear from him we will assume it's clear and take a chance — we just don't have the time to waste. If there are men there we will have to hit them hard and hope that none get away to raise the alarm.' As the banner man scuttled off, Erik swept them all with a final look. 'Is that it? Good, let's get moving!'

The sight of Arnkel and Erland jogging back to their crews had the last men at the riverside coaxing the thirsty mounts back into line, and Erik and his guardsmen hauled themselves into the saddle as Sturla returned from his task. Erik raised his head as the clatter of hooves drew his attention back to the footpath, the russet cloak common among scouts everywhere growing indistinct as the rider urged his mount beyond the woodland edge. A sweep of his eyes took in those closest to him as the pre-battle thrill put new life into travel weary men, and he did a quick check that his weapons were to hand as he watched his shipmen doing the same. Erik raised an arm in the sign that the advance recommence, and when he saw that the army was ready to ride his heels went back to send the horse on its way.

Within a mile the track was angling away from the water-course, and as the trees closed in Erik cursed as he was forced to drop the pace. Bunched together in single file, hundreds of horsemen were pounding along a woodland track more suited to the footfall of deer and men. At any moment a missed tree root or overhanging branch could take down a horse or unsaddle a rider bringing the whole column to a halt, but to his relief the trees soon drew back, and Erik's heart leapt as he saw the scout waiting patiently for him on a well made road up ahead. Bursting free from the woodland he guided the head of his horse to the north, slowing the headlong dash just enough to allow the man to slip alongside and make his report.

'The bridge is clear lord,' the youngster cried above the sound of beating hooves. 'There is no sign of man nor beast.'

Erik flashed him a smile. 'And this road leads directly there?'

'Yes, lord,' the scout confirmed. 'It is little more than a mile ahead. Cross the bridge and the road which leads to Haydon is a short distance beyond.'

The words drifted behind him along with their owner as Erik urged the horse into a gallop, and he sensed his leading men moving up to his flanks as the raiding army of Erik Bloodaxe swelled to fill the width of the roadway. A flash of light as they came clear of the trees, and the rumble of hooves became a thunderous clatter as they gained the stone bridge, crossed the Tine and swept on. Erik's eyes pierced the gathering gloom as they plunged back into the tree cover on the northern bank, but as he led the riders in a gentle turn the road which led to his destination was lit by the last of the day's light slanting in from the West. A heartbeat later he was heading east, three ships' crew of spear Norse roaring along in his wake, and Erik raised his eyes to spy out the roadway ahead as a hand moved back to loosen the binding holding his war axe secure at his shoulder.

The setting sun lay directly to the west, a bale fire throwing long shadows ahead as Thorstein and Helgrim Smiter moved alongside, and Erik felt the familiar thrill of battle building within as Sturla Godi tucked in behind. Within moments a new silhouette joined the shadows of the riders on the roadway ahead, as the Romsdaler raised the flagstaff aloft and Erik's war banner flew. With the road before them arrow straight and gilded by the sun Erik dug in his heels to goad the horse into lengthening his stride, and as the settlement grew nearer and the first signs of movement were seen up ahead Erik reached back to draw Jomal.

At the outskirts of Haydon sunlight danced on polished steel, and a lifetime of war-play told Erik that it was not the benign shimmer from helm or shield boss but the flash of spear blades being raised. These men were clearly resolute and well led, and as a volley was released to arc towards the leading riders a horn brayed a warning of their attack to the men in the settlement beyond. Erik hunkered down behind the neck of his horse as the javelins flew, firming his grip on the handle of the war axe as he willed the last few yards away. A blur as the spear flashed by a whisker away and the death cries of hirdmen to his rear told that not every man had seen the danger in time, but he was close enough now to see the terror on the faces of the enemy spearmen as they made a last gasp leap for the roadside. One left it too late, and Erik caught the dreamlike sight at the edge of his vision as the Cumbrian's broken body corkscrewed ahead of the party to be swallowed up by the shadows. Norse war horns keened their death songs now, and as the trees retreated and the charging Northmen gave voice to their battle cries, the roofs of Haydon swam into view.

6

RED BEARD

A momentary glimpse of thatch blushed honey gold in the rays of the dying sun, of horrified faces turned their way as villagers scattered like startled deer or shrank back against the walls of the dwellings. The mad drumbeat of hooves redoubled as Erik led his raiders into heart of the settlement, reverberating back from wattle and paling as he urged the horse on. Directly in his path a young girl froze in terror as the tide of horseflesh thundered towards her amid a flurry of panicky hens. Unable to steer his mount aside in the constricted space of the village Erik winced, steeling himself to hear the sound of her screams snuffed out along with her life, but at the last moment a youth shot from a doorway to snatch her to safety and Erik raised his eyes as he put the village behind him, the roadway widened, and he caught his first sight of the enemy camp.

To Erik's surprise the campsite appeared deserted and he almost curbed his mount, fearing a trap, but the distinctive smell of woodsmoke hung in the evening air and he felt a kick of excitement as he realised that he had caught the enemy at their most vulnerable. The horses barely paused as

the first of the tents were ridden down, and a heartbeat later
Erik had his suspicions confirmed when he spotted the men
of Cumbraland in ranks, their spears and swords swapped for
bowls and spoons as they waited for the evening meal to be
doled out from great steaming cauldrons.

A whoop of joy caused Erik to turn his head aside —
Thorstein had seen how the gods have favoured them, and
before he turned back Erik caught a glimpse of Arnkel's Iron
Beards hugging the riverside as they rode north to slam the
trap shut. Screams and cries told them that not all the tents
were without occupants, and Erik roared his battle cry as the
horses rode over them and the braying of battle horns filled
the air. Within moments the cry was taken up — *Blóðøx!*
Blóðøx! — and Erik cut across the camp as he saw the first
Cumbrians recover their wits, hurling bowls aside as they
made for the tent lines and the spears stacked neatly in their
racks. These were the most dangerous men, men whose first
reaction to seeing a host of charging Norsemen was not to
turn tail and flee but arm themselves and turn their faces to
the foe, and Erik left the food lines to those following on as
he hauled at the reins to cut them off. A visage appeared at a
tent flap, the confusion of a mind fogged by sleep swept away
in an instant as Jomal took the face clean off. The Dane axe
whirred through the air again as Erik came up upon the rear-
most runners, the heavy blade paring flesh and smashing
bone as the king cut a deadly path.

A handful of Cumbrians had reached the spear stacks, the
quickest and brightest among them snatching up shields as
they shuffled shoulder to shoulder and turned their faces to
the enemy. The semblance of a coordinated defence was
beginning to coalesce around a red bearded giant, and Erik
thought to retrieve his own spear from its carrying place as
more men arrived by the moment to add to their numbers. But

the distance between them was shrinking quickly as the horse cantered on, and he was forced to lay the idea aside as he realised the chance to do so had already passed.

Set in their shield wall now Erik knew that the advantages were beginning to favour the defenders; even trained war horses were reluctant to approach a tightly packed spear hedge and he urged his mount forward, desperate to close the gap before the wall could fully form. Erik continued to swing Jomal as he drew closer to the enemy, but with all his attention fixed upon the men lined up before him the first inkling he had of the counterattack which unhorsed him was when the head of his mount dropped from sight and he began to topple from the saddle. Erik kicked himself clear as the horse pitched forward, and as he crashed to the ground he was already dropping a shoulder. The instant he hit he continued to roll, springing back to his feet to take up a fighting stance as he prepared to defend himself from the follow-up strike. Held secure by its lanyard Jomal was still in his hand, and Erik swept the deadly blade in an arc as his eyes searched for the assailant. Before he could pick the man out from the crowd his ship mates had moved up in support, the king now standing like a rock midstream as they swept past to either side. Erik relaxed a touch as the threat subsided, shouldering the haft lest he kill or injure one of his own, and within moments Sturla and Thorstein had drawn alongside.

Seeing his lord fall Helgrim Smiter had taken over leadership of the main attack, and Erik watched with satisfaction as the huskarl led the crew of the *Draki* across to envelop red beard and his Cumbrians. Surrounded now it was only a matter of time before any resistance ended there, and Erik searched the meadow as more of his crewmen peeled off from the column and slid to the turf. Nearby a bloody trail led to the place where Erik's horse still screamed in its agony, and Erik saw for the first time what had brought it down. A hoof had been taken off just below the fetlock, and Erik turned his head to Thorstein as he readjusted his helm. 'What happened?'

The big huskarl spat, indicating the beleaguered Cumbrians with a flick of the head. 'While you were unsighted the big lad with the red beard came forward to hurl a hand axe — it took your horse's hoof clean off. It was a good shot too,' he added begrudgingly, 'whirling in low where you wouldn't see it coming.' Erik looked. The horse was on its side, three legs and a bloody stump thrashing the air as it attempted to right itself; but there was no hope for a three legged horse, and he trotted across to bury Jomal in its skull as the army continued to sweep through the camp. Olvir had already darted in to retrieve his lord's shield from its place on the crupper, risking a shattered skull of his own as the wounded horse had beat the air, and the Vestfolder handed the board across as Erik's crewmen began to gather about their lord.

Erik nodded his thanks as he closed his fingers about the grip, and a quick headcount told him that roughly half of the hird had witnessed their lord take a tumble and had turned aside to come to his aid. The attacking force immediately available to him had been weakened, but Erik was still confident that thirty-something spear Norse would overcome thrice their number of Cumbrians. A quick look to the west told him that Helgrim and the rest of his crewmen were already mopping up the best of the enemy fighters, red beard now the core of a rapidly shrinking band as Norse horsemen circled, spears and swords jabbing and chopping down onto the heads and shoulders of the last of his companions. Beyond them Erik caught a glimpse of Erland Torf-Einarsson's Valkyries as they galloped past the church, already nearing the point where they would begin to sweep downhill to close the net.

Reassured that Helgrim and the rest of his hirdmen would soon ride in support and mindful of the time already lost Erik snapped an order, and Sturla spat to clear his mouth of spittle as the battle horn came up. As the strident howl cut the air Erik broke into a run, the king's eyes scanning the field as he searched for the point where he could strike the enemy hardest. The ordered lines of hungry men had dispersed now that the nature of the threat had revealed itself, and Erik's eyes searched for the places where they must be coming together to begin the fightback as he ran. The best places to make a stand were to the east and west of the tangled knot of tents and guy ropes which crisscrossed the rising ground, near the little church or the waterside at the base of the slope where they could make a stand with their backs to the river — but a quick check told him that Erland and Arnkel's men were already there, working their way towards the centre of the field like beaters at the hunt. As the net drew tighter, Erik knew that the enemy had only one place to go. 'Make for the centre of the camp,' he shouted above the clamour, 'a silver arm ring for every man who takes a banner!'

The men of the *Draki* gave a roar and surged ahead as Thorstein's shout drew Erik's eyes to the north. 'There they are — they look like they are pulling the wagons together, we need to be quick!'

Several of the men who had ridden with Helgrim had already removed themselves from red beard's last stand in search of fresh opponents, riding down the final few tents as they cleared a path for their shipmates. The way ahead clear the horsemen wheeled away, and Erik cursed as he saw that Thorstein was right. Most armies collected the carts and wagons carrying foodstuffs, armour and the heavier weapons at the centre of the camp when they settled in for an overnight stop, and the Cumbrians were no different. Realising that they were hemmed in on all sides the remaining fighters had made a dash for the place which offered the best chance for survival, and they were within an ace of forming a circle with the transports, a final redoubt within which they hoped to beat back the attackers and hold out until morning. Erik knew as well as the enemy that if they failed to appear at the muster in Corebricg at the appointed time the king of Cumbraland would send men to find out why and his battle plan would fail.

In the time it had taken Erik to see the threat Thorstein was several yards ahead, men streaming in his wake as they sought to stop the final wagons from coming together to complete the laager. Erik followed on as Sturla moved to his side, a tight knot of men gathering protectively around the pair as the younger crewmen fought down the instinct to outpace the king. The last of the broken tents were behind him now, and Erik increased the pace as the wagons reared up ahead. Thorstein and his followers were already fighting in the space where the enemy had hoped to seal the wall, the flash of blades and cries of battle filling the air as they slashed and forced their way into the compound, and Erik turned aside as he saw that the arrival of the king and his supporters would only add to the crush.

Either side of the gap spearmen were lining the sides of the wagons behind a barricade of interlocking shields, and Erik let his own shield fall to the earth to take a double-handed grip on the haft of Jomal as he readied himself for the assault. Shorn of his defence the king of York was as vulnerable as he was ever likely to be to a thrown spear or loosed arrow, but his men had realised his plight and a volley of javelins drove the defenders back as he ran. As the enemy shields came up to deflect the barrage Erik's mind was calculating the distance to the nearest wheel, and he adjusted his stride as his eyes searched out a foothold.

Faces were beginning to reappear around shield rims as the last Norwegian spears thudded into the lime wood boards, but Erik was upon them now and his foot found a spoke as he launched himself upward. Jomal swung as he came up, the great blade whipping around in a savage arc, driving the nearest Cumbrians back from the side of the wagon and breaking the shield wall's cohesion. With a final push Erik was clearing the box boards to land with a crash on the wagon bed, and he let out his war cry as the Dane axe scythed the air all around. Desperate to reform their battle line before the arrival of Erik's men the Cumbrians began probing with their spears, each man waiting until Jomal's silver blade had passed by on its deadly circuit before jumping in to stab at the axeman before them. Erik was rolling on the balls of his feet as he danced between each jab, and he took a sideways step and then another as he began to work his way down the defensive line. As his axe swept the Cumbrian defenders aside the battle cry of his war band sounded again close by — *Blóðøx! Blóðøx!* — and he knew that his men had gained a foothold on the carriage to his rear.

Outflanked the spearmen lining the side boards shrank back, but the king's solo attack had bunched up the remaining defenders and there was nowhere left to hide. Jomal came around to take the nearest fighter's head from his shoulders before he could raise his shield in defence, and before the headless body even had time to fall to the boards the war axe was coming around again. Already bespattered with the blood and gore of his friend the next man in line managed to hurl himself aside, but Erik had broken the line and the first defenders were beginning to save themselves from his savage onslaught by hurling themselves over the side and into the centre of the corral. Distracted by the king's attack, those who remained were beginning to fall to well aimed spear thrusts from the Norsemen still waiting to clamber aboard, and as the last of them fell or took flight Erik paused as he used the vantage point to gauge how the assault was progressing. A glance to the left told him that Thorstein had crushed the opposition from the Cumbrians at the gap in the wagon line, and the Norwegians were successfully fighting their way into the compound itself. To the right the last of the enemy spearmen lining the wain had been driven across the back boards, and with Jomal now still the men who had accompanied Erik in his charge across the campsite were pouring across the flatbed as they came on in pursuit.

The shadow of a banner fell across him, and when the leather rim of a shield appeared to his fore Erik knew without taking his eyes from the fight that Sturla and Kolbein had finally caught up with him. Reassured by their presence and the protection of his guards, Erik lifted his eyes to scan the hillside. Helgrim Smiter had finally overcome red beard's gallant resistance and was dismounting with those of Erik's hird who had fought alongside him, rushing forward to add their weight to the attack at the compound. Further out the Orcadians had completed their encirclement of the doomed army and were rapidly tightening the net. The mounted men of the *Iron Beard* and *Valkyrie* were moving in a skirmish line through the camp, dispatching any survivors they sniffed out with spear and sword. Satisfied, the king returned his gaze to the struggle before him. The last Cumbrians were fighting back to back within a circle of beaten down grass, as warriors of the army of York cascaded over the sides of the wagon line all around them. The fighting was all but over, and Erik put aside the urge to rush forward into the fray, to be in at the kill, as he saw that he was just not needed.

On the western hill Haydon church wore a corona as the last rays of the sun threw long shadows across a field of death. The victory was total; he would seek out Oswald Thane from the mob, and together they would walk up to the kirk and give thanks before he led his heathen in a bloodier celebration.

ERIK SPOONED another dollop of pottage, forming a circle with his mouth as he sucked in air. Seeing just how hot it was Olvir paused his spoon midway to his lips, sensibly placing the bowl to one side as he waited for the go-ahead to begin his report. The mixture finally cool enough for the king to swallow, Erik gave him the nod as he dipped the spoon again.

'The enemy have reached Corebricg, lord,' the scout said, the excitement in his voice obvious to all those crowded together in the little room. 'There are three walled enclosures at the heart of the town; the flags of Alba and Strathclyde fly above those closest to the River Tine, the purple and gold flag of St Oswald of Northumbria above that which lies on the northern side of Stane Gate. There is a water meadow which slopes down to the river itself where the horses are grazing and watering under guard, with a further score guarding the northern entrance to the bridge itself.'

'What about overall numbers?'

Olvir's mouth became a line. 'The best we could do was tally the horses near the river and make a rough estimate from that, the buildings of the town itself are too densely packed to see many of the enemy themselves. We would say that there are roughly five hundred horses.' He pulled a face. 'It is difficult to give a more accurate number,' he added apologetically.

'We were taking cover in a small wood a mile away and staring directly into the rising sun. The meadow curls around the eastern end of the town, so there could be more we were unable to see.'

Erik nodded that he understood as the spoon came up again. Every man present knew that those wealthy enough to own a horse usually outnumbered the men who had to walk to the battlefield by a measure of five or six to one. That would give a rough estimation that they were facing upwards of three thousand spears. Having learnt his lesson before, Erik stilled the spoon with its streaming contents as he pumped the scout for more. 'And you sent word of this to the main army?'

'Yes, lord — Hauk and Mord crossed the river upstream, well out of sight of the town.'

Erik nodded again, satisfied. 'We know the army is camped ten miles south of the Tine and Regenwold will have his own scouts out, but it pays to be sure.'

Arnkel added a question of his own. 'What if the enemy have scouts out too? If they discover how close the Erikssons and the earls are they will likely move against them.'

Erik teased his beard as he thought. The plan was coming together nicely and he was loathe to change it now, but even the best strategies rarely survived contact with the enemy and he had always encouraged his leading men to chip in with observations and suggestions of their own. 'I think that it is unlikely any enemy scouts will ride that far,' he said finally. 'They will expect to find us cowering behind the River Tees fifty miles to the south like always. But even if they do and manage to return unscathed, it will play into our hands if we move quickly.' Erik turned his head to Oswald Thane as the men exchanged knowing looks. They had all seen Erik plotting and knew the look of old. Their king was a battle winner

— a feeder of ravens. 'You have been in Corebricg,' he said. 'What are these walled compounds Olvir speaks of?'

'The remains of three forts from Roman times lord,' the Northumbrian replied. 'You will recall Regenwold's description of the town, in the garth the morning we left York. The whole town was originally built to guard the junction of Dere Street and Stane Gate, controlling the crossing of the River Tine. It was an important town, built to cater for the needs of the smaller forts which were built the length of the wall of Hadrian. Supplies could be brought in from the South with ease, either along Dere Street or by sea via the river; the Tine reaches the sea only twenty miles to the east and is easily navigable.'

Erik nodded. 'Olvir, how far is it from the point where we will ride clear of the tree cover to Corebricg itself?'

'Just over half a mile lord,' the Vestfolder replied. 'The road dips into a small valley, crosses a beck and climbs the final few yards to the outskirts of the town.'

Erik's eyes swept the room. 'Good, we will move forward straightaway. I want to be fighting again within the hour.'

7

FLANK ATTACK

'Watch your step lord,' Olvir said. 'There is a big pile of shit just there. Bear it looks like, I almost stepped in it myself the first time I was here.'

Thorstein sniffed. 'Smells like it too — bear shit in the woods...' He threw them all a look. 'Now we know.'

Erik moved around the bole of an oak to get a better view, careful to dodge the early morning sunbeams lancing in from the East. A king of York dressed for war, even a moment's distraction could make all the difference between success or failure if the flash of light from polished steel was spotted by an eagle-eyed guard down in the town. Erik's hopes soared as the rearguard emerged from the distant wood and began to deploy on the southern slope.

'That is a show to send lightning coursing through a man's blood,' Thorstein breathed at his shoulder. 'You must be over-proud, lord.'

Erik nodded as he took in the sight. Beyond the River Tine the army of York had now spread across the width of the hillside, and the king thrilled to the view as he picked out the companies arrayed beneath their gaudy war banners. Earl

Regenwold's men astride Dere Street itself with his fellow earls Gunderic and Godfred anchoring each wing with their own contingents. The Erikssons: Gamli; Harald; Guttorm; Sigurd and Ragnfrod filling the right wing with their oath sworn, while the left was packed with the Vikings and adventurers to whom Erik had doled out good silver to fight at their side. Down in Corebricg the town resembled an overturned hive as men ran hither and yon, word spreading like wildfire that the enemy had appeared at their front and caught them unprepared. The first signs of a response could be glimpsed among the old buildings flanking the road, and Erik pulled his wolf grin as he saw that the old king of Alba was taking the bait. Erik stepped back into the deep shadow, turning his face to Olvir as the first war horns cried out their challenge. 'I am heading back to the column,' he said as the rolling thunder of spear shafts striking shield rims began to steal northwards. 'Remember my orders — as soon as Mael Colm begins to lead his Scots across the river make the signal.'

The scout gave a curt nod, the responsibility he had been given pulling at his features. Erik recognised the look, shooting the younger man what he hoped was a heartening smile. 'You are the best I have, you have proven that time and again, ever since that day outside Tunsberg when you tracked my brother Bjorn the Far Trader and saved us from ambush.' He clapped the scout on the shoulder and threw him a wink. 'You saved us from a hard fight that day, and none of us who were there have ever forgotten it. That is why I have entrusted you with this task and no other.'

Olvir's face brightened at the faith shown by his king, and Erik threw a final look down the slope to the town as they began to move away. Despite the press of buildings, it was now clear that the Scots and Britons were forming up to cross the river and confront the threat. From his vantage point Erik now had a perfect view along the east-west line of Stane Gate, and the old road was filling quickly as men poured forth from the forts and buildings which lined it, struggling into mail shirts and buckling helms as they came down to mass at the junction with Dere Street. The fortress which lay beneath the flag of St Oswald seemed unnaturally quiet and Erik wondered at it, but the time to make the attack on which so much depended was slipping away now and he pushed the thought aside. A short while later he was back in the saddle, and Erik called out to each of the men he had stationed on the road as he led his huskarls back to the place he had left the army. 'Watch for the signal — it won't be long in coming!'

Half a mile to the west the combined crews of three dragons were waiting, and the king slowed his mount as he breasted a rise and his best men came into view. Erland and Arnkel had come to the head of the stationary column to await his return with Oswald Thane, and as men rushed to don their battle helms at the sight of their king returned, Erik curbed his mount as he unhooked his own grim helm from its carrying place. 'Regenwold is in position south of the river,' he called as he slipped to the ancient setts. 'The army of York fills the southern hillside, and the enemy are making preparations to move across the bridge to engage them.' The brothers exchanged looks of glee at their king's report as Erik strode across. 'We will follow the plan of attack I outlined earlier — Oswald you will ride with me,' he said flicking at look at the Englishman. 'I will lead us from cover, sheering off as we near the defile to hit the enemy in the flank. Arnkel and his Iron Beards will follow me southwards, peeling away to seal off the northern end of the Tine bridge when I strike. The bank looks far shallower where the beck enters the river so that will help.' He switched his gaze. 'Erland — head straight down Stane Gate and cross the bridge to clear and hold the junction of the two roads. Mael Colm is a grizzled old veteran who will lead from the front, so with the Scots and their leaders stranded on the far side of the river we have the chance to isolate and destroy a third part of their army — that alone should be enough to win the day.' As the pair wished the king happy hunting and hauled their horses out of line to return to their crews, Erik turned to his banner man. 'Sturla, did you sort through the captured banners from last evening?'

'Yes, lord,' he chirped. 'Five were reusable, the others…' His voice trailed away, but he shot his king the ghost of a smile as he found the words to complete his description. 'The others would have been fine enough if they had started off blood red.'

Erik returned the smile. These were the moments he lived for, when tough fighting men hung on his every word, the raven days when he bent Midgard to his will. 'Choose five men to carry the Cumbrian banners ahead of the column; make sure they know to hold them high enough to be clearly seen by those in the town and on the far side of the Tine. The enemy will be expecting the levies from Cumbraland to join them at the muster today and men have a habit of seeing what they expect to see, especially when they have just awoken to a nasty surprise. At the very least a cloud of flags should help to mask our true identity until we split up for the final run in.' Erik switched his gaze to the East as his banner man hurried off to distribute the enemy flags to chosen men. Satisfied that the closest scout was clearly visible and alert he began to loosen his trews. 'Time for a piss I think.'

His huskarls moved across to join him, each man keen to seize the last opportunity to wring every last drip from his bladder while they still had the chance, and soon the roadside was a line of glistening arcs as Sturla's chosen banner men moved forward to the head of the column. Satisfied that he had drained the last drop, Erik retied his breeks and remounted. As he loosened the bindings which held his spears and sword secure his guardsmen were doing the same, checking chin straps and rolling their shoulders as they warmed the muscles for the hard work to come. The silence was oppressive, and Erik thought to mouth unneeded words of encouragement to those within earshot in an effort to mask the awkwardness of the moment, but Kolbein's exclamation beat him to it as he cried the words they had all been waiting for. 'There it is!'

Erik's head snapped back. Silhouetted on the lip of the rise a quarter mile distant, the flash of sunlight on spear tip showed where the scout had hoisted his weapon. The banner men had seen it too, and they turned their heads together as they awaited the order to advance. It was not long in coming, and Erik threw his closest men his war grin as he tightened his grip on the reins. 'Óðinn is with us boys, it is time to wet our spears again.' His huskarls flashed grins of their own in reply, and as the king turned back to the flag carriers his voice became a roar. 'Ride lads! Ride!'

With the king of Alba committed all need for concealment was gone, and Sturla Godi's war horn was answered by those to the rear as the advance began. Erik drew his best stabbing spear from its carrying place near the crupper, raising the gold chased blade high as the unfamiliar battle flags of Cumbraland snapped open ahead. Stane Gate rose before him as the horse gathered pace, and before the canter had become a gallop the closest scout was guiding his mount aside to allow the column through. Cresting the rise the road took a gentle turn to the south, and the horizon came into view beyond the press of banners as the tree cover thinned. Erik settled into the saddle, firming the grip on his spear as the still of the morning was shattered by the hoofbeats of his *here,* and when he recognised the next scout up ahead as Olvir he knew that the mile was up. The column emerged into a burst of light as it galloped free of the tree line, and Erik felt a kick of relief as he moved his head to peer southwards. The army of York were set their battle line athwart Dere Street, and the old king of Scots was clearly visible beneath the saltire flag of Alba as the invaders cleared the confines of the Tine bridge and began to spread across the southern bank. Despite the brevity of the look, Erik was surprised to find that a third of the distance between the place where the old Roman road exited the woodland and the buildings of Corebricg had already passed beneath the hooves of his mount, and he raised his spear and cried a war cry, confident that the men following on would do the same.

On the southern bank heads were turning their way as the flash of movement and the thunder of hooves carried across the waters of the Tine, and Erik laughed despite the tension of the moment as he saw the first spears and shields raised in acclamation and he knew that his ruse had succeeded. The slope steepened as it approached the small bridge across the burn, and Erik judged that the time had arrived to peel off and begin his own assault. A hand shot out as he hauled at the reins, the spear it held pointing directly at the place he had chosen to attack, and the clatter of hoofbeats on stone became a thunderous rumble as the horse tore across the grassy hillside. A glimpse of Arnkel at the head of his Iron Beards, the Orkneyman already beginning to ascend the shallow slope which led to the northern approach to the Tine bridge itself, and a heartbeat later the view was snuffed out as Erik's horse picked its way down into the defile.

Erik raised his eyes to scan the lip of the bank for signs of opposition as the horse leapt the watercourse, but no spearmen had appeared there and he realised that the buildings were screening the attackers from the men marching down Dere Street on their way down to the Tine crossing. As the momentum of the charge bled away and the horse scrabbled up the slope, Erik was aware of Thorstein and Helgrim Smiter urging their mounts alongside, and the trio gained the top of the rise together as Sturla Godi finally unfurled the bloodied axe banner of Erik Haraldsson to reveal their true identity.

Erik threw a look to either side as he slipped to the ground, thrilling to the sight as the men of his hird made the brow like a wave lapping the shore. He returned his gaze to the immediate surroundings as the men dismounted and his hand drifted down to his sword hilt, checking again that the peace bands were hanging loose and hooking a thumb beneath the cross guard to edge it an inch clear of the scabbard. He turned his face to Oswald Thane as the Northumbrian drew his own sword and set his features into a mask of grim determination. Erik recognised the apprehension behind the look; the man had witnessed more than sixty summers warm the air of York, but he had been adamant that he join the attack when given the choice and the men respected him all the more for it. 'Dere Street lies directly beyond these buildings you say?'

Oswald swallowed hard before replying, his pinched expression revealing the turmoil he felt within. 'Yes, King Erik, I know the town well. These dwellings are mostly workshops which open out onto the road for trade: the workers and their families live in rooms at the rear.'

Erik moved his head as he made an attempt to pierce the gloomy margin between the long walls of the nearest buildings. Crammed together and with what little space remaining between them a jumble of rubbish and filth, there was only one way to go. 'Well, they are about to have a hundred fired-up Norse trample their vegetable plots and trudge mud through their homes. Let us hope they possess the wits to hold their tongue and stay well clear.'

Erik made a fist to punch the man lightly on the arm as he fixed him with a look. 'I am glad that you are here,' he said softly, 'and Archbishop Wulfstan would be proud if he knew. Come on,' he said with a final nod of encouragement, 'let us see off those who mean us ill together.' Oswald's mouth turned up into a watery smile at the mention of his master, the old prelate now languishing in southern captivity for his part in bringing Erik back to the kingdom. Erik looked away as he saw that his words had bolstered the Northumbrian as they had been meant to do, and with the men of the *Draki* in position, poised like runners awaiting the off, Erik raised his spear and bellowed his war cry: *Blóðøx!*

As the answering roar shook the timbers of Corebricg, Erik broke into a run. Ahead of him a wooden latch went up with a *clack*, and Erik swept his shield to throw the door wide as the pale oval of a female face appeared there. The handle snatched from her hand, the woman just had time to gape in surprise at the approach of a king in his battle glory before Erik had shouldered her roughly aside. Ducking beneath the lintel he raised his chin to peer the length of the smoky room, and was gratified to see that the doorway which led to the street had already been thrown wide. Marching men could be seen there, the metal of their arms aglitter in the soft morning light, and Erik saw the questioning looks on their faces changing to horror as their minds came to recognise just what the earlier battlecry must mean. A glimpse of a young girl still abed, the wide-eyed features gone in a flash as she ducked beneath the blanket and Erik was past the hearth, clutching his spear a little tighter as he lowered the shaft and prepared to strike. In moments he was through the workshop leaving the screams of the woman and the sound of splintering pots in his wake, and Erik drew back his arm as the doorway grew to fill the view ahead.

A figure hardened from the glare as he burst into the open, the momentary glimpse of a black bushy beard beneath a cap of hardened leather, and Erik drew the first blood that day as the spear stabbed forward to disappear into the gaping maw. Erik swung his shield in an arc before him the moment he had cleared the portal, releasing his grip on the spear as he shouldered the dying man aside. The quick witted among the men of Strathclyde were reaching for their weapons before the body had hit the roadway, but Erik's sword was already in his hand and he chopped down onto shoulders and heads, driving the enemy before him as he hewed a salient for the men following on.

Jomal bounced at his shoulder as he hacked and hacked, Harald Fairhair's gift seemingly indignant at missing the fight, but Erik knew that the sweep of a Dane axe within the press of men would be equally deadly to friend and foe alike, and he took a pace forward as Thorstein's familiar war cry came to his ear. Erik risked a look along the line of the roadway as more of his men exited the shopfront to push the enemy back. To the north Erland and his men had tossed aside the flags of Cumbraland, the wild boar banner of Orkney flying proudly above them as they chased the rearguard from the junction of the Roman roads. Switching his gaze to the south, Erik saw that Arnkel and his men were having a harder time of it. Assailed on both flanks by the armies of Strathclyde and the Scots of Alba, their flags nevertheless appeared to be inching forward as they fought to seal off the approach to the bridge. When he succeeded, Mael Colm and his men would be left relying on the dubious mercy of Regenwold and his army of York to witness the dusk that day — Erik doubted they were in the mood. The sweep of his vision had spied the man he had most hoped to see above all others, and Erik called out as he set off towards him:

'There he is! To me!'

As his trusted huskarls closed around him and the hirdmen drove the enemy back from his path, Erik knew that the time had arrived to use his axe. Before he could draw the weapon a brutish warrior emerged from the crowd to bar his path, the quality of his arms and clothing, of the silver hoops festooning his forearms, telling Erik that here was a fellow Norsemen with renown to gain as the killer of Erik Bloodaxe. Erik instinctively shifted his weight forward as the swordsman prepared to strike, perfectly balanced as he waited to see which way to go. The blow when it came was pulled at the last moment, the warrior flicking a wrist to send the blade arcing in towards Erik's knee — but no king lived to an age if he fell easily for such a trick, and he was already darting in to parry with his shield before the steel could bite flesh. Erik raised his elbow high as he did so, angling the point of his sword downwards, and as Thorstein and Helgrim Smiter rushed forward to beat back the attacker's companions, the king thrust down with all his strength. The power of Erik's shield strike had forced the warrior's arm wide, his body opening up as he sought to bring the blade back under control, and Erik saw the look of disbelief that he had been bested so easily change to agonised horror as the long blade sliced into his groin. Erik released his grip on the handle, reaching up to finally draw Jomal across his shoulder as the Viking fell. The Dane axe was already screaming down as the man hit the roadway, and before he could roll away or recover the wicked steel blade had crushed his face to a bloody mash.

The length of Dere Street the men of the *Draki* were

surging forward as all hope of an ordered resistance collapsed, and Erik raised his eyes to fix upon the flag of his enemy and the gold bedecked figure at its base. 'There he is!' he cried again as his guardsmen rallied to his side. 'There is Dyfnwal of Strathclyde — Kill him!'

8

MACCUS THE EASTERNER

The army of Strathclyde, bursting with confidence as they marched to war only a short while before, had been reduced to isolated knots of desperate men by the ferocity of the Norwegian attack. Taken unawares as Erik's hirdmen had erupted from the doorways, scores had fallen before they had slipped shields from carrying straps or had the chance to bring their weapons to bear. Now the survivors were backing against the walls of the buildings on the eastern side of Dere Street as they sought to escape the carnage, and Jomal sang its death song as Erik cut a bloody swathe through those who stood in his path. The enemy scattered like ships before a storm, but as Erik grasped the opportunity to spy out how close he had come to his goal, he saw to his consternation that king Dyfnwal and the Strathclyde banners were gone. The king's retainers, his most trusted men, remained in a skjald-borg as they covered their lord's escape, and Erik pulled up short as he searched for an easier way through. The buildings on the far side of the street differed from those through which they had passed such a short while before. Larger and more widely spaced, it was obvious to the king that these were some of the warehouses and stores which supplied the needs of the workshops opposite and the wider town beyond. Those men of Strathclyde who were able were already pouring through the wide gaps between the store-houses, and Thorstein's voice sounded in his ear as they watched Dyfnwal's guards begin to back out of sight.

'If they are going, their lord is already safely away Erik.' He spat into the dust to show his contempt.

Erik nodded as he recognised the truth of it. 'The meadow beyond is one giant corral,' he agreed. 'I saw the horses from the top of the hill when I came forward with Olvir.' Dere Street was filled with his hirdmen now; never one to go blindly forward in a fight, Erik paused as his father's motto came again into his mind: *first win the battle — and then fight it.* It was pointless to blunder on and become entangled in a running fight with levy men and churls; if he vanished into an alleyway the cohesion of the attack would unravel as men lost sight of their king. Despite his blood lust, Erik knew that he must remain beneath his banner so that the men could regroup to fight again. At his side Thorstein was still speaking, and the king blinked in surprise as his hearth man began wittering on about a battle from long ago. 'So, this Dyfnwal ab Owain is even less worthy than his father then?'

Erik's eyes narrowed as his focus returned, and his huskarl explained as the last of the trapped men fell to Norwegian arms and the alleyways opposite filled with enemy dead. 'Remember when Arnkel described the battle at Brunanburh, that time in your hall in king Gorm's land?'

Erik shook his head in wonder. Only Thorstein could pause mid battle for a chat. 'That was a dozen years ago!'

Thorstein agreed. 'Aye, it was. But I had never heard of a king abandoning his men on a battlefield before, and the cowardliness of it has always stayed with me; Owain's retreat could have cost the northern army victory that day, it certainly cost the lives of a good many men who had answered his war arrow when the flags went back and the English broke through.'

Erik nodded his agreement, but his mind was already elsewhere as he put the bravery or otherwise shown by the kings of Strathclyde from his mind. To the south he could see that Arnkel and his men had managed to fight their way upslope to seal the river crossing, and the approach now bristled with Iron Beard spears beneath the Orkney sigil. As word spread of the disaster which had overtaken their king and the remainder of the column, the last of the Strathclyde fighters were streaming away from the approaches as they too placed survival above honour and raced to saddle a horse. Lifting his chin, Erik saw that his own attack had been the signal for the army of York to advance, and he thrilled to the sight as the morning sun reflected back from helm and spearpoint and they came on beneath the battle flags of his kin and kingdom. Switching his gaze back to the North, Erik was surprised to see that although Erland Torf-Einarsson and his crewmen had dismounted and secured the crossroads as ordered, there were still no signs that they had come under sustained attack. He turned back to Thorstein as he saw what he must do. 'I am going to reinforce Erland and his men. We will make sure that the forts are empty and then swing south to clear the meadow of any lingering threat there; with the alleyways blocked by the dead and dying we don't want to give Dyfnwal the chance to rediscover his manhood, regroup and rejoin the fight. Take half of the crew down to the bridge to bolster Arnkel and his lads. After going through all the trouble to divide and trap the enemy, we don't want the Scots to force the crossing and escape at the last moment.'

Thorstein could not hide his surprise at Erik's orders, and

he cleared his throat before venturing a reply. It was not the done thing to question the king, but they had spent decades together side by side in peace and war and he had earned the right. 'What if Earl Oswulf and his Bernicians are just waiting for us to split our force before they leave the fort, or offer our flank to him by chasing Dyfnwal and his men along the riverfront? Kill you and the war is won.'

Erik thumbed his nose as he thought, finally shaking his head as he confirmed his decision. 'We need to keep them on the back foot. The moment the army of Strathclyde realises just how few we are things could turn very ugly for us. Even if the Bernicians have seen which way the way the wind is blowing and decided to hedge their bets, if we can deny the bridge to the Scots my half crew and Erland's men should be enough to drive those remaining from the field.' He turned to Helgrim, Sturla, Kolbein and Oswald Thane. 'Let us see why Oswulf and his Bernicians have failed to put in an appearance. You know the man, Oswald,' he said. 'We may never again be in such a strong position — our victory here may even persuade him to join us.'

The quartet moved back to the western side of Dere Street as they picked their way through the dead and dying. The bodies were far fewer on this side of the road with just the odd man fallen here and there, the first to succumb to the initial rush as Erik and his men had burst from cover. Helgrim snorted as they walked. 'You can see where we passed by lord,' he said proudly. 'Jomal sure makes a mess.' Erik looked. A distinct ridge of bodies marked the passage of Erik and his huskarls, the lopped arms and severed heads which were typical of the war axe's savagery plain to see. A crewman came across as he saw the king, and Erik shot him a smile and a word of thanks as the man returned his sword. The bloodletting was almost over now, the few injured men remaining from Dyfnwal's invading army being dispatched to Óðinn or Christ's safekeeping by Erik's fighters, and the king returned his sword to its scabbard before resting the haft of his axe on a shoulder as they walked north. Erland had seen him coming, and the Orkney man walked down to greet his king as a great roar rent the air to the south. 'I have brought you some help,' Erik quipped, with a rearward flick of his head towards the half crew bustling along in his wake. 'You look like you need it.'

Erland appeared crestfallen as he replied. 'It is the hardest thing I have had to ask my men to do lord,' he said. 'To stand guard upon a deserted roadway while men fight a stone's throw away.'

Erik plucked at his sleeve as they made their way back to the place where Stane Gate bisected the town. 'I know that full well,' he assured his friend. 'And don't think for a moment that their sacrifice went unnoticed by the king or his men. Knowing that our flank was secure meant that we could put all our effort into driving the enemy from the roadway.' He threw Erland a look as he explained the reason for his arrival. 'I have come to see where our friend the earl of Bebbanburh is hiding — there is still no sign?'

'Not a trace, lord,' Erland replied. 'The doors have remained closed since we arrived, and we have not spotted a single spearman on the walls.'

'Have you sent anyone forward to take a look?'

Erland nodded. 'Half a dozen, mounted in case they needed to beat a hasty retreat. The northern fort is further away than the two which open onto the road on the opposite side, and I was loathe to risk any more in case it was a trap. My task was to secure your wing, and I would not do that by dividing my crew. If the Bernicians had come pouring through the doors as we approached or there were still men in the southern forts, there would have a been a good chance that they could have swept us aside and fallen on you before you knew it.'

Erik clapped him on the shoulder. 'You did the right thing, but we have seen off the army of Strathclyde and I can now add a half crew to your own. Take the lead,' he said, 'you have earned the honour by your steadfastness. Let us call on our brave lord of Bebbanburh and see what has been keeping him.'

Erland returned to his men as Erik began to address his own. 'We are going to see what is keeping our Bernician friends. I will be leading the rearguard so stay alert, especially when we pass the doorways into the other forts on the southern side of the road.' Erik raised his eyes as the men formed themselves into a column four abreast. Half a mile to the South the rival armies were about to come together, and Erik felt a pang of regret that he had taken the decision to lead the flanking attack in person. A king must lead, fighting in the centre where every man on the field could see his flag going forward or standing firm amid the onslaught like a sea stack in a storm, but he pushed the regrets aside and knew deep down that the decision he had taken had been the correct one for the kingdom as a whole.

The year following the ending of his first reign in York the armies of Alba and Strathclyde had come south, wasting the land as far as the River Tees. Flying columns had crossed into the kingdom itself, carrying away cattle and slaves as they completed the destruction wrought the previous summer by king Eadred and his southern English. Eadred's place-man Olaf Cuaran had ruled then, and the king's response had been feeble and ill coordinated. With the country devastated by invaders in consecutive years and starvation rife among the populace the traders of York, the same men who had been so lukewarm in their support to Erik, had suffered financial loss when they were compelled by Olaf to import grain and other foodstuff in place of more profitable items. Now the counter-attack was being led by the same earls whose lands had suffered the most from the Scottish harrying, and the victory when it came would boost their standing among the folk in their earldoms as the thanes and levy men took revenge for the deprivation their families had suffered. It could only help to bind men who had always shown Erik loyalty closer still — it was a price well worth paying.

Erik looked back to the junction. In the short time needed to take in the goings on to the south the Orkneymen had broken their shield-fort and reordered themselves ready for the advance, and Erik watched them move eastward until the time came to lead his own men and fall in to the rear. Stane Gate stretched before them, and Erik took in the details as the heads of Erland's men moved this way and that as their eyes probed the shadows. This close to the old forts the majority of the buildings lining the roadway were similar to those which had allowed king Dyfnwal and the remnants of his army to escape, long storehouses and workshops sheltering in the protection offered by the legions and helping to cater for their needs. Beyond them the walls of the forts themselves rose into the early morning air, and although the majority of the crenelations had long since gone the way of the men who had laboured to build them, the limestone walls still towered over the buildings which surrounded them.

Oswald Thane murmured something about the spookiness of it all, and although the observation had been made more to himself than the king, Erik moved to settle the Englishman's nerves all the same. 'You are in the midst of over a hundred of my finest warriors — you have little to concern yourself with old friend.'

The Northumbrian flushed that his fears had been uncovered and moved to ask forgiveness, but the distinctive clatter made by interlocking shields from the Iron Beards interrupted him and the apology was stillborn. Taller than most Erik could see beyond the front of the column, and he called out to let the men following on know what was happening as his hand moved instinctively to the handle of his sword. 'A dozen men have left the fort and are walking our way. They are shieldless and appear to have their spears upended as a sign they wish to talk, but be on your guard all the same.' Erik turned to those at his side. 'Oswald, they came from the fort flying the earl of Bernicia's flag. Come along with me, you will have met these men and it may help to settle their nerves if they recognise a familiar face among us.' He cast a quick look at his huskarls and snapped a command. 'Sturla and Kolbein come with us — Helgrim take over here.'

As the group made their way forward, Erik slowed the pace to ensure that the Bernicians were the first to reach the point where Erland had halted and deployed for battle. It was the first of the mind games which leaders played at such times; to keep the other side waiting, however briefly, was always a powerful and highly visible statement of relative status. Oswald Thane came to Erik's shoulder as the little group skirted the men of Orkney, falling into step a half pace behind as he craned his neck to identify the men who had come from the fort. 'The big man is Maccus the Easterner — one of earl Oswulf's leading men. The others are a few of the earl's hearth warriors I recall seeing at the fortress when I travelled there on your behalf.'

Erik grunted his thanks as he picked up the pace again. The delegation had reached the place where Erland stood beneath his banners, and Erik watched as the introductions were cut short, Maccus's face coming around to search him out as he learned the identity of the man leading the attackers that morning. Emerging from the wall of shields, Erik ran his eyes across the group as he came. They were a formidable bunch, tough looking and well provided with the accoutrements of war — it spoke of the open-handedness of their lord and brought honour to the man himself as it was intended to do. The leader was aptly named, Erik decided as he came; almost as tall as Erik himself and built like an ox. If Maccus's flaxen hair was cropped at the nape and left shaggy at the brow in the Norse style, his shaven chin and cheeks told of long years spent in the Christian lands in the South. But it was the old campaigner's garb which really indicated that his nickname of the Easterner had been well earned. Maccus shone in the morning light, the rectangular metal plates of his brynja sliding past one another like the scales of a snake as he turned. Below the war shirt the baggy trews typical of the men of Kiev and the East were tucked into calf high Russian boots. Oswulf's man was as exotic a sight as you could hope to find amid the buildings of a rundown town in northern Britain, and Erik fought down the urge to comment as he came to a halt before him. 'I am Erik Haraldsson, King of York,' he said as Kolbein and Sturla took their places at his shoulder. 'Some men call me Bloodaxe.'

The man inclined his head. 'I am Maccus Olafsson, widely known as the Easterner. It is my honour to come into your presence great king.'

Erik pulled a face, casting sideways glances to each of his huskarls in turn, before turning back and shaking his head as the thunderous crash of wood on wood told them all that the armies had finally come together on the southern bank of the Tine. 'I can see from your turnout that your garments are well travelled but they outpaced any word of your deeds, for none have reached my ears.'

Maccus slipped the shield from his shoulder, holding it forward as Erik's huskarls and the closest Orkneymen tensed at the sudden movement. The ghost of a smile flitted across the Bernician's features as he saw that he had managed to unsettle the men before him despite being heavily outnumbered, but he set his face and spoke a verse as they began to relax:

> *I bore this shield home from the strife as my*
> *share in the East.*

> *Storms with waves of swords in the southern*
> *summer gave me scales of steel.*

> *I got good weapons, a flood before it abated;*

> *I won a helm when the chieftain harshly*
> *defeated the Svear.*

'All men know of the battle-fame of Erik Haraldsson,' Maccus continued as his eyes slid across to Erik's shoulder, 'and of Jomal too. I can see from this morning's attack that the king's cunning is the equal of his fierceness.'

Erik snorted softly at the praise. A wise man knew that flattery can be as useful as a strong sword arm in a tight spot. This man Maccus possessed a fox-slyness to match his extravagance, and Erik's hopes rose that he was the type to carefully weigh the options before he made a rash move and threw his life away. Erik responded with a verse of his own as the Bernician warriors stood tall at their leader's boast:

> *He should rise early, the man who means to*
> *take another's life or wealth.*

The slumbering wolf seldom gets the ham,
nor the dozing man victory.

Maccus pulled a smile as he recognised the verse. 'A saying of the High One; Óðinn's reputation for wisdom is well earned, lord.'

'Now would be a good time for you to earn your own reputation for right-thinking,' Erik replied. The sound of fighting was sweeping across the town in waves now as the armies came to grips, and he was still unsure whether the men of Strathclyde had left the field completely or were gathering to renew their attack on the water meadow below the forts. The time for words was over — Maccus would have to choose between losing his honour or his head. 'I gather as we two are talking here that Earl Oswulf has yet to reach the town. When can we expect him?'

Maccus hesitated, but Erik's face hardened into an icy scowl which left the man facing him in no doubt that his life depended on his helpfulness. Tight-lipped, he spat reply. 'They are half a day away, King Erik. We were sent forward yesterday to make contact with the king of Alba and see to the arrangements for our lodging.'

Erik indicated Oswald Thane with a flick of his head. 'You are aware of the messages of friendship this man carried on my behalf to Earl Oswulf this summer from York?'

'Yes, lord.'

'And you know something of my proposals?'

Maccus confirmed that he did.

'Well, this moment could either become the start of our great enterprise; to reunite the old lands of Northumbria and make it the most feared kingdom in these islands once again, or the final destination in your far travelled life.' Erik reached up to draw Jomal over his shoulder, the razor sharp cutting edge and blade still spattered with gore from that morning's work. 'The choice is your own, but make it quickly Maccus — I have a war to win.'

The Easterner's gaze flitted from king to war axe, before moving out to cast a look at the timeworn buildings which surrounded him. He turned back with a sigh. 'It's not much of a death vision for eyes which drank in the wonders of Miklagard,' he said with a wry smile. 'What do you want of us?'

9

A CORPSE IS NO USE TO ANYONE

Erik came clear of the buildings and halted at the top of the rise, running his eyes over the seething mass of men and horses crowding the water meadow below. It was as he had feared. Forced to split the *here* to confront the expected attack by earl Oswulf and his Bernicians, the momentum had drained from his own attack. Now, with the pressure off and the army of York in clear view beyond the river to the south, it would be plain to the Cumbrians that the spirited assault which had surprised them on the roadway could only have come from a flying column. Sure now that he had not been outflanked by overwhelming force king Dyfnwal was clearly in view, gathering his army about the war flag of Strathclyde as his guards ordered panicked men from horseback and herded them back towards their king.

Erik's huskarls gathered protectively around him as they realised the danger; the king was less than a hundred yards from the nearest enemy spearmen, at any moment they would be spotted and a counterattack could quickly develop as men who had already lost friends and suffered humiliation that

94

morning saw the chance to repay their tormentors in kind. Thankfully Erland appeared at the head of his Iron Beards, and Erik grasped the opportunity to advance as the men of Orkney began to fill the space. Ahead two large buildings straddled the ridge line, their walls gleaming like ice under a fresh lick of lime, and Erik strode onward to take up position at the centre of the gap between them as Sturla Godi carried his war banner forward and planted it at his side. Downslope heads were turning their way, but Helgrim was at his shoulder and the space was quickly filling with Norsemen as they spilled out from the alleyways which led down from Stane Gate. Reassured by the rapidly growing numbers, Erik summoned his leading men: 'Erland! Maccus!'

The Easterner already wore the expression of a man who had gone ankle deep in pig shit the first time out in his new boots, and Erik fought down a wicked smile as the big warrior trotted across. It had taken longer than he had hoped to retrieve the flag of Bernicia from the fortress, but it was central to Erik's plan and he knew that it had been time well spent. A malicious glint came into his eyes as Erland and Maccus came up and he gave them their orders. 'Form your men into a swine head. We are attacking again.'

Despite the fact that they had been potential enemies only a short while before, the pair exchanged a look of disbelief. Erland was the first to rediscover his tongue. 'You are not planning on defending the ridge line, lord? We are heavily outnumbered, and the buildings will keep us from being outflanked. Let them tire themselves attacking upslope while we pick off their leaders with javelins and arrows — it is the perfect defensive position.'

Erik shook his head. 'The day is going our way, but our part in it is not yet over.' Three heads turned as one, and the trio gazed beyond the rapidly reforming army of Strathclyde, across the river to the southern bank of the Tine. Outnumbered and in grave danger of having their shield wall turned the Scots had pulled their wings back to form a horseshoe, anchoring each end against the riverside. On the Yorkish flanks Gunderic and Godred were already leading the levies down to the banks, curving around to cut the escape route before swinging back to assault the trapped men gathered about the southern approach to the bridge itself.

The Bernician was appalled. 'You want me to form a boar snout and attack the men of Strathclyde?'

Erik nodded. 'Of course, did you not ride here to fight? Well, this is a battle — there are no onlookers here.' He pointed out Oswald Thane with a flick of his chin. Standing alongside Sturla Godi, the old Northumbrian was gnawing at his lower lip as he stared south with a face as pale as milk; Erik immediately realised that he could have chosen a better example to show how steadfast his men were, but the words were out and there was point in wishing them away. 'That man has felt the heat of sixty summers warm his face, yet when the war horn sounds he dons a shirt of mail, hefts a spear and proudly marches beneath the banner of his lord. Would Maccus the Easterner do any less?'

The Bernician's expression became a scowl, and he lowered his voice as he replied. 'You said back on the roadway that you would value my rede King Erik, there was no mention of taking part in the fighting. You speak of lords and fealty but mine is still half a day away, I am under no obligation to fight here.'

Erik's lids narrowed as his eyes turned flinty, and his reply when it came was a growl. 'Things can change from moment to moment when armies come together. Now I need you to take your place in the attack.'

The consternation Maccus felt at being outmanoeuvred was written upon his features, and he made one last plea to rescue his honour. 'If I refuse Jomal will take my head, that much I know of your reputation Bloodaxe. That is a sacrifice I will gladly make if you vow to release my men, but I cannot attack those who I broke bread with this very same morn.'

'If that is your choice, stretch your neck,' Erik spat as he firmed his grip on the haft of his axe. 'I have no more time to waste. But die knowing that the rune sticks are already cast, that your sacrifice will be in vain.' He indicated Maccus's banner man, who now carried the flag of Bernicia within its sheath of leather. 'We have Earl Oswulf's banner, and it *will* be carried against the enemy whether you are there or not.' Erik softened his tone in a final effort to win the man over. 'The men you broke bread with this morning are beaten and fated to die. You can see the scale of our victory here today. Even if the kings survive, their power is broken; your lord will desire the friendship of the king in York, and it is within your power to deliver that.' Erik forced a smile, despite the overwhelming urge have done with it; to lop off the Bernician's head and charge downhill before the men of Strathclyde could complete their rally. He had scoffed when Gunnhild had said that age had tempered the fury of his youth, but he realised at that moment that it was true. Jomal's wide blade came down to tap the helmet suspended from Maccus's belt. 'Either don that helm or I will pass it to another. One way or another, the men in the field below will believe you are leading the charge and that they have been betrayed.' Erik spoke a verse as he saw the man hesitate:

> *The lame man rides a horse,*
> *the deaf man fights and succeeds;*

to be blind is better than to be burnt:
a corpse is no use to anyone.

Maccus's eyes flitted from Erik to Erland and back again
as he began to fumble with the bindings which secured the
helm at his side. Donning the headpiece he replied with
another of Óðinn's sayings:

For those words which one man says to
another, often he gets paid back.

Erik's eyes flared at the challenge, but Maccus had
already turned to stomp away. The king began to raise his
axe, but his companion placed a hand upon his sleeve. 'Let it
ride King Erik, the insult can be repaid when we have the
victory — we have wasted enough time already.' Erland drew
his sword. 'Not all have fed the raven today. My men are in
place and eager to fight.'

With a final lingering glare at the back of the retreating
Bernician, Erik heft his shield and turned away. 'Yes, you are
right kinsman. Let us drive our enemies from the field and
settle up at leisure.'

The altercation with Maccus had served to raise his hackles, and Erik had enough experience in war to recognise that
the man had done him a service. He cried out as he stamped
across to the battle line. 'Set up a war cry! Let us remind
those at the foot of the slope what type of men we are.' Erik's
eyes ran along the front rank as the men of his hird began to
beat their weapons against the boards of their shields, until
the faces he sought hardened from the scrum. 'Grettir!
Gunnar!'

The brothers turned, drawing themselves upright at the
call from the king. 'Yes, lord?'

'You led the swine head at Ceasterford, attacking with pluck and ferocity — do the same for me today.'

Even at thirty paces the look of joy which came upon the young men's features was obvious, and Erik watched with pride as they walked clear of the battle line and bellowed their challenges to the men below. Four years had now passed since the young brothers had first approached him, on another riverside meadow between the pitiful remains of an earl's blackened hall and the small church where Erik had just led the Christian Mass. They had been big lads then he recalled as he watched the svinfylking take shape, but the intervening summers spent raiding far and wide with their king had broadened shoulders and made ship's hawsers of their arms; the young Hordalanders were now full-grown; men to be feared.

The space between the buildings was now packed with resolute looking Norsemen, and Erik placed an arm upon Olvir's shoulder as he reached the rear ranks. 'Take Hauk, Mord and twenty good men. Go across and back up Maccus and his Bernicians.' The Vestfolder nodded and turned to go, but Erik called him back as a thought crossed his mind and he fixed the young man with a look. 'Make sure that they know you are there — we would not want them to lose their way between here and the enemy.' Olvir nodded that he understood, scuttling away as the howl of war horns resounded from the nearby walls. Erik threw a quick look along the battle line as he took his place at the heart of the boar snout. To his right Erland had reached the same position in the midst of his Iron Beards; a quick look to the left, and he pulled the trace of a smile as he saw Olvir and his lads already jogging towards the place where Maccus stood grim faced beneath the flag of Bernicia.

He still had a few moments until they were in position,

and Erik decided to put them to good use as he recognised that the men were keyed up and ready for the off. Pushing his way through the ranks Erik came out into the space between the armies, and the pulsating rhythm of spear shaft on shield rim fell away along with the siren call of the battle horn as he did so. Erik strode the front line, Jomal clattering against spear and sword blade as men craned to hear his words, and his own war lust was kindled anew as he pointed out men from the crowd, recalling lineage and past deeds as the army of Bloodaxe roared their acclaim. A quick circuit and he found himself back in front of his hearth men, and the swine head opened up to swallow their king as Erik took his rightful place among them. Kolbein and Helgrim Smiter took their places at his shoulders: it was time to go. 'Sturla,' he barked, savouring the moment. 'A king should know when he is beaten — sound the charge.'

The banner man spat as the horn came up, and an instant later the distinctive call resounded about the space. Within moments the deep-seated bay was answered by the higher pitched yap of hunting horns, and Eric raised Jomal high so that all could see as the world held its breath. The Dane axe dropped, flags tipped forward, and the hillside resounded with the crash of booted feet, the swish of mail, as the *here* began to move downhill. Slowly at first as men dressed their lines and fell into step, the advance quickened as they broke clear from the confines of the buildings and those at the rear swung forward to extend the line. Seventy yards quickly became fifty and then thirty as the charge gathered pace, and as his grip firmed on the handle of Jomal Erik raised his eyes, thrilling to the sight as he saw that his own svinfylking was heading directly for the war flag of Strathclyde and the king who stood beneath it. A skjald-borg twenty men in depth had thrown itself around the body of the Cumbrian king in the time it had taken the Norse to form up and launch their attack, with shield walls two or three men deep coming off to east and west. The opportunity was still there to smash through the weaker wings and envelop the king whether Maccus played his part or not, to break through onto the riverside where all was confusion as hundreds of horses milled about and panicky men still grappled with the urge to flee.

Erik felt the familiar sensation in the final moments before the armies clashed, an intoxicating desire to get to grips with the foe as the gods and the heroes of old looked down from their heavenly halls, quaffed mead and lay odds on the victors. An instant later the mood was shattered as linden boards met, steel clashed on steel and men roared in fear and anger in a storm of sound that tore the sky. Immediately the formation closed up, the loose order so necessary to enable heavily armed men to run full pelt downhill transforming in a moment into a living ram as Grettir and Gunnar at the point of the wedge shoved and stabbed. Kolbein and Helgrim raised their shields as they moved shoulder to shoulder with their king, their eyes darting this way and that as they guarded against javelin, spear and sword. Steel flashed in the morning sun, blades hacking and chopping to either side as the wedge drove deeper and deeper into the belly of the enemy host.

Erik's safety guaranteed by the alertness of his oath sworn, the king risked a last-gasp glance to either side before the rest of the attacking force became lost from view. On his righthand side Erik saw with satisfaction that the flag of Orkney had already broken through the thinner enemy lines there, the old tusker flying proudly above a field of helmed heads as the leading men spilled out into the clear space beyond. But if Erland's breakthrough had pleased the king, a quick look to the east caused his heart to soar as he watched the flag of Bernicia teased out in a breath of wind. Already on the point of a breakthrough, it was obvious that Maccus the Easterner and his men had accepted their lot, that the only way they would escape from the situation that fate had forced upon them that day was directly through the ranks of their erstwhile allies. Every man on the battlefield would soon know that Earl Oswulf's flag had been seen fighting alongside that of Erik Bloodaxe, and even the most complete victories rarely resulted in the annihilation of an enemy host. Soon every king, thane and earl on the island of Britain and beyond would have heard the tale.

Satisfied, Erik's head switched back. In the short time it had taken to check on the progress to either flank his own boar snout had widened as the point drove on, and the men at his side were already beginning to bring their blades down onto the heads of the enemy as they enlarged the breach. Only a short distance ahead Erik recognised the arms and armour of the men who had stood guard on Dere Street, clustering about the alleyway as king Dyfnwal had fled the carnage, and he began to drive forward as the climax of his third fight in less than a day approached. Sturla Godi raised the battle horn to his lips as they went, and as the distinctive wail rose into the air Erik raised Jomal. At the tip of the battle wedge Gunnar and Grettir turned outwards at the sound to clear a path for the king, and Erik watched gleefully as the warrior who had been channelling all of his strength into pushing back against their attack tumbled forward as the resistance suddenly vanished. Erik ground the man's face into the dirt with the sole of a boot as he forced his way through, leaving the stunned and helpless swordsman to be despatched to Christ's safekeeping by those following on. Jomal swung as the enemy came into reach, and Erik watched as the man who had been in the second rank only moments before desperately snatched his shield across to parry the blow. To the king's anger the defender was successful, and Erik felt the shock of the strike jar his arm as the battle axe buried itself deeply into the face of the shield, but if his opponent thought that he had thwarted the attack he was to be disappointed. Erik tugged at the haft as Helgrim moved to his side, and as his opponent's arm shot forward the huskarl's sword was already a blur. Erik looked on as the blade came down, and he saw the horror of the moment reflected in the guard's features as he realised what must follow. Before the man could attempt to recover Helgrim's sword blade had cut through muscle and bone, and as the fighter's roar of defiance became a scream of pain and horror Jomal finally came free. Erik shifted his grip as it did so, sliding his hands along the haft as the heel came up to pulp the Cumbrian's nose, and as the man staggered under the blows Helgrim's sword flicked out again to open his throat.

If the first to fall to his attack had provided little by way of resistance, Erik saw immediately that the man who now stepped forward to take his place in the front line was of a different mettle. Glinting jewel-like above a beard as black as jet, the eyes of a killer stared from a face that told of a life spent in harm's way, and Erik knew that it would take guile as much as brute strength to quickly overcome such a man or risk the attack stalling; he called across his shoulder as he began to swing the axe: 'Sturla — the flag!'

It was a ploy they had perfected and used time and again on battlefields from Finnmark to Serkland and Erik dipped a shoulder, skewing his body as Jomal swung. As Dyfnwal's bodyguard braced to deflect the strike the blooded axe banner of Erik Haraldsson shot forward to screen his view; blinded the swordsman never saw the moment when Erik's axe changed tack but the pain when it came was real enough, and

Erik rushed in to shoulder him aside as he tugged the axe free and stepped up to break the line.

Erik raised his chin, thrilling to the sight which met his eyes as Kolbein and Helgrim Smiter fought their way back to his side. There, not more than half a dozen paces away, the king of Strathclyde had accepted that he too must fight this day and was finally drawing his sword.

10

BONE-FIRES

E rik swung again as the men of the *Draki* began to pivot forward on either flank, the axe blade glancing off a shoulder to hew the crown from the next man in line like lopping the top from an egg. The king stepped up, plunging deeper and deeper into the enemy shield-fort as his war axe came around to strike again. Faced by a wooden wall Erik changed the trajectory of the strike with a deft flick, but if he felt satisfaction as the bearded blade bit deeply into the shoulder of the next victim to fall that morning the joy was to be short lived. A counter shove came from the men facing him, the steel dome of a shield boss forcing the breath from his lungs in an explosion of spittle flecked air. As Erik was forced to take a backwards step he watched in horror as the glittering arc of an enemy sword blade swept down towards his exposed wrist. For a heart stopping moment it appeared to the king as if his hand was to share the fate of his late opponent, to be trampled into the mud of the flood plain along with the axe it held, but the swordsman's look of triumph was extinguished in an instant as Kolbein's wide board swept across to draw the power from the strike. Seizing his chance

Erik stepped up, the steel strips of his vambrace sparking as the blade slid down and past. But if Kolbein's counter had saved the king's hand there was still a price to pay, and Erik looked on in dismay as the sword severed the leather thong which secured Jomal to his wrist, caught in the beard of the blade and forced the axe from his grip.

A spear thrust evaded Helgrim's defence before Erik could recover, the leaf shaped blade hooking a ring of mail and tearing a rent in Erik's brynja at the shoulder. With Jomal lying at his feet Erik took a pace back from the crush followed by another as the men of Strathclyde fought like demons to protect their king, moving a hand across to draw his sword from its scabbard as Grettir and Gunner closed up to remake the formation.

Erik took the opportunity to raise his eyes again now that he was out of harm's way. His frenzied assault had taken them almost halfway to the place where Dyfnwal still stood rooted beneath his banner, but he was close enough now to see the fear in the king's eyes and the realisation that death could be only moments away in those of his most trusted men. A quick sweep of the head to left and right told him that both wings had broken through the makeshift Strathclyde shield wall, and although the attack led by Erland and his Iron Beards was further advanced, both flanks were in the clear and curling around to envelop the enemy king and his hearth guard.

With the sword handle now firmly in his grip Erik returned to the fray, and as the battle horn sounded at his back to clear a path for the king, his sword chopped down onto the shoulders and heads of the remaining guards as his hirdmen heaved and stabbed all around him. Their courage already shaken by the surprise assault on Dere Street, the men of Strathclyde were streaming away as their earlier dread returned to drive them to panicked flight. There would be no recovery now, the fight was won, and Erik threw his shoulder into his shield as he sensed the hopelessness of the men facing him. As one of the largest men on the battlefield, the few paces which separated him from the last of the Strath-clyde defenders was enough to turn Erik's short rush into a bull-like charge, and as his huskarls and hirdmen roared his name they hurled themselves against the foe. Certain now that they were writing the final line of their life story, the last defenders fought back like the wildcats of their northern forests; but the Norse were swarming around them now, swords, spears and axes stabbing, slashing, raining blow upon blow as the encirclement was completed.

The foeman before him raised an arm and Erik saw the glimmer of a seax as it came up, the short stabbing sword which had given the Saxons their name and was so deadly in the press of shields. The king stabbed low to counter with his sword as his shield came up to deflect the point, but before the blade could slide into flesh a Norwegian spear jabbed to turn the defender's hate-filled snarl to pulp. Spattered with teeth and gore Erik stepped up as the attacker fell away, swinging his sword overhead to hew at the last man to stand between the kings of Strathclyde and York, but even as the guard attempted to dodge the blade swords and spears were chopping and stabbing from all sides as the Norse pack barked and snapped in their moment of victory. Erik barged the cadaver aside, locking eyes with his prize as the men of the *Draki* somehow found it within themselves to curb their bloodlust. To witness a clash of kings on the battlefield was a once in a lifetime opportunity, and the victors jostled each other for places at the front as they quickly encircled the pair.

In the centre of the ring Erik saw the fear once again as his eyes narrowed in hatred. He had the man who had thought to lead an army against his kingdom, laying waste the land and carrying off his people to fill the thrall markets of Dublin and beyond a pace away. Erik struck first, punching out with his shield arm to drive his opponent's board aside, and as the foreigner's defence was opened up Erik darted in before the young king of Strathclyde could counter. Up close now Erik could see that Dyfnwal was little more than a stripling — there was little honour to be had in slaying such a man despite his kingly title, and the big Norseman feinted with the blade of his sword as his knee came up. Dyfnwal fell for the ruse, and as his eyes rose to track the strike the Yorkish king felt the softness of his opponent's groin give way to the satisfying resistance of the bone beyond. Erik was already reversing the sword in his hand as a strangulated gasp erupted from his opponent, and as Dyfnwal's head came down the handle of Erik's sword was rising. A heartbeat later the golden dome of the pommel was smashing into the bridge of the young king of Strathclyde's nose, and Erik was withdrawing his arm to punch upwards again as bone and gristle crumpled and blood sheeted to the grass. Dyfnwal staggered under the force of the blows but the pommel was already rising again to deny him any chance to recover, and as the handle connected again Erik watched in triumph as the king's eyes rolled back in his head and his knees folded beneath him.

King Dyfnwal's fall had revealed the figure of his standard bearer, the last man standing over a circle of the slain as was right, and Erik addressed him as his hirdmen roared and acclaimed their king's victory. 'Banner man — you have stood your ground; there is no need for you to fall this day.'

The man held him in his gaze before replying with a verse, and Erik thrilled to the words as he came to recognise the man's worth:

'Here lies my king, hewn down in the dust;
in the midst of my friends, a company of
*   heroes.*

'I will not hence from here.

'I purpose to lie by the side of my lord,
a man dearly loved.'

The cries of victory had abated as men stretched their necks to listen to the exchange, and Erik replied as a murmur of appreciation rolled around the onlookers at the standard bearer's noble words. 'Your king is not dead,' Erik explained, 'but he is my captive. Go from here, tell the people at home the fate which awaits those who think it an easy thing to carry arms against the kingdom of Erik Haraldsson.'

The man shook his head as he replied. 'I'll not leave this place without my lord, King Erik — the humiliation will outlive me and bring shame upon my clan.'

Erik nodded that he understood. The exchange, although thrilling, was taking too long — he itched to find out how the battle was going on the far side of the Tine. 'Then ride south with us,' he said finally as he made to leave. 'Accompany the king into captivity if that is your choice.' The man began to unfasten the scabbard at his hip, but Erik held out a hand as he began to walk away. 'I have your word that you will not attempt to rescue King Dyfnwal?' The man gave a curt nod in reply. 'Then keep your weapons; a man of rank and honour should never go unarmed.' Erik looked across at Oswald Thane as the circle of Norsemen divided to admit him. The old Northumbrian was panting like a warhorse run hard, and Erik knew that he had found the perfect way to keep the man safely out of harm's way while assuaging any guilt he would feel at missing the fight. 'Oswald old friend,' he said brightly. 'Will you do me the kindness of looking after our newfound guests?' Erik's gaze was already elsewhere before the man could reply, and his huskarls hastened to his side as the rear ranks parted to reveal the fighting on the southern bank.

Helgrim pointed across the river as the clamour of battle drifted across to them. 'It looks as if the Scots are getting ready to counterattack.'

Erik looked. Men were hauling themselves into saddles at the centre of the position, the fineness of their arms betraying their station. In the midst of the group King Mael Colm was clearly in sight as he mounted his war horse, the members of his hearth guard crowding around as the common soldiery looked on aghast. 'No,' he replied as it became clear what they were about to witness. 'The king is about to ride away and leave his army in the lurch.'

Hard pressed by the army of York, the perimeter of the Scottish position was already reduced to little more than half its original size as the southern army tasted the iron tang of a bloody victory on the air. Already those at the rear, the late-comers and battle-shirkers, were being pushed down the muddy bank of the River Tine. As more and more men came to realise that they were about to be abandoned to the unlikely mercy of Northumbrians and Norsemen, the first swimmers were already splashing into the shallows. Erik turned his head, cupping a hand to his mouth as he prepared to fight again: 'Erland!'

The Orkneyman looked up at the sound of Erik's voice, doubling across with his bodyguards as he saw the king beckon with an arm. Erik scanned the riverside as he waited for him to arrive. The speed with which the wings of king Dyfnwal's hastily assembled shield wall had collapsed when struck by the attacks of Erland and Maccus the Easterner had meant that the losses to both defenders and attackers had been relatively light. Having fled the field of battle the last of the Strathclyde casualties, men slowed down by wounds or helping injured kinsmen or friends to safety, were just reaching the horses still lowering their long necks to graze nonchalantly on the pasture to the East. Erland stood before him when he turned back, and Erik recognised the flush of victory on his kinsman's features and knew it must be reflected in his own. 'We are not done here old friend,' he said happily, clapping Erland on the arm. 'Remake the battle line — we will advance to the river at walking pace and snap the trap shut.' Erland returned the smile, turning on a heel to do his lord's bidding, and the cry carried to the king — *Reform! Reform the line!* — as Erik began to make his way across to the man who had led the swine head to the East. 'You have played your part Maccus,' Erik said as Erland bawled his orders and the clatter of arms sounded again, 'and played it well.' Erik ignored the stern faced look which greeted him and put aside the slight from earlier. The man was still useful to his plans, and he would keep him alive for as long as that was beneficial. Erik pinned him with his gaze as he came up, lowering his voice to a monotone so that only they could hear his words. 'You need to take yourself back to earl Oswulf and let him know of our great victory here and your own part in it.'

A roar of outrage came from the men across the river, and both men looked across. It was as Erik had expected. Mael Colm and his leading men had taken to their horses, surrounded themselves with their hearth troops and were hacking a passage through friend and foe alike as they spurred their mounts towards the East and safety. The pair watched as the sheer weight of numbers and the unstoppable power of the horsemen burst through the right wing of the army of York and fled. Erik continued as they watched them go. 'Tell the earl that the power of the Scots is broken and reassure him of my friendship.' Erik's smile was ravening. 'You had better be quick about it. It would be unfortunate if the earl came across Mael Colm on the road without knowing the part his men played in the victory today. Carry the message that I invite him to be my guest in York along with as many men as he sees fit to accompany him.' Erik pinned the man with a look. 'Tell your lord that I desire his fellowship, but as you can see…' The king's voice trailed away as his eyes swept the field. Large numbers of the men of Alba had managed to take advantage of the collapse of the Yorkish flank and were streaming after their departing king in their desperation, but the flags of Gamli and Guttorm Eriksson showed where Erik's sons were rushing across to plug the rent and the Scots were still a long way from the safety of their northern kingdom. Erik doubted that many would see their homes again. He turned back, and although the words were benign the underlying menace they contained was plain. 'I desire his cooperation, but don't require it. Northumbria will be one kingdom again under my rule, and earl Oswulf has a place in the new order if that is his wish.' The rhythmic clatter of weaponry told the pair that the attack was ready to be renewed. Erik smiled again, his voice rising a degree as he injected a lightheartedness into his parting words for the benefit of those within earshot. 'Carry my message to earl Oswulf, Maccus; assure him of my friendship, and tell him of our victory here today!'

Erik returned to the riverbank, stalking across to the centre of the line without a backwards glance as he regained his rightful place beneath the sigil battle flag. Across the River Tine Gamli and Guttorm had fought their way to the bank, and large numbers of those Scots still trapped near the bridge were throwing themselves into the waters as the perimeter shrank by the moment in the forlorn hope of reaching the horses and safety. Erik looked along the line, and as weapons were made ready to stab and slash he pulled a savage grin and called the advance to the riverside.

THORSTEIN STOOD at the head of the men, beaming as Erik and the rest of his shipmates approached the bridge. Erik replied in kind as he came up, clapping his old friend on the shoulder as his eyes went to the point of the bloodied spear blade and back again. 'How was it?'

'Tougher than I expected,' the big huskarl admitted as the rest of the men began to mingle with the others of their hird. 'They fought well when they got the chance, but they were never going to force a passage through nigh on a hundred Norse spearmen on such a narrow front.' He cast a look across to the place where the men of Orkney stood in groups: jubilant and flushed with success. 'Arnkel rotated the front rank every time the Scots regrouped for another attempt at forcing a way through. We continually had fresh men in the shield wall, the going got harder and harder for them with every attack.'

Erik shared a grin and a nod of recognition with Arnkel nearby; Erland came across, and the Torf-Einarsson brothers shared a hug at surviving another fight as they began to swap stories of the day. Erik plucked at Thorstein's sleeve. 'Come,' he said, 'show me.' Erik's bodyguard slipped into his wake as the pair made their way to the twin columns which marked the entrance to the bridge itself. The Draki men and the crew of the *Iron Beard* were beginning to gravitate towards their leaders now that the fighting was over, and the way ahead cleared as they walked and men drifted away.

Erik let out a low whistle as the last Orcadians parted to reveal the old Roman highway running up to the crossing place. 'Desperate men do desperate things,' Thorstein responded as they reached the bridge. Erik placed the sole of his boot on the upper line of the rampart of bloodied torsos and gave a firm push, but the wall of death remained firmly in place.

'Have you tallied up?'

'Only a rough one,' Thorstein replied. 'This close to the river the flies and midges are never far away at the best of times.' He swept a hand across the devastation before them: 'and with all this…'

As Thorstein's words were snatched up to drift away on the breeze, Erik raised his eyes to peer beyond the span to the southern bank. A shaft of sunlight broke through to bathe the battlefield in its soft glow, the air abuzz as the warmth of the morning and the ferric tang of blood drew the first scavengers to the scene on tiny wings. Erik nodded. He had meant to camp for the day on the field of victory, to *hold the field of slaughter* as the skalds would have it. But reality, of being there and witnessing such a thing with your own eyes, the sour stench of gutted men, the limbs, the severed heads and blood by the barrel load, could sometimes plumb depths unattainable by even the most honeyed tongue and today was such a day. He would have the prisoners clear the bridge, reunite the army of York and camp on the rising ground to the south while men tended wounds, drank to forget the sights and deeds of the day or slept off the exhaustion of the fight and early morning march.

ERIK PAUSED IN THE SADDLE, savouring what men were already calling his greatest victory as the last groups made their way across to the road. The field was clear of bodies now that folk from nearby Corebricg had traded the contents of their stomach for their new king's silver, labouring to build the bone-fires they hoped would keep death and disease from their doors. Bloodaxe ran his eyes along the road as he waited, satisfied that his idea was sound. The smoke was gossamer thin now that the flames had all but completed their work, with just the incandescence at the base of the plume showing where eyes had burst from sockets, body fats run in rivulets and skulls split in the scorching heat. Soon only mounds of bone, waist high to a footsore traveller, would remain alongside the iron grey setts of Dere Street to mark the place where Mael Colm's great invading army had met its match.

But it was not the charnel heaps which had excited his senses that morning, but the idea which had presented itself in the night. Shorn of his army the king of Alba had fled back to what he assumed would be the safety of his own land. But the harvest was barely in, the weather set fair for a month or two yet, enough time he mused for a follow-up strike at the wolf's lair itself.

It was time to move, and Erik's lips tightened into a warlike smile as dreams of retribution filled his thoughts. He raised his spear, signalling the march; Sturla Godi's horn sang; the tramp of leather booted feet resounded as the army of York began the long march homeward. The king of Scots had thought to drive him from his kingdom, to harry his land and enslave his folk; but Erik Haraldsson was no Olaf Cuaran nor mere earl in Bebbanburh but a son of Fairhair — there was a reckoning to be had, and sooner than they thought possible.

11

VIKING

Kolbein sucked his teeth, shading his eyes from the glare of the sun. 'The ships furthest to larboard were a bit close to the shoals that time,' he said with a frown. 'I think that should be our last tack, Erik.'

Erik nodded, gesturing to Sturla that he join the pair on the steering platform as he dropped back to the deck. 'Signal the ships — we are going to shorten sail and run out the oars.' He cast a look back at the southern shoreline of the Firth as the sound of the war horn drifted over the fleet. 'We are close enough inshore — Oswald's men must have seen us by now.'

'And sent riders back to their master in Bebbanburh,' Kolbein agreed. 'So now they can hazard a guess as to our destination, and know for sure that the fighting outside Corebricg did nothing to sap our strength.'

Erik returned his gaze to the south as the clatter of spars being lowered all about him filled the chill air. With the sails stowed the view opened up, and Erik looked fixedly upon the distant rock and the great fortress of Eidyn which stood upon it. A golden sheen against the grey clouds beyond showed where earl Oswald's flag declared the allegiance of the men manning the burh, and Erik nodded with satisfaction as an image of messengers hastily preparing to depart came into his mind.

But if his enemies would be surprised by the swiftness of the counterattack, it was no more than that of his own men he reflected as the ships closed up to double the narrows. A day and night of feasting was all that the king allowed both himself and the cream of his army on returning to York following the victory at Corebricg. Safe from attack on all sides, Erik had gathered the best of his crews together for one last foray before the winter storms returned, one last blast of the war horn to ram home the lesson that this was not the Erik Haraldsson of his first reign in York. Then he had allowed his lust for the king helm to overcome his better judgment, and when king Eadred had attacked to restore the rule of Olaf Cuaran, Erik's support had melted away. Now with his treasury full and an army of Norse, he had returned to take back that which was his by right.

Having made sure to hug the coast on the journey northwards they had passed within a mile of Bebbanburh itself, the flags of Erik Bloodaxe, York and Orkney filling the horizon leaving earl Oswulf in his fortress in no doubt to whom this powerful fleet owed allegiance. But although the Orcadians had peeled off at the entrance to the Firth, sailing home to their northern halls to carry news of their great victory and sit out the winter with kith and kin it was not the king's destination, and the reports that the leader of the northern English would soon receive from Eidyn burh would quash any such hopes that they were safe for the coming winter.

As the sun climbed to its high point in the southern sky the Forth changed from firth to river, and the ships of the fleet formed line astern as they were channeled into the twists and turns which led to their destination. Within easy bowshot now from either bank each rower was protected by a shield wielding crew mate, and Erik paced the steering platform as the river narrowed a little more with every stroke of the oars. Thorstein and Helgrim Smiter were at his side, their eyes stabbing the riverside as they sought to protect their lord. At the steering oar Kolbein spoke. 'Do you want to increase the pace, lord? It is a well marked channel.'

Erik shook his head. 'The distance from the river mouth to Stirlin is ten miles or so by road, but double that by ship. A fast horse will alert those up ahead of the threat long before we can fall upon them and do any harm. We are not here to kill the king or carry off slaves and plunder,' he added with a look, 'but to drive home the lesson we gave them outside Corebricg. To see us appear before their most important settlement little more than a month after that defeat will let everyone on the island of Britain know that a new power has arisen here, a king who will not only defend his borders but swiftly carry the flame of retribution to the heart of their own lands.'

Ahead the river took another wide meander, and Erik left Kolbein to concentrate on steering the sleek longship as he worked the paddle blade and followed the reports of the men in the bow. As lead ship in the fleet, he knew that it was vital that they steer the correct course; run aground or block the way ahead in any way here and the entire raiding force would be vulnerable, but the cries from the prow man confirmed that the soundings were good and Erik began to relax as they neared their destination. Closer to Stirlin the woodland edge drew back to reveal stands of barley and lush green pasture, and although they had yet to catch sight of man, woman or child since they had entered the confines of the river, the fortress of Mael Colm on its rocky outcrop hove into view dominating the skyline to the west. Already dressed in mail brynja and helms, the men were giving a final sweep of the sharpening stone to their blades as they prepared for a hard fight; but Erik was less sure that a battle was in the offing, and his eyes swept ahead as the *Draki* took the final bend and Kolbein centred the steering oar for the run in. The course of the River Forth straightened as it ran past the town, and Erik scanned the dockside for signs of opposition as the steady sweep of the oars walked the longship down towards them.

Helgrim spoke at his shoulder as Erik switched his gaze to sweep the bridge upstream for any signs of bowmen. 'Perhaps we beat them home?'

Thorstein was listening in and made the reply. 'More like we left their bones piled beside Dere Street.' He pulled a savage smile. 'Not many of them got away with the king.' Erik ran his eyes across the town of Stirlin for the last time as Kolbein prepared to turn the prow towards the riverbank. A landing stage ran for a good quarter of a mile on the southern bank of the Forth, the masts and rigging of dozens of ships wooding the air against a backdrop of timber warehouses and halls. Upriver a series of boat houses and shipyards appeared abandoned, save for the miserable wretch of a dog whose yaps and barks were the first opposition they had met all day. A last look behind, and Erik thrilled at the sight of beast head after beast head swinging in as the ships of the fleet exited the final bend and pulled for the quayside. 'Lay the *Draki* alongside that knarr,' Erik said to Kolbein, and as the styrisman made the final adjustment to the longship's course with a deft flick on the steering oar, Erik gathered up his weapons and stepped down to the deck.

Erik was pleased to see that not a face was turned his way as he trod the boards, the fighting men too intent on watching the town for any sign of opposition to think to throw him a smile. Every man aboard knew that this was the most vulnerable moment of the attack, that if the buildings lining to dock-side were to spew forth defenders at any time this was it. Then it would become a hacking contest as the Scots crammed the quayside, chopping down on the heads and shoulders of the Norse as they threw themselves forward and fought desperately to gain a foothold on land. But Erik's luck held and none appeared, and a heartbeat later the prow of the longship gave the tubby little trader the ghost of a kiss. Erik leapt the gap to land with a crash on the deck of the knarr, and as his huskarls thudded down all around he was already moving forward. With the tide in flood the deck beneath him lolled like a drunk as Norsemen poured across from the *Draki*, and Erik gave thanks to Þorr for Scottish gutlessness as he gripped the backstay and swung up onto the wide boards of the quay.

A dozen paces took the king halfway to the open door of a storehouse and he thought to pause and wait for his guard, but every man in the fleet must have witnessed the king leading the assault, and even a lifetime spent in warfare offered few such moments to enhance his renown as a battle winner. Erik hunkered into his shield, opening his body to raise his spear as he sped towards the doorway, and as the dart flew to disappear inside the opening the king passed from bright sunlight into the shade cast by the building itself. Although brief, the moment was enough to allow his eyes to accustom themselves to the gloomy interior, and the instant he passed through the doorway Erik thrust out his shield to ward off any attackers. Erik's sword was already in his hand, and it scythed the air in a deadly arc before him as the first of his guards reached his side and began to fan out through the warehouse. As the gloom receded and his eyes began to see further into the building, it became obvious to Erik that the store contained nothing more than the stock of a wool merchant.

Ells of homespun were stacked on shelves to raise the valuable wares clear of the hard packed earth underfoot, and the realisation that their rapid follow up to the victory at Corebricg had caught the Scots unprepared lifted his spirits to giddy heights. More of his hird were crowding into the building as they followed their lord, and Erik, realising that the lack of opposition to their landing was no ruse to lure them into a trap, bade them follow him back out into the sunlight. 'Out you come lads,' he called as he exited the building, 'the birds have already flown.'

Back on the dockside Erik watched as the last of the ships nudged alongside, and the final waves of spearmen erupted from their sides to stream into the town. Thorstein came from the storehouse as Sturla reached the king's side and hoist his war banner aloft. 'I had a quick look once we were sure it was clear,' he said. 'They must have got the best stuff away, but a cargo of wadmal will fetch a good price back in York all the same.'

Erik nodded, and a gleam came into his eyes as he began to realise just how profitable this raid could become. Although hardly high status, the coarse woollen cloth was a staple throughout the North and used by all but the poorest for weatherproof outer clothing and hats. With winter coming on fast it would find a ready market at home, and if the other warehouses lining the landing place held as many riches, this surprise attack which had started out with little other aim than to heap further humiliation upon the king of Alba could develop into one of his most successful.

The king's ships were filling the River Forth now, seamen making a raft of the fleet as they lashed one ship to another. Erik cocked an ear, and without the familiar clangour of clashing steel and battle cries coming from the town it was as good as a direct report that the entire population must have fled inland before their arrival. Erik lifted his gaze to peer the half mile to the fortress of Stirlin, high up on its rocky crag overlooking the town. The defences sparkled like ripples on a pond as sunlight reflected from helm and spearpoint, and he was in no doubt that the best of the loot was safely out of reach along with the most important inhabitants of the little town. Erik snorted, it mattered not; the treasury in York was filled to the ceiling — this day was meant to shame a beaten king and he had achieved that aim already. It was time to fire the town and take themselves home. Denied the opportunity to display their fighting prowess the men were beginning to drift back towards the dockside, and Erik picked out the face of his eldest as he led the men of the *Vindálfr* back onto the boardwalk. 'Gamli,' he called, indicating that his son join him with a movement of his head. The king fought down the urge to smile at the look of disappointment on his son's face as he came. 'How goes the day?'

Gamli spat in disgust. 'The place is empty father, even the thralls have taken to the woods — aside from ourselves there is not a living thing in the town.' A yelp carried from the far end of the wharf as the watch dog barked one time too many, and the pair shared a chuckle and a wicked smile. 'Well — not now...'

'Who is guarding the boundary?'

'Harald has men on the roofs peering off into the distance, but there are only fields between here and the fortress — there is no chance of being surprised by an attack from that direction. The rock face is too steep, and the only way in or out runs away from the town down to the bridge.'

Erik nodded, satisfied. 'Nevertheless,' he said, 'we are leaving before dusk.'

Gamli looked surprised and Erik explained. 'The Scots have borne witness to our strength and their own weakness, both in battle at Corebricg and here at the heart of their king-dom. We have achieved all we set out to do, why take a risk?' A harsh cackle caused the pair to turn their heads skyward, and the sight which met their eyes confirmed to the king that the decision was the correct one. A skein of geese beat their way south, and within moments the sky filled with vic after vic; it was an unmistakable sign that the season of storms was fast approaching, and Gamli nodded as he replied. 'You are right, of course.' He smiled. 'Let us torch the place and be away from here, the crews need time to perform a Husting — to gather together to share the loot from this year of victories and renew their oaths for the next.' He beamed. 'Then it's a winter of drinking and feasting for the all conquering army of Erik Haraldsson.'

A movement off to the king's left caught his eye, and Erik turned his head to find a crewman from Guttorm's ship the *Crane* hovering a few paces away. Erik indicated that he speak with a nod. 'Your son sends his respects lord, and asks that you would join him on his ship.'

Erik nodded. 'Tell him I will be along.'

He turned back to Gamli, placing a fatherly hand on his son's shoulder as he did so. 'Add another ship to the *Vindálfr* and head downstream. I want to ensure that there is no oppo-sition gathering to bar our route back to the sea.' Gamli nodded, calling his huskarls Hoskuld and Svan to his side as he made his way back to the crew.

Erik raised his chin as they went, indicating to his own guards that they accompany him. He felt a pang of regret at the need, but his youth back in Norway had taught him that close kinship among kings and their offspring could turn to deadly rivalry and it was a lesson he had kept close to heart. By the time he had clambered across a handful of decks Guttorm had spotted him, and the look of pride on his son's face drew the king on. As the men on board parted at the king's approach, Guttorm called across the decks. 'We think we may have found Mael Colm's ship!'

Erik vaulted the final wale, landing amidships as Helgrim and Thorstein drove the rest of the crew back with an icy glare. Erik looked. The *Crane* was the final ship in the raft, but the only thing to be seen was a dozen Norse larking about mid channel as they seized the chance for a swim. 'Well, unless Mael Colm has use of *Skíðblaðnir* and you have it in your pocket,' Erik said, 'you will have to point it out.'

Guttorm laughed, and the honesty of the sound drove any fears of foul play from the old king's mind. *Skíðblaðnir* was Frey's ship, and was made of so many parts that the god could fold it like cloth and carry it on his person when not in use. 'No lord,' Guttorm replied. 'If we had found the best of ships, I would not have my men in the water attempting to re-float her.'

Erik's eyes widened as he thought he understood. 'They have weighted a ship with rocks?'

Guttorm nodded as he pointed out a nearby trading ship. 'You see that knarr, father?'

Erik looked.

Guttorm spoke again. 'Can you see what is wrong with it?'

The king snorted as he realised what his son had uncovered. Riding a few feet higher than those downstream, the seaweed and barnacles encrusting the part of the hull which seamen called *between wind and water* were clearly in view. It was Erik's turn to laugh, and he beamed as the first trace of woodsmoke drifted across from the town. 'They were in a hurry and used the ballast from the nearest ship to sink her midstream. They knew that we could go no further inland because of the bridge so took a chance, rowed her as far upstream as they were able and sank her in the channel.' The king turned back to his son. 'And you are sure it is her?'

Guttorm shrugged. 'Not that she belongs to the king of course, but it is certainly a very fine dragon.' He indicated the swimmers, the men Erik had taken to be fooling about, with a flick of his head. 'The lads have a good idea of her dimensions and the fineness of her decoration. They tell me that they will have her raised very soon, so we shall see for ourselves — the keel is already beginning to lift free of the ooze.'

Erik cast a look to the south. Beyond the gathering pall where the settlement of Stirlin was paying the price for its craven defenders, a lowering sun blushed the horizon. To the East the stern posts of the *Vindálfr* and Sigurd's *Auk* were past the first bend and making for the sea. If Guttorm's men could raise the ship soon they would carry her away, if not the best of the plunder now being stowed beneath the decks of the fleet would do just fine.

Thorstein spoke, as the whiplash crack of a fire ravished timber told where a supporting beam had been unequal to the fight. 'Are we destroying the bridge, lord? It will not be much fun rebuilding the span with winter coming on.'

Erik shook his head slowly as his gaze wandered across. The bridge below Stirlin burh carried the roadway across the Forth, linking the richest parts of the kingdom of Alba and the Highlands beyond. 'No,' the king answered, as cries of success marked where the prow of the sunken longship had broken the surface. 'The army will need it when we return.'

PART II

KING OF THE NORTH

12

VIGIL

I f the sight of the outriders waiting patiently for the king on the rise ahead was not enough, the land itself told the travellers they were nearing a major settlement as it always did. Woodland became pasture, pasture became cropland, and despite the mugginess of high summer the telltale earthiness of woodsmoke drifted down to them on light airs. Erik's nostrils flared as he savoured the reek, casting a look at Harald who rode alongside. 'A nice soft bed for me tonight,' he said with a slap of his rump. 'I am going to make the most of it too!'

Harald snorted. 'Erik Bloodaxe longing for his bed…' He turned his head, shooting his father a smile. 'I may be a Christian father, but you have drummed enough of Óðinn's sayings into me over the years to know that even the so-called High One despises sloth; how often have I heard you say:

> *'He must rise early,*
> *the one who wants to have another's*
> *wealth or life;*

>   *seldom does a lying wolf get a ham*
>   *or a sleeping man victory?'*

Erik laughed with delight, and a twinkle came into his eyes as he countered with an Óðinn saying of his own:

>   *'A ruler's son must be silent and thoughtful—*
>   *brave in battle;*
>
>   *each man must be happy and cheerful*
>   *until he suffers death.'*

Erik called across his shoulder as the leading group chuckled at their king's riposte. 'Harald Eriksson is reciting the wisdom of the Allfather, Oswald. Perhaps Christ is not so firmly rooted as you were led to believe.'

Harald rolled his eyes, and Erik stole a glance across his shoulder as he did so, exchanging looks of mirth with the heathen of his hird. As the warriors took up the ribbing Harald curbed his mount, drifting back to lend weight to the Christian cause. The ribaldry had drawn the attention of the women working the fields, and Erik watched as they hitched up their skirts, fleeing to the woods at the sight of armed men. Even forewarned of their coming, experience had made them wary; Erik's thoughts meandered as the sun beat down and a skylark lived up to its name, capering across a vault of blue as the horse plodded on.

The winter months following the great victory at Corebricg and the devastating raid on Stirlin had been a time of celebration throughout the kingdom of York. With king Eadred in ill health and the Scottish incursion crushed, the people could finally hope for a future free from fear of invasion. Trade picked up, despite the southern embargo and the winter storms; but if the king in Wessex had hoped to choke the life from Erik's kingdom or foster discontent with his rule he had met his match in the figure of the queen, and Gunnhild's resurrection of Erik's plan from his first reign to suspend the king's tax take for a full year had been a masterstroke. Freed from the burden every penny earned had been spent in York and its environs, snubbing the enemy and boosting the local economy at the same time.

The sale of the prisoners taken from the armies of Olaf Cuaran outside York and of Scots and their allies at Corebricg had swollen the king's money chest to such an extent that the income was hardly needed, and the widespread scowls of Erik's first rule had been quickly replaced by smiling faces every time he ventured into the city. Erik knew that another such victory would turn those smiles to cheers, and he had spent the year 953 building an alliance to ensure that happened. The pay-off for the king of Strathclyde had helped of course, the gold and silver safely stored within the King's Garth before the first winter was out. Erik snorted as he recalled the negotiations. King Dyfnwal's representatives had attempted to whittle him down, citing the difficulties of collecting the high price he demanded for the safe return of their king with all his body parts attached. *The valleys and dales are snowbound* they had squealed — but the snowfalls had magically cleared when Erik had sent word he would visit them following the Jule drinking to collect it himself. The rapid turnover of rulers in York had resulted in the king having little land to call his own in the kingdom; it was a situation which meant that kings like Erik were forced to supplement their income with yearly raiding if they were to be open handed with their gold as all kings must, and it was a thing which he would soon put right. But the victories of the first year and the king's ransom from Strathclyde had filled his coffers to overflowing, and with his borders secure the spring of 954 saw him riding north to war.

The horse breasted the ridge, and a little higher now the sight of the rooftops of Conceastre dragged the king's mind back to the present. Ahead the stone made road ran as straight as any other built by the legions of Rome, through the town and across the river beyond to disappear northwards. A cloud of gulls showed where fish were being unloaded alongside the River Wear, while to the west of the road the stone walls of the old Roman fort dominated the town and river crossing. Erik turned his head as another rumble of laughter came from the men. 'Oswald, when you are finished with your conversions I have a few questions of my own.'

The man spurred his horse, and as the reins were plucked to guide the beast alongside the king the old retainer's expression softened. 'How can I be of assistance, lord?'

'A quick appraisal of the men I am to meet over the coming days would be grand.' Erik indicated the town with a jerk of his head. 'I know we have been through this before, but neither of us are as young as we used to be,' he said with a deprecating smile. 'It would be a shame to scheme and plot for a year, only to prick a delicate ego at the last moment.'

Oswald snorted. 'There will be plenty of men who hold themselves in high regard, lord, of that you can sure.' He threw the king a sour faced look. 'If you have managed to winkle Oswulf Ealdwulfing from his shell, you will be the first king of York to have done so in twenty years.' Oswald gave a sniff of disdain. 'Oswulf — divine-wolf — the second part of his name is accurate at least. He rarely ventures from the rocky fortress at Bebbanburh, and when he does it is because he has no other option.'

The king nodded. In the distance the braying of a horn announced to those inside the fort that the war band of Erik

Bloodaxe was approaching. 'You counselled over the winter months that the earl was untrustworthy,' he said. 'But you think it could be even worse?'

Oswald pulled a face. 'My advice remains the same lord,' he replied. 'Believe only half of anything he says to have some grounding in truth, and treat that with suspicion. God may not have seen fit to cast the earl in the traditional mould of a leader of men, but he makes up for that with cunning and guile.' Erik raised his eyes at the description, but Oswald only laughed. 'You will see when you meet him, lord.'

The description tallied with those of others he had asked. It was clear that the merchants and leading men in the kingdom of York regarded the northern earl as little more than a wolf head. Erik pushed the thought aside; he was to meet up with the Bernician further north, he was a problem for another day. 'How about the bishop?' Erik asked. 'You said that he is a friend of archbishop Wulfstan. Surely he is trustworthy?'

Oswald nodded. 'Have no fear lord, Bishop Aldred is an honourable and God fearing man, the perfect host unless you happen to mention his predecessor.'

Erik's expression betrayed his interest, and Oswald's eyes sparkled with amusement as he explained. 'Bishop Uchtred had only been ordained for six months when — *poof!* — gone like a ghost in the night.' Erik took the bait, prodding him for more. Despite his best efforts at keeping a straight face, Oswald broke into a smile as he continued the tale. 'The story we heard in York, was that an earthenware jug containing a hoard of Roman coins had recently been unearthed by men digging the post holes for a new storehouse within the confines of the fort.'

Erik's mouth widened into a grin. 'And this hoard disappeared the same night as our friend the bishop!'

Both men laughed. 'It would seem so, lord. The last we heard was that he had taken up residence in the South, at a place called Medeshamstede. As you can imagine the brothers in the bishopric were rather less than pleased at their new leader making off with that which the Lord had provided for them all — it is a rather prickly subject and best left unremarked upon.'

The conversation had used up the time it had taken the column to travel the final mile of their journey, and as they came abreast of the outlying buildings of Conceastre the king's guards moved forward to flank the pair. Erik raised his chin to look along the line of the road. The scouts were clearly in sight, and beyond them he could now see the bridge across the River Wear and a handful of mast tops poking above the waterfront buildings downriver. To the left the old Roman fortress towered over the rooftops, its iron grey walls topped by a wooden palisade of Saxon work. Forewarned by the signal horn the inhabitants had taken to their homes, every door closed and barred against men they clearly considered a threat. Well, Erik mused as the turn came up, his axe had won over the folk of York and it would do so for the others of greater Northumbria; a great victory in the north against the old enemy and he would be collecting skat here within the year.

At the junction Erik guided his mount from the road, and Thorstein and Helgrim Smiter led half a dozen men forward to form a guard of honour lining the route ahead. At the top of the rise the big double doors had been pulled inward, and a small knot of churchmen had collected beneath the open doorway to welcome their guest. At the centre of the group, the sun reflecting from the mitre and crosier of a bishop showed where Aldred had stepped out to greet the king.

Erik slipped from the saddle, resisting the urge to stretch

and knead travel sore joints and muscles after a day on the road; it was the signal for the others of his hird to do likewise, and Erik walked forward as the metallic clatter of mail clad men filled the air. Oswald Thane and Harald came up, the old retainer and Erik's son taking station a few paces to the rear as Sturla Godi unfurled the bloodied axe banner of Erik Haraldsson at the king's shoulder.

The path steepened as it approached the gateway, and Erik took a moment to run his eyes over the old defences as leg muscles already stiffened by the ride began to tighten in protest. He had seen enough Roman work now to know that the forts had been built to a common plan, but after more than half a millennium exposed to the raw weather of the North the fort at Conceastre had survived in far better condition than most. The ditch and bank at the base of the enclosure remained steep sided, the lip sharply defined, and the walls themselves appeared complete with none of the quarrying for reuse elsewhere which was common in towns. He was surprised that no spire or tower reached skyward from within, the fort was the seat of a bishopric and home to the remains of a saint after all, but the time to ponder had passed and his face broke into a smile as he came into the shadow of the gatehouse.

ERIK RAN his eyes across the leaves before him, searching for the mark of his enemy. Bishop Aldred understood immediately and leaned in, moving a forefinger to underline the distinctive scrawl. 'Here,' he breathed: 'Eadred Rex.' As Erik nodded the churchman reached across to turn the page, 'and here, King Edmund, and on the facing leaf their half-brother Athelstan.' Instinctively Erik moved a hand, the pad of a finger brushing the places where the southern kings had scratched their names onto the vellum. As he raised his gaze Aldred was holding forth the quill, and Erik charged the tip before stooping to add his name to the list. His final observance fulfilled, Erik paused to take a final look about the underground chamber as the churchman crossed to the stairway. The brethren were preparing to slide the sturdy oak lid back onto the body of the casket, and Erik snatched a last look at the exquisitely bound remains of Saint Cuthbert as the wan light of a candle played across the alms inside. Among the treasures which had been gifted by important men over the centuries, those of the West Saxon trio stood out in their piety: an embroidered stole of the kind worn around the neck by Christian priests, the gold thread of the needlework breathtaking in its beauty; vestments in Kufic silk; a small leatherbound book which Aldred had informed Erik contained the Gospel of John. But the buttery light played across his own gift as the lid slid into place, and Erik reflected with satisfaction on the reaction of the bishop when he had placed the gold and garnet cross among the other offerings before bending his head in prayer.

As the coffin lid dropped down with a thunk which echoed around the cell, Erik crossed to the stair. Within a dozen paces he had led the others back up into the body of the church, and Erik cast his gaze around the room as darkness returned to the chamber below and the others began to reappear one by one. Accustomed to the opulence of York Minster, Erik could still scarcely believe that the rude hut which was the cathedral of St Mary and St Cuthbert contained the earthly remains of one of the most revered Christian teachers in Britain. But if the rusticity of the wooden posts and planking had come as a surprise it had appealed to his northern soul, and it was not the building he had sought out after all but the aura it contained. Bishop

Aldred had explained that the structure had been kept deliberately makeshift and unrefined, to remind the brothers who lived within the community and those who came to pay homage that the Most Holy Cuthbert was in temporary residence only — a bolthole within which the sacred bones and their guardians would ride out the storm, until such time as it was safe to return to the monastery on the Holy Island of Lindisfarena.

The door came open, interrupting the wanderings if his mind — specks of dust danced in a rectangle of light. Erik exchanged a nod with the brothers as he ducked out into the cool morning air. His closest companions were waiting, as faithful as any hounds: Thorstein, Sturla and Helgrim alongside Kolbein Herjolfsson, the last to remain from the meeting on the strand at Naustdal where Fairhair had gifted young Erik a fleet to prove himself a Haraldsson. As the group began to haul themselves to their feet Erik held out a hand in an unmistakable gesture that he wished to alone. 'That was deeply moving,' he said, turning his face to the man at his side. 'You have my heartfelt thanks Your Excellency.'

Bishop Aldred opened his mouth to speak, but the reply was stillborn. They exchanged the look of two men who had shared a humbling experience, before the churchman moved to return to the hall. He stopped a short distance away, turning back when he realised that he was walking alone. 'Will you not join me in breaking my fast King Erik? I have missed Matins and Lauds, I am sure that the Lord will overlook my absence at Prime after a night spent in the presence of a Saint. Later I have promised your son Harald I would show him my work, adding an English gloss to the gospel book we brought from Holy Island for safekeeping.' The bishop smiled, and a look of contentment stole across his features as he regarded the old Norseman. 'Truthfully King Erik, I had heard conflicting reports as to the depth of your devotion to the one true God, but our time together has laid those fears to rest. Your son Harald is a joy, and I am thrilled to see the descendants of the folk my predecessors were forced to flee, taking a keen interest in the word of the Almighty.'

Erik pulled a bashful smile in return. 'I should like to spend a few moments alone with my thoughts Bishop,' he said softly. 'Then I would describe the wonders of our vigil to my closest friends while they are still fresh in my memory.' Erik patted his belly, the smile widening as a growl came from within. 'As you can hear, we shan't be far behind and we can break our fast together.' Aldred chuckled and nodded that he understood, but the moment that he had turned his back Erik shot his guards a wink. To a man the Norwegians had looked aghast at the sight of their king cosying up to a Christian holy man, and it was all Erik could do not to laugh aloud at the sight despite his tiredness. But the gesture had brought the colour back to their cheeks, and Erik allowed himself a snort of amusement as he doubled the corner and picked out a spot.

It had been a long night and an even longer morning as he had squirmed and shifted to keep the contents of his ageing bladder where they belonged, and as he hurriedly loosened his breeks to piss into the ground Erik's face came up to bask in the warmth of the morning sun. It was true, he mused as he splashed the soil — the small stone room which contained the body of the saint had been imbued with a sense of power. But it was not the power of the Christian God — at least not for one with only a part-time adherence to the creed such as himself, but the dominion of earthly men. The kings of the southern Saxons who had left the treasures in the vault below had not beaten a path to the old Roman storehouse just to pay homage to the dried out husk of a man long since dead.

Scorned by his under king Constantine of Alba, Athelstan — the same king who had not only fostered Erik's half-brother Hakon, but had helped him to overthrow Erik's kingship in his homeland — had stopped by at the head of an army and fleet on the way to waste the kingdom as punishment for the sleight. A decade later Erik had watched from seaward as his successor Edmund the Magnificent had carried fire and sword against the men of Strathclyde, and following that king's murder Eadred his brother had spent a summer harrying Erik's own kingdom while he had been forced to pace the King's Garth at York in impotent rage. These were the type of men whose actions Erik wished to emulate, and if he could add the support of the Christian church to the invasion of the North then so much the better. But a heap of fire scorched brands in a bloodstained glade, and the butchered remains of a pure white stallion near York showed where his heart really lay, and he murmured an invocation to Óðinn and Þórr as he retied his trews and crossed the dewy grass to his men.

13

A WISH FULFILLED

The huskarls crowded around the king as the destination hove into view, the riders yammering in their excitement like hunters at the kill. Erik's eyes shone as they drank in the scene. Harald spoke at his shoulder. 'They made it! Now that *is* a sight.'

Away to the West the army of York stood in ranks, covering the hillside beneath wind driven clouds the colour of lead. Kolbein shot Erik a look. 'Are you sure you want this crown lord? It will be the fifth.'

Erik's eyes slid across to the old campaigner. 'Fifth or not, I shall wear it. No man lives forever.'

Bishop Aldred caught his eye, clearly intrigued by the conversation and Erik explained. 'A long time ago when I was scarce more than a bairn, I led an army to the land of the Finns to repay an injustice suffered by my father Harald Fairhair. A sorcerer named Svasi ruled a kingdom known as Bjarmaland, and he had used witchcraft to trick king Harald into marrying his daughter, a woman called Snofrid.' Erik half smiled as he saw the faces of his veterans take on a faraway look, their minds drifting back over the years to days when they had been infused by the vigour of youth and a riverside temple flanked by a ship army of Norse. 'I took the king's head and lifted the curse,' Erik went on, 'but before I did so a woodland shaman foretold that I would wear five crowns in my lifetime.' Erik rode on, but Kolbein noisily cleared his throat to indicate that the tale was not yet complete. The king laughed. 'That's all I recall.'

'If I remember rightly lord,' Sturla put in, 'he also said that you would die on a windswept fell and few would mourn it. It earned him a prick from Anlaf's spearpoint when I made his words into Norse.'

The mention of Erik's old huskarl quietened those who had known him in life, and Erik explained to the Bernician churchman as the column left the shelter of the woodland and began to descend a grassy slope. 'Anlaf Crow was one of my huskarls, my very first standard bearer. He was killed by a poisoned arrow in Dublin many years ago, but we still drink to his memory and fill a horn for him when we are at our ale.' Erik ran his eyes around the group, exchanging a look which only men who had stood shoulder to shoulder in harms way could really understand. 'Loved or not; if I die on a lonely fell, far better that than a straw death a'bed.' Death's long shadow had stolen some of the levity from the moment, and Aldred knew enough of fighting men to pull a sympathetic smile and leave them to their thoughts.

Clear of the tree cover the wind shrieked and howled, and soon the riders were dipping their chins as the first rainfall drove in from the west. Erik reflected on the journey as the leading men reached the valley floor, the horses splashing through the mire as they made for the far bank. The first morning out from Conceastre had been a pleasant ride — the skies as blue, the air as warm as the week which had just gone over. But the wind had begun to rise as they rode, and within the day dark clouds were forming a rampart over the western hills, thunder drumming along its leading edge as the storm rushed in to gobble up the sun. The storms had dogged their journey north, and although the rain had slowly eased the winds had continued to rise until the gentle breezes of York and Conceastre had turned to gales.

Erik's stallion had crossed the shallow valley as he reminisced, and as the animal gained the ridge his horse guards rode forward to form a protective screen. Up on the hog-back now the wind was a demon, and as the landscape opened up before him Erik narrowed his eyes against the blow. Away to his left the spearmen of York striped the heights, the boundary wall of a hill fort built by the ancients just visible beyond as a white line beneath the racing clouds.

The army of Bebbanburh had gathered half a mile to the East, and as Erik looked a knot of riders detached themselves and began to make their way across beneath the banner of their earldom. Erik flicked a look across his shoulder, exchanging a look with Sturla Godi as his standard bearer struggled manfully to hold the sigil of Erik Haraldsson upright in the gale. Erik drew rein, Harald and bishop Aldred moving to his shoulders as the riders approached, and as they grew nearer the king's eyes searched out the figure of the earl. A savage gust blew a curtain of rain across the group, and when it cleared Erik's eyes widened in surprise. Despite being forewarned by the bishop and others who had met the man, the king was still shocked by the sight. Oswulf Ealdwulfing was quite possibly the paunchiest man he had ever laid eyes upon, and despite the magnificence of his arms and armour Erik understood for the first time why the man had cried off accompanying the army on this summer's campaign and was thankful for it. The Yorkish outriders drew aside as the group came up, funnelling the Bernicians towards the fold in the land where the king and his party were sheltering from the worst of the gale.

The earl slowed as he approached Erik, curbing his horse several lengths shy of the king before bowing his head low. Maccus the Easterner was at his lord's side, and Erik watched for any hesitation in the man's demeanour as he followed the action and was heartened to see there was none. Erik let the moment of submission stretch until he was sure that all had seen; it had taken a year of negotiation and no few threats, veiled or otherwise, to winkle the man from his rocky bolt-hole, and Erik was going to make the fact of his overlordship plain to all whether the earl liked it or not. When he judged that the point had been made, Erik spoke. 'Earl Oswulf, this is a momentous day — the day the ancient kingdom of Northumbria is reforged under one king.' The king's words were the signal for the men before him to raise their heads, and the Bernician earl's features broke into a smile as he replied. 'It was my father's dearest wish, and his before that that they would live to see this day King Erik.' Oswulf flicked a look at bishop Aldred, and up to the cross of Saint Cuthbert on its gilt staff. 'That the Lord in Heaven should make that dream reality during my lifetime is a thing of which I am unworthy.'

Erik slipped from the saddle, gesturing that the earl join him with a wave of his hand. A flurry of movement caused the Norwegians to stiffen but Erik was closer, and he raised a hand for calm as he watched a retainer hurry forward to help the earl dismount. Oswulf just had time to straighten up before Erik was upon him, and the king embraced the earl before taking a rearward pace and regarding the man who was about to swear allegiance. Erik smiled, and the answering smile seemed honest and true; despite the well meant warnings of Oswald Thane and others, Erik had met enough men during his long lifetime to judge a man's character, and he pushed any doubts aside as he threw a look at the sky. Above them the clouds were as dark as iron, but a band of light above the distant Cheviots was coming on apace. 'Come,' he said. 'Let us do that which needs to be done — I have a kingdom to ravage, and the army to do it.'

ERIK TOOK his place on the royal seat of Northumbria and looked out to the west. The storm had cleared away but the hour was late, the horizon aglow; a little to the north, beyond the River Glein, rain fell in sheets — but the long hill on which the combined army of Northumbria had gathered was in the clear for now, and each and every man was grateful for that. The anointing already performed, Erik looked about him as the bishop approached, shifting the weight of the orb and sceptre in his hands as he prepared for the culmination of the ceremony. Ringed by the leading men — the thanes, earls and gesiths of York and Bernicia — Erik imagined the ghosts of the kings who had gone before him joining the throng, craning their necks to catch a glimpse of the golden king helm they had worn in life on this very spot named Gefrin — the Hill of Goats. The halls and buildings had long gone — burned again and again by Picts, Scots and Danes — with just the odd charred beam poking through the rain lashed grass to remind men that this had been one of the most important sites in the old kingdom. Some of those kings had been heathen he now knew, back in the days when the English had first come to this land and Óðinn, Þórr and Njörðr had held sway over their devotions. Bishop Aldred had enthused over the mass conversions which had taken place in the little River Glein at the foot of the hill, but the site was far older still, and if the land hereabouts had borne witness to a plethora of gods the fact suited Erik and a good part of his army well.

As the bishop came closer to the steps the gaggle of priests following on broke into song, and Erik allowed his eyes to savour the beauty of the golden helm of the Northumbrians as Aldred raised it high for all to see. Gleaming dully in the failing light, a circuit of decorated plates enclosed the bowl of the helm: an army of spearmen on the march; dragons writhing on the cheek pieces and nasal; boar heads guarding the eyes. But it was the crest made from the hair of the same animal which drew gasps of wonder from tough fighting men, and Erik's heart skipped a beat as the last of the day's light finally broke through to paint the bristles the colour of blood. Bishop Aldred had reached him now, and Erik straightened in the ancient seat as the man moved to his rear. This was the moment on which he had pondered throughout the upheavals of his life, the instant the fifth and final crown rested upon his head. A picture of his foster-brother came into his mind as the chants of the brethren hung on the air, and a trace of a smile appeared despite the gravity of the occasion. For a snippet in time he was back in Norway, treading the jetty at Avaldsnes as the first of the fleet turned their bows to the south and prepared to carry him into exile. Arinbjorn Thorirsson was fixing him with a stern faced glare, and he heard the words again as the song became a chant and he felt the weight of the crown rest upon his head:

'If the shaman told you anything about the future Erik, he did so out of mischief; it was a curse…'

Well, curse or not the augury had run its course, but a new *Bretwalda* - the Britain-wide-ruler of old - had risen to add his name to the great Northumbrian emperors of the past: Edwin; Oswald; Oswiu; Erik. But if the act of carrying the ancient helm from its place of safekeeping within the high walls of Bebbanburh had been a sign of earl Oswulf's submission there was one more act to follow, and the chants and acclamations of churchmen and warriors alike petered out as the king turned his eyes on the man.

Oswulf dipped his head in acknowledgment, and as he began to make his way forward and bishop Aldred came up to recover the orb and sceptre, Helgrim Smiter and Harald Eriksson hefted their spears and moved in to stand at the king's side. Sturla moved forward to fly the bloodaxe standard alongside the cross of Saint Cuthbert, and as earl Oswulf drew up before him King Erik spoke:

'Oswulf Ealdwulfing — is it your intention to offer an oath of allegiance, to forsake all others and become my man?'

The Bernician met the king's gaze and straightened his flabby shoulders. 'Aye, lord.'

The king nodded. 'Share with us your lineage — regale us with your deeds, that all may know what type of man you are.'

The request was a formality — Erik had worked ever since his return to York for this moment — and his eyes wandered across the throng as the earl said his piece, acknowledging the look of satisfaction in the countenance of the leading men in his newly restored kingdom, until they alighted on the face of the man he wished to see the most. Erik saw the pride shining in the eyes of his favoured English earl, the man who had stood shoulder to shoulder alongside him through all the trials and shifting loyalties in the madcap kingdom of York as he recalled Regenwold's fervent wish:

With Bernician warriors and Yorkish gold, a reunified Northumbria could once again become the greatest power on the island...

Oswulf had completed his boasting by the time Erik looked back, and although the wind was a cats-paw compared to the earlier gale, he filled his lungs in the hope that all would hear his reply:

'Oswulf Ealdwulfing, we recognise your worthiness. Do you swear by the deck of a ship and the rim of a shield, the withers of a horse and the point of a sword to become my man and forsake all others?'

As the earl confirmed that he did, Helgrim handed the king a fine sword which he laid upon a thigh. With the handle facing towards the supplicant Erik trapped the point between the right side of his body and arm, laying his forearm along the length of the blade until his hand gripped the hilt.

'Then speak your oath.'

Earl Oswulf knelt before the king, reaching out to place his right hand beneath the hilt. His oath of allegiance made, the man who had arrived on the windswept hill as sole ruler in these parts leaned in to kiss the hilt of his overlord's sword, and as Erik nodded in satisfaction he reached across to remove a heavy gold ring from his arm. Sliding the hoop onto the tip of the sword he held the point forward, and as the precious gift slid down the blade with a rasp Oswulf drew and raised his own. The sword points met, the ring sliding from one to the other. Oswulf retrieved the ring and slipped it onto his arm, and Erik spoke the final words of warning against the treacherous breaking of the oath just uttered as he gripped the blade with both hands and presented it to his earl:

> *Bíti-a þér þat sverð er þú bregðir*
> *nema sjalfum þér syngvi of höfði.*
> *May the sword pierce you which you draw!*
> *May it sing only around thine own head.*

A peal of thunder rolled down from the North as the king completed the curse, and the heathen among his army — already thrilled by the sound of their own tongue after all that had gone before — exchanged looks of wonder as the air crackled and fizzed. Þórr had come among them, and as the wheels of the god's goat drawn chariot rumbled across the sky again, hands moved up to clasp silver hammers and charms and the sound of thunder filled the air. Earl Oswulf withdrew and Erik raised Jomal, stalking the flatbed of the wagon which had carried the ancient king-stool of Northumbria from its usual place in York. Sturla hoist the king's battle banner aloft, following in his steps, and Erik waited for the cries of acclamation to lessen before lowering the war axe to speak.

'And so it has come to pass, the day which Archbishop Wulfstan has worked and longed for throughout the course of his honourable life — Deira and Bernicia are joined again — one kingdom — one folk — indivisible under God. Let your minds recall Northumbrians of old as we gather together at the moment of rebirth, hear again the songs, the skalds' honeyed words as they told the tale of the great deeds of your ancestors. Bring again to mind those tales, stories of the days when the English of the North — of Æthelfrith, a king mighty in memory and deed — crushed the Gododdin and won a kingdom.

'I look upon the faces before me today, here on this hill where the ghosts of those men now rejoice at the sight of a Northumbrian army under arms, and harbour no doubts the descendants of those heroes are lacking in manliness any more than the Norse and Danes who are now their neighbours and spear-brothers.

'As I speak my sons sail a mighty fleet northwards to scour the coast of Alba, the jarls of Orkney cross the Ness, and the spear and axe men of the Sudreys march eastwards to close the net.

'The men of Alba and Strathclyde have always thought it a fine thing to come south and harry our land — to kill, rape and burn — to drive off our cattle and carry away our kin to a life of hardship, servitude and thraldom.' Erik paused to sweep the upturned faces with a flinty gaze. 'It is all a bit of a lark then, a merry jaunt — but return the favour, carry fire and death to their land in return and it is no longer a game, but mournful songs and Sassenach this and Sassenach that.' Erik stopped his pacing, raising the war axe to his lips in a lingering kiss as he let the moment stretch. He turned his gaze on them again, and the king of Northumbria felt the old familiar thrill course through him as he saw that his words had ignited the flames of war in their eyes. His voice became a growl then, and Erik traced a fingertip along Jomal's razored edge before he regarded the army with the mien of a wolf. 'Well, we shall pay them a visit nevertheless. Let us gift them a reason to sing their laments and dirges in peat smelling hovels this summer, when I send this Mael Colm to the Devil and take his crown for trinkets.'

14

ALBA AFLAME

Regenwold's nostrils flared, his shirt billowing like a dragon ship's sail as he sucked in another breath. 'It is different somehow from the stench of our own crops burning, lord.' The Northumbrian opened his eyes, turning his face to the king: 'sweeter somehow.'

Erik recognised the satisfaction writ large on his features as the old warrior savoured the smell. He snorted. 'That, my friend, is the smell of conquest.'

'Aye, lord,' the earl replied, 'it is.' His eyes closed and his chest swelled again. 'It's a smell I could grow accustomed to though.'

Erik fixed the big man with a look. 'Until Mael Colm is dead or driven into exile and the folk here agree to take me in his place, I shall return every summer until Alba is nowt but a land of ash. Rest easy, while I am king of Northumbria no Scottish army shall ever raid south of the Forth again — they will bend their knee or be destroyed completely, on that you have my word.'

The pair rested for a moment, turning their gaze to the

North. The fires had taken hold now despite the greenness of the crop, sheets of flame licking hungrily at the sky beneath a billowing column of smoke. 'We will be doing them a kindness,' Regenwold said with a jerk of his chin. 'Carrying off all but the oldest and scrawniest now they have little to eat this winter.' Erik looked. Men were moving among the captives, pushing them roughly into line with the shaft of their spears as the army prepared to move off. Others were still sifting the grain from the chaff, running hands long used to gauging the value of a horse or sheep over shoulders and arms; adding a squeeze to breast and buttock of the women to weed out those too saggy and past their prime. 'The remainder can survive on fish stew and brewet,' Erik said, 'and be thankful that we have left them the means.'

Morcar Thane came across, throwing his leaders a smile as the horse came to a halt. 'The men are set King Erik,' he said, 'and await your command.'

Erik nodded his thanks before turning his face back to the earl. 'Happy hunting old friend; flush the fox from the briar and drive him towards the hounds, but remember what we agreed.'

'Don't worry lord,' Regenwold replied as he hauled at the reins, 'they will not catch us out. Whether we find the king or not, we shall harry the land between here and the Highlands, and meet you at the coast when the moon is full.'

Mindful that he was splitting his army in hostile territory, Erik ran through the dispositions once again as he watched him go. By any measure, two hundred mounted warriors constituted an army — a highly mobile, hard-hitting force — strong enough to stand and fight if the opportunity to kill or capture the king of Scots presented itself, but flexible enough to split up and warn Erik in the unlikely event that they were suddenly faced by an enemy in overwhelming numbers. With Oswulf Ealdwulfing's army of Bebbanburh already detached to scathe the Fife peninsula to the East, Erik knew that he was taking a chance; but the best of the Scots were already bone piles alongside the roadway outside Corebricg following the fighting there, and it was a risk he was willing to take. With the crown of Northumbria and the king stool now safely back in York after the crowning at Gefrin, Erik was going to disprove the Finnish curse and go in search of another.

The clatter of hooves on the sun baked ground drew his eyes to the west, and Erik watched with pride as the men of York sidestepped the encroaching flames and were swallowed by the smoke. They were, he knew, the embodiment of his new kingdom; a mingling of all that was good and martial among the disparate folk he now ruled: Angle; Norse; Dane, Briton and others. Now he had set himself the task of adding the people of Alba and Strathclyde to his empire, a true empire of the North which would stretch from the wave lashed tip of Shetland to the English border. With such a force at his back, even the king in Winchester would be wary of his power. Perhaps, Erik mused as the wail of a child stopped abruptly nearby, he would be the one to finally subdue the West Saxons and add their lands to his own, to become the first man ever to rule the island of Britain in its entirety.

The child's death had broken his line of thought, and returning his gaze to the front Erik could see that the men had finally formed the captives into something resembling an ordered group. Eager to move on now, Erik spurred his mount as he made his way to the front of the column. Ahead the roadway wound its way around a grassy knoll before disappearing into the woodland edge, and Erik drew rein as he gained the hillock and took a parting look at the devastation. The settlement had seemed an idyll when they had arrived.

Nestled within a fold of land the score or so buildings, round huts of lime washed clay beneath roofs of tow coloured thatch, had been sheltered from the worst of the winter storms which roared in from the nearby German Sea. The river which bordered its northern limit was enough to carry salmon practically to their doors in the autumn, but not so deep and straight as to make the waters navigable for seagoing keels and the Vikings they bore. Added to the bream and roach they had found drying on racks along the riverside, and the nearby woodland providing autumn mast for the hogs, the unnamed village had been fairly typical for the area.

A report carried to him across the fields as a beam gave way under the strain, and as another roof collapsed in a pall of dirty grey smoke, Thorstein sniffed at his side. 'Nice place.' Erik nodded. 'Aye, it was, and the sooner they recognise me as their rightful king the sooner it will be again.' He gave a last look before finally turning the head of his ride to the north. The tail end of the army had cleared the village, and tongues of flame among the roof thatch showed where the last of the buildings had been torched. The smoke was being driven inland on a fitful breeze; high above a white tailed eagle rode the air on outstretched wings. 'Come on,' he said. 'The settlements are clustered as thick as fleas in a thrall's breeks in these parts. Someone must know where Mael Colm is.'

THE BUZZ up ahead drew him on, and Erik's mouth widened into a grin as he crossed the ridge line and turned his face to the morning sun. Two leagues to the east, beyond the shimmering waters of a wide tidal inlet, the river banks and beaches were wooded by masts. Hauk had drawn rein a respectful distance ahead, and Erik called the scout back to his side with a sweep of an arm. Thorstein and Harald Eriksson hovered within earshot as the man came up. 'Yes, lord?'

'You have been down there?'

The scout gave a firm nod as he replied. 'Yes, lord.'

'Then tell us all you know.'

'The place had been largely abandoned when the fleet arrived,' Hauk reported. 'Apart from a few crones and men too old to fight, the inhabitants of both settlements had fled inland.'

Erik nodded that he understood. It had been the same for days now; village after village emptied of folk when they arrived, anything of value carried away or buried until the storm had passed and it was safe to return. It was hardly surprising, Erik knew; only a blind fool would stay put, as the columns of smoke which marked his progress marched closer day by day.

The scout twisted in the saddle, squinting against the glare of the sun as he raised an arm to point. 'That is Stroma at the mouth of the river, and the larger town to the north is known as Celurca.'

Erik followed the man's outstretched arm. 'One Norse, the other Scot?'

Hauk nodded. 'Stroma is a small trading port. It seems that the lord in Celurca allows them to organise their own affairs so long as they pay him the skat he is due.'

Erik's eyes widened in surprise. It was unusual for folk to be so welcoming in their land, but if he had learned anything since becoming king in York it had been that worshipping at the altar of the god of mammon was universal. If that was the case here he thought, as his eyes slid across the rooftops to tally the hulls by the harbour, it bode well for his plan to incorporate the kingdom within greater

Northumbria. 'Are all the ships we can see part of our fleet?'

Hauk nodded. 'The traders sailed for Norway when they heard that Gamli's ships were headed this way. It seems that they were in a bit of a hurry too,' he said with a smile, 'for they left a good part of their stock behind.'

Erik brightened at the news. It had been a week since the army had unearthed anything of value on the march, and although the object of the invasion was the death of the Scottish king and the harrying of his land, war was an expensive undertaking. No doubt the traders had their halls and families safely back in Norway and owed allegiance to his half-brother king Hakon, it was hardly a surprise that they had fled before the Eriksson ships arrived. Erik spoke again. 'What did they find?'

'Bearskins and antler, beaver and otter pelts mostly,' the scout replied. 'Barrels of wind dried cod and salmon too, so at least the army will eat well tonight.'

Erik nodded. 'And our men in the town told you all this?'

'No, lord,' Hauk replied. 'When we rode within a few miles of the outskirts, we came within hailing distance of several of our snekkja busily checking the creeks for any signs of enemy ships hiding there. They said they were not expecting trouble, but they were taking no chances before you arrived and have already thrown up an earthwork to defend the port.'

Erik studied the collection of halls and storehouses which went by the grand sounding name of Stroma. A ring of hard packed earth now enclosed the little trading post to landward, and although the ships of Erik's fleet spilled out to either side he noticed with satisfaction that the largest and finest drekkar were safely within the perimeter. Nearer the river, the newness of their timber stark against the weatherbeaten buildings surrounding them, slave pens awaited their footsore cargo of misery.

Hauk spoke again, and a glimmer came into his eyes as he saw the king's gaze wander back to the longships. 'They told us the majority of our fleet are safely beached, but your son Gamli has taken a flotilla and led them further north looking for trouble.'

The group shared a laugh as Harald Eriksson made a quip. 'It is unlike my big brother to be so warlike.'

Erik had heard enough. 'Let us get down there,' he said. 'If the local laird and population of Celurca have turned their halls over to us, we should show our gratitude by accepting the gift.'

Erik clicked his tongue, guiding the horse onto the track which meandered down the back slope, and his heart lifted at the sights and smells of the nearby sea after weeks spent in field and woodland. Seabirds filled the air, the cries of Fulmar, Skua and Gannet as familiar to the Norsemen as the voices of friends and kin as they dove and wheeled over a sea as smooth as hammered iron. As the final mile of their journey came up Erik put back his heels, keen to hear the tales of raiding and plundering from the lips of his sons, and as the River Esk widened into a tidal pool the king was overjoyed to see the banners of the Erikssons coming out to greet him. With Gamli away in the North and Harald part of their father's host, Guttorm led his younger brothers Sigurd and Ragnfrod out to meet the king; Erik drew rein as the walls of Stroma came into view, and his eyes drank in the sight of his younger sons as they approached at the head of their guards. Only Ragnfrod retained a touch of boyishness in his features, but his shoulders had widened after a summer at sea and the beard was thickening by the day. The sight of his sons was bittersweet to the king as he recalled the days of his own youth, but the pride he felt in them pushed the thought aside as they drew near. Soon they were before him, and Harald came up to Erik's side as his younger brother hailed the king. 'Welcome to Stroma, King Erik,' Guttorm began. 'We have prepared a hall and laid in meat and ale.' He shot his father a smile. 'We thought that you could put it to good use after weeks in the saddle.'

Erik chuckled. 'You thought right.' He urged his horse forward with a squeeze of his knees as the Erikssons fell in alongside. 'So, tell me,' Erik said as the horses walked on. 'How did the raiding go, and have you heard a whisper about the whereabouts of our phantom king of Scots?'

'The coast has been picked clean, father,' came Guttorm's glum reply. 'With earl Oswald's army scathing Fife and your *here* wasting the land to the north of the River Tay, we barely saw a soul.' He jerked his head towards Celurca — 'a bit like this place.' Perched on rising ground to the north, the location offered a commanding view over the coastline in either direction. Erik ran his eyes over the town as they came closer. Protected by a ditch and bank topped by a stout palisade, the place had been constructed to withstand a siege; that the town had been abandoned without a fight meant that the inhabitants had been ordered to withdraw, presumably by Mael Colm. Erik shook his head. 'And it was like this all down the coast?'

Guttorm nodded. 'All the able bodied had fled inland before we arrived, taking their valuables with them.'

'And no one knows anything about the location of the king?'

'If you had seen the people left behind, father….' Guttorm rolled his eyes. 'They were not the type of folk accustomed to being privy to the king's plans.'

For the first time since they had crossed into Alba, Erik began to grow uneasy. They were far to the North now, and although the Sudrey jarls and men of Orkney were drawing the net ever tighter around the places the enemy king could be, it was becoming more obvious by the day that there was a degree of control and strategic thinking behind the lack of opposition. By his reckoning he had led the army of York more than three hundred miles from home in his quest to slay the Scottish king, but although he had proven to them he was a war winner at Corebricg it wouldn't do to push their loyalty too far. Unlike his own huskarls and shipmen who were oath sworn to him personally, the men of the levy owed their service for a fixed period of time. Mael Colm's will-o'-the-wisp exploits since they had crossed into Alba was eating into that time, and as the distance from home grew and harvest month approached their anxiety grew. The messengers from earl Regenwold's column told a similar story; a near deserted countryside inhabited by the old and infirm.

In the South the stories of king Eadred's incapacity in Winchester were too widely abroad to be a ruse, but the southern English were not short of war leaders, and the distance from York to the border at Ceasterford, the scene of his own victory over the men of Kent several years before, was less than a day's ride. Gunnhild was no fool and she would put up a stout fight if the English did attack, but denuded of fighting men as it was, the city would fall. And where was Olaf Cuaran? Run out of York by Erik, the last he had heard his Norse rival was back in Dublin; but he had kin and oath men in Cumbraland to add to the men from Ireland, and it was a short hop across the sea to make them one. The last communication he had received from archbishop Wulfstan, still an enforced guest of the southern English for his part in Erik's return, had intimated that king Eadred was growing tired of supporting the usurper after his many failures to secure York as an under king; but Eadred was ailing, and although the likely successor was a mere child other claimants could very likely come to the fore the moment the king died. Of all the kings on Midgard, Erik knew full-well that the succession wishes of even a mighty king like Harald Fairhair often fell by the wayside the moment he was laid in his Howe.

Erik turned his face to his son as the worries continued to gnaw at him. His earlier joy at arriving at the meeting place had vanished like summer smoke. 'I saw that you have constructed slave pens from the hilltop. How many did you take?'

Guttorm shared an awkward look with his younger brothers, clearing his throat before replying. 'There were none worth taking father. We thought it best to keep the hulls empty to take onboard those you took inland. We fired the towns of course and took any ship we found,' he added lest Erik think he had been wanting in his duty to him, 'but we felt certain that you would have far better luck on the march than we were having raiding the coastal districts. As I said,' he offered apologetically, 'we found none but runts and hag-wives. I doubt they would have survived the journey to the thrall market, let alone fetch a good price if we did manage to keep them alive.'

Erik nodded, forcing a smile to his face to avoid the risk of revealing his unease. All the evidence was beginning to point to a trap, and he pushed down the urge to fly back south with difficulty. He would call a meeting of his sons and leading men to consider their advice, and act upon it the following morning. 'You say that I have a hall, freshly aired and provisioned for my use?'

Guttorm assured him they did.

'In that case,' Erik replied in a voice laced with a cheerfulness he no longer felt, 'what better way could I celebrate the reunion of our land and ship armies than feasting my kinsmen and oath sworn. We shall gather at sundown,' he said, as he raised an arm to acknowledge the cheers and welcoming cries of the men lining the earthen bank, 'and you can help wash the road dust from my throat, while we discuss what to do next.'

15

SKULISSONS

The king aimed a kick as the rat scurried past, exchanging a look with Thorstein as the rodent was swallowed by the gloom. He held out the cup for a refill while he had the man's attention, knuckling his lids and attempting to blink the weariness from his eyes as the ale splashed. Erik shifted again on the stool, rocking from side to side to allow the blood flow to return to one arse cheek after the other before returning his gaze to the palisade. Still nothing. He glanced up at the night sky through a gap in the ill-fitting planking. High above the moon slipped behind a bank of ribboned clouds, riming the edges a steely grey as the wind drove them on. Erik looked away to the East. This far north the summer nights were barely worth the bother of heading to your bed; already the stars were dimming as the wolf light of predawn grew moment by moment.

Grettir and Gunnar, the brothers from Hordaland who had led the boar head charge at Ceasterford and Corebricg, had been the ones to discover the preparations for the expected attack. Constantly alert to signs of danger, the pair had walked the perimeter of Celurca before daylight had faded the previous evening. In a part of the circuit all but obscured from the rest of the town by the long roof of a byre, the slight signs of a disturbance near the base of the wall had drawn them across, despite the clouds of insects and overwhelming stench from the racks of cow pats left drying in the sun. There they had discovered that one of the big upright posts which ringed the bank had recently been sawn through near the base. Although all traces of sawdust had been carefully removed and the cut itself smeared with mud and shit, the attempt at concealment had only reinforced their fears that an attack on Erik and his leading men was imminent. No one could foresee how long the king would remain in the town, so any assault was likely to take place that night, and although Erik had gone ahead with the feast he had spent the best part of the night sat in the hayloft as he waited for the enemy to make their move. He supped again as he thought, snorting softly in the dark as he closed his eyes momentarily and shifted on the stool: he really was getting a bit long in the tooth for this shit.

Thorstein's hand on his shoulder snapped him out of it, and Erik's gaze flew across to the base of the fence as shadowy figures tensed around him. At first his eyes had difficulty readjusting to the shadows, but a finger of moonlight stabbed out at just that moment and Erik caught the merest movement before the returning glow caused it to stop. A heartbeat later the light blinked out as the clouds moved back to smother the moon, and Erik gripped the hilt of his sword as the point of a dagger appeared at the side of the panel to lever it aside. Fingertips spidered into view, and as the fencing was pulled outward Erik was on his feet, flexing arms and legs to warm muscles ready for the fight. Swords were hissing from scabbards all around as the first face appeared in the gap, and Erik and his leading men looked on from the darkness of the hayloft as a leg and then the torso of a man squeezed through the crack and into the compound. In looks and clothing the intruder was clearly a Norseman like himself, but it took only a moment for the king to realise that that must be how any assassin would dress if he hoped to get close enough to strike. Another man appeared as the first slipped down the bank and into the shadows at the rear of the byre, and Erik was about to order the men outside when he stopped. The second intruder was sliding the fencing back into place, covering up the sawtooth marks as before, and Erik shared a look of glee with those surrounding him as they all came to realise the opportunity which was presenting itself to them. 'Come on,' he hissed as the would-be assassins made their way through the drying racks and disappeared from view. 'Let us make sure the lads take these fools alive.'

The men stood aside as the king crossed the loft, and within moments Erik was at the ladder. Every creak drew a wince as he made his way down, but the reappearance of men in their midst caused the cattle to stir in their stalls, smothering the sound, and Erik doubled across to the doorway as the rest of his men followed on. He drew back his sword arm, aiming the point of the weapon at the place any head would appear and waited. As Thorstein led the rest of his guard to the king's side, Erik risked a look outside. Needful of driving cattle through the town the thoroughfare was wider than most, and Erik calmed his breathing as he watched for the first sign of the intruders. Away to the East the sky was lightening by the moment: soon the cocks would crow — the killers would have to move quickly if they were to send him on to Valhöll. The moment stretched as they waited in the shadows, but just as Erik began to doubt that the enemy would appear on the roadway they sauntered into view. Despite their deadly intent, Erik allowed himself a smile at the men's composure as one acknowledged an early riser with a nod of the head. With the returning light he could see now that the intruders were younger than he had expected, not much more than lads, and he allowed the pair to get a dozen paces closer to the hall of the laird before he stepped through the doorway and hailed them. 'Would it be me you are looking for boys?'

The men spun on their heels as Erik's huskarls bustled to his side, and Erik saw the look of surprise turn to horror and dejection as they recognised who stood before them. The king's appearance had been the signal for his sons and their bodyguards to emerge from their own hiding places, and within moments the pair were hemmed in on all sides. The heavy silence which had followed Erik's question stretched as he watched the pair's indecision, but the sound of bowmen training their weapons on the assassins finally prompted a reaction from the king. 'Remove your hands from the handle of your swords, and you may yet live to see the dawn.' For a moment it looked as if the men were about to comply, but the drooped shoulders and downcast looks were overdone and it came as no surprise to any looking on when the pair let out a roar of defiance and charged. Erik planted his feet, standing foursquare as they closed, but the pair had only covered half the distance to the man they wanted dead when arrows flashed to take them in the knees. Despite the determination to keep going written on their faces the darts had done their work, and as their legs buckled beneath them to send the pair sprawling into the dust Erik moved forward to kick their swords aside. 'That was unnecessary,' he said as they gritted their teeth in pain and frustration, 'but entertaining all the same. You are fortunate that my bowmen have the wits to know I want you alive.' Erik reached down, jiggling the shaft of an arrow as his face creased into a smile. 'I have a few questions to ask of you.' Firming his grip, he pushed the head deeper as the youngster whimpered with pain. 'You can answer me now or a little later, but you will tell me all I need to know.' He paused to allow the youth the opportunity to reply, but with the agony subsiding all he received was a snarl of defiance. Erik rose to his feet. 'You had your chance, but you have cost me a night's sleep already and I am in no mood for games.' Erik indicated that his men come forward to disarm the prisoners and lead them away. 'I am off to break my fast. Other men will take care of you until we speak again.'

ERIK BLINKED as he came into the full light of day. The few short hours sleep he had managed to snatch while others more skilled in extracting knowledge from reluctant men had done wonders for his state of mind, and he was looking forward to ending their misery; they had, after all, crept into town to take his life. Thorstein spoke again, the incredulity he felt at the identity of the assassins still evident in the tone. 'Who would have thought a merchant would whelp such brave lads?'

Erik shrugged. 'I daresay the family fortune took a tumble when we fed their father to the fish. Their loss was our gain, the silver we made on the trip to Lishbunah and from Gamli and Harald's attack on the eastern ship paid for our first spell as king in York. Without it,' he said with a look, 'it may never have happened, and we would have remained forever holed up in Orkney dreaming of returning home to Norway. But the slaver only had himself to blame — if Skuli had not let his greed get the better of him, his sons would not be about to lose their heads.' Erik glanced at the southern sky. The sun was midway to its zenith — there was still plenty of time to make his plans and get the army back on the move.

While he had slept word had spread throughout the camp of the attempt on the king's life, and Erik was pleased to see that the faces which greeted him as they walked looked genuinely thankful that it had been thwarted. Despite the lack of an overwhelming victory and the distance he had led them from their farms and halls, it was plain that he still had their loyalty. 'Run through what we have discovered again,' he said, 'it will be too late to ask any more questions of them soon.'

'Mael Colm has been in the North, putting down a rebellion there,' Thorstein began. 'It seems that one of his lairds, a man called Cellach of Moray, had grasped the opportunity presented by our invasion to throw in his lot with old king Constantine's son Indulf, who has been agitating to replace his uncle as the king of Alba. Mael Colm has called out the northern levy and told them to meet him at a place called Fetteresso. When he returns the idea is that he will lead them south through the hilly country inland and link up with the rest of the army, leaving us stranded up here before we can either rejoin earl Oswulf's Bernicians or return to Northumbria via Strathclyde.'

Erik nodded. 'Do we know if the king has returned to this...' He pulled a face: 'Feserello?'

'Fetteresso, lord. Our unexpected guests say that he due to arrive back any day now.' Thorstein pulled a wicked smile. 'The Highlanders are still coming in, and between you and me I doubt that Mael Colm harboured much hope that our young Skulissons would be successful in bumping you off.' Thorstein indicated the door of a nondescript hut with the flick of a hand. 'Here we are.' He pushed the door open and stepped aside to allow the king entry, lowering his voice as Erik ducked inside. 'If I were asked my opinion, lord,' he breathed as he followed on, 'I don't think the Scots expected us to march this far north — they have been caught out and are playing for time.'

Erik only half heard. No stranger to gore and suffering, even he was momentarily taken aback by the sight which met his eyes as they grew accustomed to the gloom. The Skulisson brothers were strapped into high backed seats facing each other across the hearth. What Erik had taken to be wood chips or whittling sticks strewn about the floor revealed themselves to be the fingers and toes of the young lads, and raising his eyes to their faces he saw that the ears and noses had also been pared away. Strips of skin hung like Mayday ribbons from their upper bodies, the raw flesh abuzz as the flies and gnats which swarmed in the short summer months gathered to feast on the unexpected bounty. Their breeks had been pulled down and lay bunched at the ankles, and scorched flesh on their feet and thighs showed where a heated blade had been put to work. To Erik's surprise a Christian priest knelt at prayer in the space between the boys, unknowing or uncaring as to the identity of the men who had entered the hut. He shot Thorstein a look, and the big huskarl indicated a pair of small silver crosses which had been tossed aside with their shirts. 'It would seem that your half-brother is having more success converting the folk in Norway to the Christ than we were led to believe.'

Erik shook his head. 'I doubt that — these men are merchants. If they want to trade in Christian lands they need to be open minded in their choice of gods.' Indistinct moans came from the trussed up pair: Erik had seen enough. 'We will get nowt more of any use from them, cut their bindings and get them on their feet. We will take them down and parade them at the riverside, so that all men can see the price paid by those who wish me harm. Cross bearers or not, I will send them on to whichever god gets their final allegiance.' He cast a sidelong look at his house man. 'Moments like this tend to concentrate the mind on what comes next.'

Erik stepped outside as the men in the hut moved to do his bidding, filling his lungs with fresh sea air before spitting into the dust. The weather was fine and the hearth fire had made the air in the hut insufferably hot, but it was the cloying sweetness of tortured flesh filling the room which had caused the sour tasting liquid to pool in his mouth. The king reflected on the scene as he waited for the pair to be bundled through the doorway. The gods knew he was a hard man, a man who had sent many fine men to their graves; but although he had heard it said that men called him cruel and ravening that was a necessary part of being a king. He had never killed for the pleasure of it; every man who had fallen beneath his sword or axe had been an enemy of one kind or another.

The sound of scuffling feet brought him back from his thoughts, and Erik looked on as the pathetic bundles which had been young men in the prime of life only a few hours before were dragged out into the light. A weasel faced man, dark eyed under brows of russet-brown, the scrawniest of them all, sidled across and bowed his head before the king. Erik indicated that he speak his piece, eager to be out of his company. 'King Erik,' the man purred. 'I trust that my men have done you a service this morning?'

Erik said that they had, reaching down to untie a pouch of coins from his belt. Tossing them across, he watched in disgust as the eyes of his henchmen traced the passage of the bag through the air and into the hands their weaselly leader. Glancing back he was just in time to see the dark pools of the torturer's eyes widen at the weight of coin within, and Erik only suppressed the urge to kill him there and then with difficulty. But it was a truism of kingship that he was forced to suppress his own feelings for the greater good — he could, after all, have need of their skills again before he sat once more upon his frith-stool in York — and Erik forced what must pass for a smile to his face as he commended them once again on their morning's work.

The first of Skuli's sons was through the doorway now, the youth raising his head despite the pain to fix Erik with a stare, and as the king looked into his eyes he saw not only the hatred they harboured but the cause of their wild-eyed glare. The boys' lids had been sliced away as part of the torture, no doubt so that they were unable to close them to the pain or the glowing steel as it approached naked skin. But it was the realisation why the young Skulissons had been sat facing each other across the hearth which really caused the king to catch his breath. Unable to blink or turn away both lads had been forced to look on as his brother underwent the ordeal, and Erik knew then that they had already suffered enough. The cross of Christ had been retrieved from the floor where they had been discarded by the heathen torturers and both were now back where they belonged, at the neck of their owners. Erik watched as a shaky hand raised the pendant to blood encrusted lips, and he called the priest across as he came to accept their conversion was genuine. 'Father,' he asked when the man reached him. 'Are they shriven?'

The priest nodded, careful to avert his eyes lest they reveal his own disgust at the goings on that morning and risk joining the boys on their journey to Heaven.

'Then we shall have them bend their heads here in the town. They have acted with honour, seeking out their father's killer across the sea despite the near certainty that it would end in their own deaths.'

They were not so far from the cattle byre where he had spent the night in discomfort, and an idea came to him as he recalled a Christian tale. 'Take them to the cowshed,' he said, pointing the building out. 'I shall dispatch them there.' Erik drew Jomal as she walked, and with the haft of the axe resting on his shoulder he turned to Thorstein at his side. 'Once this is over with,' he said, 'reassemble my sons and leading men in the laird's hall.'

Thorstein's eyes shone. 'We are attacking then, lord?'

Erik shook his head, driving the joy from his old friend's expression. 'No, we are not.'

The huskarl protested. 'But we may be only twenty miles or so away from the man we have hunted all summer.'

The Skulissons had reached the cattle byre now, and Erik indicated that they be led inside with a jerk of his head. He plucked at Thorstein's sleeve. 'Let us dispatch these boys to their God, and then we will tap a barrel or two and I will explain my thinking to you all. If, after I have said my piece, you still think we should continue our march north I will welcome your rede along with the others.'

Erik entered the byre, passing the bloodstained patches marking the place where his would-be killers had been laid low by arrows in the dawn. As bovine heads looked on he interrupted the low chanting of the priest to point out a wooden feeding trough. 'That is a manger; did I have the right of it when I understood it was where your Saviour was lain as a newborn?'

The priest nodded that he had.

'Then lay their necks upon it,' Erik said as he heft Jomal. 'And I shall close the circle.'

16

THE FOX IS FLUSHED

With the orb low in the southern sky the sunlight chased the shadows from even the most wayward nook, streaming in through the open doors to paint the gable end with its glow. Erik prowled the margins as the men made their case, picking at a wedge of cheese as he listened in. The rind was as tough as old boot leather, but every morsel was precious on campaign and the king worked it around his mouth as Thorstein rose to speak.

'I say we attack,' the big man growled. 'Make ready for the march tonight, leave before dawn and our mounted men will reach the enemy while they are still half asleep.' The huskarl ran his eyes around the group as he looked for support. 'Even without Oswulf's army and Regenwold's detachment we still have more than five hundred mounted men with us, and we can send word to the earl to rejoin us as we ride. That will give us a force of eight hundred mounted men, more than enough to pin the Scots in place while those on foot make their way to the battlefield. We know that the Sudrey jarls are less than fifty miles away, and the Orkney men near the Moray Firth and marching south.' Thorstein ran his eyes around the group, seemingly at a loss to see that there could be any hesitation in taking up his plan. He turned his face to a fellow huskarl, opening his arms wide as he made a final plea for support. 'Helgrim, you must be of the same mind? We have trudged north for months, and here we are within a few miles of the man we came all this way to kill. Tell them to grasp the opportunity, now while it is there, or we shall have to return next year to hunt the man again and things may not go so easily. With a full year to prepare a defence he will be ready, and may well spring a surprise or two of his own.'

To Thorstein's delight his friend agreed. 'Yes, we have to kill Mael Colm this year. Who knows how long the southern English will be led by a weakling? What if king Eadred recovers, or dies? With more time to plan, what if our old friend Olaf Cuaran takes advantage of our absence in the North next year to mount an invasion of his own?' He paused to swallow a mouthful of ale, before flicking a look across to the place where Erik was washing the last of the cheese from his mouth with a draught of his own. 'Thorstein is right, lord,' he said. 'We must attack.'

Keen to hear the views of his most trusted men Erik had withheld his own lest he sway them either way, but as he prepared to share his thoughts the man whose rede he was beginning to value above all others rose to say his piece. 'What do we know for certain? What more do we know now of the whereabouts of Mael Colm, that was hidden from us when we arrived at this place?' Harald Eriksson looked about those seated around the hearth and gave a shrug: 'nothing…' Before anyone could counter he spoke again. 'All we have to go on is the word of two young fools, men who thought it would be an easy thing to sneak into camp and kill the king of Northumbria in the middle of his army. What if they were expected to fail and were being used by Mael Colm to bait a trap?' Erik watched proudly as his son began to reflect his own fears. 'You both say that king Eadred is weak and ailing, but his kingdom is as strong as ever, rich in silver and men. If the southern English decide to spend a little of that silver paying for an army from Dublin or for a Viking fleet of their own, we are a month's forced march from home — by the time word reached us York would have already fallen, we shall all be landless wanderers and my father shall be a sea king once again.'

Harald's wisdom had driven some of the fire from the pair, and Erik watched with satisfaction as the men gathered around the hearth nodded their heads in agreement. Harald opened his mouth to speak again, but the words caught in his throat as the doleful note of a signal horn carried to them from the watchtower outside. Erik tossed his drinking horn aside, making for the doorway as the sound trailed away. Already on the high point of the settlement it was only a matter of moments before the king was scurrying up the ladder, and as he reached the platform the lookout raised an arm to point northwards. 'The *Vindalfr* is in sight lord,' the watchman reported as Erik came alongside him. 'And she looks to be in a hurry.' Erik looked out to sea. The Wind-Elf was leaping the waves, clouds of spray necklacing her prow as the bow rose and fell, and Erik watched with mounting excitement as the crew of Gamli Eriksson's ship worked the braces to capture every breath of wind. Helgrim had joined him on the small platform, and the pair, king and huskarl exchanged a look as the rest of the flotilla rounded the headland and the voice of the lookout told-off their prow beasts one by one: *Langháls — Skelfa — Hestr — Skær...*

Helgrim spoke as the man rattled off the identities of the longships. 'Gamli is not one to run around like his arse is on fire for no reason, Erik. It must be the news we have been waiting for.'

Erik nodded. 'Let us get down to the strand.' He threw the lookout a parting instruction as he began to descend again. 'You know my son's fleet well, that is why you were entrusted with this duty. Keep your eye on the sea beyond the headland, but don't forget to look for any sign of riders inland. We have our own patrols out, but it pays to be sure. If any ships or horsemen appear that you don't recognise send a runner to tell me straight away.' Erik was through the hole in the platform before the man could reply, and in moments he was back on the ground. The others had abandoned the hall by now, bunching at the foot of the ladder as they waited to find out what the signal horn had indicated. Erik reported what they had seen as Helgrim dropped to the ground at his side. 'Gamli is returning,' he said, 'and by the look of it the Midgard Serpent must be on his tail.' Erik indicated the little riverside settlement beyond the town walls. Men could be seen lining the brow of the earthworks, peering northwards as news of Gamli's mad dash spread. 'Let us get down to Stroma. Hopefully my son's council can help us decide whether we march the army up to Fetteresso, or begin the long haul home.'

A well-trodden path connected the hilltop settlement of Celurca to the more rough and ready trading port of Stroma, and Erik cast a wistful look at the sea as he walked. The sun was westering now, dusting salmon-pink shards over a rack of iron-grey clouds. The waves surged and seethed, spurting where they broke over rock or skerry — even in summer the sea here could be broodier than a mare in heat. With the treasury in York full to overflowing following the victories of the last few years, he had had no need to raid for almost the first time since he had left Norway; no longer a young man at first it had seemed a boon, but as the months ticked by and he had kicked his heels in the King's Garth, Erik had come to realise just how much ships and the sea had become a part of the man he was. For a moment he wished his crowns away and he was back on the beach, that first night out of Thorir's hall in Nausdal. The faces floated into his mind then, some still vivid in the firelight: Anlaf Crow; Ulfar Whistle Tooth; Skipper Alf — others cobwebby and indistinct as the relentless march of time dimmed his memory of them. And the ships: *Reindyr; Bison;* the Skipper's skei *Fjord-Ulf* and his own ship *Isbjorn*, long gone now — her back broken racing a whale! Erik chuckled at the memory, the sound breaking the spell and causing his sons and guards to cast him quizzical looks. He shrugged and snorted, pulling a threadlike smile. 'Ghost ships and dead men…'

His reminiscing had eaten up the time it took to walk the quarter mile which separated the two camps, and Erik raised a hand to acknowledge the chants of the men lining the earthen bank as he came into its shadow:

Blóðøx! — Blóðøx! — Blóðøx!

Men were rising to their feet as he entered the compound, brushing mud and grass from breeks and tunics as they watched the king pass, and soon Erik was at the waterfront, the soft pad of foot upon earth changing to a clatter as he mounted the boardwalk and gazed out to sea. The king's hirdmen Grettir and Gunnar were there, the brothers dipping their heads as he passed, and they tacked on to the throng following on as Erik made his way to the end of the landing stage. Erik threw an instruction over his shoulder as he went. 'Rustle up food and drink for the crews. They will not have had much time to eat if they have driven their hulls hard all the way down the coast.'

When he looked back the *Vindalfr* was in sight, the sleek

hull heeling as she came about on the starboard tack; shields wedged tight in their racks caressing the waves — the Tents of Battle; Wound Moons; the Clouds of Óðinn of the skalds. Erik watched in admiration as the sail was brailed, the spar rattled down the mast, and oars slid proud of the hull to row the ship home. In the shadow of the land the longship was picked up by the incoming tide, and as the lookout in the prow kept a practised eye out for sandbars and floating debris another crewman swung a line to take soundings in the unfamiliar waters of the river mouth.

With the great woollen sail safely stored amidships and the snarling beast head stowed lest they unsettle the *land-vættir* — the land spirits of the Norse or the wulvers and kelpies of the Scots — Erik was able to search the faces on the steering platform, and an involuntary smile spread across his features as he caught sight of his firstborn for the first time in months. Gamli had spotted him in return, and the grin which flashed bright in the sunlight set the old king's heart racing as the ship began to turn its prow to the bank. A flash of colour to seaward, and a quick glance to the East showed where the snekkjur were coming about, the little ships bounding the waves as they pointed their own prows to the river mouth and followed on.

In what seemed little more than an eye blink the *Vindalfr* was before them, and Erik smiled to himself as Kolbein came up to cast a critical eye over the skill of the styrisman as the big paddle blade was worked, the oars withdrawn and the larboard strakes kissed the quay. Ropes were tossed to willing hands, and as men ashore tied them off a gangway clanked on the quayside. Gamli was first off, and Erik looked proudly on as he bounded down the boards. His boy looked every inch the seafarer, from the crow feet around his eyes to the salt spray on his breeks, and Erik took up a kingly stance as his son drew up before him. 'Hail Erik Haraldsson, King of Northumbria, overlord of the Orkneys, Shetlands and Sudreys,' the lad began. 'I bring you great news father.'

Erik pushed down the temptation to tell him that he had received information of the whereabouts of the king of Scots; of the uprising in Moray and the call to arms at Fetteresso. There was glory enough to share. Gamli continued as his oath sworn Hoskuld and Svan hurried ashore and came forward to support their lord. 'Mael Colm has been in the north, suppressing a rebellion by Cellach of Moray.'

Erik nodded. 'We have heard whispers, but our source was…' He hesitated, as he searched for the right words to describe the unlikely informants. 'Let us just say that they would have said anything by the time the final toe came off.'

Gamli's eyes widened in surprise. Pitiless torture was not his father's way, but Erik shrugged it off. 'It was not my doing, but we needed to know.'

The thunk of wood being driven into wood carried across to the pair, and the mood lifted again. 'Ah,' he said, 'the welcome sound of ale barrels being tapped. Disembark your men and we shall share what we know over a horn or three.' The crowd parted to allow father and son to pass, and Erik looked on gleefully as Gamli and Harald embraced. The other Erikssons joined in the ruckus and Erik left them to it, exchanging grins with his guards as his wolf cubs yammered and yelped. A cart had been manhandled onto the dockside as Erik had awaited the arrival of the *Vindalfr*, and he was pleased to see that men were already piling the wagon bed high with bread, cheeses and oatcakes; off to the side several barrels were now tapped and ready to slake the thirst of travel weary seamen. A quick look over the heads of the others told Erik that the smaller ships were preparing to run ashore a little further down the strand, and Erik gave instructions to the men there as he filled the first horn. 'Wait until the ship-masters are ashore before you allow the crews to touch the food. They will ensure that every man receives the amount which reflects his worth.'

Gamli had extricated himself from the ruck, and Erik handed the horn across as he turned to fill another, thought better of it, and heaved the barrel onto his shoulder. 'Come,' he said as he shifted the weight and held on tight. 'Let us go aboard your ship; with the snekkje beaching themselves downriver it is about to get rather busy — the deck of a skei is the perfect place to share our news away from the crowd.' Erik indicated that the men who had followed him down from Celurca tag along with a movement of his head, and his spirits lifted another notch as he walked the plank and stepped aboard a ship for the first time that summer. As the king set the ale barrel upon a coil of rope the others trooped aboard, and Erik handed each man a full cup as they dragged the crew's sea chests into a circle and took their places. Gamli waited until they were settled, and on receiving a nod from his father the king, he began to share his news:

'A week ago we were raiding along the southern shore of the Moray Firth when we were hailed by one of Arnkel Torf-Einarsson's ships which had been sent out to waylay us. It seems that our friend the king of Alba had struck north, surrounded the hall of the laird of Moray one night and burned him in for his support of a rival claimant to the throne. The Torf-Einarsson brothers and their army of Orkneymen were within sight of the flames, and assuming it was the work of our own fleet which they had seen from the hills that day, rushed to join us. When they got there they not only discovered the truth of it but also the laird's son, a man called Crinan, who had been returning from a hunt and survived the attack. The son was able to tell them not only that Mael Colm had issued a summons for the northern levy to meet him at a place called Fetteresso on his return, but that the king himself was only a few hours ahead of them.'

Erik worried his beard as he listened in, and he inclined his head as he made a comment of his own. 'We had been told of the king's journey north but were unaware of the outcome. We also had word of the muster at Fetteresso, but your confirmation is more than welcome. Can we assume that the Orkney men are attempting to overtake Mael Colm before he reaches safety?'

Gamli nodded. 'Yes, father — and they have been joined by the men of Moray and the new laird.'

'That's good,' Erik said. 'With my own kinsmen and an avenging son on his tail, Mael Colm dare not let the pace drop for a moment. When he does arrive back, he and his men will be exhausted.'

Erik ran his eyes around the group as Gamli topped up his drinking horn, and was unsurprised to see that Harald was clearly itching to ask a question of his own. Erik nodded his assent as Gamli regained his seat. 'We have heard that this Fetteresso is twenty miles or so to the north of here. You have been up that way, can you tell us anything of it?'

Gamli smiled. 'Not only did we slow our sprint south just long enough to spy out the coastline, we overtook a fisherman who was keen to keep his head upon his shoulders in return for a description of the lie of the land.'

The men beamed and shared a look. This was just the type of information they needed if they were to head off Mael Colm and stop him going to ground. Gamli revelled in the moment before a look from his father set him off again. If Mael Colm had been chased south for the best part of a week, even on blown horses he must be nearing his destination. There was no time to lose.

'Fetteresso is situated within a maze of river courses and marshland a few miles inland from a small fishing village known as Stonehive. It's the ideal place to gather an army if there may be opposition nearby — the clans can assemble in dribs and drabs but the pathways are too small to mount a major assault. The only north-south road worth speaking of is the very same one you used to ride here. It continues northwards, passes through Stonehive and then follows the coast along an old drover's causeway across the marshes. Assuming that the Scots know that they are being pursued by the Orkneymen, this is the fastest and most likely route they will take.'

Helgrim cut in. 'Well, that is fine. If there is only one road surrounded by marsh, all we have to do is cut that road and wait for him to fall into our lap.'

Gamli remained silent, and Erik glanced across and pulled a face: 'but, there is more…' He was not to be disappointed. 'But there is the fortress at Dun Foither, just to the south,' his son continued. 'We had a good look from the sea on our way here. It is built upon a rocky promontory, precipitous, practically a sea stack, and if Mael Colm gets in before we can cut him off, well,' he said gravely, 'we will never get him out.'

Erik ran his eyes around the group as Gamli's words sank in. 'If we are to give ourselves the best chance of killing our foe, we will have to move quickly. I will leave the levy men here at Stroma to await our return, and send word to Regenwold to join us if he can. Harald,' he said, 'search out Olvir and Mord — have them ride out and find him. The rest of you prepare yourselves for a hard ride — we leave within the hour.'

17

DUN FOITHER

The horsemen drew rein as the fortress came into view, and Erik shifted in the saddle and let out an involuntary groan. 'If he is in there,' he said finally, 'I will set up camp and starve the bastard out — even if it takes all winter.' Helgrim shot him a look of surprise. 'Do you think that is wise lord? You may well find that the price you pay to take Mael Colm's head will be the crown of Northumbria. As Harald said back in Celerca, Eadred of Wessex, Olaf Cuaran or some other sea wolf is likely to take advantage of your absence from York.'

Erik pulled a roguish smile. 'I said that I would raise a siege here, not that I would be the one prosecuting it.' The smile widened into a grin. 'I would appoint someone in my stead, you know,' he said with a wink, 'a trusted huskarl or the like.'

To Erik's surprise the suggestion was not met with the look of horror he had expected, and he listened in as Helgrim took up the threads of the idea. 'It could work,' the huskarl mused. 'While we have the manpower to hand, use the York levies to throw up a bank and ditch; leave a strong force here when the others return south, and resupply them by sea.' The pair looked to the East. Before them the solid blackness of the rocky outcrop dominated the view, but to either side wide sandy bays stretched away to north and south. 'Down there is the perfect place to beach a ship — they could bring in food and news from home while rotating the men to relieve boredom and help to keep disease at bay. We will need to keep a longship or two here, despite the winter weather,' he said with a frown, 'to stop the defenders bringing in supplies or even taking the king out.' Helgrim's eyes widened and he snorted. 'We would look bloody silly then!'

Erik nodded as he ran the idea through his mind; high above the stars were paling as he switched his gaze to take in the rocky outline of Dun Foither once again. Although a good deal smaller, the great stronghold reminded him of Byrgisey up in Orkney — Fortress-Isle — the place which had sheltered his family during the darkest days following the loss of Norway. Whereas that outcrop became an island at high tide, the one before him was still connected to the mainland by a knife-edged ridge, but a quick appraisal by the king told him that it was no less formidable for that. A pathway switch-backed down from the clifftops where the men of his hird now sat patiently, bottoming out in a wide gully. From there the path climbed again before entering a narrow cleft in the sheer sided rock face which led up to the summit and the walls of the fortress itself. From the moment an attacker left the tree line to descend the slope, they would come under arrow shot from any bowmen manning the walls above. Gaining the gully would add to their difficulties, as javelins added their weight to the deadly hail. Any who had survived the onslaught thus far would now be channelled into the narrow passageway which led to the summit, and Erik harboured no illusions as to their likely fate as they attempted to force their way up and all manner of weapons, rocks and boiling liquids cascaded down upon them from the heights above. It was the perfect killing ground that had drawn the groan from Erik the moment he had first laid eyes upon it, but any thoughts of assault and siege were pushed gratefully aside as the first brands winked into life on the battlements and he came to realise the truth. Erik turned to Helgrim as shouts of alarm carried to them across the void, and his breath fogged the cool air as he spoke again. 'Come on,' he said thankfully. 'Let us return to the roadway — Mael Colm is not here.'

A SHOUTED command followed by the clatter of shield on shield told Erik that he was nearing the roadway, and a heart-beat later he rode clear of the trees. A wall of Norwegian shields lined the path, the rising sun throwing long shadows away to the west, and Erik curbed his mount's headlong dash as the men of the *Draki* spilled from the tree line. A quick scan of the men arrayed in battle order before him and the king's eyes went to the war flags of his sons; Erik instinctively passed judgement on the disposition as his own huskarls gathered around. Thorstein spoke, echoing the king's thoughts. 'There is nowt wrong with that defence Erik,' he said, the approval obvious in his voice. 'You'll not catch Erikssons unprepared for war.'

Erik ran his eyes along the formation as he slid to the ground. Thorstein was right — strung out in line of march the column was vulnerable to a surprise attack. But with Gamli and his men guarding the head of the column and Harald the track which led down to Dun Foither, the two most likely places that foemen could launch an assault were well covered. A glance to the south confirmed that the banners of his remaining sons were bringing up the rear, and as Harald came up Erik snapped out an answer to his son's unspoken question. 'He is not there.'

Harald's expression became a mix of relief and surprise that Erik was certain must echo his own as he spoke. 'You are sure, father? You were barely gone long enough to ride there and back.'

Movement to the king's right caught his eye, and Erik glanced across to see Gamli trotting back down the column with the scout, Hauk, in tow. He waited the few moments it took for his eldest son to arrive before repeating his conclusion. 'If he was heading there, Mael Colm has not yet reached the fortress,' he said to them both.

The brothers shared a look, and Erik's war lust flared as he recognised the excitement which passed between them as he explained his reasoning. 'The rock was in darkness when we arrived at the head of the clifftop path, and it was not until we exited the tree line and revealed ourselves that the guards reacted. Helgrim and I were sat on our horses in full view for some time before brands were lit and the sound of the alarm being raised carried to us. It was plain that their king was not holed up there, if he was he would have told them of the chase south from Moray and they would have been expecting the pursuers to arrive soon after.' Erik flicked a look across to the place where Hauk was waiting patiently, before returning his gaze to his sons. 'What do we know of the situation ahead?'

Gamli summoned the scout with the wave of an arm. 'Tell the king what you told me.'

'The town looks quiet, lord,' Hauk reported. 'A few early risers going about their business, but no sign of armed men and nothing which would suggest that they are expecting any.'

Erik nodded. 'Describe it to me.'

'Stonehive is pretty unremarkable — a score or so huts and a few shacks down by the beach for the fisherfolk. From what we could make out this road runs directly through the settlement and then north across the bog.' He glanced up at the rapidly lightening sky. The sun had climbed a little higher since Erik had returned and the woodland to the East was fringed with light. 'It was dark of course,' Hauk added apologetically, 'it will be far easier to see now; but I have left good men in position on the ridge above the town who will ride back and report anything significant I may have missed. We didn't want to enter the town because there were too few of us to seal off all the pathways, and it would have left us unable to warn you here if anything changed. It is only a couple of miles away at most — now that we know that our rear is secure we can be there in no time.'

Erik clapped Hauk on the arm and threw him a heartening smile. 'Lead us forward and we shall push on through this collection of hovels.' He glanced at the sky and smiled. 'With the returning light we can increase the pace — once we are on the northern causeway it will be an easy matter to block the road and wait for Mael Colm to come to us.' He returned his gaze to his sons. 'Gamli — Harald; when we reach Stonehive take your men and block the road which leads to Fetteresso, we don't want the Scots who have already arrived at the muster to attack our rear if they get wind of our presence.' Erik recognised the look of disappointment which washed across the faces of his eldest sons and he explained his reasoning. 'It will not take five hundred of our finest men to block a narrow causeway. A king must face a king in battle, and I would feel a whole lot easier knowing that my rear was secured by my best men.'

Erik crossed to his horse, unhooking his war helm from

its carrying place as the boys relayed his orders, and as the headpiece slipped into place the clearing was filled with the clatter of men doing the same. Erik threw his huskarls a grin as he hauled himself back into the saddle. 'Come on lads,' he said. 'We have a war to win.'

Gamli was just mounting his own gelding as Erik swept by, and Hauk urged his horse into a gallop as the scout led the army north. With the sun now lighting the way Erik increased the pace to a gallop, and in what seemed little more than moments the trees were beginning to give way to cultivated fields, but as the first rooftops of Stonehive hove into view he was forced to drop to a canter as a horseman came racing into view ahead.

As he drew closer Erik recognised the man as Thord, the young scout who had won a silver arm ring for spotting the ford before the attack on Haydon the previous summer, and as the rider turned to come alongside he cocked an ear to listen. 'There is a strong force of mounted men approaching from the North, lord,' Thord called across the sound of beating hooves. 'They are very close — within a mile now I would guess.'

Erik nodded that he understood as he threw back his heels. The road was stony and rutted this close to the town, but he knew that with the bulk of his army still back at Stroma it was imperative that they reach a good defensive position before the arrival of what must be Mael Colm and his raiding army or invite catastrophe. Taking the next rise at a gallop the way ahead opened up, and as the early morning light finally revealed the town and its environs, he raised his chin to look. A mile away the causeway shimmered as the sunlight lancing in from the East played upon helm and mail, and dropping his gaze Erik searched frantically for a place to make a stand. The first of the Scots were already across a wide river and coming on fast, but the nearest buildings were little more than a hundred yards ahead and he knew what he must do.

The thunder of hooves beneath him changed to a clatter as his horse crossed a rickety bridge, and a heartbeat later he was across and beginning to slow as he put the southernmost buildings behind him. In a matter of moments he had reached the far side of Stonehive, and as Erik slid from the saddle and took up his weapons the rest of his hird were fanning out to do the same. Sleepy faces stared at him from the depths of the huts, and Erik snapped a command which had them quickly melting back into the gloom. As the last of the doors were slammed shut and locking bars clunked into place the king was releasing his shield from its carrying place, and the reassuring weight of the piece firmed the muscles of his forearm as he prepared for the fight. By the time he had turned back his guards were out of their saddles and at the king's side, and Erik threw them an order as he made his way forward. 'Cut the roadway — form up between the buildings either side, we will use them as a bulwark.'

The sunlight returned as Erik came clear of the buildings, and the king forced down his disappointment as the light revealed just how close the enemy were. Mael Colm was clearly in view beneath the war flag of Alba, and although a quick tally told Erik that he would be outnumbered roughly three to one it also revealed what he knew would be his salvation. He turned aside to share his joy, and saw that Helgrim Smiter was already drawing the haft of his Dane axe across his shoulder before stooping to prop the great dome of his shield against a nearby wall. The big man planted a kiss on the blade of the axe as he straightened his back, turning his head to address his lord as the others began to pour into the clearing. 'I shall hold them at bay while the men move forward to the gully,' he said.

By the time Erik had thought to reply the huskarl was already halfway to the bridge, rolling his shoulders and neck as he warmed muscles chilled by a hard night's ride for the killing time ahead. The war axe was a two handed weapon and deadly for close-in combat, but nigh on impossible to use and wield a shield at the same time. Erik turned back, his eyes flying across those cramming the gap between the two nearest halls until they found the men he wanted: 'Grettir — Gunnar!' The brothers' heads snapped around as they recognised the voice of the king. 'Helgrim is our axe man on the bridge — take shields across and protect him from spears and arrows.' The pair nodded, and Erik added words of encouragement as they squirmed clear of the crush and trotted by: 'and show these Scots how Hordalanders fight…'

Safe for now, Erik strode clear of the buildings as he sought to use the opportunity to organise the defence. The quicker he could do it, the quicker he could recall the defenders from the bridge; he had to give them the best chance he could. A line of longhouses ran parallel to the burn, and although the watercourse was not much more than a trickle at the height of summer, the fact that the inhabitants of Stonehive had felt the need to steepen the banks to contain the flow during the wetter months should make it a formidable obstacle when the enemy attacked. Fifty yards on, what flow there was meandered across a pebbly beach before discharging into the cold blue waters of the German Sea. Several small boats had been drawn up amid the nets and drying racks of their trade, and Erik realised the danger to his flank as the last of his men surged through the gaps between the buildings and formed up.

To Erik's surprise Harald Eriksson was one of them, and

as his eyes picked out the figure of the king he hurried across. 'We have found the road to Fetteresso father,' he said, 'and it is a piddling thing. Gamli was able to set up a defence four men deep straddling the path using the crew from the *Vindalfr* alone, so I brought my men across to see if we could be of more use here.'

Erik's hand went to the silver hammer at his throat in thanks. With the majority of the Christians absent, either with Regenwold in the west or back in York with the returning Oswald Thane he felt more comfortable displaying the emblem of Þórr, and old red beard would know that the king would very soon have need of every shield, spear and axe he could get. Erik plucked at his son's sleeve, turning him to face the early morning sun. 'Take yourself down to the strand and anchor the line there,' he said gratefully. 'If you get time you may be able to drag those boats across to form a rudimentary wall, if not make sure that axemen render them unusable. In fact,' he added as an afterthought, 'stove the sides in anyway in case you are overrun and lose the opportunity. Whatever happens we cannot let Mael Colm reach Dun Foither, either by turning our flank and regaining the roadway or taking ship and doubling the headland.'

Harald gave a curt nod and strode away. Erik allowed himself a moment to wallow in self-regard despite the nearness of battle as he watched his son go. The eyes of Harald's hirdmen were eagerly following the young man as they awaited his command, and Erik let his gaze linger even as the first roar of defiance rolled down upon the beleaguered Norsemen from the Scots across the ditch. It was not until Harald reached the first of the shoreside huts that Erik reluctantly tore his gaze away, and turning his head to the north he was just in time to witness the last of the enemy exiting the causeway and dropping down onto the riverside meadow.

Erik could see Mael Colm clearly now — walking the front rank just out of arrow shot, surrounded by his personal guard as he sought to instil the fighting spirit they would need to cross the ditch and come face to face with battle hardened Norsemen. Erik smiled his war smile as he looked, and his cares sluiced away as he came to see just how weary the Scots must be regardless of their numbers. A couple of nights' broken sleep had fogged his own mind somewhat, despite the few hours he had snatched following the Skulissons' torture and demise. He was not a young man now, well into his sixth decade on Midgard so the skalds told him; Mael Colm was older still, and he had just been chased all the way from Moray. But it was not the ages of the respective leaders in the upcoming fight which had lifted his mood, but the realisation that the Scots were already hastening to form their battle lines and desperate to force the issue. If he was outnumbered here, then Erik's experience told him that was unlikely to last. To race south, throwing your army at the enemy you have avoided all summer long without taking the time to rest up or spy out the battlefield beforehand was the act of a desperate man. The army of the Orkneys and their new Moray allies were not only close behind, they must be coming on in overwhelming strength. Erik knew that if he could hold them here until the northerners arrived he would win the war — Mael Colm would die, and the crown of Alba would be added to that of Northumbria, Orkney and the Sudreys. Then, while the southern English hid behind the skirts of their sickly king, he would assemble an army from all the lands north of the Humber and add that crown too.

18

SPEARS AND SHIELDS

The cries of the enemy were building as Erik walked forward to address his fighters, and a snatched glance northwards confirmed that the Scots were on the cusp of making their first assault of the day. Time was short, but there were no novices among the ranks before him, no downy lipped boys putting on a brave face as the enemy cavorted and chanted only yards away, and at Erik's appearance before them the men quietened and turned their faces to him. The king lost no time in addressing them:

'Norsemen,' he cried, 'men of the North — Norwegians.' He smiled as he saw a hawkish look come into faces up and down the line as he did so. 'I have no need for fancy words, exhortations or appeals to your manliness, and I would not shame you to do so. The end of our summer long campaign is in sight. Yonder...' he said with the dismissive waft of an arm, 'is Mael Colm. No man remains king for as long as he without fox-cunning, but he has outrun his luck and this morn will be his last.' Erik's gaze drifted from face to face, pausing here and there to share a nod or the ghost of a smile with favoured veterans. 'We are outnumbered for now and faced by desperate men — they will hit us as hard as they can, but even so we will prevail.'

The rattle of spear shaft upon shield carried to the king, and Erik knew that the enemy attack was only moments away. Sturla Godi was alongside him where banner men must be, and Erik reached across to raise the huskarl's war horn high as he outlined his battle plan. 'We move forward to the edge of the ditch and hold them there as long as we can. It's a day for spears and shields lads,' he said with a gleam in his eye. 'The longer we hold the lip of the ditch the more of them shall fall, but their numbers may tell in the end so keep an ear cocked for this. Three blows on the horn signify the moment we retreat back to the buildings. Regain the positions you occupy now and hold them there. If there is any sign of a breakthrough or that one seems likely, three more blows of the horn will send us back to guard the road south.' Erik ran his eyes along the line, pinning men with his gaze as he drove home the final point. 'Gamli and Harald are anchoring our wings, so they will not outflank us through force of arms — but whatever happens here we must deny Mael Colm passage to the fortress at Dun Foither. If the war horn sounds a third time, fall back and form a skjald-borg on the far side of the little bridge we crossed on the ride in.' He made a fist and glowered. 'If we can pin the Scots here until the Orkneymen arrive we shall crush them in a vice, if not Mael Colm will escape us again and we shall have to return next year to hunt him down afresh.'

A cry rent the air, and Erik glanced across to see that the Scots had begun their advance, the long line of armoured men breaking into a trot as they crossed the water meadow. Erik looked back and urged his army forward with the sweep of an arm. 'To the ditch, lads — Oðinn is with us!'

He turned his attention to his bodyguards as the warriors

thundered past. 'We will back up Helgrim at the bridge. He has done his work there, denying the Scots any chance of an easy passage until we had shared our plans and made our dispositions.'

Erik threw a look away to the north as he regained the roadway, blinking in surprise as he saw how near a loping gait had carried the enemy in such a short space of time. What had been pale smudges only moments before had hardened into hate-filled faces, and as the men of the *Draki* fanned out to either side of the little bridge the first volley of javelins left the hands of his countrymen to arc through the air. A moment later the throwing spears fell among the onrushing Scots, and Erik looked on with satisfaction as men were punched backwards by the force of the strike. Those following on leapt the falling bodies of the dying and injured, increasing the pace to come to grips with the enemy before they too could be struck down by the deadly darts, and as a follow-up volley darkened the sky the leading Scots gained the ditch. A moment later the attackers were airborne, launching themselves across the gap to land among the Norsemen in a thunderous clash of wood, muscle and steel. Leading the line Erik braced as a raven haired Scot grew to fill his vision. The blow when it came rocked him back on his heels, but his huskarls were there and as the king threw his shoulder into the boards they moved in to lend their weight to the push. Despite the crush of bodies Erik worked to free his spear, twisting his grip to angle the long blade almost vertical as the man before him scrabbled to find a foothold on the crumbly edge. Unbalanced, the Scot could only look on in horror as Kolbein's hand shot out to grip the hem of his mail shirt, and as the armour was tugged upwards Erik's spear was already moving. An instant later the blade was worming its way beneath the folds, and Erik grunted with effort as he felt the point touch yielding flesh and he stepped in to drive it upwards. A gasp of rancid air washed over his face as the breath was driven from the attacker, and Erik threw his bodyweight forward to send the dying man tumbling back into the ditch.

With his opponent now bleeding out in the burn below Erik raised his eyes to seek out the next threat, but the look told him that the following wave was only just setting off across the meadow. Satisfied that the immediate danger had been taken care of Erik took a rearwards step, and he raised his eyes to scan the battlefront as a crewman slipped into his stead. The majority of the first wave had been beaten back and were now lying in a bloodied line at the foot of the slope; here and there tiny bridgeheads had been gained where the meander of the burn had closed the distance between the two banks to little more than a hop, but the resistance was fierce and he doubted that the Scottish van could force its way through before the main body of attackers arrived to add weight to the push. Erik's eyes slid across to the bridge. Helgrim Smiter and the young Hordalanders were standing mid span, the whistle of Helgrim's war axe as it arced through the morning air clearly audible above the shouts and cries of warring men. As yet the threat posed by the trio seemed to have warded off any thoughts of attack in the enemy ranks, but that would not last Erik knew, and he gave a snort as he imagined the big man's unease and embarrassment at being the only man in the army yet to wet his blade.

Erik's respite was short lived, and he firmed his grip on shield and shaft as the next wave of attackers arrived to crash down upon the Norwegian line. A yard to his right the wall was breached, and as triumphant Scots poured into the gap Erik let out a roar and counterattacked. His spear stabbed out as a face swam into view, but his opponent was quicker still and Erik felt his shoulder jar as the man's shield brushed the attack aside to send the spear spinning from his hand. Before the Scot could follow up Thorstein was there, the huskarl's desperate counterstrike enough to thwart the attack on his lord as Erik drew his sword and took a sideways step. Still hunkered into his shield as he looked to bring his spear into play, Erik's attacker had made the fatal mistake of losing sight of his first opponent, and the king took full advantage as he swept the blade in to take the man in the neck. As the sword cut a rictus and blood spurted the Scot crumpled; Erik shoved the body back into the ditch, rushing in to plug the gap before more of the enemy could leap across. A Norwegian was down in the mud, stuffing ropes of black-blue guts back into a savage rent in his belly, but Erik had no time to drag him clear of the stamping feet as he forced his way back into the front line. Before him the ditch was rapidly filling with bodies as attack after attack was beaten back, and Erik braced to meet the next as the Scots came on screaming their war cries.

As far as he could see the first waves of attackers were lying dead or grievously wounded in the ditch now, and back on the lip Erik saw at a glance that those following on were of the lesser sort. But if their weapons, leather caps and jerkins marked them out as levy men their numbers and fighting spirit were still potentially overwhelming, and Erik raised his sword as they reached the far bank and slid down the slope without hesitation. Rank after rank followed on, and Erik prepared to deal out death from his position above them as the first scrambled across the dead and dying and clawed their way up the slope.

Halfway up the rise a spearman made a lunge, aiming to catch Erik in the vulnerable spot beneath the steel plates of his greaves; it was a cunning strike, but Erik had seen too many winters to fall for such a thing and he raised his foot to bring it crashing down to pin the shaft to the edge of the rise. The attacker looked up in desperation as he worked to free his only weapon, and the surprise of the counterstroke just had time enough to register on the face of the Scotsman before Thorstein's spear blade arrived to make a horror of it. Erik raised his eyes again as Thorstein and Kolbein covered him; the Scots were pouring across the far side of the burn to crash upon the Norwegian line like a breaking wave, and he knew that he must extract himself from the fight if he was to fulfil his duty to the army. Another face appeared beneath him, and Erik's boot shot out to pulp a nose as he called to his hirdmen above the furore. 'Here, 'he said, 'step up and take my place lads.'

The moment he felt the presence of the men at his shoulders Erik took a backwards pace, and as his oath sworn slotted in to take the positions of the king and his guards they retreated into the clear space between the fighting and the huts beyond. Sturla Godi stuck staunchly at his side, the bloodied axe war banner of Erik Haraldsson flying proudly alongside the dark raven of Óðinn as the king led them across to the roadway. Raised a few feet above the level of the riverside in an effort to hold the worst of the spring floods at bay, the causeway which carried the road offered by far the best overview of the fighting tactics of the enemy to the Norwegian leader, and Erik's eyes swept the field as his guardsmen clustered protectively around him.

Straight ahead the earlier reticence on the part of the attackers had been overcome, and the blade of Helgrim's axe was cutting a bloody swathe as the Scots attempted to force a passage across the bridge. To either side the Norwegian shield wall was holding firm for the most part, but where the ditch began to peter out as it approached the sea the enemy were across in force. Raising his chin Erik could clearly see Harald and the men of the *Skrípi* pivoting as they swung inland to attack the flank of the enemy breakthrough, and although the flooding tide would help to secure their own wing for now it was plain that they were placing themselves in some danger by doing so.

The men had fought well and the little beck had become a midden stacked high with the broken remains of Alba's best, but Erik knew that the time had come to withdraw or risk being overwhelmed by sheer weight of numbers. 'Sturla,' he said, as a war cry rent the air and the Scots surged again. 'Send a runner to tell Helgrim and the boys to abandon the bridge: then make the signal to withdraw to the huts.' Erik switched his gaze to the men about him. 'We will make a stand here. It is only a few yards, but I want us to give our lads the best chance to retreat without being forced to turn their backs or fight their way out. As soon as the shield wall begins to retreat, the enemy will be on them like a pack of wolves.'

Sturla caught his eye as a spearman dashed across to the entrance to the bridge, raising the war horn to his lips as he sought a final confirmation that the king wanted the signal made. Erik gave a curt nod and the horn sang, once, twice, three times — the sound hanging like a pall over the field of battle as the first faces, pale, drawn and bloodied by the intensity of the fighting, turned his way. Sensing a break-through the signal drew a roar from the attacking Scots, but Norwegian discipline held firm and Erik watched as they retreated step-by-step from the edge of the ditch. With the shield wall intact the attackers soon came to realise that their foe remained undefeated, and as the flood plain opened up before them and the pressure to gain a foothold on the southern bank receded with it the Scots began to disengage, falling back to regroup before renewing their assault.

With the men retreating in good order and the ferocity of the Scottish attacks momentarily on the wane, Erik raised his eyes to search out the far bank. The oncoming waves of spearmen were all but spent, the last of the Scots now bunching up against the far bank as they waited for the attack to begin again, but it was the absence of Mael Colm's war flag which caused the king's stomach to lurch, and his brow furrowed as his eyes searched the length of the water meadow in desperation. He gave voice to his worries, more in hope than expectation. 'Can anyone see Mael Colm?'

Thorsten and Kolbein Herjolfsson were at his side, and the pair shielded their eyes from the bright morning sun as they scanned the opposite bank. Kolbein spoke first, the old campaigner's voice betraying his unease as he confirmed Erik's worst fears. 'No, lord,' he said. 'There is no sign.'

The last of the men of the *Draki* were just reaching their new defensive position, and Erik had opened his mouth to speak when he realised that the man Sturla had sent to retrieve the three on the bridge was stood before him. A quick check told him that Helgrim, Grettir and Gunnar were standing firm, their weapons glinting mid span, and he nodded that the man speak as he watched the newcomers swell the Scottish ranks to cut off the trio's retreat.

'Helgrim asked for your leave to stay, lord. He believes that he can hold the bridge even if he is surrounded, but that if it is his fate to die here he will raise a horn to us all in Valhöll. He did try to insist that the others leave,' he added, 'but they refused. They said that it would be cowardly of them to allow him to tread the rainbow bridge alone.'

Thorstein growled at his side. 'We will see about that.' He turned to Erik. 'Let me lead a charge to get them out, lord. I'll not watch a friend of mine lay down his life for a ramshackle bridge in the arse-end of nowhere.' He cast a dismissive glance towards the enemy before speaking again. 'We will cut through this rabble and be back here before they know what has hit them.'

Erik shook his head. 'Smiter knows what he is about. Now that we know that Mael Colm has fled the field, the Scots will never break through his defence. Abandoned by the king, only a lackwit would match himself against Helgrim's axe for a forlorn cause.' He raised his eyes to scan the far bank once more, hoping against hope that he would see the banner of his enemy hove into view. He was to be disappointed. 'If the bastard has found a way to escape us again, this whole summer campaign has been a waste. We could have feasted away every day in York, and I would still have saved silver.'

As if to confirm the king's worst fears, the first sounds of fighting were beginning to drift across from the Southwest: Erik turned to look, only to find that the source of the conflict was masked by the buildings of Stonehaven. Either the king of Alba knew of another route through the maze of bogland to the west, or the men who had answered Mael Colm's call to arms had heard the fighting from the nearby encampments at Fetteresso and were rushing across to lend their weight to the assault. Neither was good news, and Erik's eyes flicked across the field before him as he pondered what to do. With Mael Colm gone the battle before him was now meaningless, but until the Scots retreated the Norwegians would have to hold their position or risk being overtaken and hacked down from behind. Erik ran his eyes over the enemy again. The demeanour had changed, the savagery of the earlier attacks had left them as word spread that their king had left the field, and Erik knew immediately what needed to be done. 'Sturla!'

he snapped. 'Sound the attack! I have had enough of skulking behind my shield, it's time these Scots discovered what type of men they are facing.'

As the low moan of the battle horn drifted above the armies, Erik walked free of the line and turned his back on the foe. With the enemy front rank little more than a two score paces away it was an act of scorn intended to put the fire back into the bellies of men unused to being on the defensive, but if any had harboured a doubt as to their mettle the Norwegian fighters quickly drove it away. As Erik raised Jomal high and the sound of the war horn lay heavily on the battlefield he called a rallying cry, turned and broke into a run: *'Follow me lads! Back to the ditch!'*

Erik powered across the clearing, sweeping his axe in deadly arcs as he did so — war horns blaring as his name filled the air:

Blóðøx! Blóðøx! Blóðøx!

Taken by surprise the Scots quailed before him, and Erik was thrilled to see the first of them abandon the field and flee across the ditch to safety before he even reached them. A moment later he was there, Jomal scything through flesh and bone in a gore spattered crescent before his foemen could cobble together an organised defence. A spearman waved his weapon in a half-hearted attempt to drive him back, but the attack was gutless and Erik let the point snag in the links of his mail shirt as he crushed the man's skull. The harsh crash of wood on wood and the softer sounds of steel striking flesh told the king that the rest of his army had reached the foe, and Erik swept out to either side as the Scots fell back in disarray. Without warning the ditch opened up before him, and Erik stood panting on the lip as he watched the last of the enemy throw themselves across the dead and dying in a desperate attempt to escape the slaughter. Erik looked to either side as his guardsmen reached him, the familiar thrill of victory sending his spirits soaring as he watched the rest of the army drive the Scots before them like deer before fire. Away to the west the first of the fugitives were melting into the reed bed fringing the wetter ground, and Erik spat his disgust as he saw that he had been right; there was another pathway which lead inland from the settlement. It was obvious now that Mael Colm had squirmed from his grasp once again, and as the realisation caused the elation of victory to drain away Thorstein spoke at his side. 'Look lord.'

Erik replied without taking his eyes from the fleeing Scots. 'Yes, I know — as we feared, there was another path.'

Thorstein spoke again. 'No, lord — look.'

Erik dragged his eyes away from the enemy and followed the huskarl's gaze. There, half a mile to the north, a party of horsemen sat highlighted against the skyline.

19

A KING AT BAY

Picking his way through the jetsam of bloodied torsos and limbs which marked the high tide of the Scottish advance Erik crossed the little bridge, shaking his head as he surveyed the carnage all around. 'What were you thinking? If we had been forced back all the way to the southern bridge, you would have been cut off and overwhelmed.'

Helgrim shook his head. 'Up here I could see more than you down on the bank,' he replied. 'I was the first to see that Mael Colm was preparing to flee to the marsh. I tried to warn you,' he added apologetically, 'but I was assailed on all sides. If I had turned my head any further, I would have been run through before I could gain your attention.'

Erik nodded that he understood, taking a backwards step as he ran his eyes quickly over the body of his friend. As was usual there were no visible wounds, and the blood which freckled his arms and mail shirt had belonged to his enemies. He turned his head, shooting Grettir and Gunnar a smile as the pair finally rested the heavy shields against the parapet of the place they had helped to defend throughout the battle. The wooden boards showed brightly where spear blades had sliced through the leather covering, and a smattering of arrowheads on hastily broken shafts showed the king how well they had fulfilled the task he had given them at the start of the fight. 'I see you were kept busy lads,' he said with a nod towards the shield faces. He ran his eyes across the dead underfoot. The majority of those who had attacked the trio were lightly armed levy men, and Erik felt a pang of pity imagining the fear as they rushed the armoured giant in a desperate attempt to swamp the Norwegians and force the crossing. Despite their bravery Helgrim's axe had made short work of them, and all that remained to tell the tale were mounds of broken bodies amid the unseeing eyes of the dead. 'No axe man can ply his trade without support,' the king said as he looked. 'You did your work well.'

As the pair stood tall at their king's praise the first clatter of hooves drifted down to them from the roadway, and Erik turned his attention to the north to see that an army had overtaken the scouts on the skyline and were approaching beneath the wild boar banners of Orkney.

The sounds of fighting which had drawn his attention earlier flared suddenly, and Erik exchanged a look with his huskarls as the oncoming riders slowed the horses to a trot. There was clearly a savage fight taking place nearby, and Erik forced down the desire to plunge into the marsh and seek it out with difficulty as he awaited the news the Orkneymen would bring. The army of York was far from home; he had already been forced to divide the invaders and it was not the actions of a wise king to blunder into fights without a plan, but he allowed himself a snort of amusement that age had tempered his hot blood even as he hoped that Gamli Eriksson would show the same restraint at his position guarding the western roadway. The leading riders were clearly in view now, and Erik painted his face in a welcoming smile as the familiar features of Arnkel Torf-Einarsson hardened from the crowd. The jarl-brother returned the gesture, curbing his mount as the king walked forward beneath his own war banner — but the smile fell away to be replaced by a covetous look as the Orcadian saw into the depths of the burn for the first time. 'You have a victory lord,' he said, forcing a smile back into his features. 'It would seem the gods are not on my side today.'

'If we did the fighting,' Erik replied, 'the victory belonged to us both. Without your pursuit they would never have paused to fight here at all. You drove them onto our spears, and I am thankful for it.' Erik turned his gaze to the West. The sound of fighting was unrelenting now, and he turned back with a question on his lips. 'I see that Erland is not with you. I take it he has something to do with the fighting in the marsh?'

Arnkel nodded. 'The new laird of Moray knew the back ways and paths to the Scottish meeting place at Fetteresso. He went to spread word among the clansmen of the king of Alba's treachery in burning in his father in the hope that they would abandon his cause. Erland went along with his own ship's crew to support them should they give any trouble.' The Orkneyman cast an anxious look westwards. 'It sounds as if they were not to be persuaded. As Mael Colm lies dead here, I would like to take the rest of our army across to help.'

'Mael Colm is not dead,' Erik replied to Arnkel's surprise. He indicated the marshland with a jerk of his head. From their position on the northern side of the burn, the trackway which had swallowed up the Scots and their runaway king was in plain sight. 'As soon as it became obvious that there was no way through here, he took off. The rest of the Scottish army made one last attack and then headed west down that track, hopefully following him to Fetteresso.' Erik cast a glance across his shoulder. Harald Eriksson had left the beach and brought his men up to the roadway, but the horses were still a good distance away in the heart of the settlement. If the king of Alba had added the remnants of his raiding army to that of the men at the muster, he could yet overcome Erland and his new ally, slip through the net, and either retreat into the interior or double Erik's position and gain the fortress at Dun Foither. 'How many men did this new laird bring along?'

'Only fifty, lord — tough men, but not all seasoned fighters.' Arnkel's face reflected the king's concern. 'No doubt the best of the fighting men perished along with their lord in the hall burning.'

Erik plucked at his beard as he thought. 'So added to Erland and his ship's crew of sixty or so, there are little more than a hundred men taking on who knows how many Scots.' It was obvious now that speed of thought and action were vital, and within moments Erik had come up with a plan. 'We have to reinforce our kinsman as soon as we can. Remount and follow the path the Scots took into the marsh. With the added height you should be able to see a good distance ahead, but be on your guard for isolated groups, traps or stragglers — they may be difficult to spot until you are almost upon them. I will mount up and move inland along the main path which leads away from the settlement behind me.'

With his brother likely facing overwhelming odds at nearby Fetteresso and having already missed the battle at Stonehive, Arnkel needed no encouragement after the rigours and privations of a week-long chase. The horse protested as he hauled himself back into the saddle, tossing its head and stamping the ground with a hoof, and Arnkel ran a gloved hand along its neck as his hearth guard swarmed around him. 'A few more miles old lad,' he said as he took up the reins, 'and then you can eat all the grass you want.' Erik and Arnkel exchanged a nod, and the king looked on momentarily as the Orkney man urged his mount into a canter and the army of the northern isles crowded in his wake.

With the chase back on and the sound of fighting still drifting across from the west, Erik turned back and recrossed the bridge. On the far side men were seeking out friends and kinsmen as they compared wounds and swapped stories of the fight, but Erik cupped a hand to his mouth as he regained the bank and called out above the din. 'There is no time to waste boys,' he cried. 'Our fighting is not yet over, the day not yet won.' He raised an arm to make himself more conspicuous as Sturla Godi struggled across the lines of dead to carry Erik's sigil back to his side. 'Leading men — cross to me!' he bellowed. 'The rest of you clean your weapons and restore the cutting edge ready to fight again.'

As the sound of sharpening stones caressing steel replaced the buzz of celebration Erik's underlings hurried across, and the moment the last of them came to a halt before him he began his address. 'We haven't much time if we want to ensure that this day is Mael Colm's last, so listen up. Erland Torf-Einarsson has taken his hird across to engage the Scots at Fetteresso, backed up by the laird of Moray and his men. If Mael Colm has gone to join them, he may very well escape again before we can cross to support our friends. Arnkel has taken the army of Orkney through the marsh, but we don't know for sure where the pathway actually leads or whether it is suitable for so many horses, so we need to get across there as soon as we can. Get your men back to the horse lines, and fall in behind Gamli at the place where the western road enters the marsh. We will advance again as soon as we are set.' Erik indicated that they return to their crewmen with a flick of his head, and as they retreated he called his son across. 'Harald — how did you get on?'

Harald wiped the sweat and grime from his face with a forearm before replying. It was clear to the king that he had had a tough fight of it. 'Three dead and a dozen wounded father,' he replied, 'although most of those are fit to fight again if called upon.' Erik could not help his eyes widening in surprise at the scale of the loss in such a short time. Harald recognised the look and was quick to defend his men. 'The lack of a ditch before us, and the fact that we had nothing but the surf to anchor our shield wall was as obvious to the enemy as it was ourselves, lord. They threw everything they had at us — but we held.'

Erik had recognised the defensive pitch of Harald's reply, and the change in address from father to lord. He placed a hand on his son's arm as he softened his tone. 'Don't take offence where none was intended, I watched your men fight and I know their worthiness. I need a good crew to double back and block the path which leads down to Dun Foither — it's vital that we keep Mael Colm from reaching the fortress. Your men have fought the hardest today, but Gamli has yet to come to grips with the enemy. If your brother of all people can keep his discipline for the greater good, I know that you can too.' Erik tugged at Harald's sleeve as the pair turned back. 'Hurry south,' he said as they walked. 'We shall return here and see to our dead and wounded when we are sure that the old Scot has gone to Hell.'

Erik's guards had hovered a short distance away while he spoke to his son, and with his honour and that of his men confirmed by the king, Harald brightened and went to do his bidding. With the king's son gone, the huskarls came across. 'We are attacking Fetteresso,' Erik quickly explained. The king looked across to the men of his hird as they began to move back into the heart of Stonehaven, cupping a hand to his mouth as he singled out a trustworthy face from the ruck: 'Hauk!'

The scout's head turned at the sound of his name. 'Yes, lord?'

'Hurry across to Gamli. Tell him to mount up and lead an attack on Fetteresso — the rest of the army will follow on.'

As Hauk scampered away, Erik was leading the men of the *Draki* back along the roadway to the centre of Stone-haven. With the midmorning sun now bathing the town in its soft light, his gaze took in the halls and outbuildings. It was clearly a prosperous place. Stone walled buildings gleamed white, and raising his eyes he saw that the roof thatch on all but the meanest buildings was in good repair. It was hardly surprising he decided, as he secured his shield to its carrying place and prepared to mount. More familiar with the wilder lands on the West Coast and the islands which skirted it he only knew the eastern lowlands from previous coastal raiding, but the interior of Alba was bountiful — lush with pasture, cropland and thickly forested. With salmon filling the autumn rivers and the offshore fisheries teeming with cod and herring, the kingdom would make a fine addition to his empire of the North once Mael Colm was dead and the inhab-itants had experienced the benefits of Erik's rule.

Erik settled into the saddle, turning the mount in a wide circle as he waited for the army to form column. Fifty yards to the east Harald was leading his men across the little bridge as they rode to block the track to Dun Foither, and by the time the horse had returned to its starting position the army was mounted and awaiting his signal. At the head of the column Gamli's face was turned his way and Erik raised an arm, holding it for a heartbeat before chopping it down to unleash the horde. Faces snapped forward as war flags coloured the air, and with a whoop of joy which was heard clearly the length of the line Gamli was away.

Within moments the entire column was following on, and as they came clear of the buildings the king threw a look across to the north. A mile or so away Erik could make out the gaily coloured banners of the men of Orkney as they rode down the fleeing Scots, and although they were still strung out in line he knew that they must be about to break out from the confines of the marshy path and join the fight. Denied the chance to come to grips with the enemy at Stonehaven Gamli was charging ahead despite the uneven path, and Erik sent a plea winging its way to the gods of war that the battle lasted long enough for his son to wet his sword that day as a reward for his patience and discipline.

The day was warming up quickly as the sun rose higher, and a glance to the Northwest showed the boar flags growing indistinct as they merged with the heat haze blanketing the reeds and bullrushes. But the look had been enough to tell the king that the leading elements were beginning to fan out as they exited the track, and a spike in the clamour drifting across from the direction of Fetteresso confirmed that Arnkel and his men were entering the fray.

The higher ground which carried the road had allowed trees to establish themselves marking the route as well as any scout, but Erik saw that the switchback path must double the distance they would need to travel before they too could join the fight. At the front of the column Gamli shone like a silver penny, the sunlight glistening on his sword as he swung the long blade in an arc, and lifting his gaze Erik's heart leapt as the fighting finally hove into view less than half a mile ahead. Short, sharp notes cut the air as Gamli's banner man raised the war horn to sound the charge, and within moments the call to arms was being repeated the length of the line as the riders spurred their mounts for the final run in.

Erik's eyes took in the details of Fetteresso as the way ahead was revealed, and his battle-trained mind quickly saw what must have been the course of events that morning as the horse rushed on. A large hall dominated the clearing, sturdily built of split boughs under a roof of hazel brown thatch, with a collection of outbuildings and corrals scattered to either side. At the arrival of Erland and his Scottish ally the defending Scots had strung formations of warriors between them, in much the same way as Erik's defenders had guarded the gaps between the buildings of nearby Stonehaven that same morning. It was a sound tactic, but the unexpected arrival of their king followed by hundreds of stragglers from the earlier fight had sown confusion where only stout hearts and a united front could hope to win the day.

At the centre of the line Mael Colm came into view, finally rediscovering the valour of his youth to fight like a king at bay beneath the war banner of Alba. Gamli swerved left as Erik looked on, taking his riders across to attack the Scottish right wing; in the mad scrum directly before Mael Colm a knot of men were hacking their way forward beneath a battle flag showing a leaping salmon, the huge two-handed swords typical of highlanders rising and falling above them. With his back to the wall and any chance of retreat slipping away by the moment, Erik called across to Grettir as they approached the fight. 'Take the crew and close off Mael Colm's escape route. I will remain here with my bodyguard, ready to reinforce the main attack if it stalls.'

Erik wheeled right as he came into the clearing, guiding his horse to one side as the rest of his crew peeled off and the sounds of battle swirled around him. The hall at Fetteresso stood on a slight hill, raising it clear of the fetid air from the

surrounding marsh; from horseback Erik could see well
enough, and as his guards came to his side Grettir and Gunnar
led the men of his hird around the edge of the fight. Erik
looked on appreciatively as his ship mates swept forward,
arcing around to close the net as they crowded about the rear
of the hall. With Mael Colm's slender chances of escaping the
fight now closed to him, Erik settled down to watch the end.
In the short time it had taken his hirdmen to reach the position Gamli Eriksson and his crew had broken through the
defenders anchored to the southern stockade, and Erik
allowed his eyes to linger on the sight of his eldest hacking
down on the heads of the enemy as they broke and ran. Still
in the saddle the crew of the *Vindalfr* were following suit,
riding their mounts into the fleeing Scots to drive them from
the field. More and more of Erik's *here* were spilling from the
marshland path, snatching up spears and shields as they
rushed to join the fight.

At the hall Mael Colm was still in sight, but the numbers
opposing his shrinking band were a tide in full flood now, and
with retreat impossible Erik relaxed a little as he prepared to
witness the thing which had drawn him north months before
— the death of the man who had thought to drive him from
his own kingdom a few years before. On the far side of the
field the flags of Orkney formed a screen to the north,
Arnkel's newly arrived reinforcements enough to turn the tide
of battle there as he fought his way to his brother's side. The
last Scots there were already casting nervous glances to the
rear, eager to tread the fugitives' path before the Orcadians
turned the flank and denied them the chance, and satisfied
that the battle would be won without his intervention Erik let
his gaze wander back to the centre. He was just in time. The
leaping salmon flag was a few paces before the king now, the
storm tide lapping at his feet, and as Erik thrilled to the sight

the Scottish standard was wrestled from the banner man and Mael Colm disappeared beneath a flurry of blows.

After all that had gone before, the plotting and planning over the course of the previous winter and the long chase north, the death of Mael Colm felt like a release to the king, more akin to being rid of a pest than the culmination of a glorious campaign, and glancing aside Erik saw the same emotion reflected upon the faces of his huskarls.

The summer-long campaign had been the first time Erik and his men had prosecuted anything on such a scale, but the king knew that the lessons learnt that year were invaluable. This was a new type of warfare to them all; grinding out a victory against an enemy who refused to give battle, withdrawing deeper and deeper into a hostile land. With the countryside stripped bare of anything useful to the invaders, Erik's thoughts had slowly turned from glorious adventure and the pursuit of an opponent to the more mundane worries of resupply and distance. Although he knew they would grumble out of earshot of their leaders the men had got by well enough on meagre fare, but the horses were a constant concern. The animals ate and drank prodigiously, and although farriers had accompanied the army north the supply of new horseshoes quickly ran out. With the horses increasingly tired and footsore, the pace of the advance had slowed to little more than a walk; scouting and raiding away from the main column had been reduced to the occasional foray, and Erik saw for the first time just how effective this new type of warfare could be. With the borders of Northumbria restored and the size of his kingdom more than doubled, it was something he could contemplate should the southern English come north again, something to consider should he lead a mighty army south of the Humber.

A savage roar interrupted his thoughts; Erik looked across

to the hall. The body of Mael Colm had been dragged into the open now, the pale cadaver reminding King Erik of a skinned eel in its nakedness as his killers cavorted and sang their songs of victory. Thorstein caught his eye, and Erik's mouth widened into a watery smile as he brought the campaign to an end. 'It's been a long summer,' he said. 'We will spend the remainder of the day building a pyre for our dead back at Stonehive, drink the night away and head back south in the morning.'

PART III

OÐINN´S WOLF SMILE

20

OLD BONES

The trio bent their heads as they came clear of the buildings and into the full force of the blow, and Erik drew his cloak tightly around him as they set out across the square. Off to the right the stony heights of the minster dominated the gloom, the muffled toll of a bell showing where a finger of wind had penetrated the tower. At his side the flames of Oswy's torch sawed back and forth in a desperate struggle for life, before a fierce gust snuffed the light completely. The Englishman threw Erik a look of exasperation as he tossed the thing aside, cupping a hand to his mouth to yell above the force of the wind. 'So much for that, lord. Thankfully we are all but there.'

Erik raised his eyes to peer across what in Roman times had been called the Forum. With the shutters fastened against the savagery of the storm the long low building which housed the ecclesiastics was a Stygian wall, the dark shape only broken at the point where an open door revealed the welcoming glow of firelight within. Outlined against the light a figure stood within the doorway, and even at a distance of fifty yards the king recognised the figure of Morcar, Oswald's thane. Despite the best efforts of the gale to drive them back the little party were soon across the clearing, and as Morcar stepped respectfully aside, Erik led them across the threshold and into the calm of the interior. Thorstein and Helgrim moved further into the room, their eyes searching the shadows as Erik made to unfasten the belt which carried his sword. Morcar Thane held out a hand. 'There is no need to disarm, lord,' he said quietly. 'Although places of worship exist within these walls, the building itself is little more than a home to the brethren — a place to eat, sleep and do God's work.' As Erik's hand went back to his side the man continued. 'I am sorry to send word during such a night, lord,' he went on. 'But I doubt that Oswald will see the morn.'

Erik nodded. 'Death rarely comes at times which are convenient for those who remain, I am sure that we have both seen enough of it over the years to know that to be true. Where is my old friend?'

Morcar gestured towards a wide passageway which led further into the building, and the thane fell in at Erik's side as the pair crossed the entry vestibule to take it. The passage stretched ahead deep into the building, and Erik took in the details as he walked. Beeswax candles lit the way, the sweet-smelling aroma welcome after the stench of York's streets; beneath his feet Erik marvelled once again at stone pavings which would have been laid soon after the Christ walked the earth, the dips and rises in the ancient stonework polished smooth by the footfall of men long dead. The starkness of the lime washed walls and ceiling was interrupted every dozen paces by the dark form of a doorway, and as the last but one was reached Morcar drew to a halt.

The final doorway shifted and rattled on its latch, but even as he sensed Thorstein and Helgrim stiffen Erik pushed any thoughts of ambush from his mind. He had heard tales of the dying room from Oswald himself; beyond the last door lay a garden, a place of beauty and tranquility where those soon to make their peace with God could bask in the beauty of His creation during their final days on earth. Morcar tapped lightly on the old panels, and the sound of shuffling from the far side was soon replaced by the soft click of metal as the latch was lifted and a face appeared. The brother dipped his head as he recognised the figures before him, standing aside to allow the pair entry into the room beyond, and Erik let out an involuntary gasp at the sight which met his eyes as he crossed the sill and came into the space. A cot rested against the far wall on which his old friend lay swaddled in blankets, but it was the vibrance of the room after the starkness of the passageway and entrance hall which had grabbed the king's attention, and Erik let his gaze wander across the walls and ceiling as he began to cross the flags.

The walls of the cell were completely covered with many of the scenes from the gospel he was familiar with from the nearby cathedral: Christ on the cross; the army of winged men he now knew to be angels marching to give battle with the forces of evil; the ark of Noah breasting stormy seas to rescue God's beasts from His cleansing flood. But if the wall paintings reflected the lessons with which the dying man would be familiar from his time in the minster, the ceiling was altogether different. Gone was the depiction of Edmund the Martyr, the last native king of the East Angles who had been put to death by invading Danes a century before. In its place was a figure who could only be the Almighty, surrounded by trumpet blowing angels as they welcomed a man into Heaven after a life of service to his God. Picked out in reds and blues and gold the scene would be the last image seen by the dying man, and although Erik could never be described as Christianity's most fervent follower he knew enough of kingship to recognise the power of the image.

A priest knelt at Oswald's side, the singsong note of his incantation pushing back the shadows, but the prayer stopped abruptly as Morcar crossed to lay a hand lightly on his shoulder and he became aware of the king's presence. The old churchman hauled himself upright on unsteady legs, and Morcar ushered him out to join those already waiting in the passageway outside. Morcar waited until the priests had left the room and closed the door before speaking in an undertone. 'Oswald received another communication from archbishop Wulfstan only this afternoon,' he breathed. 'I have not been made privy to its contents, so I can only presume that he wishes to discuss the information it relates with you alone.' The Englishman glanced across to the recumbent figure of Oswald before looking back and inclining his head. 'I will wait outside with the others, lord,' he said before lowering his voice to a whisper. 'I humbly suggest that you take the opportunity to learn all you can while the man is still conscious — he is spending an increasing amount of time asleep or befuddled.'

Erik nodded that he understood, watching as Morcar crossed the room to take his countryman gently by the hand. It was a heartfelt gesture that was clearly meant to be a final farewell between two men who had known each other the greater part of their lives, and the king returned his gaze to the murals to spare them all the embarrassment of having him witness the tenderness of the moment. Their farewells exchanged the Englishmen parted, and Erik exchanged a nod with Morcar Thane as he made his way from the cell. As the heavy door closed with a thud and the latch dropped into place Erik crossed the room to kneel at the bedside, forcing down a grimace at the iciness he felt when his fingers curled around man's hand. Oswald had noticed the slight change in the king's expression, and he pulled a thin smile as the king drew near. 'I know I am not long for this place, lord,' he cawed. 'But I rest here content that I go from a corruptible world to the incorruptible.' The smile widened, and a glimmer returned to Oswald's eyes as his mind fought against the gathering darkness. 'Christianity is a wonderful thing, lord,' he said softly. 'You should try it.'

Erik opened his mouth to protest, but his friend waved the words away before they came. 'It is not me you have to convince King Erik,' he said. 'But I will put a good word in for you soon enough.'

Oswald rummaged beneath the blanket as he talked, finally withdrawing a rolled parchment into the light. He passed it across with a trembling hand. 'Here,' he said. 'The latest communication from my lord archbishop.' Erik reached out, and seeing the wax seal already broken he unfurled the roll and angled it towards the light. After a moment's study he pulled a face. 'I was hoping it was written in English,' he said, 'my latin is a little rough and ready, and I would hate to miss anything of importance. Could you?'

Oswald motioned towards a cup and pitcher as he attempted to raise his head on the pillow. Erik poured, cradling the old man's head as he took a sip. 'There is no need to read the message in its entirety,' Erik said as he returned Oswald's head to the pillow. 'You have already read it I see — just tell me that which I need to know.'

Oswald nodded weakly. 'The archbishop is overjoyed at your actions in the north, and he wants you to know that you have his undying thanks and admiration for reunifying the realm of Northumbria,' he wheezed. 'There is disbelief and consternation in the south that you should have such success at the time when king Eadred is clearly dying, but their greatest fear is that you ally yourselves with the Scots rather than attempt to impose your own kingship upon them.'

Oswald closed his eyes, his breath coming in short rasps as the effort overwhelmed his mind and body. Erik looked shamefaced that his own inadequacies was forcing the man to endure such torment in what was clearly his last hours. He laid a hand on the Englishman's shoulder. 'That is enough old friend,' he murmured. 'Gunnhild or Harald can read me the letter in full.' Oswald's eyes opened and he nodded towards the cup. Erik cradled the dying man's head as he sipped. 'They want you tied down in the north, lord,' Oswald whispered as the spark of life returned to his gaze, 'and they will spend as much silver as it takes to bring that about. For the first time in my life the West Saxons fear us, and I give thanks to the Lord that I lived just long enough to see this day.'

GUNNHILD HELD the parchment close to the flame, screwing up her eyes as they wandered across the glassy surface. Raising her chin she looked at her husband. 'There are parts which have been scraped clean and written on,' she said.

Erik shrugged. 'That is not unusual.'

The queen lowered the message, running the pads of her fingers lightly across the surface as she traced the words and letters. She exhaled slowly as she thought. 'Let us compare the two again.'

Erik sat down beside her, unrolling the earlier communication and offering it up to the new. 'The writing style looks the same,' he said. 'The quill strokes which formed the archbishop's name are identical, and look,' he said moving his own parchment across to the candlelight, 'there are patches which have been scraped clean on this message too.'

Gunnhild sighed as her gaze flitted from one to the other. She had not laboured for nigh on forty years to advance the fortunes of her husband and offspring to fall easily into a trap. Erik nudged her and smiled. 'You are right to be suspicious — you are a sharp minded woman, that is why we are an unstoppable pair.' He gave her biceps a squeeze as his smile widened into grin. 'Brains and brawn, that's us. I have the brains…'

Gunnhild rolled her eyes. 'Then we *are* doomed.'

Erik chuckled happily before continuing. 'There is nothing in the latest message which would endanger our position here if we acted upon it — no pleas to attack at such-and-such place on this date if we want to kill Eadred, and even if it did I would ignore it for we are far safer with the wretch alive. The letter congratulates us on our victories, and tells us of the panic which they have caused in Wessex that we might ally ourselves to Indulf mac Constantine. It also adds that we have little to fear from Olaf Cuaran who is tied down in Ireland fighting my old friend Conalach Cnogba, the High King who attempted to double-cross me when we attacked Dublin all those years ago. That at least we know to be true, due to the traders who pass through York from the place. You forget that Wulfstan is being held against his will out in the wilds somewhere,' he explained patiently. 'I rather doubt that king Eadred has supplied him with a healthy stack of freshly prepared parchments in case he wishes to communicate with old friends here in the North — it is only down to the wiliness of our archbishop that we receive word at all.'

The sound of something heavy skittering along the roadway outside interrupted the king, and the pair shared a look. 'I was lucky to get back unharmed,' Erik said. 'There is thatch, roof tiles and all sorts flying about the city.' They paused to listen as the wind howled about the ancient stones of the King's Garth. Gunnhild spoke again. 'It reminds me of winter nights huddled around the hearth in Orkney.' She shuddered. 'It is not a memory I treasure.'

Erik gave her a nudge. 'Why be so downhearted? We are back in York and I have defeated every enemy sent against me. Wulfstan even remarked upon southern fears that I will form a northern alliance against them now that I have disposed of Eadred's lackey Mael Colm.' Erik rose from the settle, crossing to the side board. Filling two cups from a pitcher he handed one across. 'But we had already decided that we would attempt such a thing; it makes perfect sense to do so. I cannot take an army north from York every summer to subdue Alba — the distance is too great and the hinterland offers too many places to hide. If Eadred recovers or Olaf Cuaran defeats the high king in Ireland their armies could be in York before I even got to hear of an invasion.' Erik drained his cup as he paced the boards, turning aside for a refill before continuing. 'Tell me more of this Indulf son of Constantine — why should I withdraw my support from Crinan mac Cellach, the man who actually lopped the head from Mael Colm's shoulders? If they are acceptable to the Scots either man will make a suitable ally, and we can reform the alliance which threatened to overrun the southern English twenty years back.' He smiled. 'That will certainly give them something worth worrying about.'

Gunnhild tossed the parchments aside, taking a sip from her wine cup as she ordered her thoughts before replying. Erik swigged a mouthful as he waited, noisily swilling the drink back and forth over his teeth before gulping it down to belch. Unlike other husbands Erik had always sought her advice in all things, and if the gods had not seen fit to endow her with the brute strength and coarseness of her menfolk, the queen knew the workings of her mind were just as important to the success of them all. She was aware that he had heard the whispers that he was hag-ridden, but he had never wavered in his determination that she act as caretaker for the kingdom both here in York and earlier in Norway despite the scoffs and sniggers, and she loved him all the more for it. A further sip of wine and her mind had distilled her advice down to a short statement. 'Crinan mac Cellach is the son of a minor noble from an earldom situated far from the centre of power — Indulf mac Constantine is the son of a king, indeed a king who still lives.'

Erik clicked his fingers. 'Of course! King Constantine still lives — the one who renounced the throne to see out his days in the monastery at Saint Andrews what — ten years ago?' Gunnhild nodded as a look of puzzlement came into Erik's face. He had always left the more tiresome duties of kingship to Gunnhild, matters of importance which were nevertheless as dry as old bones; things like who married whom and why — she seemed to revel in them. 'So why didn't Indulf succeed his father back then?'

'Because he was a toddler.' Gunnhild smiled: 'let me explain. At the turn of the century a king called Domnall was killed fighting against invading Norwegians led by their own king Harald, known to men as Fairhair.'

Erik beamed — his father had been a rampaging bull of a king, and he loved to hear accounts of his deeds. Gunnhild chuckled as Erik's aged features took on a boyish mien again, before moving on with her tale. 'Domnall's son Mael Colm was little more than a bairn at the time of his father's death so the crown passed to the dead king's cousin Constantine. Constantine's rule was long and successful, but he allowed himself to be drawn into an invasion of England which resulted in the death of his son and heir.'

Erik scowled. 'The battle at Brunanburh; I recall Athelstan's offer of the king helm of York as his underling following the victory there, but I will be nobody's liegeman — I rule alone or not at all.'

Gunnhild cocked her head. 'May I continue Great King?'

Erik laughed as his humour returned. 'Please do.'

'The death of his favourite son did for the old man, and a few years later he, as you said, gave away his throne and retired to a monastery where he still resides today praying his life away. His nephew Mael Colm was rewarded for the loyalty he had shown the king and restored the line of Domnall, but Constantine had another son, a toddler named…' Gunnhild let the sentence hang in the air until Erik supplied the answer. He smiled as he began to unravel the weft and weave of the tale: 'our new friend Indulf mac Constantine. So considering that my father killed Domnall and I harried his son Mael Colm to his death only this summer past, it is fair to say that I will struggle to attract much support from that side of the family. However, by supporting Indulf I will restore the line of the popular and holy Constantine, Crinan can carry on as earl of Moray and everyone should be happy.'

'There is one more thing,' Gunnhild added with a look.

Erik's expression went deadpan as he answered with a sigh. 'There always is…'

'Indulf's mother was a woman called Ealdgyth.'

'An Englishwoman?'

Gunnhild nodded. 'Ealdgyth is a daughter of Ealdwulf of Bernicia, so also the sister of your new vassal in Bebbanburh — the aptly named Oswulf Ealdwulfing.'

Erik nodded that he understood. 'So that makes Oswulf and Indulf kin, and potentially a threat to us here in York.' He cursed. 'So all the tales of harrying by Oswulf's Bernicians in Fife last summer could have been just that — tales. For all we know they were guests at Indulf's hall, having a fine old time and plotting our downfall.' Erik's expression darkened. 'That changes everything. If Oswulf is untrustworthy he will have to meet his end sooner than I had planned for.'

A sly look crept into the queen's features. 'We could invite the earl to be our honoured guest over Juletide,' she suggested. 'He would suspect nothing; he submitted to you between the armies at the beginning of summer, and you are barely back from leading his thanes to war in Alba.'

Erik nodded his agreement. 'We will make the arrangements. It would seem that Indulf mac Constantine will become king of Alba whether I like it or not, but if I allow him to remain so he shall not have a kinsman ruling in Bebbanburh, and his southern border shall be firmly on the Forth and not the Tees.'

21

MORNINGS

E rik threw back the shutter and stared downriver. A knarr had slipped its moorings in the night to drift beam on to the flow, and the king watched as men aboard struggled to bring the bows about before rowing her back to her berth. The town-outside-the-walls which had been added between the River Ouse and the Foss by the conquering Danes, had stood up surprisingly well to the battering it had received during the night he decided, no doubt sheltered by the walls themselves from the full fury of the gale. But if the buildings had been spared, the same could not be said of the beasts which lived off kitchen scraps in the yards and thoroughfares throughout the town or grazed the fields beyond. Already the first bleats and cries were rising into the fresh autumnal air, and soon the town would reek of blood, offal and shit as those animals earmarked for the pot during the dark months met their end.

It was the fourteenth day of October, nine hundred and fifty-four years since the birth of Christ. It was also the first day of winter — what Erik knew as the beginning of the season of *Gormánuður*, slaughter-month, the local English

Blotmonath or Blood-month. All across the land freshly butchered meat joints would be salted for the coming winter, and ale-wives would begin to prepare the Jule ale which would be consumed during the festival which was now little more than ten weeks away. A low moan drew his attention, and he turned back to watch as Gunnhild fought her way clear of the bedcovers. 'Close the shutter Erik,' she groaned, 'and feed the fire, there's a good lad. It is cold enough, without throwing the screens wide.'

The light was snuffed out as the latch dropped into place, and back in the gloom of early morning Erik crossed to the hearth. Sparks and embers glimmered as he stoked the ashes, and as the wood caught and fresh flames lit his features with a fiery glow he turned his face to the queen. 'After you had retired, word came that Oswald Thane had gone to God. It seems that I was the last to have any meaningful words with him before the end. It was fitting really,' Erik said sadly. 'He was the first Englishman I ever spoke to.'

Gunnhild propped herself against the headboard, tugging the covers up to her chin to ward off the chill. 'If he was always the archbishop's man, he was also of use to us,' she said. 'We should mark his passing in some way Erik, perhaps we could build a church in his memory? He would have liked that.'

Erik snorted. 'I think that York has enough churches already.' He crossed to the settle and sat at the foot. Illuminated once again by the flickering flames, the figures on a wall hanging came to life as threads of gold and blue shone in the firelight. It was one of the tapestries he had brought out of Harald Fairhair's hall in far-off Avaldsnes, the day that he had been forced from his first kingdom by English gold and scheming. Known to all as *Völuspá* — Prophesy — Óðinn sat at the feet of a seeress as she answered the Allfather's questions of the creation, destruction and rebirth of everything. He spoke a passage as his eyes fixed upon a scene:

> *'She saw Valkyries arrive from afar,*
> *ordained to ride to the race of the gods.*
>
> *Future clasped a shield, Stabber was another:*
> *War, Battle, Weaver and Spear-prodder…'*

Erik's face lit up as his wife completed the passage:

> *'Now they are counted,*
> *the war-maker's handmaids;*
> *Valkyries fated to ride the ground.'*

'The old days,' he lamented as the pair shared a look, 'when the world was a simpler place. It would be quicker to heap earth over his corpse, to build a barrow like my father shared with his own though no less costly. If I filled it with gold it would be only part payment for the services he has rendered me over the years. But I have already thought of a fitting tribute to the man,' he added, 'over the past few days when it became obvious that Oswald's time here was coming to an end. He told me once that he had but one remaining kinsman, a younger brother — a leper who lived off alms at a monastery outside Hrypum. The rest of his family had been taken by plague and warfare, so the church took them in as children.'

'All dead? So much for a merciful God,' Gunnhild scoffed. Swinging her legs clear of the bed, she reached for the pot. 'Christ may be winning the war for men's hearts, but I think that the old gods still have the best tales.' She rolled her eyes as she pissed. 'Loaves and fishes…'

Erik shrugged. 'The gods have their own reasons for doing things, and sometimes just for the fun of it. They scheme and plot just like men. If Oswald's family had survived and he had grown to take over the running of the farm or whatever their trade was, maybe we should not be living here in the King's Garth.' He continued his tale as the queen covered the pot with a linen kerchief and slipped back beneath the blankets. 'Thankfully the place was spared when Eadred's army torched the church and town during our first reign here, and I thought that a purpose-built wing to house the sufferers could be added in Oswald's memory. I will speak to the abbott later today when I return the thane's body for burial, and if it pleases him I will arrange for building work to begin in the spring.'

Gunnhild's eyes widened in surprise. 'You are still going north, despite all we said last night? What if all this talk of the day of the wolf does not refer to the plots of archbishop Wulfstan and the sword arm of Erik Haraldsson? What if it is Óðinn's trickery to add that sword to the *einherjar*, his army of the battle-slain, while you are still of fighting age?'

A thunderous look had flashed into Erik's features, but the queen carried on, determined to make her point. 'Oswulf is a wolf too,' she said, 'as was his father Ealdwulf — the old wolf. And who is Ealdwulf's grandson other than Indulf — soon to be king of Scots? Wulf — Ulf, they both mean the same, perhaps the Allfather means the day to be theirs?'

Erik had heard enough. 'I have already accepted the invitation to feast, and I am not about to disappoint a man who has shown me nothing but loyalty and steadfastness in peace and war for fear of our fat friend in Bebbanburh, nor his Scottish kin. Once earl Oswulf has been disposed of Indulf will either come to heel, or he will discover that this summer's harrying was little more than a nuisance raid.'

Her worries had taken the king by surprise, and he struggled to hide his irritation. 'You expect me to cower in York because you fancy there may be a plot against us in Bebbanburh or,' he snorted, 'in Valhöll?' His expression clouded and she knew that she had said too much, but she had made her fears known and all their futures were now in the hands of the gods. 'Hrypum is only twenty miles from York, and Regenwold's hall outside Catrice only twenty miles beyond that,' he snapped. Erik sighed as the anger left him as quickly as it had arrived, his shoulders slumping in regret. 'I am sorry,' he said, turning his face to her. 'A foul temper can help to earn you the reputation of a fighter as a young man; later in life it just makes you a bore. I know you mean well,' he said. 'But some things are more important to a man than the number of days he can eke out his lifespan.'

Gunnhild sat upright, leaning forward to kiss him lightly on the cheek. 'You will never be a bore to me Erik Bloodaxe,' she breathed, 'and I would not trade a moment of our time together for another hundred years of life.' The movement had freed her breasts, and for once the cool air was welcome as she felt them firm. Despite the years of childbearing, Gunnhild had always ensured that nursemaids had helped her retain a youthful figure. She cared not what Erik did while he was away Viking; but in York she was his queen, and she would use every womanly wile to remain so. Erik cupped a tit, moving closer as all thoughts of plots and memorials were driven away. Gunnhild's breath quickened as she ran her fingertips along his inner thigh. 'Why don't you come back to bed,' she cooed, 'and show me how sorry you are?'

. . .

THE DAY OF THE WOLF

THE HEAVY OAK door closed behind him with a thud, and Erik exchanged smiles with the men as he crossed the frosty grass and came back to the camp.

Thorstein carved a nugget from the dried meat in his hand, popping it into his mouth as he handed the rest across. 'Eat well, lord?'

Erik pulled a face as he took out his knife and pared a sliver of his own. 'You know the answer to that question full-well. As an honoured guest I was offered something called a pittance, which was little more than a palmful of black bread and a rude clay cup of water.' He frowned. 'It was either that or some muck they called dowcet made out of milk, cream, fruit and egg. They only eat one meal around midday, other-wise as the abbott kindly explained: *the brethren are too satisfied to concentrate on their prayers.*'

Thorstein laughed at Erik's impression, the sound drawing the rest of his huskarls across. With the promise of a weeklong bout of feasting, drinking and fine entertainment in the offing, Erik's kinsmen Erland and Arnkel had tagged along with their own huskarls. The sound of laughter had them turning their heads, and the pair threw Erik a wave from the horse lines as they helped to remove the blankets from the beasts.

Thorstein had seen them too, and he made a remark as the Orcadians rolled up the sheets and began stacking them on the wagon. 'I will wager you slept better than the rest of us though lord, it was bloody freezing last night.'

Erik feigned concern. 'Since you are so fretful, yes it's true I slept like a bairn. The abbott was most pleased with my plans to become a benefactor of his little community, so much so that he insisted that I take over his own private lodgings for the night.' Erik threw his huskarl a wink. 'It is a privilege of rank — I *am* a king you know.' Beyond the tents and horses the eastern hills wore a crown of their own, as the celestial horses Arvak and Alsvið drew the sun's chariot back into the sky to herald the start of a new day. Nearby the lads had tapped a barrel, and Kolbein sauntered across with a horn of ale for his lord as the others exchanged small talk. Erik took it with a smile of gratitude. 'Another dawn,' he said. 'How many of those have we seen in together old friend?'

Kolbein returned the smile. 'Not enough Erik — let us drink to a few more yet.'

Erik snorted. 'Aye,' he said raising the horn, 'let us do just that.'

The others had seen Kolbein at the tap, and they waved their cups to-and-fro as they called across for a refill. Erik left them joshing, taking the opportunity to walk through the camp as he worked the dry meat around his mouth and washed it down with a gulp of his own. He had been a leader of men long enough now that he could move among them exchanging quips and banter with barely a thought, and his mind began to wander as he went. A hundred and fifty horsemen was considered a *here*, a raiding army in the laws of the southern English, and it had been enough to lay Gunnhild's worries despite her fears the previous morning. That he had agreed to leave the elder Erikssons back in York had helped, with only the youngest Ragnfrod tagging along to show the northern earl honour at the feast. With such a large following Olvir had been dispatched to ride the twenty miles along Dere Street to Catrice, sent north to warn Regenwold of the number of bellies he would be expected to fill over the next few days. Erik let out a snort of amusement as he imagined the frenzied preparations which would have followed the news, but he would be sure to restock the earl's larder from his own before the Jule ale was tapped.

The sun had cleared the hills now, and he paused to

breathe in the cool morning air as hoar frost was shaken from guy ropes and tent panels, and icy water was carried from the nearby burn to extinguish the campfires with a hiss. The scouts Hauk and Mord appeared before him, and Erik's mind returned from its journeying as the welcome sound of leather tents clattering on flatbeds came to his ears. He smiled. 'All set lads?'

The pair nodded happily. Independent and as reliable as night following day, they had been his eyes and ears for as long as he could recall.

Hauk answered for them both. 'Yes, lord, all saddled up and ready to go.'

Erik's gaze dropped to the satchel at his side.

Hauk patted the bag and pulled a cheeky grin. 'Just a few things for the journey, lord,' he explained. 'A joint of swine flesh, and a fresh loaf from the town.'

Erik opened his mouth to protest, but the look in the scout's eyes stilled his tongue before he uttered a sound. The trio shared a laugh, and all about men exchanged smiles to see their king in such a fine mood.

Mord indicated the wagon with a flick of his head. 'We brought back a couple of sackfuls for the rest of you King Erik, enough for the men to share a good sized chunk apiece.' He smiled. 'Most of the loaves should still be warm, despite the chilly start — a sacrifice worthy of a silver penny.'

'Aye Mord,' the king replied, 'you have the right of that!' Erik placed a hand on each man's shoulder as they walked across to the horses. 'Don't be in too much of a hurry lads,' he said. 'It has been light, what? An hour or so? That still leaves us a good ten hours to cover the twenty miles to Catrice before dark. We will ride at the pace of the wagon and give Regenwold and his household a little more time to prepare for our arrival.'

The pair hauled themselves into the saddle, guiding the horses onto the path which led eastwards back to the Roman road as the king turned away. Eager faces greeted him, and now that he knew the reason for their good humour he gave a nod that they should recover the bread sacks from the wagon and share the contents among them. 'We will eat in the saddle boys,' he called as the first of the loaves sailed through the air. He took a final look around him as Sturla Godi, as attentive as ever, began to lead the king's horse across. Erik mounted as the last of the tents and cooking pots were loaded, and as his guardsmen rode on ahead Ragnfrod guided his horse alongside the king. The youngest Eriksson cast a look across his shoulder as they began to ride away. 'Did the abbott agree to the building of a hospital father?' Erik nodded. 'There is a suitable stretch of ground on the far side of the cloister.' He turned back, stretching an arm to point out the place. 'On the level ground between the monastery buildings and the burn. I even had a conversation with Oswald's brother.'

Ragnfrod's eyes widened in alarm.

Erik laughed. 'From a distance!'

'How was he?'

'He has leprosy — he looked like shit.'

'You know what I meant — how did he take the news of his brother's death?' Before Erik could reply Ragnfrod threw his father a stony look. 'And please don't say that he laughed his head off or some such thing — I know that you are tempted, and temptation is the Devil's work.'

Erik chuckled happily at his son's dry wit. Lepers often shed body parts as the disease spread, usually extremities like ears and noses. 'Surprisingly calmly,' the king replied. 'When I told him about my plans to have a leper hospital built in memory of his brother, the man was positively jubilant.'

Erik's son was delighted. 'That was the Holy Spirit; Oswald's name will be remembered for all time, and men's prayers of thanks will raise him up to the Lord's right hand.' He glanced across as the wagon waddled across the field to the track, the ox's breath pluming as it shouldered the load. 'For a grizzled heathen, you do much that is good father.'

Erik snorted. Of all his sons only the eldest, Gamli, had spurned Christianity completely. But he knew their devotion to the eastern god was a necessity — the gods of their forefathers were receding everywhere like a passing storm on a summer day, and his sons would need to follow the Christ if they were to have any future in the rich lands of what Oswald had called Christendom. 'I am honouring a friend,' he replied, 'nothing more.'

The pair rode on in silence as the wagon made the track, the only sounds left to disturb the tranquility of the morning hoof falls and the rumble of wheels. Within a few miles the ash-grey line of Dere Street came back into view, and as the sun rose higher to burn off the frost and the fields disappeared beneath a vaporous brume, the column turned their mounts to the north. With the king's scouts already sent on ahead, Erland's man Arnald Styrsson led a handful of Orkneymen a half mile or so forward to spy out the roadway, and with a full belly and the promise of a raucous night to come Erik settled down to enjoy the ride.

Within a few miles any chatter had died off, and Erik took in the fields and woodlands of his kingdom as the clatter of hooves filled the vale. It was a fine land, wealthy in a rugged sort of way, and if the inhabitants were less ordered and dutiful than their counterparts south of the Humber he liked them all the more for it. With the wan winter sun warming his back the miles sluiced away, but if the king's mind was at peace his reverie was soon shattered as the scouts came back into view. Thorstein and Helgrim appeared at his side as they too recognised the urgency in their movements, and the sound of weapons and helms being taken up replaced the steady ring of horseshoes on stone as Erik's guards rode forward to form a screen. Within a few moments the onrushing horsemen were curbing their mounts as they approached the forward defence, and closer now Erik felt a stab of unease as he recognised his own man Hauk among them. Despite the disquiet he felt Erik forced down the urge to hurry forward, drawing rein as the guards satisfied themselves the riders were friendly. Erik's closest men had identified Hauk now, the rider's drawn features betraying the nature of his message, and they guided their horses aside as the scout trotted forward to make his report. Erik gave him permission to speak before his horse had come to a halt.

Hauk swallowed. 'Regenwold has been burned in, lord,' he blurted. 'It is all ash: hall; barn; everything.'

Aware that all eyes were upon him and mindful of his outburst with Gunnhild the previous day, Erik took a moment to quell his anger before replying. 'Have you seen the earl's body?'

Hauk shook his head. 'No lord — the moment we saw what had happened, we shied away and took cover in a nearby copse.'

Erik's eyes widened in question at the action, but he had known the man half of his life and trusted that he had good reason. Hauk had seen the look, and he supplied the answer quickly. 'Scouts don't blunder into places of danger, lord,' he said. 'Our job is to gather what information we can without getting caught or killed, and report back to our leaders.'

Erik nodded that he understood. 'Where is Mord?'

'We split up,' the scout explained. 'Mord went forward to see what he could find out, while I raced back here to warn you. They must have left a trail, and Mord is as good a tracker as any man alive.'

Movement all around him caught the king's eye, and Erik glanced about to see that he was surrounded by his leading men. 'Regenwold's hall has been burned, but there is a chance he has been taken.' As the riders shared horrified looks, Erik spat a promise through gritted teeth. 'When I find whoever has done this, they will beg for death long before I grant it.'

22

HANGI

He could smell smoke on the wind before the remains of the hall came into view. With his mind clouded by thoughts of vengeance Erik had charged ahead, oblivious to the cries of his huskarls as they spurred their horses in his wake.

Dressed for speed and lightly armed Hauk was already in the clearing when he arrived, and Erik swept the perimeter for signs of opposition as he hurled himself clear of the saddle. Moments later the oppressive silence was torn asunder as heavily armed horsemen spilled from the tree line to send a cloud of crows and magpies cawing with annoyance into the air, the riders cleaving to left and right around the figure of the king as they enclosed him in a ring of steel. Jomal was in his hand, and Erik stomped across to the smouldering remains of Regenwold's hall. Hauk dropped to the ground as he passed, his eyes already lowered as he read the telltale marks in the grass, and as his huskarls reached his side Erik's gaze took in the devastation.

A latticework of blackened beams lay at crazy angles, the

floor knee deep in ash; at the centre a withered arm rose into the air, the hand which topped it pointing claw-like towards the heavens. Erik crossed a ridge of scorched clay, all that remained from the exterior daub of the hall crunching beneath the soles of his boots as he went. He took another pace forward to overturn a heavily charred beam with the sole of his boot; immediately small flames flickered into life as they hungrily fed on the cool morning air.

Every man knew what that meant, and Ragnfrod shaped their thoughts into words. 'This happened last night.'

Erik stood tight lipped, eyes blazing as his son's conclusion caused any further comments to be stillborn. It was obvious to each man there that the casual ride from York and stop-off at Hrypum had very likely cost the life of one of the king's most ardent supporters, and men lowered their eyes as they awaited his reaction to the sobering realisation. To their surprise the king remained calm as he looked back from the ash field. 'This is an act of war,' he said, his speech monotone. 'And war is a bloodthirsty thing. Men die, but it is up to those who remain to take the blood price for those who are no longer able to do so.'

Erik lifted his chin to scan the clearing. A beck bordered the steading to the north, the southern bank a wide boggy pool where the floodwaters from the great storm were making their way from the high hills to the distant sea. Westward the woodland edge lay a short bowshot off, while to the south strips of ploughed earth on the gently sloping hillside showed where in happier times the earl's thralls and farmhands had harvested barley and spelt for his table. Erik was about to move further into the building, to sift through the ash for the body of his friend, when Kolbein called out from the southern boundary. 'There was a fight here, lord.'

Erik looked across. 'Blood?'

Kolbein nodded: 'bucketfuls.'

The king walked across, his huskarls and leading men following on as they went to inspect the scene. It was as his styrisman had said. Midway along the south facing wall the bare ground around the doorway to the hall was a crimson soup, and Erik ran experienced eyes across the scene as his mind worked through the details of the fight. There was no sign that Regenwold had led his men out to form an orderly defence of the doorway in the time-honoured way, the scrap had been a disorderly brawl. It could only mean one thing, and Helgrim confirmed the king's conclusion before Erik could give voice to it. 'No messing about — straight out through the doorway and into them,' he said. 'That means that the hall was already in flames — there was nothing to defend.'

Erik nodded. 'That is the death path any of us would have taken given the choice.' Runnels in the courtyard showed where bodies had been dragged by the scruff of the neck through the muck, and as Erik lifted his eyes to follow the tracks he found that Arnkel was already there. 'If you are wondering where they are King Erik,' the Orkneyman said. 'We have found the earl and his men.' He turned to point. 'Over there, at the woodland edge.'

Erik looked and wondered that he not noticed before, now that it was clear it had been an easy meal which had drawn crows to the place of death as it always did. A path cut the tree line to the west, and littering the sturdier branches a dozen naked cadavers swung gently in the light morning airs. Erik walked across, fixing his gaze on the dead as he went. The birds had already made a mess of the faces. As he had expected all were eyeless as the jelly they contained was a well-known crow titbit, but it was the heaped up offal in the underbrush and the vivid red gash in each belly which really drew his attention. 'We are being sent a message,' Erik said as they walked. He threw Arnkel a look. 'Can you hear it?'

The Orcadian was quick to reply. 'They are goading us, and coming this late in the year they think it unlikely we will retaliate immediately. It is no way to treat brave men Erik. I had a quick look while you came across — any wounds from the fight are to the fore, none behind.'

Erik nodded. 'I knew the earl and his men, I would expect nothing less. But if they think I will sup the Jule ale and feast house guests while my greatest earl goes unavenged they are in for a shock.'

Arnkel glanced across in surprise. 'A winter campaign? Coming so soon after the fight at Corebricg and the Scottish war, you may struggle to raise another army, lord.'

'Not an invasion, a quick strike with handpicked men.' Erik nodded towards the woodland path. Hauk was there, the scout crouching low as he brushed the earth with a hand. 'Let us see if we can catch them first. If they are only a few hours ahead we may not need a winter raid at all.' Erik came to halt before the body of his earl, biting down on his anger. Regenwold was unmistakable, despite the absence of his eyes, ears and nose, if not for the great size of his body then the distinctive cut of his hair. Practically alone among his English subjects Regenwold had always styled it in what church and laymen alike described as the Viking way, cropped at the nape with a shaggy fringe, and although his devotion to the Christian God was never in question, Erik knew that the earl had enjoyed the disapproval it had brought about and liked him all the more for it.

A brief look was enough and Erik moved on. He was no stranger to the dead, whether he had counted them among his friends or not; but he let out a sigh of regret, raising a hand to touch Olvir's blackened foot as he passed. The scout had been a loyal member of his hird from way back, and for a moment Erik's mind was back on a sun blushed field outside Tunsberg. He saw again Olvir in his youth, riding through a field of rye to bring him the news that Erik's brother Bjorn was raising an army against him, and he was sure to guard against a tremor in his voice as he walked on and spoke again. 'Cut these boys down,' he yelled. 'Bury the Christians for now and make a pyre for Olvir, but be quick about it — we are not finished today.' Erik crossed to the track as men hurried to do his bidding. Hauk was still squatting on the path, and the king hailed him as he came. 'What can you tell me?'

Deep in thought, Hauk looked up for the first time as he recognised the king's voice. Rising to his feet he let out a sigh, clucking his tongue as he thought. Finally he pointed to the hoof prints which had churned up the mud all about. 'They came in here and left the same way, but there is something I can't quite get.' A moment later he clicked his fingers as the answer came to him, and he turned his face to the king as he explained. 'More horses left than arrived — I thought at first that they had met others here.' He pointed across to the main path which led down to Dere Street. 'It could have happened like that, we would have trampled the evidence after all when we arrived, but I don't think it is.'

'How do you know?'

Hauk bent down, tracing the outline of a horse shoe with a forefinger. 'I was puzzled at first because the prints leading into the clearing are shallower than those leaving. That is usually the sign that the horses are riderless and can point to a ruse, but that was obviously ridiculous,' he replied. 'Horses as a rule don't burn folk in. Then I remembered last night's frost.'

Erik nodded that he understood. 'The earth was frozen hard when they arrived, so the prints were shallower. What about the numbers?'

'It looks like they carried Regenwold's horses away as plunder, lord' he explained. 'I would say that fifty or so arrived and a few more left, but there is another thing.' He bent again to dip a finger in the mud before holding it up for the king to see. Erik smiled for the first time since Hauk had told him of the attack, back on Dere Street an hour before. 'Blood — so they carried the dead away with them. That answers two questions,' Hauk said. 'What happened to the bodies of the men Regenwold and his lads killed and injured, and whether it was an attack by Olaf Cuaran or any other Viking or Dubliner — they are not going to carry their dead away if they are returning to a ship, so the attackers must have come from this side of the sea.'

Erik's guards and closest men were gathered nearby, and Ragnfrod Eriksson asked questions of his own. 'You are sure that they all left this way? As you say, we could have trampled the evidence of them leaving to head north along Dere Street on our way in. And where is your friend Mord? It would be good to get another opinion if we are to have any chance of catching them.'

Hauk raised a finger, walking across to brush the undergrowth with a booted foot. Within moments he was stooping to pluck something from the grass; turning back he tossed what looked to be a pebble into the air and snatched it back. 'This may look like any other,' he said as his hand went to his sark, 'and that is the idea.' Hauk pulled a white stone from a pocket and held it against the first. The pair formed a perfect whole, and the scout held it up for all to see. 'We carry half each me and Mord, so we can leave them for the other to find if we are split up. After all,' he said, 'who would suspect a stone as a messenger? This tells me that Mord has read the same story into the hoof prints here, and that he has not only gone on to track them, but he has done so freely and not been taken captive.' He threw them a smile as he explained further. 'Because if he had he wouldn't drop the stone, and even if they searched his pockets it would just be taken for a lucky charm. This track,' he said with a glance westwards, 'crosses the beck a little further up and takes you to a place called Hindrelag on the far bank of the River Swale. There it joins a wider road which cuts the corner between Dere Street and the road across Stainmore to Cumbraland.'

Erik thought he knew it. 'The road with the Roman marching camp at the summit? The one we stayed in before the attack on the Cumbrians the year before last?'

'That is right, lord — Hreyrr Camp. It is important that scouts learn all there is to know about the layout of the surrounding land, so we spend most of our spare time riding the roads and byways of the kingdom.'

'There is something equally important here,' Erik countered as he scuffed the ground with his boot. 'If the path had softened enough for the hoof prints to deepen, that means that the sun had risen high enough to burn off last night's frost before they left. You had a lucky break, they cannot have left much before you two arrived.' The realisation was all that Erik needed to decide what to do next, and his voice became a bellow as he began to retrace his steps to the place where the horses were bunching together as far away from the scene of death as possible. 'All of you,' he cried to the men there, 'mount up! The killers are not far ahead of us, and we still have the chance to avenge our friends.'

Kolbein fell in at the king's side as he crossed the clearing, and as men flew to their horses he spoke to the king in an undertone. 'Is this wise Erik?'

Erik was taken aback by his styrisman's words, and he stopped dead midway to the horse line. Turning to Kolbein, he spoke of his surprise. 'Is what wise? Taking the opportunity to avenge our men while we have the chance?'

Kolbein fingered the hammer of Þórr at his neck as he spoke again. 'The gods are against us lord,' he said with a nervous glance towards the cadavers. 'They have handed us great victories since we returned, but maybe they think they have done enough?'

'The gods are with us old friend,' he scoffed. 'If Mord and Hauk had not gone into Hrypum and purchased fresh bread this morning they would as likely as not reached Regenwold's hall before the killers left. If that had happened they would have died here with the others, and we would have journeyed here at a leisurely pace being none the wiser.'

Kolbein was not to be so easily dissuaded. 'Think about it Erik. After harrying your foe for the best part of a year and barely losing a man, three of your closest companions have died within days of one another — Oswald Thane and now Regenwold and Olvir. I gave Harald Fairhair an oath more years ago than I care to admit, back on the strand at Nausdal, that I would always protect you in word and deed and this is my rede.'

Erik threw a quick look around the clearing as the man spoke; men were in the saddle, casting expectant looks his way as he stood chatting after the call to action which had gone before. He could see their confusion and ached to leap into the saddle but Kolbein was right, his old companion had fulfilled every oath to both himself and his father for longer than many men lived and he deserved a hearing. 'Sturla Godi owns rune sticks,' Kolbein was saying. 'Why not let him read them? What harm can it do?' His hand went back to the pendant at his neck as he cast a nervous glance about the clearing. 'Old Hangi is here Erik,' he whispered, 'I can feel his presence. Óðinn is the god of the hanged, and he has come to claim his own.'

Erik shook his head. 'We have wasted enough time already, whether Hangi, Óðinn or whatever name the Allfather chooses to go by today is here or not — if we don't leave soon we will never catch the killers; Hauk says we outnumber them three to one, we must grab the chance to overtake them while it is there. How can I yell at everyone to mount up and then stop to read the runes? What impression would that give?' He placed a hand on his huskarl's arm as he guided him towards the horses. 'I want to leave a couple of men to keep the crows and animals away from the dead until we return,' he said. 'Pick a few men to do that for me and remain here with them — if things are as you say and the gods have deserted me, I can think of no one better to carry the news back to Gunnhild and my sons in York.'

Faced with the possibility of being left behind, Kolbein finally relented. 'And break my vows Erik? I have given you my advice, and that is all I was obliged to do. Come,' he said with a smile as he accepted his fate, 'let us see what the Norns have in store for us. I will detail two men to finish up here and you give the lads a speech.' Erik mounted as Kolbein picked out two of the youngest from the mounted men nearby. 'You and you — down you get; the king has a job for you.'

As the chosen pair exchanged mortified looks Erik took up the reins, walking the horse forward before turning about to face the warriors. A grim faced host stared back; Erik hawked and spat to clear his throat:

'Look behind me at what remains of our friends, strung up and butchered like swine.' Erik paused as their eyes swept the woodland edge. 'Hauk tells me that they cannot be far away so I will keep this brief. We outnumber them by a margin of three to one, and we know they have had a hard fight here and suffered death and injury. What is more,' he said with a look, 'both they and their mounts have been awake throughout the night; they are carrying wounded and will be tired from the journey and lack of sleep. The pathway behind me leads away to join up with the old Roman road up onto Stainmore and the West, so we don't know yet whether we will be facing Norsemen, Cumbrians or Scots.' He threw them a hellish look. 'But whoever it is, I could not have hoped to meet them with better men at my side.'

Erik wheeled his horse as the men bayed their support, pointing the beast towards the place where the track arced away. With a last look at the bodies of his friends swaying from the boughs nearby he plunged into the shade, and as the trees closed in and the still of the woodland was shattered by the hoof falls of an avenging army he followed the path towards the beck. With the waters in flood the bed this close to its source would be strewn with rocks and other debris carried downstream by the force of the flow, and Erik slowed his mount to a walk as he forded the swollen burn with care. But if the waters were deeper than usual the banks here contained them, and he was soon across, scrambling up the far side as he spurred his horse clear. Away from the riverside the trees drew back, and with the pathway opening up before them Helgrim and Thorstein urged their mounts forward to ride at his side. Scattered woodland become pasture as they moved further from the waterway and Erik rode on, urging the horse into a canter as the land began to trend upwards.

Within a short while they were approaching the brow of the hill, and Erik slowed the horse again to a trot as he prepared to spy out the way ahead. With the momentum bleeding away the rest of Erik's huskarls came up, and as the king's group crested the rise together they saw the first signs that the invaders had not had things all their own way that morning. Half a mile distant, beyond the ford on the River Swale, bloodied torsos lay scattered like poppies in a wheat field.

23

CENWULF THANE

The water fell in sheets as Erik rode from the ford, and as the land began to trend upwards he caught the first glimpse of movement ahead. Men were there, shield and spear carrying men ready to fight again in defence of their kin, but the leaders had already recognised one another and Erik hailed the man as he approached. 'Cenwulf Thane,' he said. 'We have had a grim morning, you and I.'

The man walked forward, and Erik noted the blood tainting his sark as he did so. 'You carry a wound?'

Cenwulf shrugged. 'It is nothing compared to the feeling of dread in my heart King Erik.'

Erik grimaced as he confirmed the thane's forebodings. 'Your earl was slain fighting to defend his hall like a hero of old, but I promise you that his killers will not outlive the day. What can you tell me of them? Do you know who they are?'

The Englishman's shoulders slumped as his worst fears were realised, and he crossed himself as he replied. 'Men of Strathclyde lord, led by king Dyfnwal in person.' Cenwulf indicated the town with a jerk of his head. 'They tried to ride through Hindrelag on their way back home, but a shepherd boy had seen the glow of flames in the southern sky and rushed to warn us. Lucky for us that he did,' the thane added, 'for it meant we were out of our beds and ready to repel the bastards when they arrived. Earl Regenwold's hall is the only building in that direction, and we were saddling horses to come to his aid when they appeared.' He sighed. 'At first I had hoped that we would arrive to help the earl fight a fire, but when Dyfnwal and his raiders crested the hill opposite I feared that it was a hall burning and my lord was already dead.'

Erik cursed. 'I should have killed the brat long ago,' he spat, 'the gods know that I have had enough opportunities. How many men accompanied him?'

The thane's features became a frown. 'Forty or fifty? It was difficult to tell King Erik — not only was the sun at their back as they tried to force their way through, there were also riderless horses among them.' Despite his wound, Cenwulf puffed out his chest. 'They attempted to hack their way past us, but we kept them out. In the end they had to bypass the village,' he said as he raised an arm to point, 'down there, to the West. That was an hour after dawn, although a lone rider followed on an hour or so after that. We would have ridden to the earl's hall, but with raiders in the area I had to look to the safety of the families here before I went chasing off over the hill with the able bodied men.'

Erik noted the hint of shame in the man's voice and moved to lay his fears. 'There is no blame attached to yourself or your men, you did well to deny them passage through your village; who knows what destruction they would have caused had they got through. As for the lone rider, he was one of my scouts. If it is Dyfnwal we seek, the bastard will be looking to cut the corner before taking the old road across the moors to get home by way of Cumbraland. How far away is the road from here?'

'Only five miles,' Cenwulf replied. 'Follow this track north and it will lead you directly to it. With your permission King Erik, I will send out riders to muster the fyrd as I recover the body of my earl and his friends.' The thane fixed his king with a look of determination as he went on. 'Even if I arrive too late to witness the death of my lord's killers, I should like the satisfaction of gazing upon their corpses.'

Erik replied with a curt nod. 'You would be welcome — no leader ever complained that his army was too large.'

Recognising the figure of the king and thankful that they would be spared a fight against such overwhelming numbers, the shield wall barring the way ahead had quickly broken up, and Erik guided his mount aside with a tug on the reins as he glanced at the position of the sun. It was already the third hour, he was at least a couple of hours behind the men he wanted to kill. 'If I am to catch them I need to keep moving,' he said, clicking his tongue to urge the horse forward. 'I have left two men with the dead back at the hall. Have the Christians buried at the church here, and I will attend to the heathen upon my return.'

Erik rode forward, past the lines of grateful men and into Hindrelag itself. The usual gawping faces staring from open doorways and he was through, the king urging his horse into a gallop as the path ran directly across what would have been a field of sun kissed barley only a few months before. Away from Hindrelag the fields gave way to woodland, and as the trees crowded in and the shadows lengthened it became a simple thing to follow the tracks of the invaders as the pathway turned muddy. Twin hills channelled the track as Erik led the army northwards, and as the gradient increased the trees drew back once again to reveal the figure of Mord on the skyline ahead. Erik urged his horse up the final slope, and as the men of York spewed from the greenwood behind him he reined in and pointed to the West. 'That way?'

The scout nodded. 'Yes, King Erik — we are chasing fifty armed riders from Strathclyde led by Dyfnwal.'

Erik nodded. 'Yes, I know. We were told their identity by Cenwulf Thane back in Hindrelag. How far ahead are they?'

'I left them resting at a place called Bogas, but the conditions hereabouts make them difficult to track.' The scout cast a contemptuous look at the surrounding countryside. 'The moors are too open with barely a tree,' he explained, 'and I was forced to leave the road and use what cover I could find — dips, gullies and the like. Luckily they do not appear to be in too much of a hurry, the majority of the time I was observing them they were riding at little more than a walking pace.'

Erik's eyes flashed. 'I had hoped as much. If they had had any idea I was in the area they would not have gone ahead with the attack — this time of year they expected that I would be keeping snug and warm in York. Now they are making for home on tired mounts, without an inkling that I am on their trail.' Erik's mind was working as he spoke, and he seemed to recall the name of the place where Dyfnwal and his men had camped from the last time he had ridden the road — on his way to rest up at the big Roman fort at Hreyrr before the battles at Haydon and Corebricg. 'Bogas?' he said. 'Is that the place with the stone bridge?'

Mord nodded. 'That's right lord. The English call it that because the bridge is bow shaped. There are a couple of huts and the remains of a smallish fort, nothing grand, just folk eking out a living offering food and shelter to passing travellers.'

'And how far away are we?'

'About ten miles, but most of the route is through patchy woodland so we can use the road for speed without fear of being spotted. The final few miles will be in the open as the path begins to climb up towards the summit, so we will have to assume that we will be in for a tail chase once their guards see us coming.' Mord sighed. 'I wanted to stay and trail them, but I couldn't be sure you knew who we were facing. Once they reached a stone sett road they could have gone in either direction without leaving any trace, and with Hauk now swinging from a bough we lost our best tracker in the fight at the earl's hall last night.'

Erik slipped a silver ring from his forearm and handed it across to the scout's obvious surprise. 'Humility is a Christian trait,' he said, 'and I don't recall seeing you at any service I have endured, but tail chase or not they are weary men riding tired horses. We shall run them to ground long before they can reach the western dales, avenge our friends, and feed the carcasses to the crows.'

In the short time it had taken for the scout to make his report the rest of the army had made the roadway, and Erik wheeled his horse as they fell into line and issued a curt call to battle. 'A short while ago they were resting ten miles ahead of us,' he snarled. 'We outnumber them three to one, so bring to mind the sights which met us back at Regenwold's hall and leave none alive.' By the time the words were out his horse had turned full circle, and Erik threw back his heels as his huskarls rode to his side. Before the crash of hooves on stone could drown it out Erik thrilled to the sound of his battle banner snapping free from its ties, and as the column picked up speed and the trees closed about them once again the greenwood quickly became a blur.

Within a short time the woodland began to thin, and despite the steepening slope Erik urged his horse to make an extra effort as he sought to bring the murderers beneath the blade of his axe before they could escape. As the trees fell away behind him the gradient increased again, doglegging to the south as it traversed the hillside before straightening out once more to head for the summit now clearly in view. Erik cursed as the turn sapped the momentum from his ride, and his worst fears were confirmed within an instant as the blare of a warning horn drifted down from the heights above. The sound came again as he reached the turning point, the *yip-yip-yip* more urgent now as the upslope filled with his men, and Erik tugged at the reins as the road changed course for a final time to run the last mile to the bridge.

In the clear now Erik reached back to retrieve a javelin from its carrying place, raising his eyes to catch a glimpse of the enemy as the first wisps of smoke were teased from the lodges at Bogas by a freshening wind. The leading men were clearly in view half a mile ahead, crouched forward as they urged tired mounts into a gallop, but closer still Erik thrilled to the sight as the last of the raiders gained the approach to the bridge and the first lick of flame began to show at doors and windows. They were obviously the men who had been ordered to fire the buildings before they followed on, and Erik shifted the weight of the spear in his hand as he grasped the chance to bring a horseman down despite the distance. Erik's arm went back the instant he found the point of perfect balance, and a moment later the breath exploded from him as he channelled all of his strength into the throw. The king was already reaching for another as the javelin flew true, but as he watched the point of the spear began to trend downward and he knew it would fall short. Moments later the blade of the weapon was striking the setts a glancing blow, skipping along the ancient surface in a welter of sparks before disappearing into the grass at the roadside. The attempt had not gone unnoticed by the enemy horseman, and Erik watched with satisfaction as the rider bringing up the rear looked back, the pale oval of his face betraying his fear even at a distance.

As the last of the enemy cleared the apex of the bridge and dropped from sight, Erik led the men of York past the aged ramparts of the old Roman fort and through the burning buildings of Bogas. Scattered about the bodies of the inhabitants lay like bloody rags, but Erik's horse paid them little heed, barely breaking its stride as it picked its way between them. With the settlement behind him the land steepened again as it approached the bridge, and higher now Erik could see that Dyfnwal and his raiders were little more than half a mile ahead.

But if the change in tone told him that he had gained the bridge, the sight which met his eyes as he crested the high point caused the king to gasp in horror. Certain in their minds that they could never outrun the pursuers on weary mounts, the rearguard had turned back to face down death rather than be hacked to pieces from behind as they fled. Taken by surprise, Erik instinctively hauled on the reins as the wall of shields appeared before him blocking the exit to the bridge, and he let out a curse as the horse struggled for grip on the slippery setts. An instant later horse and rider were going down, and it was all that Erik could do to snatch his leg away as the animal crashed on its side and began to career towards the enemy. The points of their spears were less than a dozen paces away, beyond them the grim faces of men who knew they were about to die, and Erik knew that he would have to act quickly if he were not to beat them to Heaven or Valhöll. The torso of his horse had begun to spin as it careered onward, and Erik pulled his knees into his chest as he waited for the rump to come around. The moment it did so his feet shot forward, and as he felt his slide towards certain death begin to slow his hand had already found the grip of his sword. Erik drew the weapon in a flash, opening his body as he prepared to fight back, but even as he did so a glimpse was all it took to show that his horse had already started the killing. Spinning like a top the beast had crashed into the defenders, bowling men aside as it crashed through their ranks, and as Erik looked on a flailing hoof shot out to shatter a skull with an audible *crack!*

A heartbeat later Erik's world darkened as his guards swept over and around him, and as the clash of steel replaced the clatter of hooves the king scrambled to his feet. Bodies appeared at his side as the rest of the men dropped from their saddles to rush to his defence, but as he prepared to lead them in a charge Erik saw that he was already too late. With their last-ditch defence shattered by Erik's horse, the men of Strathclyde were now reduced to fighting singly or in pairs as the king's veteran guardsmen chased them down. Helgrim Smiter was moving among the fallen, his bloody axe blade rising and falling as he stove in the skulls of those who had been crushed or thrown aside by the skidding horse. As the last defenders fell and his mount finally regained its feet to trot aside Erik stomped forward, bellowing his orders as he went. 'Somebody get my horse — and the rest of you remount,' he cried with a sharp look. 'Every moment we spend here allows the enemy to draw further away.'

Back on his feet and with the way ahead clear, Erik was able to see the carnage which the horse had caused among the enemy defenders for the first time. Several bodies lay twisted and broken, and bloody streaks on the roadway led to the place where one of the men had been pinned beneath the body of the horse as it slid across the setts. The horse had quickly recovered from its ordeal, lowering its neck to pull at the roadside verge now that the fighting had ended, and Erik rushed across as he sought to chase down the fleeing king of Strathclyde and his gang of murderers.

Erik cursed as he ran his eyes over the wounded beast. Raw flesh glistening in the pale light of a northern winter day showed where patches of skin had been pared from the horse's flank, and further down the belly strap hung by a thread where the weight of the horse had ground it against the roadway. Even if the animal was still up to the chase there was little chance that the saddle would hold together, and his eyes flew to the raiders' horses as he raged at his luck. Kolbein's words of warning back at the hall came to mind, but the die was cast whether Óðinn was with him or against him, and he was about to throw himself into the saddle when Ragnfrod appeared and dropped down at his side. 'Here father,' he snapped, 'take my mount. A king needs to be seen to lead, and this old nag will never keep up. Besides, horses are not without feelings — they have looked on as the men they knew and trusted were chopped to pieces before them, and he may not be prepared to give his all for his master's killers. Your horse looks a bit battered, but I doubt there is anything badly wrong with him. I will check him over while one of my lads replace the saddle with this one — it will only take a short while, and we will follow on.'

Erik grabbed the reins, hauling himself into the saddle as Sturla rushed over to transfer the king's weapons from one horse to the other. Glancing down Erik spoke to his son as he prepared to ride. 'So, you know what a horse is thinking now eh? That must be more Christian wisdom.'

Ragnfrod smiled as he slapped the horse on the rump. 'Common sense father — get going, the army is waiting for you to lead them. I will catch you up as soon as I can.'

Erik clicked his tongue, guiding the horse across to the roadway as his huskarls threw themselves onto the backs of their own. Within moments the soft thud of hooves on grass changed back to a stony clatter, and as Erik's body craned forward and his heels went back the horse sped away. After the zigzag which had caused them so much trouble when they exited the tree line Erik was pleased to see the road ahead ran as straight as a spear shaft towards the distant summit, and as the horse flew westwards he screwed up his eyes as he attempted to pick out the fleeing men of Strathclyde against the muted tones of the hillside. Instantly he had them, the raiders a ribbon of gaudy colour less than a mile ahead, and although his own horse was still gathering speed he could already tell that he was gaining on them.

Erik lowered his head, hugging the horse's neck as he sought to gain every advantage in speed that he could, and as the hummocky outlines of a drumlin field flashed by to either side he snatched another look. To his great joy the wild ride was about to reel in the last of the raiders, and with the gradient increasing as they approached the summit the gap was narrowing with every passing moment. As the first fugitive came within reach Erik drew his sword, ready to strike, but at the very moment he unleashed the blow the rider threw a rearwards glance. The look came just in time, and if the horseman had been slow to realise how near the enemy had come his reactions were whiplash fast, and Erik's powerful sword strike became little more than a glancing blow as the man ducked and squirmed from its path. Erik reversed the sweep as the horse thundered past, the blade whistling as it cut the air, but although he missed again a snatched look told him that his opponent's deliverance had been brief as the rider was engulfed by an avenging Norse army.

Witnessing the fate of their countryman the riders ahead were urging their horses on, gruff voices in a foreign tongue and the crack of the lash making plain their desperation, and

Erik brought his blade up as the next enemy came closer. The sword flashed again, and there was no mistake this time as Erik felt the blade drive through mail, leather and woollen undershirt to cleave muscle and backbone. As the foeman crumpled and fell away with a yell Erik raised his gaze, desperate to see how close he had come to the man he wanted dead most of all. But if he had thought the day almost won the sight that met his eyes came as a shock, for the rampart of Hreyrr Camp — a dark line against the lighter clouds beyond only moments before — was now black with men.

24

SVINFYLKING

Dyfnwal and his guardsmen were already coming within arrow range of the fort's defenders, and Erik spat a curse as he wheeled the horse to the right and came to a halt. Within an instant he was ringed by his huskarls, and as Sturla Godi carried the king's war banner to his side a ring of shields was drawn tightly around the body of the king. Experienced eyes were already scanning the walls of the old marching fort as they measured the scale of the threat, and Helgrim Smiter spoke as the rest of the army left the roadway to deploy to the rear. 'I make it one hundred and forty manning the walls, plus a further forty or so remaining with the column.' He spat his contempt for the numbers opposing them. 'If that is supposed to be an ambush, they might be in for a shock when we get among them.'

Kolbein added words of caution. 'Who can say if what we see before us is all the spears they have? Not only could an army be forming up within the fort itself, why are they there at all?' Erik listened as the veteran went on. 'There are too many to supply remounts or meet the king and escort him home, so why not take the whole lot down to burn in Regenwold?'

Thorstein chipped in with a reply. 'Because they would never have crammed so many horsemen into a small space like Regenwold's courtyard. They were in hostile country, they needed to be in and out before they were spotted, and fifty men were enough to do the job.'

Erik listened in as his men offered their opinions, but time was against them and his mind made up. Aware that precious momentum was bleeding away from his attack with every passing moment, the king made his decision known. 'Everything you say, for and against an attack, is good advice and you have my thanks. It is true that I am not the same man who was the first over the walls of Dublin, but if age has dulled my senses and chipped away at my strength my heart remains that of a Haraldsson. The truth is that if I had not listened to Gunnhild and brought along more men than I intended, we could not have pursued them at all and their plan would have met with success.' Erik turned to Kolbein and winked. 'Maybe Óðinn can wait awhile yet to add our little company to his army of heroes.'

The screech of a golden eagle interrupted the king, faces turning skyward as one as they watched the bird soar against a backdrop of wind shredded clouds. Erik smiled as his closest companions looked back. 'If it is a sign its meaning is lost on me, and we have not the time for Sturla to read the runes. If they thought to trap us here they have made a mistake; we know the layout of this fort as well as any men alive, for we spent the night within its walls before the attack on the army of Cumbraland not so long ago. Our horses have been on the road since dawn, and we must assume that the majority of those facing us now are fresh; we cannot outrun them, even if we wanted to — we must attack.'

Erik eased his horse free of the crush, hauling at the reins to ride along the front of the army as he raised a bloodied sword aloft. 'Follow me lads,' he called as he rode, 'draw your weapons and follow me!' Erik left the roars of his army behind as he angled across the slope, Thorstein and Helgrim Smiter moving up to screen the king from arrow and spear fall as he rode. The ground underfoot changed from coarse grasses to moss and lichen as he rode, and soon the horse was picking its way through the marshy ground Erik recalled from before. As the taunts and jeers of his enemies died away and the rumble of a horse army filled his ears, Erik pointed the head of his mount towards the West. This late in the year the ground was a stony marsh, but he urged the horse onward as he sought to gain the gap before the enemy could react. The pale orb of the sun peaked through leaden clouds throwing long shadows away to the north, but if the sunlight only lasted for an instant it was enough, and Erik saw that his memory had served him well. Ahead the eastern wall of Hreyrr Camp ended abruptly, and as he rounded the corner he saw again where the ancients had trusted to the boggy nature of the ground to act in place of a full-scale bulwark.

With the northern limit defended by a sporadic bank and ditch Erik led the men of the *Draki* into the enclosure, sliding from the saddle as his eyes took in the details. Outflanked by Erik's tactics men were tumbling back into the interior of the old fort from the eastern wall, and a quick look across to the place where the enemy were beginning to form up told the king that no hidden force awaited them. As Erik's fears of an ambush subsided the king took heart, and his confidence soared again as he saw now that he had run Dyfnwal to ground. If his Norwegians were outnumbered it was only two to one; soon Ragnfrod would arrive with his men, and though the numbers would still be against them, a Norseman had never shirked a fight with any Briton for want of valour. Within moments the width of the fort had filled with his army, and Erik thrilled to the sound of pommels and axe hafts beating a tattoo on lime wood boards as the men of his army set up their battle cry:

Blóðøx! — Blóðøx! — Blóðøx!

The enemy were flooding the southern end of the fort as they strove to regroup before the imminent attack, and Erik allowed himself a nod of satisfaction as he saw that his calculations were correct. They may be outnumbered, but the constrictions placed upon the opposing war bands by the walls made it unlikely that either could be outflanked. Nevertheless, until Ragnfrod arrived with his crew there remained a couple of yards of empty ground between each Norwegian, but Erik knew the perfect answer and he held up his hand for silence as he turned to face the men. As the chants trailed away he drew Jomal with a flourish, calling out as he walked the ranks.

'Axemen — step forward!'

The men walked proud of the line, scything the air in great arcs as they loosened muscles for the hard fight ahead. Erik spoke again as they came. 'The rest of you form two svinfylking alongside Arnkel and Erland's Orkneymen.'

Erik threw a look across his shoulder as the remaining men hurried across to do his bidding. Less than a hundred yards away the men of Strathclyde were still dressing their lines, and he could imagine the disappointment among them that what appeared to be a carefully prepared trap had been so easily defeated. No fighting man is very comfortable with the thought that his leaders have been outwitted, and shorn now of the protection of the bank and ditch of the Roman wall, the first doubts would begin to chip away at their confidence despite their numbers. But he had to attack, and quickly, if he was to take full advantage of their disarray, and the king loped across to take position at the centre of the axemen as the twin swine heads took shape. Erik felt a moment of regret that he did not have *ulfhéðnar* or *berserkir* to lead the assault — after all Óðinn's wolf-warriors and bear-shirts lived for days such as these; but they were not the sort to invite along to the beery feast where he had expected to be, and he pushed the thought aside as he raised his war axe, gave voice to his battle cry and snapped into a run.

As the answering cries from the men at his back filled the bowl, Erik increased the pace. One hundred yards quickly became eighty and then fifty as he closed in on the enemy, and Erik scanned the formation ahead as he sought out the ideal place to land the first blow. As the distance narrowed he found it, the terror in the man's expression obvious as he struggled to bring his shield up in the disorganised crush, and Erik angled his run towards him as Jomal began to swing. In a panic the enemy spearman dragged the shield fully up to cover his head, but the action had left his midriff exposed as Erik had known it would, and he adjusted the pace to take full advantage of his enemy's mistake. Unsighted the Strathclyde warrior was unable to react as Erik launched himself into the air, Jomal scything around to clear a path through enemy spears as he did so. Within a heartbeat the sole of Erik's boot was sinking into the defender's belly, and as the man was driven back into the second rank Jomal continued to move. Erik's shoulders pivoted as the axe cut a murderous swathe through the front ranks, and as blood and limbs flew all around him he hit out to either side, broadening the breach. As the enemy shrunk back before the sweep of the axe, Erik snatched a look to the West. All along the line the axemen had sown death and confusion in the forward ranks of the defence, and with the imminent arrival of the swine heads

Erik knew that it was time to withdraw lest the swing of his axe disrupt their attack. A rearward step took him free of an enemy wall now broken and disordered, and as the Dane axe slowed and came to a halt his huskarls rushed forward to envelop their lord in a protective wedge.

At the same moment the first svinfylking smashed into the wall fifty paces away, and Erik watched as the leading men took full advantage of the mayhem caused by the axemen's attack to drive deep. Erik's hopes of a decisive victory rose as the men of Strathclyde wavered and appeared on the verge of breaking, but more and more were rushing forward to shore up the defence and raising his gaze Erik saw why. Beyond the place where king Dyfnwal stood beneath his war flag men were pouring into the fort through a western gate, and although their numbers were far from overwhelming the steady stream was having an affect. Men on the cusp of retreat rediscovered their courage as the numbers swelled, and Erik took the snap decision to re-enter the fray before the shock of the Norwegian attack subsided. A curt command from the king was all that was required for the formation to slide smoothly into being, and as Thorstein stood in his customary place of honour at the head of Erik's own scaled-down swine head Grettir and his brother Gunnar slipped in behind. With Kolbein Herjolfsson as his right hand man and Sturla Godi to his rear, Helgrim Smiter slipped in to make the wedge formation complete as Erik prepared to advance again. The king cried out above the din, as shields were raised and swords drawn. 'Thorstein! We are aiming directly for Dyfnwal — kill the king and they will break, whatever the numbers.' Without taking his eyes from the enemy spearmen only a few paces away his huskarl gave a nod of recognition, and Erik spoke to his banner man as he prepared to drive forward again: 'Sturla!'

'Yes, lord?'

'Make the signal for the axemen to renew the attack!'

Sturla was close enough for Erik to feel the war horn brush the back of his brynja as it came up, and he prepared to move forward as the bugle was turned aside and the rising note filled the air. The moment the familiar sound came Thorstein burst forward, his sword blade a swatch of silver-grey in the sunless gloom of a Pennine winter day. All along the line axeman and spearmen attacked again, throwing themselves forward as they sought to stop the enemy line reforming. Reaching the enemy Thorstein's sword became a blur as he hacked and hacked again, and within moments he had broken through the faltering defence and was cutting a path towards the king. Grettir and Gunnar joined in as their swords came to bear, and soon Erik was preparing to burst forth from the wedge as the king of Strathclyde grew closer. For a moment Erik's heart came into his mouth as a line of spearman appeared on the ramparts and he feared he had been undone; but he recognised the war flag of his son Ragnfrod before he could wheel to face down the threat, and he urged his guardsmen on as his own reinforcements began to tumble into the fortress.

Ragnfrod's shipmen slammed into the right wing of the Strathclyde defence, and as the Britons staggered under the blow Erik looked again at the enemy leader. If he was not surprised to see the king of Strathclyde in retreat the manner of it struck him as odd, and the first inkling that something was not quite right began to pluck at his thoughts. Rather than a panicked flight the king and his guards were retreating in good order, and lifting his chin to peer beyond them Erik saw the reason for the first time. Fresh warriors were still entering the fort through the western gate, but unlike the first to come through at the start of the fight who had hastened forward to shore up the defence, the newcomers were busily forming a new wall of shields fifty yards to the south. A battle horn sounded then, and as he watched the wings of the Strathclyde army in contact with Erik's men contracted to form a protective horseshoe around their king. The reorganisation had caught the Norwegians by surprise, and thinking the enemy on the point of breaking the compact wedges of the svinfylking broke apart as the men they contained prepared to chase down the fleeing enemy.

Only Erik appeared to have realised that the retreat had been a carefully planned manoeuvre, and he quickly saw the danger as the cohesion of the Norwegian attack began to unravel. He snapped an order to Sturla at his rear as he scrambled to retrieve the situation: 'Sturla — sound the recall!' As the horn came up and the long falling note drowned out the premature roars of victory, the first battle cries that day came from the men of Strathclyde standing in rank before them:

Mar-wol-aeth! — Mar-wol-aeth! — Mar-wol-aeth!

Erik looked at the faces of his army, gauging their reaction as the sound was amplified by the walls of the old fortress. If the confidence displayed by the enemy had come as a shock to many Norse, the fact that the Britons had taken their word for death as a prearranged battle cry clearly filled them with foreboding, and Erik realised that he must rally them quickly if he was to have any hope of winning the day as enemy numbers continued to grow. The axemen took too long to array, and with the disintegration of the swine heads all order had gone. Erik cried above the din as he ordered them back in line, pointing out the men who were to lead the follow up assault as he went: 'Orkneymen — reform the svinfylking behind your leaders to the west; men of the *Draki* we take the centre; the rest of you form up behind Ragnfrod to the east.' Erik called again as the men rushed to do his bidding. 'One last push lads — pin them with their backs to the wall and we have them.'

Ragnfrod hurried across as the battle wedges began to reform, and the army of Strathclyde remade their lines two score paces away. 'There are other war bands abroad father,' he said ominously. 'We could see them coming from the East as we rode to overtake you.'

Erik nodded that he understood. 'Be that as it may, we need to attack again while the men still have fire in their blood. Let us see if we can hack our way through to the man we came here to kill — do that and the army of Strathclyde will break. When the man who killed Regenwold is dead, we can decide whether we stand and face any newcomers or take to our horses.' He clumped his youngest son on the arm as a realisation lifted his spirits. 'Who knows they may well be friends? Cenwulf Thane raised a hue and cry after we left; I witnessed the man's worth and the love he had for earl Regenwold during the campaign in Alba this summer past. He told me he would follow on when he had raised the local levy, and I trust his word. Nevertheless you are right to be concerned,' Erik said, flicking a look at the walls which hemmed them in. 'Attacking within the confines of the fort may have been to our advantage, but now that we know there are other war bands about I should have liked to have been able to see further.' His gaze crossed to the old lookout station then, the tumbledown building still dominating the skyline as it had since the days the fort had echoed to the vulgar latin of the legions. 'Station a keen-eyed man on the rampart where you came in until we can push the enemy back beyond the tower. As soon as we take it, we can recall him and post lookouts at the top.' Seeing the king's confidence, Ragnfrod brightened. 'It is as you say lord,' he chirped, 'they may be friends.' He shot his father a smile, and Erik's heart lifted with the pride he felt as his youngest added a rejoinder. 'One last push to finish the day then, lest we are forced to share the glory with Englishmen.'

Erik watched his son as he trotted back to his men. The trust that he displayed in his father's abilities was touching if a little starry-eyed, and he felt a pang of regret that he had brought him along despite his brave words. Maybe Gunnhild and Kolbein were right he reflected, as spear shafts began to beat out a thunderous din and the men in both armies exchanged war cries and javelins — he was not the wolf after all, and Oðinn was up to his tricks. But the self-doubt only lasted a heartbeat before the Erik Bloodaxe of old reasserted itself, and he allowed himself a snort of derision at his moment of weakness as his older sons came to mind. If men *were* referring to his reign as the day of the wolf, then Gamli Eriksson was his wild cub. With no desire for the responsibilities which went with a kingdom of his own the young man had all the makings of a fine sea king, a raider to terrorise the shores and rivers of Christendom and beyond. Harald would be a king and rule a kingdom, Gunnhild would see to that — and a fine king he would make Erik decided as the battle cries rose to a crescendo all around him. Raised within the bosom of a loving family the younger lads would at least live long enough to find their rightful place in the world, unlike the offspring of Fairhair who he now realised had pit cub against cub, while up in Orkney folk said that Ragnhild was her mother's daughter, and there was no greater praise to be had.

Erik's mind came back from his reflections as he saw that he was now surrounded by a wall of steel, and a glance to either side told the king that the swine heads were complete and awaiting his command. Ahead the men of Strathclyde were beginning to quieten as they prepared to face another attack, and Erik smiled his war smile as he raised his sword aloft. The very air seemed to still as the blade pointed skyward, and Erik savoured the weight of the moment. Despite his misgivings he had always prized days like these above all others, the fleeting moments when friend and foe alike held their breath and turned their eyes to him. Occasions such as this only came a handful of times in a lifespan, and then only to a favoured few. But he had been one such man, one of the very best, and if the Norns decided that his days were spent he knew that he would never have changed a thing.

The blade chopped down, and as the pent-up tension was released in a howl of war lust, the sawtooth blade of the Norwegian assault began to move forward again.

25

TREACHERY

The first few steps were at walking pace, the leading men reining in the desire to spurt forward with difficulty as those at the rear dressed their lines. If the swine heads were to punch through to the enemy leaders they would have to arrive as one hard blow, a mailed fist to the guts which would knock the wind from the front rankers and open the way through to the softer belly beyond. Erik ran his eyes along the enemy formation as the pace quickened. The shouts and taunts from the men of Strathclyde had petered out as they conserved their strength for the fight which was now only moments away, and as he raised his eyes to look beyond the spears and shields of the front row Erik saw to his disappointment that Dyfnwal was now encased within a protective screen fifty men deep. The formations were moving at a fast jog now as the enemy grew in their sight, and as spears and arrows crisscrossed the rapidly shrinking gap, Thorstein hurled a cry of dedication to Óðinn into the raw mountaintop air and broke into a run.

Erik's shield came up to swat an arrow aside as they ran,

and as Thorstein's blade swung in arcs to silver the air the svinfyliking hit. The wedge came to a juddering halt as the enemy line bowed inwards to soften the blow, but as the salient widened and his crewmen brought their spears and sword blades into play they began to inch forward again. At the head of the formation Thorstein could still be seen, fighting like a berserk as he hacked and stabbed at anyone in sight, and behind him Gunnar and Grettir jabbed blades into faces and necks as they strove to guard his flanks with more measured strikes.

Erik grabbed the last chance to gauge the success of the assault, snatching a look to either side as he came closer to the fighting. The rise and fall of sword and axe blades showed that both wings had advanced further than the central attack, and the king's hopes of a quick victory rose as he saw that the boar banner of Orkney was almost up with the squat platform upon which the signal tower stood out as a stark column against the lighter clouds beyond. Very soon the defenders at the foot would find themselves pushed back into the ditch which ringed it, and with it any chance of an organised defence would vanish. When that happened Erik knew that men of Arnkel and Erland's experience would wheel their army eastwards, rolling up the line and threatening Dyfnwal's guards themselves. With Ragnfrod's attack gathering pace on his left flank, Erik turned his attention back to the fight before him as his confidence soared. King Dyfnwal and his henchmen were well within spear shot beneath the war banner of Strathclyde, and despite the fact that upwards of a hundred men still stood between them, Erik was convinced that a breakthrough was only moments away.

As if to confirm his conviction the wedge surged forward again, and as the advance carried him level with the foremost enemy he gripped the hilt of his sword a little tighter as Helgrim Smiter lunged outwards at his side. A gap opened up where his huskarl had been, and Erik grabbed at the chance to make a contribution of his own for the first time since he had stowed his war axe following the opening attack. Erik's sword stabbed out as a spearman reeled beneath the ferocity of Helgrim's charge, and the king had the satisfaction of feeling the blade burst through mail and leather as his foe crumpled to his knees. Helgrim was cutting a deadly swathe through the enemy, and Erik stepped up to widen the rift as his shipmates rushed forward in support. Across the breadth of the old fort Norwegian blades were driving all before them, and as the defenders tried desperately to retreat in good order, Erik felt the springiness underfoot replaced by the unyielding feel of stone as they gained the roadway. With the change came the realisation of just how far the Norwegian onslaught had pushed back the foe in so short a space of time, and the king took a rearward pace to extract himself from the fighting as he sought to gauge the progress elsewhere. As he did so the men of his hird rushed forward to renew the pressure on the foe, and safe for the moment Erik threw a hopeful look to the West. He was not to be disappointed. The Orcadians were already across the road, the leading fighters now trading blows with Dyfnwal's bodyguards as the men who had failed to halt their advance fled the field. The surviving enemy were now squeezed into the final few yards of the old fortification, and although the remains of twin gateways in the southern bank still offered a means of escape to the beleaguered force, Erik looked on wolfishly as a breakout by a party of Orkneymen moved up to seal them off.

Erik switched his gaze to the East, his conviction hardening with every passing moment that the men who only

hours before had burned in and mutilated some of his closest
friends were about to pay for the act with their lives. Ragnfrod's advance had ground to a halt now that the enemy were
pinned back into the angle of the fort, but on the roadway
beyond a flash of colour drew his attention and the king's
confidence took a knock as he saw the first signs of movement through the eastern gateway. Erik's eyes narrowed in
suspicion as mounted warriors swept by, and his head shot
across to the top of the rampart as he searched for the lookout
his son had set to watch the road. Spearmen were in his place,
their weapons wooding the air as they welcomed the
newcomers to the fight, and Erik's eyes now widened in
alarm as he came to realise the significance of the sight. With
every Norseman bar the horse guard heavily engaged it could
only mean one thing, and the king felt a knot of fear tighten
in his guts as he looked. Erik's eyes flew back to the place
where the Roman road cut the walls, and he spat a name as
his worst fears were confirmed by a familiar face hardening
from the ruck: 'Maccus…'

ERIK WITHDREW from the fighting as he waited for the
newcomers to enter the fort, pushing his way through to the
rear as the men of the *Draki* continued to throw themselves
upon the enemy. Confused by the retreat, his bodyguards
detached themselves from the front ranks and followed on as
best they could, but for the moment at least the king was
accompanied only by his standard bearer as the first of the
riders swept into the interior. Riding beneath the flag of St
Cuthbert Maccus the Easterner was near the head of the
column, and Erik fixed the man with a stare as he attempted
to divine his intentions. He barked a command to his banner

man as he did so. 'Sturla — lower my war flag for the moment. Let us see where they head…'

Maccus's eyes swept the interior of the fort as horsemen continued to pour into the clearing, and as the riders began to fan out and haul the heads of their mounts to the south Erik turned and bellowed a command. 'Rear ranks! Turnabout and form a skjald-borg!' The first of his men were already turning as more Bernicians entered the confines of the fortress, and the thunder of hooves began to drown out the clash of steel on steel; but if the king's command had caused them to exchange looks of disquiet their discipline held, and a flash of colour lit the scene as the boards clattered into place. The movement had caught Maccus' eye, and Erik watched with interest as, convinced now that the man had come as an enemy, the Bernician's head snapped around. With the defences now in place, Erik spoke again. 'Sturla, raise the banner — let us see what he does.'

The effect was immediate, and Erik watched with a curious mixture of regret and satisfaction that he had been right to doubt their loyalty as the Bernician force wheeled about and drove directly for him. Despite his disappointment, Erik knew that the act of revealing his whereabouts while the enemy were still in line of march would be a success. Not only had he saved the unsuspecting rear ranks of all three swine heads from suffering a surprise attack from horsemen they had every right to regard as allies, but he knew that the attackers would arrive piecemeal before his own defences and suffer accordingly. Denied the opportunity to wheel and canter the length of the line, stabbing down on the heads and shoulders of the defenders as they went, the Bernicians would now be forced to come face to face with their intended victims. Unable to manoeuvre, and with the length of the horses' head, neck and withers between them and the defenders, they would be leaning forward as they struck — opening up their bodies to the defenders' spear thrusts and depriving their own counterstroke of much of its power.

The distance between the two forces shrank rapidly as the horses came on, and Erik called a final order as they prepared to fight again. 'Keep your shields tight lads, and use your spears to hold them off. Frustrate the attack and they will be forced to retreat and dismount.' The final words had barely escaped his lips when the latest opponents were upon them, and Erik hunkered into his shield as the head of a horse loomed over him. His spear stabbed out as he did so, the wickedly sharp point sliding easily into the flesh of the animal's long neck, and as it screamed and shied away Erik was already dragging the blade clear to send the follow-up strike knifing into the soft tissue beneath the horse's jaw. The blade powered through skin and flesh until the king felt it jar against the base of the horse's skull, but the delay was momentary as bone shattered and the point punched through. Erik swished the blade back and forth as he made a mash of the animal's brain, and as the horse's eyes went wide and its legs began to buckle, the king withdrew the blade in a gush of gore-flecked blood. Unable to keep his balance as the horse writhed beneath him the enemy rider took a wild swing with his sword, but even before the king could bring his spear shaft across to deflect the blow, the point of Erik's war standard had taken the man in the throat to send him flying backwards to the ground.

Along the entirety of its length the shield wall was holding firm as the experience of the Norwegians told, and the king looked on in satisfaction as Maccus realised that there would be no quick victories here and hauled at his reins to canter away. To the south the Orkney attack had ground to a halt, no doubt Erik knew, in a mixture of horror and confusion as they saw the cross of St Cuthbert and realised they had been betrayed. He turned aside to snap an order as the men of Strathclyde, trapped and in desperate straits only moments before, filled the bowl of the fort with the heartfelt cries of the saved. 'Sturla — make the signal to retreat to the watchtower.'

Three short notes on the war horn had heads turning his way, and within moments the sigil war banner had described a series of circuits in the air before lowering to point out their destination. As the disparate parts of his army began to move, Erik looked again at the gate through which the army of Bernicia had ridden a short while before and his expression became a snarl. It was, he grudgingly admitted, the perfect place to snare an army. Isolated on the crest of a long ridge behind high ramparts it was impossible to see in any direction once engaged, added to which the fortress itself had been built with almost a dozen points of entrance, any one of which could be used to outflank a smaller force at any time. But if the look had raised his hackles it had at least confirmed that there were no more enemies entering through the old gate, and Erik tallied the numbers as the men began to march. With the Bernicians still in the act of dismounting it was difficult to judge, but it looked as though the Easterner had led a further two hundred men to the fight, and Erik congratulated himself on suppressing his initial thought to launch an attack on the newcomers before they could settle. A quick look across to the buoyant men from Strathclyde, now gingerly edging forward as the Orkneymen retreated before them, confirmed that their numbers were much reduced by the fighting. But they could still bring fifty or sixty spears to the fight and he would have already lost men of his own. Despite the bravery and heroism of his army, they were still outnumbered at least two to one.

The western flank of the army were approaching the environs of the watchtower now, and Erik took a last look to remind himself of the layout before it disappeared from sight beneath booted feet. A defensive ditch ringed the whole, inside which the remains of an outer wall lay scattered about where it had been robbed out for stone over the centuries. Beyond that the signal tower stood on a raised plinth, rectangular in shape and perhaps shoulder high for the majority of its length, with the building itself rising thirty feet into the air above it. It was not only the perfect defensive position for a force his size, but would offer Erik the chance to see beyond the walls and far into the countryside in all directions for the first time since they had entered the fort, and he sent a prayer of thanks to Christ and Óðinn that they had seen fit to bless him with such a thing within easy reach. The realisation that the gods were still on his side raised his spirits as he marched, and with his enemies content to hang back until they could join forces, it was plain that the three elements of Erik's army would reach the sanctuary of the watchtower with few if any losses.

The first of his crewmen had reached the new position now, and Erik watched as they crossed the ditch, scrambled through the rubble field, and began to make way for those following on. The king was soon up with them, his calf muscles tightening as he scaled the far side, and as Erik entered the fort-let he barked out an order. 'This is our perimeter lads,' he said. 'Form up shoulder to shoulder and prepare to fight again.' As his loyal hirdmen bent to the task, others manhandled the scattered blocks to form a rudimentary wall at the lip of the drop, and satisfied that all was in order Erik turned back as he waited for the others to arrive.

Ragnfrod's division had had the furthest to travel to get to the new redoubt, but they had only taken part in one attack that day and were in better shape for it. The obvious belligerence had clearly dissuaded the Bernicians from launching a flanking attack despite their overwhelming numbers, and Erik looked on with pride as his son led a rearguard to protect the main body of men as they gained the ditch and scurried across. Sure that Ragnfrod's men would soon be inside the redoubt, Erik switched his gaze to the south. King Dyfnwal's raiding army had taken a beating and the Orcadians appeared to outnumber them for the first time that day, so it was no surprise that the foreigners appeared content to let the tough islanders withdraw without renewing the fight. The Torf-Einarsson brothers were already across the Roman road and approaching the outer ditch, and Erik allowed himself to relax a touch as he saw that the warriors in all three svinfylking had managed to extricate themselves from a potential disaster without losing another man.

With the central area of Hreyrr Camp now clear of Norwegians the Bernicians came forward to link up with the remnants of king Dyfnwal's raiders, and Erik looked on in disgust as the two leaders gripped each other by the shoulders before sharing a warm embrace. Their underlings were already busy parcelling the army into three equal parts ready to launch an assault, and as the enemy began to curl around the ditch the last of the Orkneymen made it home. Now that the battle lines were drawn Erik turned to run an experienced eye over his own dispositions as the first chants filled the air, and was pleased to find that they were as he had expected to find them; set in their divisions, shields and spears to the fore and ready to renew the fight.

As the rival armies glared across the old ditch and the enemy leaders busied themselves celebrating a trap well sprung, Erik grasped the opportunity to speak with his leading men. Threading his way back through the packed ranks he was soon scrambling up the inner mound on which the watchtower itself had been built. A quick look told him that the enemy spearmen were still forming up, and reassured he called the men to him before ducking his head inside the structure of the building. The interior was the same as before of course, the day he had stood on this spot with Oswald Thane and the Englishman had described the fort before the ride to Haydon. The rubble and detritus of centuries filled the ground before him, all that remained from the original stair-case and floors; but if the walls had lost their plaster and were little more than roughly hewn stone they suited his needs well, and he was already thinking of the best men to send aloft as he came back out into the light of day. With the ancient roof now a scattering of rotten beams and broken tile in the well of the building, there was room at the summit for several bowmen to ply their deadly trade as they kept a watch over the surrounding moorland, and Erik began to call the best men to him as he awaited his friends.

Erik raised his chin to peer above the grassy banks thrown up in an afternoon much like this a thousand years before, out across the wind driven wastes of Stainmore, the stony moor, as they came. Nestled high up on the saddleback the land dipped away to fore and aft, restricting the view; clouds of bluish-grey scurried across the sky as the fine drizzle began to thicken and whiten in the chill. Overhead the eagle had been joined by a handful of ravens as they awaited the feast to come, but as far as he could tell there appeared to be no more war bands in the immediate area, no sign of Cenwulf Thane and his host of spearmen, and he turned away with a wistful sigh.

Satisfied now that he would be forewarned when the lookouts reached their lofty perch, the king relaxed as friendly faces hove into view. Erik threw them all a grin as they reached him, and as they responded in kind the king felt the familiar thrill of being among trusted companions facing a hard fight. He reeled off their names, as much to hear them spoken aloud as to welcome them to his presence: 'Arnkel and Erland Torf-Einarsson; Ragnfrod Eriksson...'

26

TODAY IS FULL OF SURPRISES

E rik motioned towards the doorway, lowering his voice as they came. 'Place your friends as far in as possible lads,' he said. 'We may lose a few more men yet.' Erik looked back. The forces ranged against them had taken a beating but then their leaders could afford the loss, and Erik let his eyes take in the men who ringed the defences below him as the wounded carried those less fortunate past him and into the well of the building. They were fighting well, and a quick count of the bodies slowly filling the ditch before them told the king that his men were killing the enemy at a rate of three or four to one. But the Norwegian success could very well lead to their undoing if no help arrived soon. Despite the difficulty negotiating a causeway made of the dead and dying, to do so would be far easier than facing down a barrage of Norse spears and axes rained down upon their heads from the lip of the defences above, and Thorstein confirmed Erik's fears as he made an observation of his own. 'One more attack like that and they will break through,' he said. The huskarl turned his face to the king and his expression hardened into a frown. 'The lads are tiring Erik — and they are thirsty…'

Erik nodded. Norsemen or not they had been on the road since sunup, leapt from the saddle to carry out two frontal assaults of their own and beaten back a handful since they had retreated to the old signal station. In their haste to overcome the enemy the Norwegians had left their water skins and other supplies festooning the saddles, and with the horse guards now bloody mounds on the grass and the horses themselves in the hands of the enemy the situation was grim.

Erik paused to think before offering a reply, but in truth he was as tired as anyone in the Camp. War was a young man's game, and although he still considered himself a match for any man one on one, there was a reason that men approaching their seventh decade were rarely seen in the front ranks after the opening moves in a battle. But Erik knew that Thorstein was right in what he had said, as he watched his opponents make a great show of emptying water skins and drinking horns and the men of Norway threw them covetous looks. Warriors on campaign or engaged in a standup fight can go days without a crumb, but deny them ale or fresh water for an hour or two and the situation can quickly become desperate. Hacking and slashing in the push of shields is thirsty work, and Erik and his leading men had shared looks of concern as the shouts of defiance coming from the Norwegian ranks had lessened with each attack. With throats and mouths as dry as a summer beck the men were silent as the enemy made a show of their abundance, sinking ale by the barrel load as they taunted their parched opponents. Erik knew that the time was fast approaching when he would have to abandon his original plan — to hold out until the expected arrival of Cenwulf and his levy men, if they were stand any chance of victory.

The wintry showers of earlier had retreated as they fought, and with it the commanding view from the ridge top had returned. A quick look out past the southern boundary of the camp, across the valley and the moorland beyond to the upland he knew was White Brow, showed where a westering sun was gilding grasses made slick by the earlier sleet.

The short winter day was far advanced, but as Erik began to accept that a breakout may be the only option left to him a shout from the stonework above had the king turning his head. Riders were coming from the East; Erik beckoned him down, and hearing the shout Kolbein and Helgrim Smiter came up as Norwegian faces turned their way in hope. Within a short while the lookout had negotiated the rocky wall and stood before them; but if the steely look on the face of the man told them all they needed to know, Erik nodded that he make his report anyway as the expectation that the oncoming horsemen were friends began to recede.

'There is a large column heading this way lord,' the man said, 'at least fifty strong but possibly many more. It is difficult to tell,' he added apologetically, 'the slant of the hillside obscures the tail end of the column, and the gathering dusk is throwing the eastern slope into shadow.'

Erik nodded. 'We may not have a full idea of the numbers involved, but I can see by your glumness that you consider them foes.'

The watchman opened his mouth to reply, but the sound of a bugle caused him to pause as the enemy warriors lining the eastern rampart cried out in joy and stabbed the air with their spears. Kolbein answered the question in his stead as all their hopes were dashed. 'You have your answer Erik,' he said grimly. 'It looks like you have a decision to make.'

Erik nodded in reply, but his mind was now elsewhere as he scanned the ranks before him. Already outnumbered two to one, it appeared that the odds were lengthening again. Hearing the lookout's cry and seeing the reaction of the enemy the jarl brothers had come across, and Ragnfrod also joined the group as the king thought. Erik's son gave voice to questions of his own, the exasperation he felt dripping from every word. 'Where are they all coming from? How do they know we are here?'

Erland Torf-Einarsson answered as an enemy runner scrambled down the far bank and made his way towards Dyfnwal and Maccus. 'The smoke told them kinsman…'

Ragnfrod's eyes narrowed in question, and Helgrim expanded on Erland's clipped reply as the king's mind continued to plan. 'When Dyfnwal and his men rested up down at Bogas they were not surprised to see us appear at the woodland edge after all, they had been waiting there for us all along. By firing the buildings and slaying the occupants they were not harrying for the sake of it, they were signalling to other war bands that they had your father on their tail.'

Thorstein chipped in. 'The smoke columns could have been seen for miles. Who is to say that this war band will be the last?' He spat in disgust. 'Today is full of surprises — all of them nasty.'

Another shout came from the top of the tower, and the group craned their necks as the lookout cupped a hand to his mouth to call a report. 'I can see the newcomer's banner now lord,' the man said. 'It is the golden cross of St Cuthbert again.'

Thorstein spat. 'Earl Oswulf come to be in at the kill.' He threw Erik a sour faced look. 'He must be confident of victory to risk his neck so close to the fighting.'

Despite the realisation that this day was beginning to look very much like the last, Erik was surprised to discover that the arrival of the man who had so publicly pledged his allegiance only a few months before between the armies at Gefrin had served to clear his mind. He turned his face to the others, and their conversations ended abruptly as they saw that the king had reached his decision. 'We take the fight to them,' he growled, and Erik's spirits soared as he recognised his own eagerness reflected in the faces of his closest friends. 'I want to ensure that one man gets away,' he added as his eyes flitted from face to face, 'so it is important that all our efforts are directed at getting him a horse.' As Erik's gaze alighted on the face of his son he saw the consternation written there, and pride welled up within the king as the young man blurted his fear. 'Not I lord,' he pleaded. 'If I escape from here while my father lies dead, the shame of surviving even a single day will be too long!'

Before Erik could reply, Kolbein Herjolfsson had added a plea of his own. 'I may be but a withered husk of the man I once was Erik,' he said, 'but I gave my word to your father that I would never to leave your side and I mean to keep it.'

Erik held up a hand to forestall any other arguments. 'There is no time to discuss things; this is my last order to you all — do as I say.' His eyes went to his banner man, and he saw the man blink in surprise as all faces turned his way. 'Sturla — I don't want my war banner carried off as a trophy or trampled in the mud. Carry it back to York; tell Gunnhild and my sons what has happened here and to look to their own safety.' As Sturla made to protest, a look from Erik cut him short. 'You are far more than my banner man,' he explained, 'you are my friend and skald. Use your skills to weave a poem so that men far and wide will know of the treachery of our enemies and the bravery of our fight. Take ship to the hall of my brother in Avaldsnes — tell him of the manner in which our father Harald Fairhair's favoured son met his end, that he learn the truth from one who was at my side and not the lies of lesser men.' Erik let his gaze wander across the warriors still stood in ranks a few yards away as he continued. 'Many back in Norway will have brothers and fathers here on this hilltop. From your place at my side you will have witnessed acts of heroism, both on the ramparts below and in the earlier fighting; make sure to put names to those acts of courage, that kin and others shall celebrate their worth the length of Norway whenever folk gather to hear tales of fighting men.'

Erik's stare flitted from face to face, and he broke into a smile as he took in the familiar details for what he was sure now was the final time on Midgard. Beyond them sheeting rain moved in to cloak the southern summit, and down in the western vale a rainbow arced as the dying sun painted the horizon a bloody red. Erik's smile broadened into a grin, and the joy was reflected in the faces of his friends as they realised its meaning. 'Move among your men,' Erik said, 'and tell them of my intentions. One last charge and we sup with the gods.'

Cheers and taunts were coming from the enemy ranks now, the raucous sound rolling around the cup of the fort as the drumming of hoofbeats grew louder. A very few steps and Erik was with his crewmen, the men of the *Draki* turning their faces together as their lord came among them. 'We are making a break for it boys,' Erik explained as he walked. 'Find yourself a horse and ride like the wind.' He came to a halt in their midst, his eyes searching the ranks until they settled on the chosen pair. 'Grettir and Gunnar,' he said, slipping gold arm rings from his forearms and handing them across. 'When I give the command drive the svinfylking straight at the enemy leaders, but keep an ear cocked for Sturla's horn and prepare to change direction — one long note veer left, two short notes veer right.' The brothers nodded as the rings joined those already wreathing their arms, and Erik took a backwards pace as the change in tone told them all that the first horsemen had come through the gate.

Thorstein and Helgrim took their places before him as Kolbein and Sturla came to his side, and as the men prepared to attack Erik's gaze moved out to search the riders as they spilled into the clearing. A full score were inside the walls of the fort before the bloated figure of Oswulf Ealdwulfing, earl of Bernicia swept through the gate, and Erik's eyes narrowed in hatred as the man spotted Maccus and guided his mount across.

All around the king the men of the *Draki* were tensing — the fingers curling and unwinding on spears, sword handles and axe hafts the outward signs of the tautness within. A moment before he slipped from view the Bernician earl raised his chin to peer across at the rump of the Norwegian army stranded on their little mound, and for a heartbeat he and Erik's eyes met across the heads of the fighters. It was only a fleeting glimpse, an instant in time, but the Englishman had not ruled from his northern fastness in a world dominated by Norse, West Saxons and Scots without sniffing out danger with a look. Erik knew that he had to move quickly as the earl's triumphal aura vanished like woodsmoke, and he barked a command as the last of the enemy riders cleared the gate:

'Grettir — Gunnar: *Go!*'

For a brief moment the pair slid from view as they launched themselves onto the body field below, but as the rest of the crew began to feed through and the way ahead opened up Erik's hopes leapt as he saw that they were already through. As the Hordalanders vaulted the far bank and the men of the *Draki* bounded across in their wake, Erik reached the drop. Thorstein and Helgrim were the first to go, the

Norwegian giants placing their feet unerringly as they used the backs of the dead like stepping stones to ford the gully, and as Erik dropped down to follow on the first sounds of renewed fighting told him that the tip of the swine array had made contact with the enemy. Intent on reaching the far bank Erik slipped on the gore spattered pathway, but Kolbein's hand shot out to grasp his lord by the sleeve and halt his fall, and with a downward glance Erik placed his foot squarely across the unseeing eyes of a vanquished foe as he recovered his balance. A handful of steps and the king was climbing from the ditch, and a thrill coursed through him as he saw how far his shipmates had already driven into the enemy ranks as he did so. He knew then that his plan had been sound, to strike the foe at the very moment their victory had seemed assured, to hit them hard as the newcomers slid from saddles and the spearmen had turned in welcome. It took a great fighter, one of the very best, to switch back in an instant from joyful relief to steadfastness as a beaten and cowed enemy suddenly became an army of raging madmen, and Erik knew full-well that any army contained only a very few.

With the need to block off any escape and the losses already incurred that day, the ring of steel enclosing the watchtower on its grassy knoll had grown thinner and thinner, and although the best of the enemy were naturally concentrated around the leading men at the centre Erik saw to his glee that the svinfylking had already hacked their way halfway to the enemy standards. To either side the men of his hird were stabbing and slashing with spear and sword blades, driving the lesser warriors back, widening the breach, and Erik's gaze flew across to the eastern rampart in hope. All of his planning rested upon this moment — but he had left his refuge now, there was no way back, and as he raised his eyes to peer across the heads of the enemy he took in the situation with a single look. Arnkel and Erland had already smashed through the northern shield wall and were curving around to threaten the enemy rear. To the king's right Ragnfrod Eriksson had done likewise, Erik's son clearly visible beneath his war banner — fighting like a wildcat against the enemies of his kin.

With the opposition in disarray and the far side of the fort awash with panicked and abandoned horses, Erik gave his final order to the man who had shared his disasters and triumphs since the day they had met on a Finnish beach, where a shaman had lost his head and a war axe gained a name. As the battle horn came up and two short notes drifted over the heads of fighting men the Finn's prophesy came into his mind, and Erik snorted at the foresight contained within as the swine head began to turn:

He says that you will be five times a king, but that you will die on a windswept fell...

Taken by surprise by the change in direction the enemy were slow to respond, and by the time they had rallied the flanks of the boar head were an impenetrable line of inter-locking shields. Within moments the final opponents had been swept aside, and as Erik's men poured through the gap to spill out into the clear space beyond a bugle call told him that the enemy leaders were beginning to recover. Spearmen were hastening across, throwing a wall of shields across the interior of the fort to deny the Norwegians an escape, but a handful of horses remained within sight and Erik looked on with satisfaction as Gunnar and Grettir used their initiative to race across and cut them off from the herd. Erik moved in as the men on the flanks curved forward to corral the animals against the eastern wall of the fort, making a grab for the reins as he calmed a skittish horse with the stroke of a hand. Turning to Sturla he handed the straps across. 'Off you go,' he said, 'while the enemy are still off-balance.' Sturla glanced down at the king's hand for an instant as he wrestled with his conscience, but his discipline returned in a flash as he took the reins and hauled himself into the saddle. His eyes slid across to Kolbein at the king's side, and before Erik could intervene he had tossed the bloody axe war banner across to the venerable huskarl. 'Carry our lord's banner before him in his last fight old friend,' he said with a look of anguish, 'that no man can ever say they saw the war flag of Erik Bloodaxe flee from war-play.' With a tug at the reins the head came around, and as the horse began to move Sturla threw them a final wish before the emotion of their parting overwhelmed him. 'Save me a place on old one-eye's benches,' he croaked. 'For I have no wish to be far behind.'

Denied passage through the gateways by the swelling ranks of the enemy Sturla turned the head of the mount to the east, and with a kick spurred the horse up and across the old rampart. As the skald's head sank from view Erik realised for the first time that one of the younger members of his hird was stood before him, patiently waiting for the king to mount the horse he had seized to enable his escape. Erik threw the man a fatherly smile as he passed an arm ring across. 'Mount up Thrand,' he said, 'and live a long life. Tell every man who will listen that you were given this ring by Erik Haraldsson in his last fight at the Hreyrr on Stainmore, and you will never spend silver for ale again.'

Erik turned back before Thrand could reply, and his eyes drifted across the ranks of foemen as his huskarls clustered around. 'No straw deaths for us lads,' he cried as he heft Jomal; 'pissing all night, and dozing all day. Tonight we drink in Valhöll!' Erik looked about him as his closest friends pulled savage grins and said their farewells. Away to the north the Torf-Einarsson brothers were fighting back-to-back beneath the wild boar of Orkney, while to the south Erik looked on with pride as Ragnfrod and his hirdmen wheeled right to shatter the Strathclyde line. Beyond them the clouds had shredded, and the sky was brightening despite the late hour. A sunburst showed where the rainbow had come closer, and Erik thrilled to the sight as Kolbein raised the war flag and handed him a spear. Erik looked at it in bafflement and the old styrisman explained with a smile. 'You will recall your first Viking, Erik?' he said. 'When I guided a young prince to a foreign shore and we sacked the monastery together.' Kolbein's eyes slipped across to the West, over to the Vale of Eden and its arch of many colours. 'Well, the old one is listening now — it would be a shame to miss the chance.' Erik snorted, hefting the dart as the memory returned. The spear flew, and the king's dedication to the Allfather rang out as Norsemen chanted a verse and ash shafts clattered against lime wood boards.

27

ERIKSMÁL

Palatium Apostolicum Lateranense
The year of our Lord 960

The archbishop swept through the entrance, his eyes drinking in the splendour of the triclinium as he walked, and as the great doors closed behind him and the hubbub drifting in from the atrium beyond was snuffed out he recalled the events of the previous day with satisfaction. They were approaching the very spot where Pope John had presented the Englishman with the pallium, the Y-shaped woollen cloak which symbolised the authority of his office, before the assembled bishops and higher clergy of both Rome and those from his own land who had trodden the path across the Alps alongside him that spring. Empty now save a few guards, Dunstan had time to take in the mosaics lining the walls and niches as footfalls echoed like thunderclaps in the heavy silence. One in particular had caught his eye the previous day, despite the dignity of the occasion, and he paused for a moment to savour the image as his guide began to explain. 'Ah,' the man purred, 'this mosaic is also a favourite of the Holy Father; you have fine taste archbishop.'

Dunstan's eyes widened at the remark as he feigned annoyance; but in truth there was very little which could dampen his spirits on a day like this, and he smothered a wicked smile as he supplied the obvious conclusion to the Roman's statement. 'I have fine taste — for a northerner you mean?'

The man's mouth gaped momentarily at the slip, but there were no tongue-tied rustics within the Lateran Palace and Dunstan was impressed as the retainer's glib demeanour returned in a flash. 'Good heavens no, archbishop,' he said as a pained look washed across his features. 'There is not a man in Rome who is unaware of your personal qualities, and the fervour with which you do God's work.'

Dunstan's face broke into a smile. 'I already know of this image,' he said as a hand moved up to point out the details. 'In the central alcove the figure of Christ hands out tasks to the Apostles.' The archbishop's hand wafted from side to side as he described the images on either flank. 'To the left St Peter receives the keys to his kingdom, while on the opposite side Christ confers the stole on Leo and a standard to Charlemagne, King of Franks.'

Dunstan noticed the faint whiff of disappointment steal into the Roman's features at the depth of his charge's knowledge, and he was quick to make amends as the pair walked on — he was a guest after all, and manners were the mark of a man. 'This is a wonderful building,' he said, craning his neck. 'I have heard it said that it has stood for the best part of half a millennium.'

The guide's face lit up, the underestimation allowing him the opportunity to correct the archbishop as the Englishman had fully meant it to do. 'Oh, it's older still archbishop,' he chirruped happily, 'as is the adjoining basilica. You will have seen the obelisk in the square outside of course. Now that was brought to Rome from Egypt, and is of almost incalculable age…' Puffed up with pride at the achievements of his ancestors the guide wittered on, and the archbishop's mind began to wander as they turned aside and made their way through the room beyond.

If the journey from England had been long, arduous and more than a little unsafe — only the previous year a predecessor, Ælfsige, had frozen to death making the same journey — it only mirrored the passage the country had made through the turbulent years that had just gone over. But the new king Edgar was a fine young man who was already bending the country to his will Dunstan reflected as he walked, and the churchman sent a prayer to God the Father in this most Holy place that the latest scion of Wessex to hold the title *Rex Anglorum* be spared the tribulations which had plagued his predecessors. The soft shuffling of feet dragged the archbishop back from his thoughts, and Dunstan saw that he had reached Pope John's private chambers as the guards came to attention and the doors were drawn inward. The light was dazzling as he came into the room, the combination of a wall set with high windows and the brilliance of the southern sun momentarily blinding eyes more accustomed to gloomy days and gloomier interiors; but the figure of the Pope hardened from the glare, and the Englishman brightened as he saw again the warmth in the younger man's smile. 'Dunstan,' the pope beamed, 'welcome to my chamber.'

Dunstan lowered his gaze in supplication, but before he could utter a word the prelate rested a hand on his shoulder and spoke again. 'There is no need for formality here, we are the same you and I — men in the service of God. Come,' he said, guiding the archbishop towards a shady corner, 'let us take refreshment away from the sun's glare.' Dunstan cast a look about the room as he sank into a chair. Every surface in the long rectangular room was covered with scenes from the Holy Bible, every projection, ledge or shelf gilt as shafts of light striped the floor. The pope settled into the chair directly opposite, and he shot the archbishop a smile as he patted the familiar stack with a hand. 'You have my thanks Dunstan,' he said, 'for bringing this story to me.'

Dunstan inclined his head. 'If it is far too good a tale to destroy out of hand, it is far too dangerous to remain in the North, Your Holiness. I rather hoped that you could find a home for it in the papal collection?'

Drinks appeared on the small table at each man's shoulder, and as the servant bowed and backed away the pope smiled his thanks. Pope John took a sip of wine, but as the Holy Father's eyes flicked up the archbishop flinched inwardly as he caught a glimpse of the man within. Not only was Pope John XII a fighting man, a warrior Pope who was frequently at war with the neighbouring Italian states, but a young man who found it difficult to resist temptations of the flesh. Only that summer he had led a papal army against the Lombards, and the Englishman had heard it said since his arrival in the city that the palace was known to the locals as the finest whorehouse in Rome. The pope transferred the manuscript from the table to his lap as they drank, and Dunstan watched with interest as the head of the church flicked through the leaves. 'This Erik Haraldsson was quite a man,' he said finally. 'Indeed, five times a king. I have to admit that the tale of his life kept me from my bed until the wee small hours.' Pope John lifted his gaze, fixing the older man with a look. 'I wonder if he was aware of how close he came to realising his dream of an empire of Britain? If king Eadred had not been so open-handed with his silver to buy off this Bernician earl and his Scottish nephew, how likely is it that the English south would have returned to barbarism?'

Dunstan shifted uncomfortably as he sought to reply with more confidence than he felt. 'It is true that Eadred had been ailing,' he admitted, 'and was fated to die soon after Erik's own death. His brother Eadwy who inherited the crown was a disaster who only succeeded in dividing the kingdom. But the Lord ensured that the tyrant's rule was brief,' he said earnestly, 'and our new king Edgar is strong and just.'

'But imagine if Erik had lived but a few more months, to the following spring or summer — what then?' The Roman patted the parchment again, and as a flash of mischief came into his eyes Dunstan realised with a jolt that the pope, God's representative of earth, saw the hoary Norseman not as the Devil made flesh and bone but a kindred spirit worthy of admiration. Pope John raised a forefinger, and as a servant detached himself from the shadows he handed the book the monks in Glastonbury knew by its Norwegian name *Eriksmál*, the Lay of Erik, across. The brothers' fervour for the tale and the poems it contained had been the reason that Dunstan had decided to bring the manuscript to Rome; even in death the deeds of Erik Haraldsson inspired men to hanker for more in their own life, and kept the God-fearing from their devotions.

John spoke again as the servant awaited his instructions. 'And Wulfstan, the archbishop of York, never suspected that his communications were being intercepted by your men during the entire course of his incarceration?'

Dunstan smiled at *that* memory. It had been one of the greatest services he had bestowed upon his king and people, and instrumental in the Norseman's death on the wintry ridge top that day. 'It would appear not, for both Erik and Wulfstan are long dead and earl Oswulf has ruled in York as a liegeman of the king of England these past six years. Northumbrian independence died out with the pair,' he gloated. 'They have finally been brought to heel, and we shall ensure that they never rise again.'

Pope John nodded. 'I can see that you are wary of them, and you are right to be so. But before Erik's story is consigned to the vaults, perhaps we could listen to a snippet or two? It is doubtful that it will see the light of day again.' John turned his face to the servant waiting silently a dozen paces away, and Dunstan found that he approved of the choice as the pope spoke a command. 'Read a passage from the missive to archbishop Wulfstan by Erik's widow; skip the lamentations at the beginning, and take up the tale where the skald Sturla Godi described the king's death.' The Roman turned his head, and archbishop Dunstan nodded his agreement at the words which followed; the Norse may be untamed heathens, but he would willingly admit that the best of their poetry contained more than a dash of brutish charm. 'Transition as seamlessly as possible into the part of the skald's poem where Bloodaxe leads his men into Óðinn's hall if you would.' The churchmen shared a look, and as they raised a glass in celebration Dunstan nodded again. 'We are both in accord,' John confirmed. 'That would be a fitting place to leave Erik's tale, after all that has gone before.'

The retainer shuffled the leaves as he sought to follow his master's instructions, and as pope and archbishop sipped, he cleared his throat and began:

'Norwegian battle cries filled the air behind me as the horse skidded down the face of the bank, and by the time we were across the ditch the sound of fighting was beginning to build again. It was the matter of a few moments before I had gained the roadway, but casting a look to the East I saw to my dismay that the high point from which I had intended to witness the battle was denied me as yet more horsemen were making their way to the fort up the road there. With the westward route through Hreyrr Camp blocked as Ragnfrod Eriksson and his men fell upon the enemy wing, there was only one place to go if I was to witness the final battle as was the king's wish, and I hauled at the reins, guiding the horse down into the gully which bordered the fortress to the South, across the beck and thence up on to the crag known as White Brow. Looking back I realised at once that I had reached the promontory with little time to spare, as a spear flew from King Erik's hand to signal the beginning of the attack.

'Erik Bloodaxe led the final assault in person, striding clear of his oath sworn to take up position at the head of the svinfylking, and as his huskarls moved forward to protect my lord's flanks his jog became a sprint. The crew of the *Draki* channelled into the king's wake as he gathered speed, and before the wedge was half formed he had crashed into the enemy line. Jomal swung then, and as shields and heads alike were riven and splintered by the king's whirring axe blade the men of Strathclyde recoiled in terror. Erik's bloodied axe war banner, the sigil I had proudly carried in battles across the northern lands showed where Kolbein Herjolfsson was fulfilling his vow to die at our lord's side, and as the forward momentum drained from the attack and numbers began to tell, I looked on sadly as the Norwegians were enveloped.

'More foemen were entering the fort as parties of riders reached the place of battle, and within moments the Norwegian attacks had been reduced to clusters of heroes as their enemies swarmed and jostled to be in at the kill. Very soon the king's swine head had been parcelled up into small knots of fighting men, and as my lord's battle flag fell and the last stand was overwhelmed I took a final look before riding away.

'All across the interior of the fort the enemy were in the ascendant as numbers triumphed over valour; but at that moment in the western sky the setting sun broke free of the clouds, and as a shameful roar told every man within earshot that a giant had fallen I witnessed Bifröst, the rainbow bridge to Asgard, harden from the gloom.'

> Ravens cawed, a wolf growled: men were
>   treading the quivering road. Óðinn's eye
>   opened; the High One spoke:
>
> 'What kind of dream is this, that I was a little
>   before daybreak preparing Valhöll for an
>   army of the slain?
>
> 'I awakened the heroes; I asked them to get
>   up, to strew the benches, to rinse the
>   drinking cups; Valkyries to bring wine as if
>   a leader should come.
>
> 'I expect certain glorious men from the world
>   of the living, so my heart is glad.'
>
> 'What thunders there as if a thousand were
>   stirring — a mighty host?' said Bragi.
>
> 'All the bench planks creak, as if Balder were
>   coming back into the halls of Óðinn.'
>
> 'The wise Bragi should not blather,' replied the
>   Allfather, 'when you know the truth full-

well: the clamour is made for Erik, who
must be coming here, a prince into Valhöll.

'Sigmund, rise up quickly and go to meet the
ruler. Invite him in, for it is Erik I am
expecting now.'

'Why do you expect Erik,' asked Sigmund,
'rather than other kings?'

Óðinn smiled his wolf smile. 'Because he has
reddened his blade in many lands, and
borne a bloody sword...'

AFTERWORD

We know so little of the events which occurred throughout Erik's long and active life, that historians cannot even agree when he reigned in York. As in the previous volumes in this trilogy, I have thought it safest to base the timeline on the only contemporary record for those years to have come down to us in full, the various annals known collectively as the *Anglo-Saxon Chronicles*. Here Erik's second period as ruler is bookended by the following entries:

952: In this year the Northumbrians drove out king Olaf and accepted Erik, son of Harald, as king.

954: In this year the Northumbrians drove out Erik, and Eadred succeeded to the Northumbrian kingdom.

It is hardly expansive, but fortunately we have a few later sources which add snippets of information to the bare-boned records of the day. Archbishop Wulfstan of York was seized upon visiting the southern English kingdom, for what a contemporary recorded as: "accusations had often been made to the king against him." William of Malmesbury writing in the first half of the twelfth century with the aid of documents now lost to history could add: "He is said to have connived at the shifts of allegiance by his compatriots." Wulfstan may have been held in the south for the entirety of Erik's second reign in York, and although he was released soon after Erik's downfall he was never allowed to return to Northumbria, dying within a few years to be buried at Oundle in Northamptonshire.

But if the southern English appear to have been militarily paralysed by the ongoing illness of king Eadred, their wealth could fight almost as effectively. The *Annals of Ulster* mention a great battle late in the year 952 in northern Britain between the Norse and an alliance of Scots, Welsh and Saxons, ie the Britons of Strathclyde and the English of the old kingdom of Bernicia ruling from Bamburgh. The battle ended in a crushing victory for the Norsemen, and although the commander of the army is not named, it seems clear from the fact that Erik remained king in York following the fight that he had been the leader of the victorious force.

If the invasion of 952 *was* aimed at the removal of Erik, he was not the kind of man to take such a thing lying down. The counter invasion I have based on a passage from the *Saga of Hakon the Good*, Erik's half-brother who we saw replace him on the throne of Norway at the end of book one, Bloodaxe. Here it states that: "Erik became very bold and had a large army, and could rely so much on his men that he drove far inland, where he harried and pursued folk…"

Erik had of course already been accepted as overlord of the Orkneys (which included the northern part of modern day Scotland as far south as the Moray Firth), the Western Isles and the adjacent mainland by this time, so with Erik now king in York it can reasonably said that the kingdom of Alba was now surrounded by hostile armies. If the campaign of 952 had been intended to stop this situation developing, the scale of the defeat placed the Scots and their allies in a precarious position, and a retaliatory invasion on three fronts would have been a distinct possibility.

Erik Haraldsson did visit the shrine of St Cuthbert, then situated in modern day Chester-le-Street, and signed the Liber Vitae of the community, a kind of visitors book where his name can still be seen. The gifts I have described in the tale are also still extant, though who gifted the gold and garnet cross we will never know. Similarly the crowning as king of a reunified Northumbria on the site of the old royal hall at Gefrin is invention on my part.

The king of Alba, Mael Colm (Máel Coluim mac Domnaill) escaped the battle in 952, but he was clearly facing a challenge to his authority at home. Whether this was a result of his defeat or an inability to defend the kingdom from Erik we cannot now say, but it seems that there was a rival party developing around the person of his cousin Indulf. This situation appears to have come to a head in 954. In this year, The *Chronicle of the Kings of Alba* records that Mael Colm took an army into Moray "and slew Cellach," one of Indulf's supporters, while the *Annals of Ulster* add that the king was killed late in the year at Fetteresso, and it seemed not unreasonable to link the two in this novel.

The various genealogies and kinship arrangements outlined by Gunnhild in her conversation with Erik in Chapter 20 were reality, and with the rise of Indulf mac Causantin in Alba and the encouragement of the southern English, earl Oswulf in Bamburgh seems to have been the prime mover in Erik's ultimate defeat. An Icelandic account known as *Fagrskinna* appears to form the basis of most of the subsequent saga references to Erik's fall, and the document is believed to have drawn on the now lost eulogy known as *Eriksmál*, part of which was quoted at the very end of Chapter 27. Thought to have been composed in Orkney shortly after the events they describe for Erik's widow Gunnhild the original is now unfortunately lost, but in addition to the Lay quoted in part at the very end of my tale, the following passage sheds a little light on Erik's last fight:

"Erik had so great an army that five kings followed him because he was a valiant man and a battle winner. He trusted in himself and his strength so much that he went far up country, and everywhere he went with warfare. Then came against him king Olaf (there are various theories as to who is being referred to here), a tributary king of king Edmund (in reality the English king was of course Eadred). They fought and Erik was routed by the army of the land; and he fell with all his force."

The *Saga of Hakon the Good* appears to have used the same source when it describes:

"A dreadful battle ensued in which many English fell. But for every one who fell three came in his place out of the country behind, and when evening came on the loss of men turned against the Norsemen and many were killed."

Among English sources the *Anglo-Saxon Chronicles* are of little help as we can see from the entry at the beginning of this Afterword, but Roger of Wendover's *Flores Historiarum* of all the later records is unequivocal in naming Erik's opponent and the location of the last battle:

"King Erik was treacherously killed by Earl Maccus in a certain lonely place called Stainmore...betrayed by Earl Oswulf, and then afterwards King Eadred ruled in these districts."

By describing Eadred's subsequent rule as *in these districts,* this passage lends weight to the theory that Roger of

Wendover had access to local documents now completely lost to us, almost certainly a copy of the *History of the Ancient Northumbrians,* a contemporary work which was compiled in York itself. We can only mourn its loss, but it does serve to elevate the reliability of this passage, and Roger's work in general, above the majority of our sources for this period.

Even today Stainmore is a remote area where the modern counties of Cumbria, County Durham and North Yorkshire meet. The modern A66 Trunk Road shadows the route of the old Roman Road and crosses the Pennines via the Stainmore Gap, where substantial remains of the old Roman marching camp can still be seen after surviving almost two millennia. Known as Rey Cross (Royal Cross) after the stone cross erected within the walls of the fort by William the Conqueror and the Scottish king Malcolm III as a border marker between their respective domains, local legend held that the mound upon which it stood was the burial place of Erik. Although this was disproved in the twentieth century when the weathered stump which is all that remains of the cross was moved to accommodate road widening, it does show that there was still a memory of Erik's last fight in the area up to the present day, and it seemed the ideal location in which to describe the king's last stand.

With Erik's death, earl Oswulf became the sole ruler of Northumbria as a sub king of the southern English. Indulf became the king of Alba and the lands of Lothian, including the hill fort of Eidyn burh (Edinburgh) passed from English to Scottish ownership the very same year — an event which looks very much like the sharing out of spoils between kinsmen and allies, now that Oswulf's power base has shifted south to York.

And so Erik Haraldsson became the last king of an independent Northumbria — but what became of the other major players in our tale?

Gunnhild and the remaining Erikssons almost certainly left York immediately and went to Orkney. Here they seem to have taken over the running of the earldom for several years, turning their attention back to Norway and attempting to recover the throne from Hakon the Good. Gamli Eriksson was killed in battle there, fighting against king Hakon at the battle of Rastarkalv in 955, but with the accession of Gunnhild's brother Harald Bluetooth to the throne of Denmark around the year 958 the family gained a powerful new ally. Several invasions were attempted over the following years, culminating in the Battle of Fitjar in 961. Hakon died of wounds received during the fighting; but before he did so, apparently having never married and being without a male heir, he elected to 'keep the family business going' by nominating Harald Eriksson as his successor. Harald reigned as King Harald Greycloak until 970 when, frustrated by his refusal to rule as an under-king after the help he had been given and eager to assert Danish dominance over Southern Norway, Bluetooth lured Harald to Denmark and killed him in an ambush.

Guttorm Eriksson died Viking in the Baltic while Sigurd, now labouring under the unfortunate nickname Slobber, was killed by a hersir named Klyppr for abducting his wife. Erik and Gunnhild's daughter Ragnhild remained in Orkney, where according to the sagas her scheming resulted in several deaths among the nobility and others. Erik's old rival for the kingdom of York, Olaf Cuaran, remained heavily involved in the warfare and political machinations in Ireland for the remainder of his active life. Defeated in battle in 980, he handed *his* family business over to a son and retired to the monastery on Iona where he died soon after. And what of

Gunnhild Gormsdottir? For a time she ruled Norway at Harald Greycloak's side in much the same way she had the young Erik Haraldsson all those years before, but following her son's death she too was lured to Jutland by her brother Harald Bluetooth and drowned in a bog.

If the story of Erik Haraldsson which I have reconstructed from the sources available is naturally fiction, I hope that I have managed to get as close to the actual course of events as possible. The evidence for his life is simply too fragmented, contradictory and unreliable for it to be otherwise: brief entries in journals; sagas written more for entertainment than historical record, hundreds of years after the events they portray. But if the dates and details of Erik's life have become little more than an echo of an echo, they were the final gasp of the barbarian Europe which had replaced the order of Rome. Christendom was advancing everywhere, with men like Erik and Olaf Cuaran fast becoming anachronisms in a world ruled by those twin pillars of civilisation, organised religion and nation states. Erik Bloodaxe was likely a shrewd enough character to realise this, but *Eriksmál* I think showed where his heart and those of his closest followers truly lay. That the skald had Oðinn choose Sigmund to welcome Erik to Valhöll was a deliberate act. In the epic *Saga of the Volsungs* King Sigmund, after a lifetime of victories, fights against an old man in battle who is really Oðinn in disguise. Oðinn shatters Sigmund's sword and immediately disappears, and as the defenceless king falls to his enemies Valkyries arrive to escort the king to the hall of heroes to prepare for Ragnarök.

So perhaps it is fitting to end our tale by returning to *Eriksmál* and the threshold of Valhöll as Sigmund, another battle winner hand-picked by Oðinn to fight alongside him at the end of days, cries a greeting to Erik, Helgrim, Thorstein and the rest:

> *"Heill thu nu Eirikr, vel skaltu her.*
> *kominn! Ok gakk i haoll, horskr."*

> *"Hail to you Erik, you are welcome here.*
> *Come in! Enter the hall, valiant King."*

Cliff May
East Anglia
May 2020

CHARACTERS

Arinbjorn Thorirsson - Erik's foster-brother.

Arnkel Torf-Einarsson - Brother of the Orkney Jarl and kinsman of Erik. Dies alongside Erik at Hreyrr Camp.

Conalach Cnogba of North Brega. High king at Tara.

Crinan mac Cellach - Avenges the death of his father by killing Mael Colm at Fetteresso.

Dunstan - An English churchman. Archbishop of Canterbury 960-988 — canonised by the Roman Catholic church in 1029.

Dyfnwal ab Owain - King of Strathclyde. Defeated and taken captive at Corebricg, he later burns in earl Regenwold and leads Erik into a trap.

Eadred - King of the English. The sickly king in Winchester.

Characters

Erik Haraldsson - Bloodaxe - King of Northumbria, overlord of the Orkneys and Sudreys.

Erland Torf-Einarsson - Brother of the Orkney Jarl and kinsman of Erik. Dies at Hreyrr Camp.

Gamli Eriksson - Erik and Gunnhild's eldest son.

Godfred - a Yorkish earl. Leads the left wing at the Battle of Corebricg.

Grettir - brother of Gunner, Erik's hirdman.

Gunderic - a Yorkish earl. Leads the right wing at the Battle of Corebricg.

Gunner - brother of Grettir, Erik's hirdman.

Gunnhild Gormsdottir - Erik's wife and queen. Daughter of King Gorm the Languid and sister to Harald Bluetooth.

Guttorm Eriksson - Erik's third son.

Hakon Haraldsson - King of Norway. Erik's half-brother by their father Harald Fairhair.

Hauk - A scout and member of Erik's hird.

Helgrim Smiter - Erik's huskarl.

Harald Eriksson - Erik and Gunnhild's second son.

Hoskuld - Gamli Eriksson's huskarl.

Indulf mac Constantine - son of the old Scottish king Constantine and kinsman of Oswulf of Bernicia.

Kolbein Herjolfsson - Erik's huskarl and styrisman.

Mael Colm - Mael Colm mac Domnall - King of Alba. Killed at Fetteresso.

Maccus Olafsson - the Easterner - Earl Oswulf's right hand man. Betrays Erik at Hreyrr Camp.

Morcar - Archbishop Wulfstan's thane.

Mord - A scout and member of Erik's hird.

Olaf Cuaran - Also known as Amlaíb Cuarán/Óláfr Sigtryg-gsson/Olaf Sandal. Erik ousts him from York with the help of archbishop Wulfstan.

Olvir - Erik's scout and hirdman. Killed alongside earl Regenwold.

Oswulf Ealdwulfing - Earl of Bernicia.

Oswy - Archbishop Wulfstan's *gesith*.

Oswald Thane - Archbishop Wulfstan's right hand man and Erik's trusted advisor.

Ragnfrod Eriksson - Erik's youngest son. Dies alongside his father at Hreyrr Camp.

Regenwold - A Yorkish earl. Burned in by Dyfnwal of Strathclyde.

Sigurd Eriksson - Erik's fourth son.

Sturla Godi - Erik's banner man and skald. Survivor of Hreyrr Camp and author of the heroic poem Eriksmál.

Svan - Gamli Eriksson's huskarl.

The Skulissons - sons of the slave trader Skuli — killed by Erik following a raid on Dublin a decade earlier.

Thorfinn Torf-Einarsson (Skull-Splitter) - Jarl of Orkney.

Thorstein Egilsson - Erik's huskarl and prow man.

Wulfstan - Archbishop of York.

Wystan - Archbishop Wulfstan's *gesith*.

PLACES/LOCATIONS

Bardolfsby - Barlby, North Yorkshire, England.

Bebbanburh - Bamburgh, Northumberland, England.

Bogas - Bowes, County Durham, England.

Byrgisey - Brough of Birsay, Mainland, Orkney.

Catrice - Catterick, North Yorkshire, England.

Ceasterford - Castleford, West Yorkshire, England.

Celerca - Montrose, Angus, Scotland. (see Stroma)

Conceastre - Chester-le-Street, County Durham, England.

Corebricg - Corbridge, Northumberland, England.

Dun Foither - Dunnottar Castle, Aberdeenshire, Scotland.

Eidyn Burh - Edinburgh, Lothian, Scotland.

Fetteresso - Kirktown of Fetteresso, Aberdeenshire, Scotland.

Gefrin - Near Wooler, Northumberland, England.

Haydon - Haydon Bridge, Northumberland, England.

Hindrelag - Richmond, North Yorkshire, England.

Hreyrr Camp - Rey Cross, County Durham, England.

Hrypum - Ripon, North Yorkshire, England.

Miydilsburh - Middlesbrough, North Yorkshire, England.

Stonehive - Stonehaven, Aberdeenshire, Scotland.

Stirlin - Stirling, Stirlingshire, Scotland.

Stroma - Montrose, Angus, Scotland. (see Celerca)

Werchesope - Worksop, Nottinghamshire, England.

York - North Yorkshire, England.

ABOUT THE AUTHOR

I am writer of historical fiction, working primarily in the early Middle Ages. I have always had a love of history which led to an early career in conservation work. Using the knowledge and expertise gained we later moved as a family through a succession of dilapidated houses which I single-handedly renovated. These ranged from a Victorian townhouse to a Fourteenth Century hall, and I added childcare to my knowledge of medieval oak frame repair, wattle and daub and lime plastering. I have crewed the replica of Captain Cook's ship, Endeavour, sleeping in a hammock and sweating in the sails and travelled the world, visiting such historic sites as the Little Big Horn, Leif Erickson's Icelandic birthplace and the bullet scarred walls of Berlin's Reichstag.

Now I write, only a stone's throw from the Anglian ship burial site at Sutton Hoo in East Anglia, England. The Day of the Wolf is my twelfth full length novel, following on from the bestselling alternative history collection of short stories set around the events of the Norman Conquest of England in 1066 — Spear Havoc.

ALSO BY C. R. MAY

SPEAR HAVOC

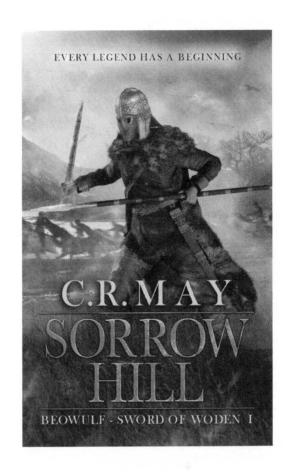

EVERY LEGEND HAS A BEGINNING

C.R.MAY

SORROW
HILL

BEOWULF - SWORD OF WODEN I

SORROW HILL

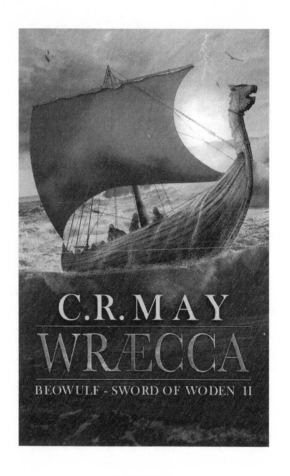

C.R. MAY
WRÆCCA
BEOWULF - SWORD OF WODEN II

WRÆCCA

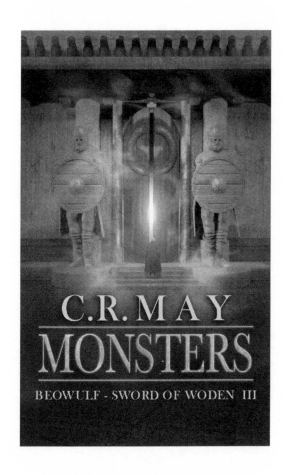

MONSTERS

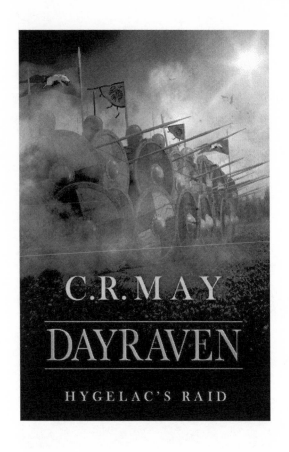

DAYRAVEN

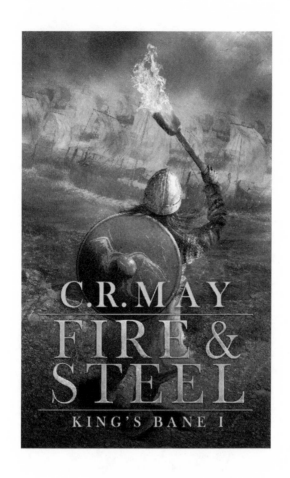

FIRE AND STEEL

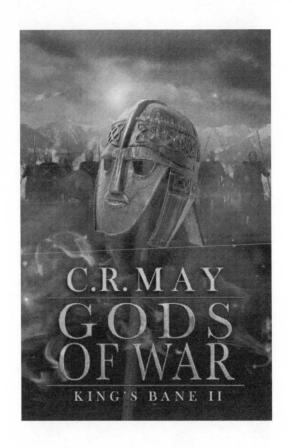

GODS OF WAR

THE SCATHING

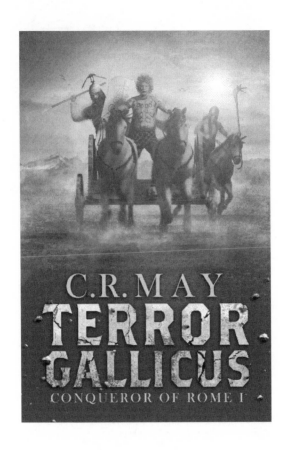

TERROR GALLICUS

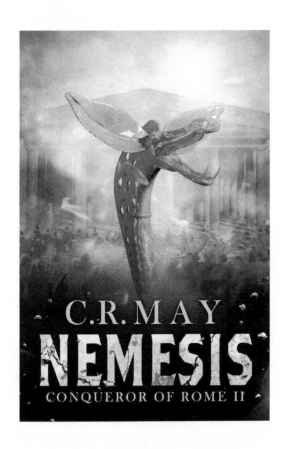

NEMESIS

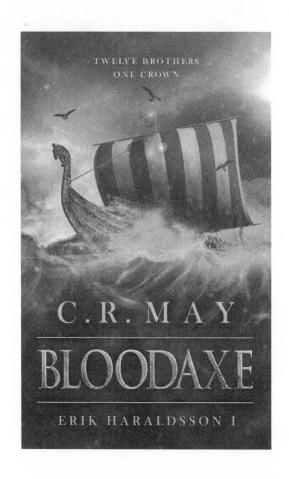

BLOODAXE

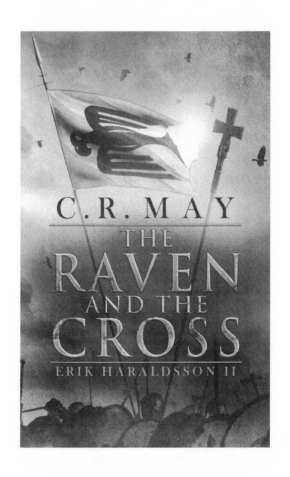

THE RAVEN AND THE CROSS

Made in the USA
Columbia, SC
19 May 2021

38184065R00207